Also by Storm Constantine

The Enchantments of Flesh and Spirit
The Bewitchments of Love and Hate
The Fulfilments of Fate and Desire
Monstrous Regiment
Hermetech
Aleph
Burying the Shadow
Sign for the Sacred

Calenture

Storm Constantine

First published in 1994
by HEADLINE BOOK PUBLISHING

First published in paperback in 1994
by HEADLINE BOOK PUBLISHING

A HEADLINE FEATURE paperback

10 9 8 7 6 5 4 3 2

All characters in this publication are fictitious and any resemblance to real persons, living or dead, is purely coincidental.

ISBN 0 7472 4553 3

Typeset by
Letterpart Limited, Reigate, Surrey

Printed and bound in Great Britain by
Cox & Wyman Ltd, Reading, Berks

HEADLINE BOOK PUBLISHING
A division of Hodder Headline PLC
338 Euston Road
London NW1 3BH

This book is dedicated to
Vikki Lee France and Steve Jeffery,
for all their kindness and support,
and whose work on Inception
is invaluable.

ACKNOWLEDGEMENTS

With thanks to my editor – again – Caroline Oakley, for her continuing faith in my work; Mark, for being there, and the plot and ideas he contributed; Steve Jeffery and Paula Wakefield for their pre-editing editing and appraisal; Mark Haines and Neil Flinn for their fecund imaginations and contributing ideas; Flo Freeman and Ben Fouracre for making sure I got fed during the final stages of writing this book; Lynn for the late night chats in moments of desparation; and finally, to Debs and Tigger, as always, for being weirde sisters.

For information on Storm Constantine's work, write to:

Inception
c/o Vikki Lee France and Steve Jeffery
44 White Way
Kidlington
OX5 2XA

CALENTURE

1. A disease incident to sailors within the tropics, characterised by delirium in which, it is said, they fancy the sea to be green fields and desire to leap into it.

2. Fig. and Trans.: Fever; burning passion, glow

'Knowledge kindles Calentures in some . . .'
John Donne

Chapter One
Frozen Spires

Rising at dawn, Casmeer found one of them hanging in the nets outside again. It was dying, a broken thing. Would they never learn? It clacked its beak at him in a last defiant, mocking gesture, shook its shaggy, dirty-white head, tried to manipulate its skinny elbows.

It had come for the roche that stood on Casmeer's roof, attracted by the scintillant sparkle in the crystal depths, filled with a lustful urge to steal. Casmeer avoided the birdlike, childlike gaze of its eyes. He sent a current through the net and watched it burn.

'Damn plumosites!' he said.

The net could be repaired, a morning mist of deodorant vapour could eclipse the burning stink. The silent motionless citizens of Thermidore would be kept safe. Casmeer, alone a moving thing, was their protector.

It was the first time one of the plumosites had ever attacked Casmeer's house. Greater booty for the taking could be found elsewhere in the city, such as in the market-places – where shining, coruscating roches clustered around the neglected booths, like giant diamonds and rubies and sapphires – or in the theatres and courthouses where they grew over the seats, encrusting everything with a glittering salt. Casmeer was alarmed a plumosite had raided his modest roof garden. He passed the roche, nervous of examining it, in case he found damage. Relieved to find there was none, he let his hand linger close to its shimmering surface. 'Elini,' he said. Perhaps he should have tried to move her inside after all, but he'd always been afraid of breaking her. Roches could be so friable.

He went back through the roof door into his house to begin his daily rituals. All the nets had been checked, the dials read, the watchtowers adjusted. Now, Casmeer could retire for a precise breakfast: eggs and barrel mushrooms. He avoided eating plumosite eggs. After breakfast he would read through everything he had written the day before; he was compiling his own history of Thermidore. It was a never-ending job because the history of the city seemed to change as he wrote it. His research produced endless new stories, new legends. After the note-reading, he would consult his maps and decide upon which parish of the city to patrol that day. In his mind's eye, he kept visualising the straight narrow streets of Jassica's Parade. He hadn't visited that place for a long time, had avoided its stern white façades, its watching façades, since he had seen that staring face pressed against a clouded upper window, looking down.

He knew there could be no staring face; it was impossible. He alone in Thermidore had a face. He did not want to believe in ghosts, and feared his own madness. It was best to shun such places. But they summoned him as if they yearned for his observation, as if, without it, they could not be real in this world, or would decay. Sometimes they had birthed new myths for him to catalogue.

Casmeer had a duty. Sometimes it was onerous, but it could not be neglected. He patrolled the city to keep it alive, even though he lacked the power to wake it.

The walls and floors of his four-storied, narrow house were adorned with elaborately worked rugs which he had woven in the days when rug-making had been his profession. The colours were fading now, and wool-beetles had made assaults upon the fabrics, but still the scenes of past life reassured him, hanging around him, concrete memories. He ate with his back to a depiction of Asserock's Market. On the opposite wall, a line of smirking priestesses fanned themselves with incense smoke. The smoke had been worked with silver thread, now tarnished. Casmeer often looked at that rug while he chewed his food, wondering why the women looked so dislikeable. What mood had been upon him during the time he'd created that scene? Had he suffered a broken heart?

It was a warm day, late-spring. Casmeer put on a long, light coat of brocaded fabric. He'd stolen it furtively from a house in a richer district some years before. He had lived alone in Thermidore for four hundred and forty years, five months, six days, and yet his appearance hadn't changed over the centuries, other than the normal changes one expected in a healthy human body: his hair and nails grew, sunlight darkened his skin in the warmer months. Apart from these fluctuations he was frozen in time, and sometimes he was afraid of seeing his reflection. There were few lines on his face, but his eyes were depthless with memory. Casmeer occasionally changed his appearance by allowing a beard to grow on his chin – scant but neat – or by cutting off his hair. He did this when anger came to his soul.

Only recently, during the last hundred years or so, had he begun to loot his environment: the still, breathless houses, the sombre museums, the dark, mousy-smelling shops. Sometimes, being able to (a mercy), he slept for weeks, perhaps months, at a time, but felt guilty doing so. Often, when he awoke, feeling remarkably refreshed, almost eager to live again, the plumosites from beyond the city walls, those scabrous crag-dwellers, would have breached all his defences and made off with vast amounts of spoils. They came for the roches, never stealing a whole one but breaking off arms, feet, noses, hair, burrowing into the shining stone to remove a crystal heart.

The roches were Casmeer's responsibility. Once, they had been his neighbours, friends, and clients. Further away, in other streets, higher up, were those who had made the laws, implemented them, those who had feasted in high, white mansions, laughing in yellow lamplight while Casmeer had worked his rugs below, in the artisan quarter. Now they were roches, stilled forever. Casmeer walked among them and felt his mobility strike their silence and stillness like a current. They felt his presence too, those who were left. They perhaps acknowledged him as sentinel and caretaker, perhaps they hated him for his mobile immortality. Sometimes Casmeer loved them, sometimes not, but he protected them always from the magpie urges of the plumosites. It had become his profession, for there was no one left to buy his rugs.

Outside Casmeer's front door was a brass plaque which read: Casmeer Brume, Rug-maker (by appointment to Sir Quallom). Every morning, Casmeer rubbed it gently with his sleeve to keep it bright. In all these years he had never managed to rub the words away, almost as if he was a ghost himself, lacking sufficient substance to abrade them. Perhaps the words would disappear overnight one day, time catching up.

Casmeer ventured into the street.

It was called Womber's Yard, even though it was fairly narrow and quite long. The street was tidy and reasonably free from weeds, as were all the other streets of Thermidore. The power of dissolution held its breath in this place. Plants grew, animals bred, but slowly. Casmeer's gaze, his memories, kept the city tidy. He sometimes felt he held it together by will alone. One moment of lapsed concentration and the tide of the years would come crashing in, obliterating everything. The roches would crumble to fragments and Casmeer would mummify in an instant, dust blowing down the street in seconds, his papery fragments blending with the jewel-dust of the others. At first, he used to wonder what kept Thermidore intact; now, he feared to think about it. Some silly superstitious fear. Wasn't he sure, in his heart, that Thermidore was eternal?

Jassica's Parade had drawn him. He stepped on to the wide, white thoroughfare and relaxed into the ambience diffused invisibly from every stone. Lady Jassica, a creature of ancient myth, had been the daughter of incestuous union. She had walked the far-forgotten streets of a nameless city, conjuring stars in the sky. On the street named after her, an observatory had been erected for public use. Sometimes, Casmeer visited it and looked at the daytime sky. He never ventured from his house at night. There were too many unexplained noises, too many echoes, too many vacillating shadows.

All the streets in Thermidore celebrated an ancient myth. Long ago, when King Pelotzo had commissioned the construction of the city, many architects had submitted plans for his inspection. All had bored him, until a young man named Tranquillo Origan had unrolled his splendid ideas upon the King's table.

'Why not build a city,' he said, 'whose spires, alleys, catacombs and buildings recreate all the myths of the world?'

'Why not?' King Pelotzo had responded, smiling at his chamberlains.

'It can be done,' Tranquillo said, and pointed to his coloured plans. 'Look at my ideas! My city could not help but be conducive to creative thought. Who knows what new myths might spring from the juxtaposition of so many fabulous designs?'

King Pelotzo had been at first intrigued, later inspired, finally convinced. Thermidore had been built. Then . . .

Where is Tranquillo Origan now? Casmeer wondered. Does he survey his handiwork still from some high spot, or has his changed flesh been plundered by the raiding plumosites, his eyes taken?

On a wall close to the observatory Casmeer noticed something new. Text cut into the wall. He went to peer at it. A new facet of Jassica's legend? The names in the text were unknown to him. Sister Lamanny, Squire True, a hound named Lasper . . . Making small sounds beneath his breath, Casmeer removed a notebook and pencil from his coat and annotated what he read. Near the end of the story, Jassica's father was mentioned. It was an elaboration, then, of the original story.

As he walked away, down the street, Casmeer thought, Perhaps I didn't notice that last time I was here? Walked past. It isn't new. Can't be. Nothing new comes to Thermidore.

As he passed between the shadows of the building, never looking up, he discreetly examined the palms of his hands. That was where it started in Elini; the roching. The process had been slow at first; a stiffening. Then the feelings would simply disappear, lulling the victim into believing they had merely suffered a temporary muscular ailment. True roching had taken them swiftly after that, taken them in waves, in batches, the survivors believing, each time, that they had been spared, that all the people who would roche had already done so. A fruitless hope. As the warm and living population diminished into cold and silent roches, the dwindling group of unroched saw their hopes become fears. All had succumbed eventually. All. Until Casmeer had been left alone in the city, listening only to a sour wind and the quiet inner throb of his own grief.

Would it come to him, ever? His footsteps echoed, presences bore down on him from the windows he would not raise his face to. Eventually, he left the Parade and crossed a cobbled square.

Come evening, Casmeer had shuttered himself in his house and had consumed a dinner of fowl-meat and sautéed greens. He had become a good cook, he thought. The upper farming terraces below the frowning slabs of the Overhang Crags were still a rich source of food. Once, they had fed a city, now they sustained only Casmeer; he had plenty to choose from. The Thermiddians had not refused to eat meat, but only enjoyed the flesh of birds and fish. Geese, chickens and quails occupied the abandoned farms, feeding themselves from the same harvests Casmeer lived on. Long, thick black fish bred in the shadowed pools beneath the mountain. Casmeer occasionally caught them, although once he'd thought he saw a pale elfin face looking up through the water at him, so refrained from taking too many of the fish. He feared invoking the displeasure of some water sprite.

I don't believe in water sprites, Casmeer told himself now as he chewed his chicken.

After dinner, he retired to his study, lit the lamps, drew the long curtains against the long windows. Oh, it was so silent at night. Why did he have to think that every time? Later, when it wasn't silent, he would be afraid. Was time progressing for him, or did he live the same day every day, just changing his spatial location in it? He had lived so long, he must be mad. Dismissing such thoughts sternly, Casmeer sat down and opened the book he was gradually filling with text. A clean, creamy page awaited his pen. It was the fifty-eighth book he had worked on. Behind his desk on shelves fifty-seven massive, hand-written volumes encroached across the wall. He wrote them slowly, taking many years to complete each one. This new book, only a dozen or so pages in, was different to all the others. In this book, Casmeer had deviated from cataloguing his memories of history, the city's memories. In this book, he had begun to create. The thought of this excited him, made him chuckle aloud. He dared to think he felt like a god, doing this. Casmeer dared not venture beyond the walls of Thermidore. Although he sometimes dreamed of doing so, of scaling the murderous crags of Overhang, of reaching another civilisation beyond the bleak rocks, he became breathless and panicked away from the city. He had tried it several times during the first fifty years of his solitude. Each time, he had been forced back, gasping, as if his body was unable to breathe the air outside. To begin with, he'd been able to wander up and down, keeping the city walls in sight, without a tremor of unease, but eventually even that freedom had been denied him. Now, he was embarking upon the next best thing. He was inventing the world beyond, peopling it, making them live.

Casmeer had been born in Thermidore and had no memory of the place before. He knew its name – Varaval – and was aware of all the historical events which had led to his people migrating into the mountains into their hidden fortress of a city. He knew a little about the land that had been left behind, although in his youth, he had never ventured far from Thermidore's walls. Therefore all his knowledge of the old land was gleaned from books. He knew that it had been a wide, flat country, its expanse occasionally punctuated by gentle ranges of ancient hills. He also knew that the land was completely surrounded by mountains, the ring of Overhang that sheltered forgotten Thermidore. He'd read of a couple of inland seas, although the flat lands were isolated from the great oceans, which were described in the travelogues of long-dead Thermiddian explorers. Thermidore's history, he thought, was tragic. It was a testament to humankind's curiosity, and perhaps their courage, but also their folly, their desire for the unattainable, their yearning to become as gods.

Hundreds of years before, in the great Combined University of Varaval, scientist scholars had researched ways through which human beings could attain immortality. Obviously, they were loth to test their elixirs and powders on human subjects, especially their own people, so took their test subjects from a species of quasi-sentient creatures, which had been discovered by Varavallian explorers in the far crags of Overhang. These creatures were dubbed plumosites. They resembled a bizarre mating of bird and monkey forms, and after prolonged study of the species, Varavallian scientists declared that all human life must have evolved from a similar animal. Plumosites proved to be ideal substitutes for human beings in the testing of immortality philtres. A great many substances were invented and tested, all of which proved fatal, or at least unsuccessful, when tested on the plumosites. Then, one fortunate day, a gifted young woman named Eclipsia Fontile created a substance that appeared to work. Laboratory specimens dosed with the stuff suffered no immediate side effects and, after three years, exhibited no signs of ageing. Cautiously, the Varavallians waited seven years, ten years, and more. Other kinds of animal were tested and, when Eclipsia Fontile was in her sixty-first year, the scholastic elite of Varaval, sanctioned by King Pelotzo, considered the drug safe enough to try on humans. Nobody appeared to suffer any ill effects and, after all the professional classes had partaken of the miracle substance, workers and servants were also given the drug. The King ordered a new city to be designed and constructed for this new race of immortals, in which they could all ponder the secrets of the universe for eternity. Many architects submitted plans to the King and his council, all of which narrowly failed to fulfil the King's dreams. All that is but for the designs of a young man named Tranquillo Origan. Unfortunately, after the city had been built and the people had moved into it in a spirit of great celebration, an unexpected, long-term side effect of the immortality drug manifested itself. After forty, fifty or even sixty years, the flesh of someone who had taken the drug began to crystallise. The domesticated plumosites and other animals were affected first, vitrifying until they could no longer move and became crystal statues. In terror, the scientists tried to discover how they might avert the same fate befalling the human population, but to no avail.

'Gradually,' wrote Casmeer, in the first of his volumes, 'the people froze, until only one remained. I, Casmeer Brume. I am the inheritor of Thermidore, frozen in my thirty-first year.'

Only Casmeer had benefited from the drug in the way it had been designed.

He knew little of what his people had been like before they'd migrated to Thermidore. The old libraries were full of historical books, but they were all of ancient history, of myth. When they'd come to occupy the city, the Thermiddians had virtually discarded their own past, perhaps feeling it was inferior to the future they had shaped for themselves. This made Casmeer's task of annotating the whole history of his people difficult. He was intrigued by the abandoned flat-lands beyond the mountains, and often wondered wistfully what it would be like to travel there, perhaps find people, learn to interact with others again. To him the flat-lands symbolised movement; a contrast to the frozen life of Thermidore. He had never been there, but he visualised swift movement across the uncluttered countryside. Perhaps even the settlements of the people who lived there were mobile? What could keep still upon such a land? Not even a great city, surely. There would be no louring mountains to block sight, progress, light.

Casmeer knew he must be lonely. He talked aloud to the house, Elini's roche, the plumosites as he killed them, the feral animals that slunk from his path as he patrolled the city. Still, it had become hard for him to imagine what it had been like to have human company. In his memory, Elini was as two-dimensional as the priestesses stitched on to his wall-rug. He had held her once, smelled her skin, heard the sounds she could make. Now, he could only recall the memory of that. So sad. And yet, despite the long absence of human warmth, he did not often crave it, and his lonely fantasies were enough to sustain him. His interest in other people was purely in what they might be seeing or doing, and it was easier to invent such things than to brave a journey into the unknown, to face the terrors of agoraphobia.

One summer evening, Casmeer had sat upon his roof with the slowly sinking company of the sun making fire in Elini's facets. If he gazed at the roche through half-closed eyes, Casmeer was just able to make out the vague contours of Elini's internal organs. She was a transparent statue; a clear rose-pink on the surface; muted blues and yellow within. Here a trail of broken ochre intestine, there the cobalt stones of kidneys. It no longer disturbed him to contemplate the roche in this way.

As he'd gazed at the roche, he had heard the high, raucous hoot of a plumosite from the west. No doubt it was trying to break through his defences. Lying back in his patterned hammock-chair, Casmeer wondered what the plumosites did with all the fragments of roche they made away with. He decided that they must take them back to their nests of scrub and thorn, where they would hold them up to the sky in order to gaze at the fire within. As his imagination took over, Casmeer invented a dark religion for the plumosites. To appease their god, who would naturally live deep within the black mountains, the plumosites would drop the roche shards into echoing shafts between the rocks. As the shards clattered down, the plumosites would hear the rumbling growl of their god's approval. They would hear a deep and distant crashing sound; the power of the god. In their ignorance, the plumosites would not realise the sounds they heard advertised the presence, not of a crotchety deity, but of a great subterranean torrent.

The shards would tumble and splinter their way between the sharp, cutting banks of the underground river. They would emerge beyond Overhang as glittering stones, twinkling in the bright sunlight, cast out into another world. What then?

Casmeer leaned back with closed eyes, trying to visualise the world the roches would find themselves in, the world of the flat-lands.

He imagined that the horizon would be far distant, double that which he could comfortably visualise, and it would merge with a dirty blue haze. The people who lived there would find the shards. They would wonder what they were, perhaps use them as precious stones, adorn their throats with them, their hair. No . . . They would realise the power of the shards, the remnants of sentience they contained. The shards could be used by the people.

But how?

Casmeer closed his eyes. He saw a woman, gaunt and tanned, standing as small as a pin in a great immensity of space. She held a shard of roche in her hand. She held it up to the sun, and it coruscated with energy. How would the stones be used, how would their power be tapped?

A huge silhouette crawled across the vista in Casmeer's mind. He saw minarets, flagpoles, campaniles, hanging terraces, ranks of columned temples. A city. Then he knew.

Great moving cities prowl the flat-lands. They are drawn along lines of glittering stones which are planted by a race of people who, steeped in their own mystery, direct the motions of the cities. These people are called terranauts. The cities are vast; huge leviathans that carve a deep wound in the earth. They accomplish movement because of the vast array of perambulatory mechanisms that adorn the inverted pyramids of their bellies; stampers, crawlers, wheels, punch sticks, skis. Their undersides are a forest of hanging pipes, conduits, nets, spouts, baskets and storage tanks. They pause to drink at any water the stones lead them to, dipping their myriad hoses into rivers and lakes, drawing up the sustenance their inhabitants need. Most of the cities grow their own produce and raise their own livestock in terraced fields around their perimeters, while other cities, being smaller and therefore more fleet, plough through the flat-lands at a smarter pace, their inhabitants gathering food, or bartering it, as they move along.

Casmeer experienced this vast and fully-formed visualisation as overwhelming stimuli to his senses. He could see, smell, taste and hear these cities. They had names as magnificent as their baroque forms. He already knew some of these names: Zanymandias, Frenepolis, Concatadore. And what was this smothering shadow that rippled over the ground, darkening his cities as they lumbered along? Ah, he could see now. It was a city in flight: a monstrous, improbable, impossible sight. Casmeer chuckled to himself. The city of Min. A city that always flew.

This was the world Casmeer Brume created, the world he would never see in reality. At night he dreamed up stories about it, and eventually he began to write these stories down. An alternative history book. Sometimes, he read the stories aloud to Elini's roche, and liked to hear the sound of his own voice. He felt he read aloud very well. Describing the cities, however, soon became tedious; he needed more. He needed individual characters to populate his new world. Idly, he made pencil sketches in the evening sunlight, to help him focus his thoughts about the matter. His protagonist was male – he felt that strongly – but there were other characters of both sexes, whom he felt were struggling, pinned beneath his pen, to emerge, take breath.

I must make my character begin to move through his world, Casmeer thought. He must be compelled to travel, to become the biographer of the flat-lands for me. How shall I do this? He pondered, and then smiled to himself, picked up his pen and began to write.

'The flying city was unthinkably ancient . . .'

Chapter Two
The Flying City

The flying city was unthinkably ancient. As its tidal shadow dappled the land beneath in a groping, amoebic progress, the city too was always reshaping. Ground-dwellers clustered like abscesses on the hempen ladders hanging down like entrails from the city's belly. Many made the climb. What they found in the city depended entirely on what they had recognised within themselves. Some saw only the weaponry – long abandoned – and they speculated. Some saw the maps on alleyway walls; maps which didn't tell them where they were, but simply indicated somewhere for them to go to. Some gravitated to the humid forest that flourished beneath a range of glass domes. Hidden among the trees there was a lake. It had flooded only once, during a storm, when the highest panes of the domes had shattered. Market stalls surrounded the forest in a hectic ring. The hub of hot leaves and noise and animal smells was surrounded by wide radials, slanting upwards, away from the city centre. These were the avenues of commerce, lined by businesses; some with buildings of their own, some without. The avenues were crossed by a warren of narrower streets; the habitat of performance, ideas, experiences and knowledge. The higher the street, the loftier and more abstract its creativity. On the next tier up, the family homes and civic buildings were to be found. The highest building was lair to an unconscious militia of social valuers, and from here a soul might rise to the stars, into dreams. Wide-winged birds soared frenziedly around this building – indistinct scraps of white among the rusting iron scaffolding – as though startled by a threatening sound. The only sound that startled anyone in this city, however, was the whirr and chirring of the birds.

The city kept pace with the sun overhead and now followed it into the evening. The silhouettes of black birds wove a febrile pattern around the stark, crenellated towers. Long horns blew mournfully and red and gold flags, bearing the emblems of the ruling families of the city, lifted sluggishly in a warm breeze. On the streets, people made genuflexions to welcome the night. Some kissed the stone walls around them, the Mother's flesh. Halfway up the second tier of the city, a small ritual was being concluded within a tiny room of one of the dwellings. Sounds, recently uttered, faded to silence, exhalations hung on the air. The glimmering light of tiny floor-lamps blossomed gently around the silhouettes of two people; one a young priest, kneeling; one a dead child, flat on his back. The priest was tired – his shoulders slumped. His hands shook a little upon his thighs. His long golden hair hung towards the grey, rug-covered flagstones like precious rags torn from a queen's train. He was slim and of medium height; his face was beautiful; his hands long-fingered and elegant. He had been working hard.

Now, he was thinking, listening, waiting for the ghost that always came to stand at his shoulder after his work was done, after the spirit had left the body of his client. Every time he was asked a question by a disembodied voice in his memory; the ghost of his work. He was sure that this voice had once belonged to someone, and perhaps still did, somewhere else. He knew the question had never been asked in reality and it was beyond him to gather up the pieces, the fragments, in his mind, and recognise the voice. It was always too close, as if a whispering mouth was pressed up to his ear. And yet, as he heard it, as he was held beneath its spell, he could almost remember the warmth of breath pouring along the nape of his neck, and a fragrance of birdwine in the air.

'What do you get from this?' The question was sarcastic, and the questioner, whoever or whatever they were, seemed to assume he had an intense motivation to carry out his work, or was at least party to an agreement. His lips echoed the question but he never had an answer. Neither could he move, nor go home, until the ghost had spoken its line and withdrawn.

'What do you get from this?'

Outside, a siren fluted into the night. A signal. It was over. He was a priest kneeling next to a corpse. He had extinguished life in the manner of his sacred profession, and it was time to leave.

The priest packed away his trappings, neatly and without haste. He turned off the music-maker, hanging on the wavy pound of the skin-bell, the delicate rapid chime and hum, as it faded on the memory of a harmonic. He picked up the sleepy-jar that contained a blue powder as light as dust, as fibrous as thick hair that had been finely diced. The music-maker and jar went into the bag which hung over his shoulder. Then the rest of his equipment went into a silk scarf; plain black with a fringe. These things were a glove made out of fur and a glove made out of snakeskin. The snakeskin, as usual was wearing thin; its scales shed themselves too quickly. He was always having to order a new one, because people liked that glove a lot. He left the tiny lamps behind; a gift, for remembrance. The scarf was stuffed into a pocket of his trousers. Tidied and ready to leave, he then drew the sheet up over the body on the bed. The dead face was smiling, but that was not unusual.

Relatives and loved ones tended to sidle into the room some minutes after his music faded to the silence of death. He was waiting for the door to open behind him and it did.

'May we give you something?' It was a woman speaking, her face tight with some unnamed emotion, her lips white. Her eyes were reddened, but from the effects of intoxicants rather than grief. She would contain her grief until the priest had gone away. Relatives of the dead often wanted to give him some kind of payment, as if to appease the limbs and fingers of the Death Woman, keep her far from their doors for a while.

The priest smiled at the woman gently, seeing his own face mirrored in the relaxation of her features. 'Not now,' he said, and reached out to touch her arm lightly. The woman nodded at him, fingers laced beneath her bosom. He bowed his head and with no further words or gestures left the house. He was never part of the mourning process. There were other functionaries to attend to that.

His name was Ays. He was a Priest of Hands, and he lived in a city named Min; a city that always flew.

What did he get out of his work? Sometimes, Ays would ask himself that question again as he sauntered back to his own community, in the honeycomb warren near the Temple itself. That he should receive some kind of gratification seemed absurd. A job was a job. Each to their own crack in the stone. Death did not frighten him, of course. Perhaps that was one of the rewards? Nobody had to pay for his services because the talents of Temple priests and priestesses were part of the community amenities. Ays had been indentured to the Temple all his life. He did not know who his parents were, but liked to believe they were city-hoppers who, having stayed in Min for a while, had fulfilled their fiscal obligations by delivering a child to public service. Not many people who'd been born in Min ever abandoned it, because they would miss the sensation of flight. They knew that relocating to a passing ground city would leave them feeling empty.

Sometimes, nagged by the receding effects of the drug in his blood, Ays had experienced an urge to travel, but it was always slight. He and Min were part of each other: its wood, clay and iron seemed like his own flesh in another form; his sensory organs were extensions of the city's heart; his work was a manifestation of nurturing concern for its inhabitants. To be apart from Min would be like dying for him, and no gloves of fur and snakeskin could stroke away the pain.

Ays lived on the second tier of Min and his chain of narrow rooms snaked rockwards towards the city's warm heart. The main room, in which he relaxed, ate and entertained friends, was at the front of the chain and had round windows that let in a clear natural light. His kitchen area was small, a curtained niche in the main room, but also boasted a window. His bedroom and bathroom, farther back, were lit by gas lamps; he never let the lights go out. The walls of these rooms were of rough-cut rock, the porous morphacite of which Min was constructed. Ays had hung coloured rugs on his walls, except for the one where a pale and sparkling vein of thremite ran through the rock. This, he lit to best effect. At night, when the lamps were low and starlight came like a spear through the window, the vein of thremite seemed to move. Ays liked to watch it with half-closed eyes.

Back in his own setting, he removed his pale ritual

clothing and dressed himself more comfortably. Not that his uniform was uncomfortable in itself, but he would feel odd doing mundane things while wearing it; not sacrilegious or heretical, just insignificant, as though he wasn't really there at all.

There might be messages waiting in the chute of his auroscope; news of another commission, a few words from a friend. The chute was connected to the city network, a tangle of tubes through which the voices of the people whispered and hummed, relayed by the passeteers, invisible presences stationed in hanging cubbies along the network. A system of mirrors relayed the image of the caller, but the voice was never theirs; they were a gesturing ghost ahead of their stolen words.

Ays kept his auroscope mirror in his living space, balanced in a long-legged dish. Other people fixed theirs to the wall for safety, but Ays liked to see it standing there, poised on the edge of destruction. Light from the window came in behind it, entering the silvered scales that made up its deceptively smooth surface. It directed splayed beams of light into the room, which looked as if they were searching for something hidden within the walls that Ays had never found. If there were no messages in the chute, he would blow into the tube hanging down from the wall, to open a passage to the Temple. 'All finished,' he would say to whichever Brother or Sister appeared in the mirror, half obscured by a disjointed window view.

'Another commission just came in. Can you take it?' they might say, or 'Nothing else for you today.'

If there is no further work, he would always add, 'Not yet.' And the Brother or Sister might smile thinly. 'It is, of course, impossible to predict . . . We'll call you.'

''Til then.' His communication finished, he would close the tube to break the connection and flick the mirror with his fingers to tilt it around a little. He didn't want any bored passeteer spying on his privacy.

After this, he would go to wash his hands. He'd take his snakeskin glove out of its wrap and hold it up to the light for inspection. Sometimes, if it had reached that state where it was as transparent as a soul, he would toss it into the waste channel straight away (where small scavenging mammals would drag it off for tidy consumption), and order another. 'Skin me a snake,' he'd say to the auroscope. It usually arrived within an hour, delivered by shute.

Min was flying low over the yellow land, into the sunset. Ays was out walking after his work was done. Above his head, the city was an abstract pattern of angular metal skeletons, clutching at gentler wooden shapes that looked like the silhouettes of vast, mechanical devices. The high buildings were all connected by a branching network of covered bridgeways that hung their shadows over the lesser roofs of stone and clay below. Winds whistled in the suspension ropes overhead as he walked the narrow streets. The skyline was dominated by a cluster of huddling glass domes, around which a mass of birds soared and dived. Amongst the ragged flocks, cagekites bobbed and dipped. They were the skycraft of small, agile children who, windblasted, were poised to capture the birds with nets.

Ays strolled down a steep rampway, out of the natural light, into the intestinal stone labyrinths of the inner and under city. He was fond of walking there, following the rise and fall of the circling paths. He descended a throat-like tunnel of orange light that led him out into one of the cold, blue-white crystal chambers where Min's water was stored. Towering, pale ranks of moist, fleshy fungus grew quickly in the breathing dark amidst the patter of scurrying claws. Despite the whispers of furtive activity in the shadow, Ays found these chambers very tranquil, and he had need of tranquillity that day. He was unable to dispel the image of the young boy he'd had to visit earlier. The child had only been twelve years old, his sickness pernicious. Still, despite these bad days, he knew his work was necessary. The boy would have died whether Ays had visited him or not, and had at least been eased into death in the proper manner. Ays calmly reminded himself of this, several times, but it was difficult to dispel a nagging uneasiness; something he'd never experienced before. After a few moments' quiet meditation, he left the Heartplace of the city and directed his steps rimward.

Ays was often drawn irresistibly to the city's rim, where he could watch the dark shadow of Min crawl hungrily over the ground beneath. The rim had its own community. Some people sat along the rails, telling stories to the passers-by; others painted or wrote, inspired by the vertiginous view, while others merely stood against the rail, staring silently at the ground below. Ays had his own rim ritual. People knew who he was and allowed him a few moments' solitary privacy when he arrived. Eventually, when they judged the time was right, the rim-watchers – young and old alike – would come to lean against the rail beside him. They might share their food with him, if they had any with them, and then ask him jaunty yet frightened questions about his work, even though they knew he was honour-bound not to answer them. Ays remembered their faces; he liked their company.

As he mounted the wide worn steps that led to the observation rails, he became aware of a strange, fluttery feeling in his belly. At first, he thought this must be yet another unwelcome reaction to his most recent work. Then, just as he'd found a comfortable space for himself beside the rail, the youngest rim-watchers all started jumping around, pointing out over the rim. Ays recognised the disturbance in his body for what it was: precognition of shift.

He squinted his eyes against the blood-and-daffodil light of the sinking sun, and could see that, down below, one of the ambulatory ground cities had become static, a diamond-shaped leviathan, balanced on its apex. It had been travelling along a long, deep valley between softly undulating hills that were misted with lavender flowers and dark green shrubs. Steaming waste fluids spattered down from the motionless city's pipe-coiled underbelly, puddling in the torn and muddied earth. People could be seen slipping down rope ladders hanging from beneath the city; others were already scurrying around in the valley, gathering whatever plants and animals they could find before their city recommenced its lumbering journey.

Ays peered through one of the many public telescopes situated along the rail, and noticed a cluster of dark brown canopies on the slope of one of the hills that advertised the presence of a terranaut camp. Terranauts were a secretive, nomadic race who caused the cities to move by planting lines of crystalline pilot-stones in the ground which the cities were then mysteriously compelled to follow. By arranging the stones in a significant pattern, the terranauts could also cause the cities to halt. The mysteries of the pilot-stones were guarded fiercely, so that only the terranauts understood how and why the cities obeyed the stones' invisible power.

Ays could see a thick ring of pilot-stones around the city beneath which had clearly caused the stoppage. As he scanned the landscape with his telescope, Min was drawn towards the panting city beneath and hovered over it, smothering the distant streets and towers with its shadow. Min had no option but to pause for a while as well. Everyone took these conditions for granted, even though, when the cities stopped moving, strange events could happen. Displacements, also known as shifts, occurred – distortions of things, time, or people. Some people believed that during a displacement terranauts could travel unseen between the cities, but no one knew for sure. A few Minnians, like Ays, had the ability to predict the shifts, rather like others could predict the coming of storms. The Temple was pleased Ays had this ability; it was as much a part of the regalia of his work as the music-maker, the jar of blue powder and the gloves.

Ays returned home to await the shift. As usual, he sat down in a chair to prepare himself for it. He felt the tug when it came, a crystalline fracture deep within the flesh – it was the only way he could describe it to himself. It reminded him of the thremite; he felt like a vein of brightness in starlight. Afterwards, just a few moments later, Ays blinked, and found the shade over the gas-lamp opposite was now in the shape of a glass lizard. Before, it had been a simple globe. He approved of this change. The furniture had altered its colour slightly, but had undergone no drastic modifications. The rugs beneath his feet felt a little softer perhaps, and the quality of the light was different; faintly pink.

In the bathroom, it was a different story. The bath was full of baby lemurs, a softly undulating foam of fur. Ays smiled and put his fingers against his mouth, wondering whether he should strip off his clothes and climb in among them. A bath of fur might feel quite agreeable.

He pondered, quite wistfully, how he would feel if one day, after a shift, his bath was full of terranaut; a lean young male with long black hair, or a wild-woman with flashing eyes and predatory fingers. Ays had always been intrigued by terranauts, even though he had never seen one close to.

During his meal the auroscope chimed, not only to advertise the arrival of a new glove through the shute, but also to indicate an incoming call from the Temple. He flicked the mirror into position and uncapped the tube, taking his new glove from the delivery slot as he did so. He wasn't annoyed at being disturbed. The very nature of his work meant that his days could never be planned.

'Here,' he said to the Sister in the mirror. She was unveiled, but her face was mostly covered by a fringe of beads which depended from a skull-cap.

'Brother Ays, a commission,' she answered, brushing aside the strands of beads, her mouth moving ahead of the words. On this occasion, the passeteer speaking was male.

'Location?'

'A transients' hostel . . . Thoroughfare Steep Steps. The hostel is called Resting on the Hop.'

'Oh?' Ays raised his brows at her image, to show her that more information was required. 'A transient? That's unusual.'

'He came in with the shift.'

That was more unusual than Ays thought. 'He climbed up to us?'

The Sister shook her head, and the beads caught the light from somewhere behind her. It looked as if she was shaking a bright spray of water from her head. 'From his condition, it would seem unlikely. We can only assume he was caught in the displacement unwittingly and was transferred here, perhaps from the city we're over. I expect he's a traveller.'

Ays walked around to face the mirror squarely,

trying on his new glove for size. 'And he's dying? How odd!'

The Sister nodded. 'An unexpected failing, true, but the hostel patron feels that we should offer his guest all of the city services, yours included.'

Ays looked at his fingers in their new snakeskin glove and flexed them slightly, watching the scales glimmer: 'I'll go right there,' he said. 'Oh, I need food for breakfast tomorrow. Any chance of a shrinee slipping out for me? Seeing as I'm working . . .' When the message reached her, the Sister raised her eyes for a moment, manifesting wry patience. That was a not uncommon request from Ays who made no secret of the fact that he was impatient with the market. Lesser minions could shop for him; he was a prestigious person, after all.

'Leave a list out,' said the Sister, '*and* the wafers. I'll see what I can do.'

Ays blew a kiss at her image to show appreciation. 'Blessings, Sister.'

The Sister shook her head, smiling. 'I hope it will be some time before I need *your* blessings, Brother.'

So did Ays. He quite liked her.

Evening was coming down. Ays put on a thick coat of hempweave before going outside, because there was a chill breeze squirming through the streets of Min. He put as many of the baby lemurs as he could comfortably carry into a large embroidered bag which he carried over his shoulder. Mounting the steps to the third tier, he paused for a moment to let the wind snag his hair and gazed out towards the rim and the dark horizon. Min had moved on. There were no cities near, no sign of life at all other than a few root bladders, half deflated and empty of passengers, drifting on the air currents to a final, distant landing and decay.

Ays felt excited and intrigued by this new commission. Wanderers, travellers, transients – whatever name they were known by – were always mentally abnormal in some way, because as the cities themselves travelled constantly, to leave home for a while and find your way back again was a difficult task. If being unconcerned about that wasn't abnormal, what was? Generally, transients were individuals following bizarre and esoteric quests that most people could not even begin to understand, never mind be sympathetic towards. Many were the victims of the calenture – a deluded state, which induced a fevered desire to leave the city of their birth. In the grip of this dementia, they forgot their homes, their origins, or even if they didn't, eventually became ignorant of where their homes might actually be. Some were mystics – a category Ays preferred to think his own parents must have belonged to – and some had important, but mysterious, purposes. Terranauts, of course, were eternal wanderers, like the cities they led, but no one thought of them as abnormal. However, barring unforeseen accidents, visitors to Min rarely needed the attentions of the Temple. Transients who were ill generally migrated instinctively towards the special sanatoriums where they could be properly cared for. If they were lucky, their feet would lead them to a suitable place before it was too late. These sanatoriums could be found in ground cities having a reputation for inordinately frequent displacements. Quite often, after a shift, a person might find they were no longer ill. True, it was also possible for such people to disappear completely from their current location's reality, but most invalids considered this slight risk to be worth taking. Ays thought his new commission must involve someone who had fallen sick unawares, or perhaps he'd find they were one of those extreme crazies who simply didn't care what happened to them?

Resting on the Hop, a narrow wafer of stone, nestled between two more imposing hostelries whose facades were clay-scaped with concealed amenity-pipes. In contrast, the Hop's wall was braided, almost carelessly, with rubbery heat conduits that sprouted from the pavement, breathing the warmth of Min's heart to the water tanks and cosy-stones of the inn.

Ays put his hand upon the door, but before he could push it open he heard an abrupt hissing whisper just beside his ear. There was a powerful sensation of someone very tall standing next to his shoulder, of sound being sucked away. He turned swiftly, his flesh freezing, but there was no one there. Yet still the feeling of being observed, of being somehow *touched*, did not abate. Odd. Ays shivered. Perhaps he'd experienced a flashback to his earlier working? He wondered if he was failing in some way, becoming prey to the melancholy that sometimes assailed the Temple staff. If any strange feelings recurred, he would consult a therapist to be on the safe side. This resolved, he directed his attention to the door once more, yet found he was reluctant to open it. The evening seemed to hold its breath around him.

Enough of this! He pushed the door roughly and stepped over the threshold.

Inside, the proprietress was waiting for him, a large woman whose age-sculpted face spoke of a character impatient with nuisance and pettifoggery. After a formal greeting, she offered Ays a biscuit and a mug of curds to augment his strength. Ays' stomach was already full, but he respected the ritual and took a single bite and a single sip. He offered the woman the baby lemurs, for which she was grateful. All of her mantises had disappeared with the shift.

'How urgently is my attention required here?' he asked.

The woman frowned. She didn't know. 'Retching,' she replied, and made a harried gesture with her hands. 'Blood. Foam. Refuses a physick. Says no one can help. I'm no healer, but I'd say time is limited.' She exhaled a weary snort. 'I don't need this tonight. There's enough kerfuffle as it is with the displacement.' Beyond her statuesque frame, Ays could see that her tap-room was empty of patrons.

He inclined his head in sympathy. 'Perhaps you had better introduce me right away?'

The proprietress nodded and preceded him into a shadowy, upward-sloping passageway. Lighted bowls of oil set into the wall did very little to dispel the gloom, but the atmosphere was oddly homely.

'Came in with the displacement, I heard?' Ays said to the broad back ahead of him.

The woman grunted an affirmative. 'Found on the street outside. No currency on him and no indication of a name.'

'The sickness could be infectious,' he said, a slight note of censure in his voice. The inn really should have called in a physick, whatever protests had been made.

'No, the rats were already trying to get at him. They know whether flesh is bad or not.'

He could not contest that. 'Are you sure he's dying?'

'You'll see.'

The proprietress took him into a room that was hardly more than a cell, and had perhaps once been a bone-cupboard, but it was warm and the oil-bowl was freshly fragranced. Immediately he stepped over the threshold, Ays sensed a difference about this commission. The room felt breathless, *waiting*, as had the air outside. For an instant of time, a fleeting impression, which he could only define as an awareness of power and indifference encompassing the entire city, blazed across his mind. Hela flashback. Must be. He willed his mind to clear, and it did.

The bed jammed against the far wall of the room was extremely narrow, because of the confined space, but the sheets were glaring white and the downy-sack plump. Within it lay a dying man, his breath liquid in his chest. His face was yellow and damp, but it was easy to see that at one time he'd been handsome. He had good bones, wide brows, a well-shaped jaw and deep-set eyes. His hair was dark brown, nearly black, but a grey streak grew back from the left temple. It always saddened Ays to see what sickness could do to a human frame; vitality and beauty were stripped away. It reminded him how essential his work was, how merciful. The man in the bed appeared to be clinging to the last vestiges of life with great effort. Ays had not come too soon, it seemed.

He became aware of the proprietress standing just behind him in the doorway, her deliberate silence. She was hoping Ays would forget she was there because she wanted to watch him at work. People always wanted to watch. Ays had no personal aversion to this, yet somehow felt instinctively that his work should remain secret, like the moment beyond death itself. He looked over his shoulder at the spectator until, with a disgruntled frown, she closed the door and went away. Then, he unpacked his equipment. He watched himself doing it; his hands moving too slowly, his mind racing ahead.

He opened the lid of the music-maker and a thin sound came out like a question. He put it on the floor. He took out the sleepy-jar, the picture on its lid long worn away. When the lid came off, a thick earthy-sweet scent spilled out into the room and he poked his fingers into the swirling blue dust within. Next, he unwrapped his gloves. Snakeskin for immortality of the soul, the essence, the invisible bird of spirit. Snakeskin for the place beyond life. Fur for protection by winter beasts, earthy reality; the luxury of fur, its sensuality. Ays knew his symbols.

He put some of the sleepy-mix inside a sticky tissue, and rolled it into a narrow cylinder which he lit with a flare-pin. He took the first lungful of smoke, sucking it down into his body, closing his eyes, visualising the silvery-purple cloud sinking into his blood. The effect was instantaneous; the world flexed around him. The thin sound from the music-maker became briefly strident; an insect din. Expelling smoke through his nose, he drew on his glove of fur, over the fingers of his left hand. Then he had to speak.

'I am Ays,' he said to the man lying on the bed. The man's eyes were closed, his face expressing no pain, although fluid leaked between his lax yet bitten lips. For a brief moment, Ays wondered whether the man was already dead and reached out to touch him with his ungloved hand. But the eyelids flickered open, revealing dark, clouded eyes that were full of confusion.

'I am from the Temple of Mother Darkness,' Ays said. 'I am a priest.' The skin on his back was prickling; he felt unnerved.

'They sent for you.' The man's voice was young, although whatever sickness convulsed his flesh had stripped the youth from his face.

'Yes,' Ays answered. 'I am here to travel with you for a while.'

The man sighed and his mouth smiled a little. 'Then I must be dying.'

Ays squatted down beside the bed. He could see the man was looking at his gloved hand in an intense manner. Ays felt absurdly ashamed. 'What is your sickness?' His voice came out more sharply than he intended.

The man screwed up his eyes. 'It is . . . a fading.' Then a flicker of panic twisted in his eyes. 'Where am I? Why am I here? What is this place?'

'Hush,' Ays said, putting his ungloved hand on the man's shoulder. He could feel, he thought, a fever heat. 'You are in the flying city of Min. Are you a traveller?'

'I don't want to die in an unknown place. I don't want to die at all!' The outburst sounded absurdly artificial, as if the man knew he was not dying at all.

Ays had to repress a shudder. He was gripped, briefly, by another cramp of unreality. 'That is why I am here,' he murmured gently, 'to help you die. That is my function. I soothe away the terrors of it.'

The man laughed weakly. 'You cannot do that. I am a stranger.'

'It makes no difference. Lie back. Be still.'

Ays drew the downy-sack away. Beneath it, the man's thin, damp body had been dressed in a clean, woollen night-shirt, which Ays guessed had been donated by the Hop's proprietress. As was the custom, the body had been bathed and oiled, ready for his attention. The dying man's long hair had been tied neatly back behind his head. As a priest, Ays was not to be bothered with such sordid tasks.

Before touching the recipient further, Ays sucked a mouthful of smoke from the smouldering sleepy-mix. He wanted to leave the room, leave the job incomplete, but knew he could not. Steeling himself with another inhalation, he leaned over the dying man, offering his puckered lips in a kiss, filling the invalid's sour, dry mouth with the smoke. His cracked lips trembled beneath Ays' own; Ays could feel the ailing lungs spasm beneath his breath.

The man lay back, blinking, his mouth slack, and Ays gently untied the laces of the night-shirt, peeled it aside. The skin was like marble, slick and pale. He did not want to touch it. Hurriedly, he pressed the glove of fur against the damp belly. It would feel like a cat rolling over and over. The contact re-established the routine; uneasy feelings ebbed. Ays' animal hand traced the line of ribs and sinew, the hollow, the torso's throat; beneath them, the hard, rippling landscape of stomach and loins.

'Your breath, it is strange,' mumbled the man.

'Mmm.' Ays did not want to encourage him to talk. He did not like his recipients talking. Soon, the sleepy-mix would eclipse, by degrees, the memory of his life. The images would fade away, until all that remained was death, a blankness. Having been raised in the Temple, and fed raw mara hela – the plant from which the sleepy-mix derived – from an early age, the drug could not kill Ays. He was addicted to it, but it brought him only well-being in a swiftly flying world. He flew on its tide in his body. He would die without it now.

'Murderer,' said the dying man in a soft voice.

Never had Ays heard such quiet conviction. His hand stopped moving. 'Be still,' he said.

The man tried to laugh. 'You have filled me with death, with your breath of death.'

'Hush, don't be afraid. Relax.'

A hand, surprisingly strong, shot out and grabbed Ays' wrist.

'Your poisonous smoke brings visions to me!'

'It is supposed to,' Ays said, attempting to free himself. This had never happened before. No one had ever resisted him, or the beckoning of the Death Woman.

'Visions, yes!' the man cried, his grip becoming harder. 'Let me tell you this: she writhed as she lay in the blood of your birth. She called upon every known god, and every unknown one, to curse you! She was a fine woman, but mazed; crazed by the lands between. She had more lovers than she could remember.'

'Be quiet!' Ays said. The man had pulled him close, so their faces were nearly touching. Ays was afraid he'd see the centres of the man's eyes spinning like kaleidoscopes, but he could not look away.

The man laughed, a strong, soft sound, and pushed Ays back a little, although he did not let him go. 'No, you must indulge me. After all, the visions speak to you, not me.' He sighed, his eyes rolling. 'Such a thin trickle of time, so scant, so vanishing. She thrust you from her arms. She strode away, her hair like a winnowing of flags. She was taller than the earth, with limbs like trees. She cursed you.'

'Who?' Ays couldn't resist asking, even though he knew he should stopper these words with smoke as soon as possible.

The man fixed him with eyes that were suddenly bright and clear. 'Your mother. Who else?'

Ays' heart seemed to freeze in his body. He yanked his hands away from the dying man's grasp, denying the conviction he was only free because he had been allowed to escape.

'You sometimes wonder about her, don't you?' said the man.

'I have nothing to wonder about,' Ays replied. His eyes felt hot. 'My mother lives here in the city.'

'Of course she does,' murmured the man.

Ays wanted to hit the cracked lips, silence them. 'You know nothing about me!'

'Do I not? I know you were left on this city as a babe. I know everything.'

Ays was silent for a moment, then asked the inevitable. 'Who are you?' The first thought, almost exultant, strangely, was that this man might be his father, but of course he was too young.

'I am your desire. Rotting. Dying. You can name me if you wish.'

Ays' ears had begun to sing with horror. He scrambled backwards on the floor.

'Say it,' said the man, and grinned. The face was death now; hollows and shadows; the void.

Ays' voice felt thick in his throat. He could barely speak, and when he did the word came out in a hiss. 'Die!'

The word was blasphemy, a denial of his art, but he could not even hate himself for it.

'Die, yesss . . .' The man's eyes rolled upwards until the colour disappeared. 'She is standing there smiling. Can't you see her?'

The chime of the music-maker seemed insignificant against the true silence of the room. Ays resisted the urge to glance over his shoulder into the shadows. He thrust his hands between his legs. 'Just die!'

'You will never forget me,' said the man. 'But neither will you remember me.'

Ays squeezed his eyes shut. For a moment, he wondered why he was letting the raving of a dying man affect him so much. He was just another recipient; a stranger, undoubtedly demented even before his sickness had taken his mind. His revelations were simply wild guesses, nothing more.

For a moment there was silence, then the man sighed deeply. 'You neglect your duties,' he said in a faint voice, raising a limp hand from the bed.

'I have no duty to you.' Despite these words, Ays knew he should administer more sleepy-mix, finish his work, if only to give himself respite, yet he balked from touching the stranger again.

'No, you have no duty to me.'

Without taking his eyes from the bed, afraid to do so, in case the man rose up from it, Ays scrabbled to re-light the sleepy-mix, as if his life depended on it. His hands trembled. He took a long draw of the smoke.

'You are not long for this world,' said the man.

Ays ignored him and concentrated on filling his lungs with more smoke. He would administer a dose that no one could survive, even if it knocked him silly. And yet the man's countenance seemed to have changed. As Ays leaned over him, his face was at peace. There were no more threatening utterances. He accepted the smoke from Ays' lips and his eyes were clear yet dark; the darkness of midnight.

'Finish your work,' he whispered.

I have been wrong, Ays thought. He is a sick man, nothing more. I should pity him. 'There is no obligation,' he replied warily. 'You are an outsider. If you have your own rites, there is no need to endure ours.'

The man blinked slowly. 'No, give me your absolution.'

Blearily, he watched as Ays stroked him with reluctant hands, stroked him further away from life. He seemed content to allow Ays to wallow in the swell of hela-strike. His words were stilled.

Full of a sleepy haze, Ays concentrated on dispelling the negative feelings he had just experienced. Perhaps it was still possible to kindle the specific sanctity of the moment. Intoxicated by the robust dose of hela, he become nothing more than a body of smoke. The music-maker hummed upon the floor, curtains at the tiny window trembled in a breeze and he was empowered by the stillness of his art, called up from the core of him. This success, the banishing of the hostile atmosphere, filled him with a piercing rapture. He swayed, let his hair fall upon the body beneath his hands, stroking away the life of it. Listen to me, beloved, listen to the rhythm of my blood, my calling.

It was time for the glove of snakeskin.

The moment was stillness itself as Ays peeled away the glove of fur. It fell to the floor; a beast sucked dry of life. A skin without quickening. His left hand squirmed into the scales, and the air was full of curling smoke. The man was watching him, watching him, the essence of his dying soul condensed into his eyes.

As Ays touched the stranger lightly with his fingers, the man made an unexpected sound. It was a crystal sound that cracked across the sound of breath, of the music, of the infinitesimal hiss of the smoke.

It was the sound of laughter.

Ays felt as if he was made of glass, some brittle substance, and the laughter cracked him. He felt the power of his skill drain out from his body, out like a thin, rancid liquor, down through the cracks in the floor.

What have you done to me?

'Oh, pretty boy,' gurgled the man. 'Let me tell you this. I see a new horizon for you. Not this world. Not this one. No wings on it. You do not even know what you are. Ah!' His body arched and his head pressed back into the pillows. 'I know your creators,' he said. 'Know them well. They are dancing for me now. I see them. I see them.' His eyes, suddenly bright with a feverish light, fixed on Ays' face. 'You will not forget me. Never. Remember this.' Then, his body expelled a last gust of breath.

Presently, he died.

Outside, a forlorn, fluting sound filled the evening, and the shadow of a gigantic root bladder slipped between the crenellated spires. Travellers, mazed-people, going somewhere.

The stranger had brought time into this room, but it was not the present. He'd been looking into the past.

Ays shivered. He felt unsure of what to do. This

man had managed to fight against the traditional ministrations. In the end, Ays felt sure he'd somehow conjured a death rite of his own.

The music-maker hummed a pretty, weightless tune and Ays knelt upon the floor, his back rigid, his stiff arms plunged between his thighs. He was cold. He could not look at the dead man.

Fleeing the hostel before the proprietress could accost him, Ays ran into the night. As he ran, he relived in his mind the events of the last hour. Why had he allowed it to affect him so badly? He was filled with fear. The man's garbled words could be interpreted as a forecast of death, Ays' death. Death Woman. Mother? Had he spoken of symbols or real people?

Ays' frantic flight woke the birds that lived among the eaves of the buildings. They screamed in protest, wheeling round his head. Somehow, he found his way along the twisting alleys and walkways to the home of his friend, Louette. She was not indentured to the Temple but, in a back room of her narrow house, painted icons which she sold at market. Another friend of Ays', an angular, unpredictable woman named Umbilana, made the frames for the icons and planed the wood for Louette to paint upon. Ays was relieved Umbilana wasn't there when he stumbled into Louette's parlour. Umbilana was always impatient with emotional upsets. Louette, on the other hand, thrived on them, and clearly relished the prospect of fussing round Ays, a person she had hitherto believed to be unshakeable.

'Are you ill?' she demanded, pressing him into an abundantly cushioned sofa. Her parlour was dark and hot, like a womb.

Ays tried to fight her off, but his attempts were feeble. 'I'm not sure.'

'Hot tisane!' Louette declared, apparently to herself.

'That will help. A strong beverage, perhaps a pinch of blane cast into the steam.'

Ays grimaced and gestured emphatically with his hands. 'No. Tisanes are for babes and virgins. Give me arabisth!'

Louette's eyes opened wide. 'Oh, too strong! Certainly inappropriate for distress. Don't you know it causes contractions of the blood?'

'I care not! Don't you have any?'

Louette pursed her lips in disapproval. 'I have some,' she said reluctantly, and went into her kitchen to fetch a glass.

Ays sipped the fiery, ostensibly illegal but easily acquired, liquor gratefully. Its insistence on numbing human flesh as quickly as possible was a balm to his addled nerves. Louette had at least refrained from diluting it with cordial.

As he sipped, Louette watched him intently, pointedly nursing a cup of tisane on her lap. 'So?' she enquired at last.

'I met a man today who claims to have known my mother.'

'Oh? Is that possible?'

Ays grimaced. 'No . . . I don't think so. He was dying, his mind wandering. I think he cursed me.'

Louette's face fell. 'You must tell me,' she said.

Haltingly, Ays related what had happened. It seemed absurd now, spoken into the hot air of Louette's plush, enveloping parlour. Perhaps he had overreacted after all? And yet . . .

'You fear omens,' Louette decided. 'Of course. I suppose I would too, but as a friend, I have to say you must disregard this fool's outlandish last words.'

'But he told me there was another world for me.'

Louette shook her head vigorously. 'He was raving, speaking of his own death-fears.'

'I don't think he meant death, not really.'

'What else? What else?'

Ays was reluctant to speak the word. Would speaking it invoke a new future for him? 'Below!'

'No!'

'He spoke of my mother.'

'He was frightening you, Ays, resentful of your health, your life beyond his death. You *must* see that!'

'But the hela . . . It warps perceptions, alters consciousness, perhaps gives access to knowledge otherwise denied us?'

Louette stood up and went to her hearth where a tisane-bowl steamed luxuriously beside the fire. She took a deep, shuddering breath, as if to calm herself. 'If anyone could have visions of your mother, it would surely be you.' She poured herself another cup. 'You know what travellers are like; all mazy-minded. I'm surprised you've put so much store by his whifflings.'

Ays knew she was simply saying the things she considered most therapeutic for him to hear. Louette was a highly superstitious individual. Her honest instinct would probably be to have hysterics on his behalf. He noticed she could not face him to say these words.

'Well, I have set store by them. I had a precognition before entering the inn, but disregarded it.' Ays leaned back into the cushions and closed his eyes. 'Perhaps I should have contacted the Temple then, got someone else to do the job?'

'Too late for that talk,' Louette said briskly. She settled herself on the rug beside the hearth. 'Ays, you must forget it.'

He put his fingers against his eyes. 'Lou, I can't. As every moment passes, I feel something growing stronger inside me – a change.'

'This is ridiculous!' Louette's voice was shrill. 'Drink more arabisth. Relax!'

Ays shook his head. 'I can't. You don't understand. He's changed my life, I know it.'

There was a moment's silence and then Louette asked fearfully: 'What are you going to do?'

Ays sighed, blinked at the ceiling. 'I suppose I must visit the Inner Place, speak to the Mother herself, but I am reluctant. This could be seen as a transgression.'

'I can't see how. You were only doing your job.'

Ays sat up straight, seemed to compose himself, and lifted his glass. He took another sip of the arabisth. 'This man . . . he affected me in such a strange way. I think I treated him very badly. I even told him to die! If I visit the Mother, I will have to confess this, although I am sure she is already aware of it.'

'And waiting for you to come to her, perhaps?'

Ays nodded. 'Yes.' Suddenly, he felt suffused with a dreadful, yet undeniably languorous, feeling of grief. 'Lou, I get the feeling . . .' He could not continue.

She stared at him. 'Don't say it,' she said, and her voice was husky.

'I have to,' Ays said, 'because I feel it so strongly. I will leave Min.'

'You won't,' Louette said, reaching out to touch him. 'You can't. Visit the Mother. She will tell you your fears are groundless.'

The outer court of the Temple was chilly and blue. Ays found himself at the threshold, breathless, unsure of how he had got there. It must be the effects of the arabisth. He remembered stepping out of Louette's humid room into the cold night, but little else.

Mist-robed noviciates glided across the long corridor before him, as insubstantial as ghosts, intent on their own thoughts. He felt invisible. The air vibrated with a subliminal hum, the vespers chant of the sancted.

Ays whispered into the air. 'What is happening to me, Mother?' His breath steamed before him, but he could not augur the answer to his question from its shape.

The air of the temple smelled of hela, and also of a violently scented disinfectant which masked the smell of ritual essences rising from the drains. Bulbous coils of insulation tubes clung to the walls like distended intestines, silver where moisture had collected in their creases and folds. Three clockwork priests stood motionless around a low shrine, where feathers had been burned earlier in the day. The marble floor around their feet was strewn with ribbons, offerings from the people of Min in gratitude for the predictions the priests had divined from the smoke of the feathers.

Ays ventured down the corridor, which was more like a tunnel, towards the inner sanctum, the Inner Place, where the Mother of Darkness ruled in moist, heated dimness, attended by her small, brightly attired consort, the Lord of Forgetting. Ays knew this visit was inevitable, but still feared the Mother's censure. Mother . . . He could not visualise even a phantom of his real mother, because his earliest memories were all of the Temple, its dormitories and gardens, its rituals and safe foreverness. Nevertheless, Ays knew he had a past before this time, a past of which he should surely remember some brief images. He knew he had not been born in Min. Part of his training had included instruction in causality, so he supposed the events of this day indicated that some vast unknown stone, which bore the story of his life, had just rolled ponderously forward to reveal a different face that was etched with new markings. All this was meant to happen and had been caused to happen by events in his past. Nothing was accidental.

As he was swallowed by the dark tunnel that led to the queen of Min's belief system, Ays attempted to concentrate on the Mother's form, to conjure her from imagination to reality.

Mother of Darkness with her gnarled brown skin. Not old but weather-sculpted, dryad-faced, pointed mouth and chin. Her eyebrows, black and bushy as feather-thorn nuts, yearned towards each other above her black, black eyes. She dressed always in fallen leaves, the wings of moths, things brown and dusty. A cloak of black chiffon was woven together with twigs and dead insects. Mother of Darkness. Mother of all. Sweet Sister of Sighs. The Grave Whore. The Great Eclipser.

The tunnel disgorged Ays into a vaulted, brown shrine where he went down on his knees. The dim yellow light did little to dispel the darkness there. Did anything lurk in the shadows? Drunken priestesses cackled in the distance. There was a rustling as of swept leaves. The incense smoke smelled of bonfires.

Ays composed himself, steadied his breathing. 'Mother, I wish to speak with you. It is Ays, your son.'

Silence in the shrine now. No hisses or distant laughter. Ays wondered whether he could sense a listening ear. It was impossible to tell. The Mother might be lying in her brown, inky pool deep inside the Temple, her sculpted demon face covered by an oily film. There might be no one listening, no one at all. Ays rarely went to the Temple. He had grown away from it, cast off the trappings. Now, he lived in air. And yet who else could answer his queries and soothe his troubled heart but the Mother incarnate, the High Priestess of All, whose will alone was legended to keep Min aloft?

Where is my history? Upon the ground, beneath some distant sea? Where? Am I of high birth? People say my hands are noble. Who was the woman who carried me in her body, nurtured me, drew me forth into the world, and dropped me here, high above the world? Did I mean nothing to her? And what of my father, what . . .? Is the world below, the world I was conceived in, calling me back to it? Why are these thoughts coming to me now?

Something groaned and shifted and slapped within the walls of the temple. An echo maybe, of something deeper.

'*The child wakes.*' There was laughter, a gritty, gurgling sound.

Mother! Ays bowed his head to the floor, felt the cold black stone against his brow. The Presence was all around him, enveloping, moist warm.

'*Is this truly the first time ever you have asked yourself these questions*?' The voice of the goddess, the priestess, was nourishment, dripping with nectar, dark and holy. Terrifying succour.

'Yes.'

'*Strange.*'

'I had no need before. Today . . .'

'*I know what happened today.*'

'Mother, do you know the answers?' Ays' voice sounded timorous and young in his ears. He liked the way it sounded; the dark columns threw it back to him. Was there movement in the stifling shadows?

Ays heard a monstrous sigh that shivered through the Temple walls, vibrated the massing columns, parted the incense smoke above him. '*I know all! All! But Ays, my pretty smalling, can you pluck the knowledge from my breast, my brow? No! I cannot bestow such privileges with abandon.*'

'Are you angry with me?' Ays murmured, his heart beating hot and wild in his ribcage.

'*Angry? No*!' roared the goddess.

'But I mistreated a recipient today.'

Ays was answered only by an indecipherable, rumbling sound.

'Then perhaps I am wrong to ask all these questions? I should perhaps just accept things as they are? But that man today . . . he spoke of new horizons for me, Mother, he spoke of other worlds. Of death. He said there would be no wings. I don't understand this, or am I afraid of the obvious answer? Is it necessary to take heed of his words? Should I act upon them? They seem to be acting upon me . . .'

'*Questioning, in itself, is not a terrible thing. You asked the questions and they must be answered, but not by me. I heard the stranger speak, but I did not hear death in his words. No, no. Something else.*' The temple throbbed to the sound of a monstrous sigh. '*You are growing now, growing forth, and your shoots must spread until they touch the knowledge.*'

'But how?' Ays pleaded. 'Where do I look?'

'*In stone, in cloud. In the smiles of passing strangers, the earth.*'

'Below,' said Ays miserably. This apparent confirmation of his fears gave him unexpected relief. There was no further response to his words. He felt the tides of goddess draw back, until the Temple was empty of Presence.

'Below,' said Ays again. He sighed, kneeling upright, his hands upon his thighs. A breath of cold was uttered by the stone around him. He stood up. Retraced his steps. Of course, he had already known the answer.

Casmeer

The hands of a priest, exquisite hands.

Casmeer sighed. He scribbled idly on his blotter with

his pen, observed the ink spread and smear. A beautiful boy; a priest. Casmeer wasn't sure whether he wanted to have created a priest. It seemed an austere and callous calling. No, it was not enough to have created this boy of Min. Besides, Casmeer sensed the priest was cold, somehow malformed in spirit.

I am a novice story-teller, he thought. That is all. He had wanted a passionate individual to roam his flatlands, someone with whom he could identify. And yet, even as he acknowledged the thought, he knew that cold Ays was very much a part of him already. Lonely Ays, imprisoned in an icy structure he had built around his own heart. Casmeer did not like this person, but neither could he abandon him. Not yet. Ays had a story, a life. It had to be written. A history had formed for Ays, a changeable history. Where had it come from?

Idly, Casmeer sketched upon a scrap of paper beside his book. He wanted to invoke a different being, a new personality. Ays was not enough. Casmeer would not abandon him – could not, now – but Ays was insufficient for his needs, unsatisfying as a creation. Despite this, Casmeer could not rid himself of the image of Ays' face as he drew. He created a darker Ays, more weathered. A wild creature of mystery and sudden impulse. As the picture took shape, acquired dimension, images began to pour through Casmeer's mind. The new Ays danced along lines of glittering stones. He spun in a frenzy beneath a hail of moonlight. A ground-dweller. Not a priest. A terranaut.

It could be no other.

Chapter Three
Travelling Time

They had no roots, the terranauts; no, none at all. Roving, tumbling, they moved across the land, strewing pilot-stones to draw the cities after. They were merry, irreverent, untrustworthy even to one another. In their veins spumed travelling blood that was drawn ever onwards like a tide, obeying the pull of sinister moons too distant to be seen.

Finnigin danced upon a large flat stone to the tune of double flutes and drums. He was surrounded by a circle of terranauts, younger than himself, and just beyond the stone a vigorous fire threw sparks at the sky. The watching terranauts were all male, and clapped in time to Finnigin's dance. They too were intoxicated, but there was a faint atmosphere of uneasiness beneath the music, as if the celebration was a sham, or perhaps a party thrown for a condemned man, scant hours before his execution.

Finnigin, however, seemed oblivious to any undercurrents in the air. He was young and drunk, mad with life, with the star-shine above, the glinting eyes and teeth of his fellows around him. He held a bladder of hotsup in one hand, slopping sweet sticky juice over his sleeve and upon the stone beneath him. He danced a man's dance, signalling a birthday. Terranauts did not have birthdays every year. They kept no record of age as such, but the star of Finnigin's birth had reached a certain point in the sky, which signalled that the time for his first wander had become imminent. All terranauts were cast out from their troupes when the first of these astral events occurred – generally after sixteen years or so – in order to learn about survival and resourcefulness. Some did not survive the experience. The brief ceremony that preceded this expulsion was the only time when male and female terranauts separated. Men expelled boys; women expelled girls. As to why this should be, no one really knew. It was perhaps their only tradition and they adhered to it through habit rather than choice.

There was little grace to Finnigin's dance, hardly any rhythm, only an obedience to a manic urge. He kicked his feet high and grimaced, swigging from the hotsup bladder. His friends laughed at his antics, but their eyes, as they glanced at one another, were furtive, nervous. Very shortly, many other boys would undergo the same expulsion. It was difficult to laugh at Finnigin with this in mind, which was why they were all so drunk. Older men, sitting beyond the light of the fire, smiled fiercely in patient endurance. Soon, they would rise and chase the youth from the fire, send him out, scrabbling, into the cold shadows of the night, into the dark blue and grey, the hint of white, the stone, away.

The older men had all been through this rite of passage; cast out from the tribe that had reared them, the indifferent care of women, the treacherous friendships of other men. Cast out, to wander, to learn, to find their souls, entrap and wear them. Eventually, they had found other wandering tribes, joined them, taken mates and lovers, had bred with them and moved on. Individuals, both male and female, often came and went swiftly in the troupe.

Finnigin danced and, as he danced, he smiled. A

pilot-stone had been embedded in one of his sharp teeth earlier that day; it would be his badge, his emblem. Licking it would remind him of who he was, should he feel the need to remember. Now it glittered in the bare moonlight, drinking the beams.

Some distance off, the women and male transvestites of the troupe sat swaying in a circle. Some might mourn the loss of sweet Finnigin, so pleasing to the eye. Later in the night, some might spit at the place where his feet had danced. Broken hearts: there were many of those among the terranauts. Their hearts were as brittle as crystal shards, yet just as sharp and hard. They broke easily into a thousand fragments, and each of those fragments was a new heart, keen enough to wound and tear. Emotions ran hotly, like lava. Eyes glittered as sharp as hearts. Often, the air around the camps smelled of dripping musk, of repressed heat, of danger. Vicious they were, vicious and swift and careless. Children were often lost in the barren lands between the cities. Later, they might be found again, feral and feline, clambering up the hoses and conduits of a passing city, to dwell among the people there, break hearts, move on.

In the shadows behind Finnigin's dance, the men stood up and advanced towards the flat stone. They had been smoking mara hela, or chewing it; their movements were slow but inexorable. Finnigin seemed not to see them, his attention turned nowhere, neither outward nor inward. He staggered as the men pushed him from the stone. He grinned at his giggling friends, pulled a rueful face.

'Go now!' The ritual was scant; no pretty words. The night looked cold and hard beyond the camp; the moon stared cruelly. Finnigin shivered at the edge of the light, the light of the fire. The men pushed him further, without violence, but without remorse.

'Go!'

Turning their backs, they gathered up the other boys and shepherded them back towards the waiting women. The heat went with them; embers sputtered. Someone had kicked soil over the remains of the fire.

Finnigin, left alone, hiccuped to himself. The whistling quiet of the night bore down on him. He felt his flesh about his bones. He made a whining sound. The hotsup was finished, gone, the fire withdrawn, friendship severed. He might die in the wilderness, or not. He would certainly mature, through privation, fear, loneliness.

Earlier, before the hotsup, Finnigin's carer, Leeara, had placed a bundle of his belongings beyond the perimeter of the camp. He had kissed Finnigin's brow carelessly. Too big for him to care for now; a man justabouts. Begone, grown child. Finnigin had forgotten about the baggage. He stumbled drunkenly into the cold moonshadows and curled beneath a rock, vomiting warm hotsup on to the gritty soil.

In the morning, the terranaut camp had disappeared, moved on, and the huge, shadowy outline of an approaching city could be seen in the east, haloed by a heat-haze. Finnigin sat up among the scrub. He smelled his own vomit, felt his head pound with pain. He remembered the baggage and went to find it. Afterwards, he nosed through the scant remains of the camp. But there was little left behind: for all their carelessness, the terranauts did not leave mess in their wake. A row of pinky-mauve pilot-stones glittered in the dawn, converging to a single point in the vanishing distance.

Terranaut children knew little about the function or placing of pilot-stones. Such secrets were reserved for when they attached themselves to a terranaut group, after their first wandering. Then, the young adults would be given instruction in the practices of stone-placing. There were no rites associated with this training, for terranauts had no religion as such. We are born, we live, we die, was the terranaut philosophy. Finnigin did not know who his parents were. Leeara, a beautiful young man who dressed as a woman, had been appointed his carer from when he was a baby. One day, when Finnigin was trotting beside Leeara as he'd been planting stones, a huge query about the world and his place in it formed in Finnigin's mind. The air was full of the soaring songs that the terranauts sang as they handled the stones. The songs had no words, only sounds.

'How does it happen?' Finnigin had asked. 'How can a little stone drag a big city along?'

Leeara had held a stone up to the sun and told Finnigin to squint at it. 'What do you see?'

'Little flames,' he'd answered.

'It is life,' Leeara had explained. 'And cities need life.'

'But why do *we* plant the stones?'

Leeara carelessly tossed the pilot-stone into the air, caught it. 'Because we have a feel for it, and the numpkins on the cities don't.'

Finnigin frowned. 'Why should we care about them? Why can't we have our own cities?'

Leeara shrugged, grimacing. 'We don't care about them . . .' He curled his hand around the stone. 'We need the feel of the stones. It's in our blood. We need them.' Then he pulled a wry face. 'And why would we want cities? We already have hundreds of them.'

'The cities belong to us?' Finnigin sounded dubious. On the occasions he climbed aboard a city, he'd felt very alien, and certainly not at home. Home to him was the rolling land, the wide sky, the musty tents.

'Cities belong to nobody,' Leeara said, 'but we are

part of them, as they are part of us. We are related.'

'I don't understand,' Finnigin whined. 'What do you mean?'

'Enough!' Leeara clipped his ear. 'It's not your business yet. Go and play. Don't pester me when I'm busy.'

Finnigin had retreated. He knew when Leeara had had enough of him.

Finnigin and his companions sometimes conjectured about the secrets of adults. 'They can't have sex if they don't plant stones,' one girl said. 'That's why they do it.'

'What's sex?' asked several of the boys, and the girls swapped looks and grinned at one another.

The world is made up of people keeping secrets, Finnigin thought.

Now, he knew what sex was, and that it had nothing to do with pilot-stones or cities. He supposed, vaguely, that he would discover these more arcane things upon his journey. Why else would young terranauts be cast out into the world alone?

The sounds of the city broke the stillness. Wattle birds ran gaping across the land, their flightless wings held wide like open coats. Finnigin shaded his eyes. It would be at least three days before the city reached him; time enough to grow hungry. He began to walk towards its advancing bulk.

Chapter Four
Down

Ays walked the rim of Min, his hand upon the polished rail. Sudden squalls of wind seemed to talk to him, pluck his hair in a spiteful way. His hood had fallen back. How strange his body felt, how liquid, not of air as he was accustomed to feel. It was as if his legs already strode the world below. Fluid preceded rock. Below, he would become heavy, clay-like, still. An airy sigh puffed from his lungs. He threw back his head, looked up. Birds above him wove an esoteric pattern through the winds. Children hung from towers, spreading nets into the sky. Could he bear to leave this place? If he cut off a finger, would it be any less painful, any less threatening to his reality, his image of himself? He looked at his hands and imagined one of them gone, both of them. To cut himself from Min might be like that, too terrible to imagine, too grotesque.

Images of cutting had plagued him since his visit to the Temple. He had dreamt of it. Walking through the streets he had noticed knives more keenly; the sharpening stone turning outside the butcher's cell, the serried razors of the barbers chiming in the wind. These portents were not lost on him.

Then why leave? What did it matter where he came from, who had carried his forming flesh within her body? What did the dying words of a maze-mind matter? The man had also figured prominently in Ays' dreams, and yet, as had been predicted, Ays could no longer remember his face, only the feel of him. He wished now that he'd learned the stranger's name.

Ays leaned back against the rail, spread out his arms, looked up with streaming eyes at the limitless sky. He felt angry about the man who had inadvertently changed his life. This interloper, to whom he had meant nothing, had expelled his last breaths upon a curse. Ays wondered whether the man had realised it, whether his soul remembered this act, whether it felt remorse. What was I to you? Ays thought fiercely. Nothing. Yet you have ruined my life.

Then ignore what he said, a cool inner voice murmured in Ays' heart. Stay here. Return to the Mother and tell her you have resolved your troubles, silenced the questions.

That would be the easy way, surely. To leave Min would be to step blind into the unknown. Different rules would hold sway upon the ground, rules of which Ays was entirely ignorant. It was possible he'd blunder to his own death within hours of leaving Min. Then, his departure would all have been for nothing. The dying man had spoken of death. Was that the destiny awaiting Ays? If so, it would be senseless to leave the flying city. He did not even know what he'd be looking for, down there upon the static ground. His mother? His babyhood? No, something more. Despite the arguments he'd conducted with himself over the past few days, Ays could not shake the conviction, the *faith*, that there was something waiting for him: a concatenation of events, significant experiences. All it would take for him to begin the process was to leave the flying city. He could not understand why he should be so sure of this, but there it was: a certainty. Someone had once said to him that belief itself was a sickness, a dead end for the questing intelligence of the human mind. It seemed he'd infected himself with a debilitating dose. There is something out there for me, he thought, and then chided himself for the melodrama of the idea. There is something for everyone, everywhere, if they have the courage to look. He knew he was no different from anyone else. Perhaps he had simply become the victim of calenture, and had not realised it? He did not feel fevered and yet his compulsion was undeniably mazy.

There were also practical considerations to be dealt with: mara hela. Lovely hela, sweet insinuation on the mind, relentless captor of the body. Although his flesh had learned to endure her mordant embrace, he paid a price for that immunity: without the hela, he would die. In order to leave Min, he would have to take his cruel seductress with him. Mara hela was a drug whose use was not confined to Min, but Ays could hardly risk setting foot upon the ground without access to a plentiful supply. He knew that many travellers were also addicts of the drug, and they solved the problem by sowing hela spores into the lining of their coats or shirts. Ays would have to emulate this practice. Nourished by the heat and steam of his travelling body, a network of fronds would develop within the cloth, which could be harvested regularly. But what if the spores should die, the fronds wither? What then? A slow, agonising death? A frantic, delirious search for wild hela? Ays shuddered. He could not bear to think about it.

The shadow of the city moved slowly over the land below, fingers of it creeping into the creases of the shallow hills. Ays looked down, and tried to imagine himself rooted there. He did not want to tell his friends about his new obsession, but it would seem impolite, uncaring, just to leave them without a word. Louette was aware of the situation, of course, but had been sworn to secrecy. Ays trusted her. She was the only person he knew who kept a confidence. When he'd told her what the Mother had said to him, and the conclusions he'd drawn for himself from Her words, Louette embraced him and began to cry.

'I will miss you,' she said. That was all, at first. Meagre words to a person who, as far as she was concerned, had more or less announced he intended to kill himself. He appreciated the fact she made no allusion to a possible brain-fever.

Umbilana was the next to know. Being an unpredictable creature herself, she did not appear to be surprised by Ays' announcement, which he delivered in Louette's parlour where he had called a gathering of his closest friends the night before he'd decided to leave the city. Because he knew Umbilana would be scathing, he told her his news before the others arrived.

She inspected him silently for a few moments, and then said, 'You don't have the *look* of calenture, but are you completely sane, Ays?'

'Yes,' he answered shortly. 'It is not a mind-fever. The Mother Herself suggested I leave Min.'

'Of course, you realise this means we shall never see you again?' Umbilana drawled, her words wrapped in a wreath of blane smoke, which was her favourite intoxicant.

'Don't say that!' Louette hissed, flinching from the truth.

'Why not?' Umbilana's tone was blunt. 'Ays knows what he's doing, I'm sure.' She laughed dryly. 'Or at least I hope he does.'

'Your hopes are fulfilled,' Ays said with a gracious inclination of his head. Many found Umbilana a grating presence, but he'd always admired her for her wit, her courage and her blistering honesty.

'How kind of you to give us so much notice!'

Umbilana said. 'At least we don't have to spend weeks bemoaning your imminent departure. Other friends would not have been so considerate.'

'You can be so hard, 'Lana!' Louette complained. Ays merely smiled.

His friends arrived in couples and groups, until Louette's parlour was full of people and the air became almost unbearably hot. Ays sat before the fire and told everyone what he intended to do. This was met with exclamations and tears, concern for his state of mind. As he reassured them on the latter count, he considered he really must be maze-brained to leave all these people who cared for him so much.

As if divining his thoughts, Umbilana made a remark. She tapped her pipe against her teeth. 'Well, Ays, there are significant absences here this evening!'

'Yes,' Louette agreed, her voice surprised as if she'd only just realised it. 'Where are Borora and Ingo? Have you told them already? Are they too sad to come?'

Ays shook his head. Borora and Ingo were his lovers, though less close to him in spirit than his friends. Would he miss them too? Borora was a beautiful priestess, with haunted eyes and hair like a swatch of raw, red silk, who wrote sad poetry for him, and languorously tormented his body with the subtlest of caresses in their bed of love. Ingo, on the other hand, was a lanky bird-catcher, too old for his craft perhaps, who took Ays fiercely to his bed, bruised him, alarmed his nerves. He had already decided he would not tell them he was going. Why this was so, he could not identify exactly. Perhaps he feared protests or, worse, the possibility they might insist on accompanying him. With the decision to leave Min had come the certainty his relationships with Borora and Ingo were over. They had never touched his heart particularly. It was far harder to bid farewell to his friends.

In the mists of morning, as Min skimmed lazily over the land, gentle hills beneath, Louette and Umbilana walked with Ays to the rim station. The ground was hidden in fog; nothing could be seen there, nothing. They listened for the hoot and grind of a passing city, but there was no sound.

'What will you do?' Louette whispered, her hand tucked through Ays' elbow. 'Just walk until you find a city, or . . . something?'

Ays shrugged. He could not say he was allowing himself to fall backwards into the arms of Fate, which he hoped were already there to catch him. He felt sure he had to do nothing more than simply descend to the ground. The rest, whatever it was, would follow naturally. Perhaps it was cruel of him not to let Louette know how he felt. If he could infect her with his irrational confidence, maybe she would not worry for him as much.

'I feel sure our friend Ays will survive,' Umbilana said. 'Look at him! He will enchant the first person he meets and make them fall in love with him.'

'That person might be a lunatic,' Louette couldn't help saying. She shuddered. 'Do you have any weapons with you, Ays? You should take weapons!'

'I have a dart-blower and a selection of knives.'

'You should have acquired a blast whistle and some earplugs,' Umbilana advised casually.

There were many stations situated around the rim of the city, but not all of them were used. These were the places where itinerants climbed aboard Min, or else, far more rarely, inhabitants left for the ground. Each station consisted of a round tower with a walkway around the summit, which was a landing terminal where travellers could embark on to, or disembark from, wind vehicles. There were several varieties of these conveyances, the most popular being the inflatable vegetable bladder, but Min itself manufactured disposable balloons, thus advertising the one-way nature of any departure from the city.

Louette and Umbilana accompanied Ays up the steps of the tower. The station-mistress had already been advised of Ays' requirements and was still in the process of inflating a large, black balloon, which was moored to the platform of the terminal. One of her staff, a young girl, was busy attaching a fine net of ropes to a wicker basket provided for the traveller's comfort, even though the descent would be fairly swift. The balloon would nestle beneath the net, slowly exhaling its brief, vital breath. Ays felt slightly sick to think he would soon have to step over the edge of the tower and into the basket.

As Ays and his friends mounted the platform, the station-mistress gave Ays a swift assessing glance, barely concealing her disapproval. She was used to welcoming people, not to bidding them farewell, and wondered how a Priest of Hands, who appeared to be perfectly well balanced, could harbour the maziness of wanting to leave the city. Wasn't he aware of his responsibilities or, even more unsettling, had he been partly mad all the time? She hoped he'd not attended the deaths of anyone she knew or was related to. The balloon and basket were expensive; they would not be returned, after all. Few baskets were ever sold for this purpose. Mostly they were used for lowering the remains of the dead to the ground, after all liquids useful to the Minnians had been decanted from the corpse.

Before climbing into the basket, Ays gave the remainder of his tokens to his friends. He would not be able to use them on the ground; other currencies were used there.

Louette looked frightened, her dark eyes round and damp. Her lips were trembling. Umbilana stood back, smoking blane, her eyes narrow against the smoke.

'Ays, I beg you, think again,' said Louette miserably, holding out her small, white hands.

Ays shook his head. No. If there was a time when he could have been dissuaded, it had passed.

'You are dying for us,' said Umbilana coolly. 'The moment you step off the rim, you might as well be dead.'

'We shall think of you often,' said Louette, pointedly ignoring her companion's grim pronouncement. 'We shall imagine where you might be. Who knows? One day you might return.'

'Who knows?' said Ays. He was more inclined to espouse Umbilana's view.

Looking down, over the platform rim, Ays could not see the ground. He felt numb, unreal. Was this what death felt like? His coat hung heavily around his body. He carried a generous supply of chopped hela in his pocket, and already young fronds were sprouting from the spores he had stuck to the lining of his coat.

'What if you lose your coat!' Louette gasped, as if aware her friend was thinking about the spores.

'Guard it well,' Umbilana advised, and grinned.

'I will.'

The station-mistress interrupted in a sharp voice. 'It's ready for you, sir. Pass me your baggage so I may stow it securely.'

Without further words, Ays passed his belongings to the station-mistress and climbed into his conveyance, his stomach lurching as the basket momentarily sank beneath his weight. Above him, the balloon bobbed on the misty air, tugging at the ropes that confined it. The station-mistress finished strapping his baggage to the basket, and then waved coloured flags at the sky, uttering resonant calls in case there were any other mad travellers hovering near the city.

At the station-mistress's signal, her assistant released the balloon from its ropes. At first it plummeted wildly, and all Louette and Umbilana could see was Ays' terrified face looking up at them, disappearing into a grey fog.

'Take our love with you!' cried Louette, leaning over the rim. Umbilana pulled her back.

'You'll fall!' she said sharply.

During the first few seconds of descent, Ays was convinced he was about to die, to be smashed to pieces on the ground. He crouched in terror on the floor of the basket, gripping the leather hand-holds, wondering when the basket would tip and spill him out. Then, as his heart and his senses came into balance, the balloon seemed to sigh, to find its own gentle pace. Ays felt disorientated, as if he was floating in nothing. Soon, the underside of Min disappeared from his sight, and he was enveloped by a dense cocoon of grey mist. There was no sound but for his own agonised breathing and the creak of the wicker basket beneath his body.

What am I doing? he thought. Someone stop me, pull me back!

In his mind he could hear himself crying out for help, he could see the black, snaking rope that the station-mistress would throw out for him, his own desperate scrabbling to take hold of it. But it was all in his mind. He did not cry out, barely moved. The balloon exhaled gas in small spurts, the basket descended; swiftly, then not at all, then swiftly once more. The quality of the air changed, new smells invaded Ays' senses; a dry, spicy aroma, a reek of burned earth. He could hear something that sounded like a wind instrument being played; gentle fluting notes.

He braced himself for a landing, but all that happened was that the basket settled itself gracefully upon the ground, with only a cursory jar to his body, and the spent balloon drifted with a final exhalation to the side.

For a few moments, Ays remained rigidly in the basket, too nervous to move. The journey had been swifter than he'd imagined. He'd not prepared himself mentally for the landing. After a minute or two, as nothing untoward occurred, he found his courage and stood up. The mist was swirling, here at ground level, like hela smoke. It was patchy and in places Ays could see through it, catch glimpses of peculiar silhouettes. And what was that strange beast? The fluting sounds were coming from it.

Gingerly, Ays stepped out of the basket, removed his luggage and settled it on to the frame he'd earlier strapped on to his back. He realised at once he'd brought too many things with him, because the weight of the backpack nearly thrust him to his knees. Terrified of hunger, he'd mainly packed it with supplies. He'd thought about bringing changes of clothing with him, but there had seemed little point to that. He could not imagine being in a situation where he would wear his leisure garments, expecting travelling to be hard. Itinerants in Min had always been travel-worn and scruffy; he felt it would be the same for him now. Vanity, as well as comfort and security, must be a thing of the past.

The strange, musical noises waxed and waned through the mist. Ays took a few cautious steps towards the sounds, and was soon close enough to the music's source to identify it as an abandoned wind orchestra; struts and vanes and hollow pipes vibrating in the wet breeze. Someone had left it there. Who? And why had it been constructed in this desolate place?

Ays peered through the jutting structures and then jumped back with a start. Although indistinct, it appeared that a motionless figure was standing among the ruined strings of an air-harp a few feet away. Ays froze, but after a few moments the shape, whatever it was, had made no movement. He peered again. Was it really a figure, or just part of the instrument? It was tall. Just as he was about to move forward and investigate, virtually convinced it was no living thing, the figure moved. Ays' flesh began to prickle as he became aware of scrutiny. He wondered whether he should feel afraid now. The unknown person – or creature – could be dangerous, could kill him. Was his journey to end so swiftly? The figure seemed slowly to raise an arm, to point directly at Ays, then . . . there was nothing but the mist.

A trick of the eye. A phantom.

Ays sighed and laughed softly to himself. He would have to harden himself to fear. He walked over to the air-harp and touched its scoured surface. There were traces of carvings in the wood. Ripples of faint music emanated wearily from what was left of its strings. The sound surrounded Ays and, as he listened to it, a strange feeling built up within him, like a wave about to crest. He almost shook with its creation. Looking down, he could see the imprint of booted feet in the dusty ground. He shuddered, suddenly and irrationally convinced the figure, now vanished, had been waiting there just for him.

With this realisation, as if it was a cue, or a key, to the next phase of Ays' journey, a memory was kindled in his mind. It was a memory of sound. Ays could see phantom lips pursed around the lip of a little pipe.

Fingers moved over a series of holes and music came out. *My mother.*

Casmeer

My mother.

Casmeer's pen was poised above the page. He felt a constriction of unshed tears in his breast. He heard again the little pipe his mother used to play over his crib. The memory of that sound was itself a comfort, as it had soothed and eased his night-time terrors as a child. What had made him recall that now? Surely it was not a part of what he was trying to create?

He sighed heavily, laid down the pen, rubbed his tired eyes with his hands. Loneliness hung heavily upon him that night. His loneliness was Ays', or vice versa. Ays is my lost soul, he thought, my lost soul wandering.

It was in his mind to strike out much of what he had inscribed, for he felt he was being cruel to his creation. He could feel the weight of future torments building up within him. They would spew forth from his hurrying hands to fill the blank pages with anguish and despair. Don't do it.

Change it now.

He couldn't.

Ays is not looking for his mother, he thought. He believes he is, but I know that isn't so. I couldn't make it so even if I tried. Even if I erased every word I have written about him and began again. What I have written is reality. It can happen no other way.

He knew he could not get close to Ays, for Ays was the part of himself that was distant. He could only ever be a phantom in Ays' reality, reaching out to touch, to communicate, yet fruitlessly because he was mute and limbless. In some strange way, even though he knew himself to be the author of Ays' life, he was but an observer on the boundary of it; helpless.

If Finnigin was to be Casmeer's peaks, then Ays would be his hollows, and for all Ays' distance, it was easier to be with him than with the flickering presence of the terranaut.

The night was deep, unending. Casmeer decided he would sleep when the light came. Until then, he would explore his new world. He would reach out.

Chapter Five
The Beautiful

On the day before his expulsion from the troupe, Leeara had said to Finnigin, 'It will be easy for you to drift from city to city. Don't do it.'

He'd looked at Leeara sharply. 'Why not? Where else should I go?'

Leeara had shrugged, and Finnigin had sensed an evasive answer was imminent. 'When I undertook my first wandering, I decided I would learn more by venturing into unknown territory. And what is unknown in this land?'

Finnigin pulled a face. 'I don't know.'

Leeara snorted in exasperation, and cuffed Finnigin's head. 'Dim boy! The mountains, of course, the mountains!'

'The mountains? How would I climb them? There's no way in.'

Leeara shook his head. 'There is for those who look carefully. A different way of living can be found there. It is very interesting. People live in static cities, ones that cannot move, and they are rooted into the rocks themselves, I think.'

'Do you want me to go there?'

'It's your decision,' Leeara said abruptly. 'That was just a suggestion.'

'All right, I'll go there,' Finnigin said, to please him.

'As you wish,' said Leeara.

As a child, Finnigin had heard tales around the fires about the mountains and their peoples. The carers had many tales to tell, most of them unconvincing. They spoke of cannibalism, bizarre customs, fearsome battles. One man once said that gods still lived in the mountains, which everyone laughed at, including the story-teller. Terranauts scorned the idea of gods, although secretly Finnigin thought he'd like them to exist. The mountains were a long way off yet. Even when he squinted into the distance, Finnigin could perceive no hazy outlines of peaks or spikes. Therefore, he would have to find some form of transport. He knew this need could be satisfied within the moving cities, and chance had laid an approaching city in his path.

As the great cities crawled across the flat-lands, residents often came down to the ground in order to gather brushwood, animals, stones, vegetation – and in some cases even wandering travellers – that could be hauled back to their homes via the complicated system of ropes and pulleys that hung from the undersides of all the cities. Sometimes, they would barter with groups of terranauts or nomad ore-scrapers, and it was through the accumulation of goods in this fashion that the cities could expand. Metal was needed to augment the under structure, to create new platforms for building and farm-terracing. The inhabitants of every city were driven to enlarge and embellish their home town, and each one was marked by the inner symbols of the collective psyche of its natives, thus giving birth to a unique appearance, a singular ambience.

The city that Finnigin approached during the first days of exile from his troupe was crowned with a chaotic thicket of wide metal sickles; great blades that caught the sun; scimitars for cutting light. The city's silhouette was therefore spiky yet voluptuous against the sky; a bizarre combination of shapes. Finnigin could only guess at the purpose behind this design; it could be inspired by a religious belief system or a particular fashion in architecture. City-dwellers were often superstitious and feared the day when their home might shudder to a halt and spill them over its side. In order to appease invented gods who might postpone such a calamity, the cities were sometimes nothing but a vast and complicated Temple, each structure significant in its shape and position within the whole. Finnigin thought that he perceived a shape within the pattern of the sickles that suggested a secret meaning, but it was only a hint and as such held his attention only briefly. The leviathan lumbered towards him, dragged by the allure of the pilot-stones in its path.

It took Finnigin three and a half days to reach the city, slightly longer than he had thought. During this time, he had wondered whether he should attempt to make plans for his future, but had abandoned the idea after he became bored with it. Worrying about forthcoming situations was not a characteristic of Finnigin's. Sometimes he had blundered into difficulties because of it, but so far, in his relatively short life, the dangers had all been social rather than physical.

As he and the city drew nearer to each other, Finnigin noticed clusters of cages hanging from its gargantuan underbelly. Closer inspection revealed that they contained corpses in various degrees of decay. Slogans attached to the cages advised any onlookers of the crimes committed by the malefactors who had been sentenced to death by starvation and exposure.

As no arcana of stones had been placed to stop the city in its journey, when telescopic walkways would be lowered to the ground, Finnigin was obliged to grab hold of one of the many waving rope ladders that hung from its gut. He winced slightly as a breeze reached his nose that had clearly passed by the caged corpses. The bulk of the city enfolded him, as he climbed into a noisy dark. The nether-life of the city, comprising homeless urchins and vagrants, who had suspended themselves in leather harnesses, shouted encouragement and abuse to Finnigin as he climbed. Some pleaded for him to swing his way towards them, offering services both carnal and practical. Finnigin was familiar with such types, having come across them before. Generally, those who lurked among the city's bowels were either outcasts who had been forced into permanent residence among the hanging straps, or else engineers, mechanics and breakdown-diviners whose function was to service the city's viscera and be persistently alert for malfunction. Most of the flat-lands peoples shared a common language, with slight local variations. Those who now addressed Finnigin all spoke in a clipped patois. Some of them seemed so embalmed in the oily juices continually spattering from the city's waste conduits and lubrication ducts that their flesh resembled that of the less uncorrupted inhabitants of the malefactors' cages nearer the ground.

Finnigin ignored them all. He was lithe and strong, and his corded arms hauled his body aloft with little effort apparent. Despite the effects of the hotsup he'd consumed two days previously, he felt very much alive, trembling with energy, excited by the cries and calls of those he passed.

Eventually, after wriggling up between the coils of a section of heating pipe, he found himself in a long vertical conduit which was dripping with soiled water and crawling with bald rodents. A metal ladder was set into its side, and Finnigin swung perilously for a few terrifying moments as he transferred himself from the rope ladder. Looking down, he could see a patch of ground very far away, and a face looked up at him from an opening some metres away, grinning a spike-toothed leer. Finnigin closed his eyes and caught his breath, allowing the chill of fright to melt from his limbs. An echoing, spiteful laugh rang out, bouncing from coil to coil beneath him, eventually swallowed by the thump, churn and hum of the city's mechanisms.

After a tortuous climb up the metal ladder, Finnigin emerged through a trap-door into a small, dark booth that led on to the street. A middle-aged woman with a shaved head and tattoos across her cheeks was on duty in the booth, observing, and perhaps obstructing, anyone or anything seeking ingress into the city. She was stationed behind a counter whose surface was hidden beneath a muddle of papers and disintegrating bound registers. Although Finnigin received an impression of light and bustle beyond the door, the booth's atmosphere was one of breathless stillness. It smelled of musty wood.

Finnigin shook wet locks of hair from his eyes. He felt both physically and socially uncomfortable, which in itself was a new experience for him. Rarely had his heart beaten so fast, and moments of terror in his life to date had been remarkably few. His clothes were damp and stained, and his baggage had become unbearably heavy upon his back owing to the fact that it had been soaked during the climb. He was surrounded by a pungent aroma of dirty oil and stagnant water.

'Where am I?' he asked.

The woman surveyed him with stony eyes, her mouth chewing rhythmically. Her nose twitched in polite aversion. 'Terranaut,' she observed, and her voice was coloured both by contempt and awe.

Finnigin was unsure whether that was a question or a remark. 'Where am I?'

The woman leaned forward on powerful folded arms. 'Zanymandias,' she replied. 'If you are a terranaut, you may enter our splendid city. But if you are something else, a worthless vagrant, for example, you must pay me for the privilege of stepping forth from my booth.'

'As you guessed, I am a terranaut,' Finnigin said, with a measure of pride.

The woman shrugged. 'In that case, you must show me your stone. It is mandatory. Deceit in these matters in not unknown.'

'I am not lying!' Humiliation was another new experience for Finnigin.

'Then show me the stone.' She stood up and picked up a pen. 'It is of no consequence to me whether you reveal the stone or pay the toll.'

'And what is the charge for entrance?'

Again, the woman shrugged, as if nothing were of less importance to her. 'Naturally, Zanymandias has its own currency, therefore visitors have to barter for entrance. Generally this involves voluntary labour for a specified period.' She paused. 'Do I take it you do not wish to display your stone? Shall I call the path-wardens to take you to an induction centre?'

Her words conjured up unpleasant images in Finnigin's head. 'No, you may examine my stone.'

Like all terranauts, he was coy and prudish about his body with anyone not of his own kind. Grudgingly, he offered forth his face, and the woman peeled back his lips. She nodded to herself, tapping the tooth where the pilot-stone was embedded with the end of her pen. 'Hmm. Seems in order.' She smiled, most of her reserve forgotten now. 'Forgive the indignity but we have to check. You never can tell. Not really.'

'Is no one but terranauts allowed freely into your

city?' Finnigin asked. He had not heard of Zanymandias before.

The woman shrugged. 'That depends.'

'On what?'

'My opinion, the analysis of my intuition. For only crazy people walk the spaces between. Crazies and . . .' she smiled crookedly '. . . terranauts.'

Finnigin was not inclined to comment. 'Then I am free to go?'

'Well, first I have to inform you that we tolerate no misconduct in our city, and your being a terranaut does not exempt you from that. If you wish to feed, you must barter for it. Likewise for accommodation. You are lucky. Most establishments are proud to have a terranaut wash their pots for a couple of nights. Or . . .' she gave him a pointed glance '. . . you could acquire currency through other means. There is not a person of my acquaintance who would say no to a night of dalliance with one of your sort, and most will pay for the favour.' She grinned, causing Finnigin to bridle in outrage.

'My needs are modest. I'll exchange labour to get what I want.' He felt annoyed with himself for even acknowledging the woman's remarks.

In response, the booth-keeper waved an arm towards the starkly lit opening to her booth. 'In that case, Zanymandias lies before you. Enjoy!'

'Thank you.'

For a moment, Finnigin paused at the threshold of the booth. He looked back, but the woman had dismissed him from her thoughts and was now concentrating on some torn and muddied papers on her counter. Finnigin found he was slightly nervous of going out into the city. He had visited cities before, but always in the company of other terranauts who had offered an invisible caul of protection. The prospect of entering unknown territory, where he would have to use his wits to find shelter and food, was unnerving. He had taken so much for granted among his troupe, and this was only the beginning of his journey. Still, there was no point in delaying. Heaving his back-pack into a less uncomfortable position, he stepped out into the light.

Finnigin was unaware of the attention he attracted as he walked up one of the main thoroughfares of Zanymandias. He had arrived in the middle of the Vitris District, where shops selling exquisite glassware fronted enormous studios and workrooms where the glass was blown. Counter assistants looked out of their windows and saw him, customers turned their heads to see what was coming down the street to arouse such interest. They saw a rather scruffy, slim young man of middle height, whose long tawny hair hung down his back. At first glance the sight was unprepossessing, until a girl of some perceptiveness said wistfully, 'It is as if he is muscled with springs.'

'A terranaut,' said her manageress. 'That is obvious.'

'Such a lovely face,' murmured the girl.

'Eyes wide-spaced,' observed a customer, peering through the window. 'As with them all, his hands are long-fingered and inquisitive.'

The girl sighed. 'I have heard such tales!'

Her manageress snapped in irritation: 'Dust those bowls, Mirrem! Enough of day-dreaming!' She herself turned back to the window to watch Finnigin leave the street.

He was ignorant of this response to his presence, believing himself to be an unappealing sight. Terranauts scorned fashionable dress, and their clothes were functional rather than decorative, although they were fond of jewellery. In comparison to the residents of

Zanymandias, Finnigin felt he looked like a vagrant. When people stopped to stare at him, his flesh shrank because he thought they found him objectionable. He did not realise how striking he was, how the mark of his people upon him set him apart, surrounded him with an ambience of otherworldliness, something bewitching. This lack of self-awareness itself contributed greatly to his allure.

To those who watched him, he appeared to dance as he walked.

Zanymandias was a city of towers and blades, and its streets were straight and radial. Finnigin left the Vitris District and came to a market area where silken canopies filled the streets. The natives, as was common among the cities, all had a unique appearance that marked them as Zanymandian; they were tall, thin, and had long noses. Their mouths, to Finnigin, looked like beaks. The men were stooping and appeared cadaverous inside elaborate flapping garments, while the women were angular and bony-looking, as if carved inexpertly from hardwood.

Finnigin passed many hostelries, cafes and inns, all of which emitted tempting smells that tormented his empty stomach, but he felt awkward about entering any of them, knowing he'd have to confess to being penniless. He had no confidence in the booth-keeper's advice that he could work for food and shelter. What if they expelled him from their premises with scorn? He smelled bad and looked so poor. Finnigin was quickly learning he was a proud creature, and for that reason would back away from confrontation with those who would look down upon him. Eventually, however, after walking about for most of the day, weariness and hunger forced him to go into one of the inns. It was late-afternoon. He chose an establishment which looked as if it catered for a distinctly low-incomed sort. Rehearsing a script in his head, he approached the counter, but before he could speak, the landlord, a lanky, skinny man, exclaimed, 'Oh, terranaut!' and came out from behind the bar. 'Let me help you with that!' He was already undoing the buckles of Finnigin's back-pack.

Finnigin made a few mild protests and uttered the words 'work' and 'meal', but the man paid no attention, calling to his wife who was somewhere nearby in the building.

'Aranda! Come here! A terranaut! We have a terranaut!'

Eventually, a typically Zanymandian woman of gaunt bones slid into the room and, upon seeing Finnigin, raised her long arms above her head. 'Oh! Oh!' she cried, and began jumping around in a rather inelegant caper, as if something extraordinary had just happened.

Finnigin was perplexed by the excitement. 'I have no money,' he said lamely, but the landlord propelled him heedlessly towards a worn wooden table near the window. 'Sit here, sit here! A terranaut! Here! Oh, we'll have custom tonight!'

Finnigin sat down. 'Well, thank you. But . . .'

'You are hungry, I'll fetch food!' declared the woman.

'And ale!' added the man importantly. He stood with his thumbs in his belt, grinning down at Finnigin.

'I . . . er . . .' Finnigin wriggled awkwardly. 'Would you like me to work for this? Some task . . .?' For a dreadful moment, the words of the booth-keeper came back to him. The man was running his eyes over Finnigin's body in a decidedly greedy manner.

'Work? Oh no, no, no!' he insisted. 'We've never had a terranaut grace us with their presence before!

And believe me, having you here will increase our trade. There's no charge.'

'Oh . . .'

The woman came hurrying out from the kitchen bearing a laden tray. 'Eat! Eat!' she cried, in a high fluting voice. Rather unnerved, Finnigin did so.

His appetite appeased, he was ushered into the most sumptuous of the inn's hire-rooms – which was barely comfortable – and allowed to sleep. The landlord, named Mooman, was explicit about how Finnigin would have to grace the saloon with his presence later in the evening, so that the clientele could look at him. Finnigin felt unable to complain. Aranda's cooking, though basic, had been like nectar to his hungry body.

Later on, Mooman came to wake him up, and Finnigin groggily descended the stairs into the saloon. It seemed the effects of the hotsup had finally caught up with him; his stomach burned with acid. The inn was packed and, behind the bar, Aranda's thin face looked almost plump with pleasure.

'Am I this good for business?' Finnigin asked warily.

Mooman propelled him towards the bar. 'Yes! Yes! This good!' He laughed. 'Ale or wine?'

'I don't mind.' Finnigin sat down gingerly on a stool. The patrons of the inn had fallen quiet, every eye turned towards him. He took the mug of wine Aranda offered him and politely toasted all those who were staring at him. This broke the ice a little and murmurs of appreciation surged round the room. Two women were brave enough to come and speak to him, ask him questions about his life and the ways of his people. He answered obliquely, something he'd learned to do at an early age, but which more than satisfied the women, who expected him to be mysterious. More and more people came to speak with him and buy him drinks, and Aranda, perhaps anticipating he needed something to line his stomach, placed a plate of bread and sausage on the bar before him. Finnigin could barely concentrate on what was said to him. His body still wanted to be asleep. This life had been thrust on to him brutally and without warning; he needed time to digest its newness.

Late in the evening, Mooman pushed proprietorially through the group that still clustered around Finnigin, and began to shoo them away. He took hold of Finnigin's arm. 'A customer has requested your presence,' he said in a low voice. From his tone, Finnigin deduced the customer must be important.

'I'm very tired,' he began, but Mooman, surprisingly strong for his build, was already dragging him across the room.

An enormous fireplace dominated the far wall and someone was seated in the inglenook. Finnigin caught a glimpse of firelight reflected in a large, round glass. He saw the hand that cupped the glass, an enormous silver ring set with a glittering black stone upon the second finger.

'My lord,' Mooman said, with an over-enthusiastic bow.

The man in the inglenook dismissed him with a gesture.

Finnigin stood dispiritedly before the fire, hoping he would not collapse before this person had finished amusing himself at Finnigin's expense.

'Sit down,' said the man. His voice was low-pitched, tinged with humour. Finnigin thought he smelled danger. He sat down on the floor, too tired to speak.

'I have paid dearly for your time,' said the man, 'therefore I would like to get my money's worth.'

'You have paid me nothing,' Finnigin said hastily.

The man laughed; a dry, unconvincing sound. 'You are a guest of this city, at this city's pleasure. Your people never have to lift a finger for their keep here.

Be so courteous as to indulge me.'

Finnigin shrugged. He could see little of the man other than the shadow of a face, dark garments, the long, expressive hands. His black boots were polished to a high, silken lustre, the feet crossed at the ankles.

'I can offer you more pleasant accomodation than this,' said the man.

Finnigin looked up sharply. 'I am quite comfortable here. Anyway, I shall be moving on in the morning.'

The man laughed again. 'Ah, yes, the quest for experience!'

Finnigin was discomfited. Only terranauts should know about such things. Was this man a terranaut too? He had heard that some of his people came back from their solitary travels ineradicably changed. Sometimes, they shunned returning to their own people and attached themselves to one of the cities. It was seen as a kind of madness, or a failing. The exile from their people was a way to weed out the weak, to cull the disloyal. Still, as far as he knew, no rogue terranaut ever divulged the secrets of his people to city-dwellers. There must be some loyalty then, some unbreakable tie. He narrowed his eyes at the man. 'Who are you?'

The man leaned forward. It was easy to see then that he was not Zanymandian; the face was too sculpted, not long enough in the jaw. 'Call me your friend,' he said.

'I don't know you.' Finnigin hesitated. 'Are you . . . were you . . .' It seemed obscene to say it, but the man appeared to understand the question.

'Let's just say I know enough about you.'

Perhaps he missed his own kind? Finnigin wondered whether he possessed the ability to feel charitable, be friendly towards this stranger.

'Come with me,' said the man.

Finnigin paused only a moment before responding. 'Very well.'

Aranda and Mooman seemed disappointed that Finnigin was leaving their humble establishment, but were obviously too much in awe of the stranger to complain. The man threw a handful of glittering coins on to the counter before he left. Finnigin hurried to his room to gather his belongings, and then followed his new patron into the street. His head ached with weariness and the effects of alcohol, but he did not feel drunk. The stars wheeled over his head and in the silence of the night, it was possible to perceive the grumbling rhythm of Zanymandias' mechanisms far beneath his feet.

'What is your name?' Finnigin asked.

The man was tall, shrouded in a dark cloak, his face now hidden by a wide-brimmed hat in which reposed a single magnificent blue feather. 'Names, names,' he said. 'Odd that they should be so important. Necessary things, I suppose, for the purpose of this story.'

'Story?' Finnigin asked.

The man nodded. 'Yes. I believe we are all characters in a story.'

Finnigin laughed. 'Whose?'

The man merely shrugged. 'It is a topic for lengthy conversation. Perhaps we can discuss it later. You may call me Varian.'

A short way from the inn, in an area reserved for public vehicles, Varian had left his carriage. Although Finnigin had noticed, earlier in the day, that Zanymandias had steam vehicles, Varian's carriage was drawn by a team of eight enormous black dogs who were sitting licking their paws and dozing, awaiting the return of their master. There was no driver, and Varian did not mount to the driver's seat himself. He ushered

Finnigin inside the carriage and then climbed in behind him, to sit on the opposite bench.

'The animals know the way,' he said.

'You are not Zanymandian,' Finnigin said, resting his head on the cushions behind him. 'Are you a resident here now?'

'I have a home in every city,' Varian replied, somewhat enigmatically.

Finnigin sniggered. He did not believe it.

Some time during the short journey, Finnigin fell asleep without realising it, for he was abruptly woken by the sound of dogs baying. The carriage had come to a halt, and Varian was opening the door.

'We're here!' he said.

Finnigin grabbed his backpack and staggered into the road. Clear moonlight bathed the cupolas and towers of a magnificent building. It appeared to be the only house on the street which was wide and lined by lofty trees whose leafage whispered in a gentle breeze far above. In Finnigin's experience, which he admitted was limited, so much open space was distinctly unusual upon one of the cities where every inch was usually utilised and developed. The house before him stood in its own park. Perhaps it was a public building?

'It's a palace!' Finnigin exclaimed. 'Do you live here?'

'Not often,' Varian replied, 'but it will be adequate.'

'You must be very rich.'

Varian only laughed politely. 'Nothing so simple!'

'You are a strange person,' Finnigin remarked as he followed Varian through the gates of his residence.

He raised an elegant hand. 'No stranger than anyone else. No stranger than you. Come.'

Inside, the house was no less splendid than it had appeared from the road, but there was a marked lack of servants which Finnigin felt would be needed in such a massive menage. There were neither gas-lights nor electricity to illuminate the looming halls, but a profusion of candles, all of them red and offering orange flames.

'You must bathe,' Varian said. 'Then we can talk.'

'I'm too tired to talk,' Finnigin said.

'I won't keep you awake long.'

'A bath will send me to sleep.'

'Then it shall be sprinkled with energising herbs.'

Sighing, Finnigin followed Varian upstairs where he was left alone in an enormous marble bathroom in which a bath stood waiting for his immersion, already full of steaming water and fragrant leaves. As he took off his clothes, Finnigin actually considered his immediate future. It seemed clear to him that Varian would want something from him, most probably some carnal gratification. Did the thought of that cause him unease? It was best not to think about it. Decisions could be made later if the situation arose. In the meantime, Finnigin elected to enjoy the comforts that had been offered to him. He was grateful for the deep, aromatic bath, so perhaps it would not be a good idea to question things too much. He lay in the water with only his face exposed, and wondered, as his hands moved slowly against the licking pressure, if it was possible he was, in reality, lying unconscious in Mooman's inn from too much wine, and this was all a fantasy. Best just to enjoy it while it was there.

Clean and refreshed, Finnigin dressed himself in the red towelling robe that had been left out for him and wandered out of the bathroom. Only a few of the corridors were lit, and these efficiently led Finnigin to an upper parlour where Varian sat reading before the fire.

'Ah,' he said as Finnigin came to haunt the edge of the room. 'Better?'

'I'm awake,' Finnigin replied. 'What do you want of me? Something obvious?'

'I wouldn't be so crude. Come. Sit down.'

He indicated the floor by his feet, but Finnigin elected to sit in a chair on the opposite side of the fire. Varian did not comment.

'Don't stare at me,' Finnigin said after a while, when the silence had become uncomfortable.

'Why not? I'm staring at a creature, exquisite in its creation, who will soon be adrift in a world completely alien. I want to enjoy these moments of stillness before that happens. Look upon it as a few scant hours of bliss before things get unpleasant and challenging for you.'

Finnigin squirmed in his chair. How could he have been so stupid and mindless as not to realise what the realities of his expulsion from the troupe would mean? For the first time since he'd left them, he missed the presence of his companions, the presence of his carer. In his mind, he could see Leeara's hands, long and scarred, brown-skinned and calloused. Those hands had held him close throughout his childhood, kept him safe. He felt a pang of coarse and terrible longing. He might never see Leeara again.

'In this city,' Varian said conversationally, 'there is a penalty worse than death for the most evil crimes.'

Finnigin raised his eyes but said nothing.

'It is banishment,' Varian said. He picked up a pipe from the hearth and lit it. Finnigin recognised the scent of hela. Varian *was* a terranaut, then. No one else could safely withstand the effects of hela.

'Banishment,' Varian repeated dreamily, sucking on the pipe. 'In a world where only the insane set forth upon journeys, leave home, where the fear of losing contact with the familiar is very great, it is not surprising to find that the worst form of punishment is casting out; yes, much worse than death.'

Finnigin had met many wanderers who were not terranauts. Not all of them were insane. Most were simply people who wished they were terranauts. Banishment, in reality, need not be more terrible than death. 'Some people say banishing is a blessing,' he said. 'I have met them.'

'And now you too have been banished from all you find familiar,' Varian remarked. 'Do you consider it a blessing?'

'Is isn't like that. You know it isn't.'

Varian offered Finnigin the pipe, but he shook his head. His mouth was too dry to take it.

'Of course it isn't,' Varian said. 'I did not mean to make an analogy. I simply meant that, in this city, the banished are sent away harnessed to vegetable air bladders. The information might be useful to you. They say the high air currents all flow towards the mountains.'

'I might not be going to the mountains.'

'Aren't you?' Varian grinned. 'As luck would have it there is a banishing taking place tomorrow morning. Perhaps you should visit the penitentiary to witness this barbaric act, and also to secure transport of your own.'

'I suppose I could,' Finnigin said. He wondered how old Varian was; it was impossible to guess. He seemed both young and old at the same time.

'Tell me about your childhood,' Varian said.

'It's not that interesting. I can't remember much about it.'

'Do you want me to remember it for you? I could invent it.'

Finnigin laughed nervously. Varian was clearly unbalanced; he came out with such strange remarks. 'If you want to. You said you were paying for my time, so do as you please.'

'Ungrateful pup!'

'I don't mean to be.'

Varian suddenly leaned forward in his chair. 'I can interfere in your life at any time,' he said in a fierce, low voice. 'At any time!' He sat back. 'Remember that.'

'Whatever you want.'

Varian sighed. 'Now you are afraid.'

'I'm not.'

'You keep looking at the door, considering whether you can make a run for it.' He laughed. 'Would you run out into the world owning nothing but a red dressing-gown, I wonder?'

Finnigin felt his face flush; he looked down at his hands, which were clasped together in his lap. 'That does not sound like a sensible idea.'

'I agree. It does not. Ah!' Varian sighed and extended his legs before the fire. 'If only we could communicate. If only.'

Finnigin looked up at him. Varian's eyes were closed. His long dark hair spread out round his head, clinging to the tapestry of the armchair; it looked faintly malevolent. His body was lean, and the sight of it made Finnigin homesick for his people. He saw, in his mind's eye, Varian's long-fingered hands planting pilot-stones. 'I'll do whatever you want me to,' he said.

Varian did not open his eyes. 'Go to bed,' he said. 'That is all.'

Finnigin stood up. He was glad to be dismissed, yet disappointed too. 'My childhood?' he said archly.

'Nothing to get excited about,' Varian replied. 'Nothing out of the ordinary.'

'Then I'll bid you goodnight.'

'Sleep deep,' Varian said. 'Use the room second door on the right from here. It's the last time you'll sleep in comfort for a long while.'

★ ★ ★

In the morning Finnigin could find no trace of Varian, even though he searched the echoing halls from top to bottom. Nor did he find any personal effects, which might have given some clue as to Varian's character. The rooms were exquisitely furnished, ready for habitation but unlived in. Varian had left very little mark on the place.

Finnigin found a parcel of food upon the table in the main hall, which he presumed was for him to take. He'd hoped Varian might give him new clothes to wear, but although his own had been mysteriously cleaned during the night, there were no further gifts. If he'd hoped for bounty, he was disappointed. Even the food he'd been given was basic and plain.

Finnigin let himself out of the towering front door with a strange mixture of emotions fighting in his chest. He felt he'd been cheated somehow, that Varian had toyed with him deliberately. Perhaps that was how the rich amused themselves? Still, he would have liked to know the truth about whether Varian had once been a terranaut or not.

Remembering the information that had been given to him, Finnigin asked directions from passers-by that would take him to the penitentiary and law-courts.

'Ah, you want to view the banishing!' one woman declared.

'Yes,' Finnigin answered. 'That's right.'

The woman pantomimed a theatrical shudder. 'Strange, isn't it, how we can't resist?' Then she narrowed her eyes. 'Well, you're a terranaut, aren't you?'

'We like to watch banishings too.' Finnigin hurried away from her into a gathering crowd that was heading in the same direction as himself.

Above the penitentiary roof, where sickles on spires all pointed downwards, vegetable bladders jostled together on the wind, trailing a web of roots. The scimitared towers of Zanymandias occluded any sight of the wilderness beyond the city, so there was rarely any sense of being on a moving thing. Zanymandias surrounded its inhabitants; massive, seemingly immovable. In comparison, the squeaking bladders were alien to this territory, restless and full of threat.

It seemed the banishment was already in progress. On a platform near the penitentiary roof, two officials were thrusting a bound man into the harness of an inflated bladder. Nearby, a struggling, squawking woman was being restrained by two female officials. The woman wept and pleaded, held out her arms through the limbs of her oppressors.

'Not this! Not this!' she cried.

Finnigin watched from the edge of the crowd, his face impassive. He eyed the mottled bladders rubbing against one another. That would be the way for him; he'd skim the wind, fly.

The ropes of the vegetable bladders were tied around an enormous brass ring set into the wall of the building. At a signal from some robed and medallioned official, a dour-faced man applied a long knife to the appropriate rope, and the doomed man flailed aloft. A frozen tableau of distraught relatives, grim officials and gruesomely delighted onlookers, shaded their eyes to follow his flight. Finnigin wondered what the man had done to deserve such a fate; he seemed to have enough supporters with him. After the convict had become nothing more than a dark dot in the distant sky, and people were beginning to comfort each other, or gossip together, and move away, Finnigin strolled up to the heavy-faced man who had cut the cords of the vegetable bladder. He was fiddling with one of his baroque inflation pumps, a mechanism comprised of wheels and pipes.

'How much?' Finnigin asked, pointing up at the bladders.

The man looked him up and down, clearly establishing almost instantly exactly what Finnigin was and what he wanted. Only a terranaut would come asking the cost of his wares. His eyes said, 'Mad fool!' but simultaneously his mouth smiled and he said, 'You'll have no money on you. Why ask?'

'I have hela.'

'An imbecile's pleasure! Death to anyone but an addict, and I am not such a creature.'

'A shard of pilot-stone.'

'Colour?'

'Lapiz.'

The man considered, sucking his upper lip for a few moments, and then nodded with the words, 'Help yourself!' He waved towards the bladder ropes with one hand, while holding out the other to take the shard. Finnigin gave him a piece of crystal, which was a fragment of a sky-stone that his carer had found in the desert some months back. It was not a pilot-stone, but what did that matter? It was pretty enough, possessing an imitation of pilot-stone fire in its depths, and the man would not know the difference.

Finnigin hung in the air, surrounded by the earthy smell of the vegetable bladder. It squeaked and wheezed as it courted the wind, its progress erratic, almost sentient. Somewhere ahead, the banished man would be no more substantial than a wail disappearing into the distance. When his root bladder eventually shuddered and perished, he would fall to dementia, isolation, and probably death, unless he had the intelligence to conquer his fears of the land.

Finnigin hummed as he floated along. He surveyed the ground beneath through a spying glass he always carried in his pocket. By tweaking certain lines that connected him to the bladder, he could influence the direction of his travel to a small degree. Travel, in any direction, would lead him to the mountains eventually. It was instinct rather than tradition that urged him to follow the steps of previous terranauts into the unknown, motionless territory of the mountains. City-dwellers shunned the region; cities balked and shuddered at its boundaries, no matter how many pilot-stones attempted to lure them to the rocky shores. Rather, they would career off the looming shadows of the rock, and be propelled back into the yellow flat-lands, with their more gentle curves and softer flora.

In certain of the moving cities, there were legends that those who were brave enough to look might find a terranaut citadel among the forbidding crags; a place where some dour terranaut god or dictator directed the lives of the flat-land people. Many believed that via some sinister power, the terranauts shaped reality. The terranauts among whom Finnigin had grown up were aware of these legends, but paid them scant attention. Leeara had told Finnigin the stories were all untrue anyway. There was no plan, he said, no design to the terranauts' activities as the city-dwellers perceived it, and he had most emphatically pointed out that they had no god, no ruler to guide them.

Finnigin, riding the winds high above the flat-lands, felt very much aware of himself; his flesh, his thoughts. This was an unfamiliar sensation, and he wondered what had initiated it. Before he'd visited Zanymandias, had he been nothing more than a hollow shell, a network of instincts, of sudden desires? Was it possible the meeting with Varian had affected him more deeply than he'd thought? He realised he had no philosophy to follow other than the demands of his flesh and its immediate needs. His hands, his most sensitive organs, would learn to intuit the song of pilot-stones, but did any subtler sense ever attune itself to the song, or find inspiration within it? The rituals of his people were few and rarely connected with the stones or their placing. Suddenly, Varian's voice resounded inside Finnigin's skull. It seemed he said: 'Still, they are a beautiful race; swift, lithe and dashing. Finnigin is a prime specimen of his kind. It is supposed he will live a long life.'

Finnigin wondered if, somewhere, in one of his palaces, Varian had just said those words to someone.

Finnigin dozed in his harness throughout the night, embraced comfortably by the padded straps that attached him to the bladder. At dawn he awoke and ate some pieces of dried meat from the package Varian had left for him. He watched his own shadow ripple over the land below. There was too much time to think, up here in the sky. He remembered Varian asking him about his childhood; he had not lied when he'd said he couldn't remember it. Did people normally remember that far back? And what did Varian's remarks about being able to invent a childhood for him signify? Simply maziness, or a self-aggrandising need to impress?

Later, he passed over a massacre, some strange event where displaced people appeared to be murdering one another in the sandy scrub. Thin screams reached him, less distinct than the cry of birds. The tragedy was left behind, perhaps having lost its sole witness. After this, Finnigin passed over a swift, darting hamlet, a citykin. Some believed these hurrying townlets were the growing stages of greater cities. A benign air current wafted Finnigin low to the ground, so he could easily see that the citykin's people were small and pale, moving quickly and purposefully through the narrow, pitted streets.

Finnigin's passage was so low, his shadow prompted the inhabitants to look up, make rapid genuflexions, utter cries against misfortune. Finnigin opened his trousers and pissed down on to the street, enjoying the blissful experience of flying and unconstrained urination at the same time. Thin, aggrieved laments followed his departure. He smiled to himself, weirdly satisfied, as he left the hamlet behind.

On and on. A stately matriarch of cities surged past below him. She wore a crown of crenellated towers, of silken flags and pennants. The heat from her gigantic body caused the vegetable bladder to soar abruptly over her streets and plazas, her raised terraces and yawning lawns.

And then, nearby, as if courting this grande dame of the flatlands, was a dark and masculine cityscape, moving deliberately, covered by small squat towers of black stone. His progress was slower; he would never catch the beauty ahead of him.

In between these giants of human habitation, small groups of terranauts planted stones, danced in spirals, moved on. Finnigin passed over several of these groups, but did not feel moved to call their attention to him. Neither did any of them chance to look up and see him.

I am alone, Finnigin thought, tasting the words in his mind. For a moment he was filled with panic; if something should happen to him, something perilous, he could die and no one would ever know. His death would be as pointless as the massacre he had passed over earlier; a grand tragedy without onlookers. No one to grieve. The fires of his troupe seemed very indistinct in his memory; faces were already fading from his mind. All he could remember of warmth and comfort was Varian's dream palace and his words before the fire: 'I'm staring at a creature, exquisite in its creation, who will soon be adrift in a world completely alien.'

He had not lied.

Casmeer

That day, Casmeer had come across a small, framed portrait of his mother's sister. There had been legends concerning this girl, family tales. He had met her only once, and had been too young to remember much about the experience.

The picture had been wrapped in muslin and packed in a chest in Casmeer's attic. He remembered dimly that it had once hung in the shadowed hall on the ground floor, and that Elini had disliked it. 'That woman looks like a mummified corpse,' she'd announced, and taken it down from the wall, to reveal a pale ghost of its shape behind. Casmeer had never seen the picture again and had quickly forgotten about it. He had been looking for something else, his teenage diaries, but had not found them. Instead: the picture.

His aunt Damia. She had died in her twenty-first year, supposedly of a blood complaint. Casmeer's mother had told her children, rather cruelly, that Damia had died of a broken heart. A man had done it to her. Heed it well, my darlings. Beware the fragile hearts of women. If you break them, they might cut you.

Casmeer put the portrait of Damia in his living room, propped against a wall. Time had not improved her sour visage. He found it difficult to believe anyone could have loved her. She should have been striking, for her dark colouring was dashing, she had good bones, and her hair was a luxuriant black mane. Unfortunately, her sour and pinched expression disfigured her face. Her mouth was tense, and thus rendered mean.

Casmeer drank wine and stared at the portrait. If Damia had had another life, would she have blossomed? Had her heart been in the early stages of breaking when the portrait was painted? She already seemed bitter, her pain caught in the careful brush-strokes. It was almost as if the artist was fond of her, so faithfully was her image represented. He tried to remember his meeting with her, but it was so long ago, the details had faded from his mind. All he could recall was her smell; unperfumed, slightly oily, a redolence of fur.

He half-closed his eyes and imagined Damia climbing from the painting. I could give you another life, he thought.

Chapter Six
Wind Music

Ays walked among the forest of membranes, struts and vanes, his whole body vibrating in tune with the subtle music emanating from the abandoned orchestra. As the dawn became morning, the fog began to dissipate and a concert of winds harried the dry, sandy soil up into a parade of vortexing dances. Ays felt very much alone, which was a novel experience, but in its way somehow empowering. Deep within him lurked a conviction that he would not die, would not starve nor be murdered. The compulsion to come down from Min and walk the flat-lands had been too strong, too significant, for his journey to end in failure or death.

I have a purpose, thought Ays. I *am* a purpose. And the winds sang their mournful tunes through the sand-scoured pipes and sails, conjuring a salt-sweet memory that surely must be false. A woman's song; a melody. The feel of sand and dry air. A sense of tombs, of ancient dust.

Ays closed his eyes and squatted in the eye of the music. The memory fragments trembled like rags upon the wind, blowing away. Soon all he had left was the memory of a memory; what he had felt like a moment before.

Sighing, he stood up and shifted his luggage baskets into position upon his head and shoulders. He wrapped a muffler veil across his lower face, and peered into the morning. Which way to go?

As if in response, he heard the yodel and rattle of a faraway wind-train. Nearby lay a section of dull-gleaming ski-rails, partly buried by gritty sand. As the train approached, the rails began to vibrate, throwing off puffs of light sand. Ays could feel the future rushing towards him. All he'd have to do was reach out and leap aboard it. The train was real, but Ays' feeling encompassed more than actualities.

Ays had often seen wind-trains dashing by below when he'd stood at the rim of Min. Some of them had been quite exotic in appearance; not like trains at all, but something half animal, plumed and spined. Of course, the Minnians had many tales concerning the trains, and before this point in his life, Ays would have laughed at the notion he'd one day be contemplating riding on one himself. This was because it was believed that no one who rode the rails ever knew where they might end up. The rails were as unpredictable and capricious as the cities themselves, always moving, shifting direction. Fools and pilgrims rode them, bent on their own visions of eternity, but not level-headed city-dwellers. Ays smiled as he remembered he was no longer part of this category.

A short distance away, the wind-train *Whiteknuckle Rush* screamed across the desert strip, towards her rendezvous with Ays, the erstwhile Priest of Hands. Streamers of ivy hung from her flanks; mementoes of an earlier landscape. In the flat-lands, the terrain was not sculpted by the weather, but something else. Desert sands fingered their way into the skirts of forests, green hills arose abruptly from barren heaths.

Aboard the third carriage of the *Rush*, the passengers had been discussing the nature of their world. Unlike the city-dwellers, whom they despised as brainless halfwits, they theorised constantly about the universe. Some of them had read ancient books in mountain cities, where a slower pace of life, a static dependability of the world, had allowed their philosophers to develop convoluted theories. The wind-trains, for all their outward hectic rush, were themselves quite motionless within. Their passengers were reporters, chroniclers of the flat-lands; observers all.

A tall, fadingly beautiful woman of early middle years, named Mariet Crane, leaned back in her ripped velvet armchair and said, 'But it is obvious, our world is a vast mind, and each area of it is but a different image. We are thoughts dashing through it.' She smiled and sipped absinth, loathing the taste but prepared to swallow it for effect. It was like admitting defeat, that taste.

Odo Grind, sitting opposite Mariet but across the carriage aisle, pouted and frowned as he considered her remarks. He was a large man whose frame never diminished, despite long periods of hunger, who told anyone he met about how he used to be a jeweller in Prudenscion – before being caught crafting hatpins from pilot-stones and banished. This confession was always delivered with pride, as Odo liked to think himself rather a rogue. Having been sipping at absinth himself for quite some time, he was now drunk. 'But whose mind?' he asked. Neither he nor Mariet had ever visited the mountains, and were still caught in the belief that they were impassable to humankind, a legacy of the cities they had left behind them.

'The mind of a sleeping lunatic, of course!' she declared. 'Who else could devise such a hectic world? It grieves me we are trapped within their wayward thoughts!'

Odo sniggered, believing Mariet's remarks to be

facetious rather than academic; he was correct in his assumption.

A young girl came creeping out from one of the chairs, where the others had supposed she'd been sleeping. She was a dark, saturnine creature, whom Mariet thought resembled a stunted witch. The girl was a fairly recent addition to the occupants of carriage three, having arrived only a few days previously, when it seemed she'd been swept onboard by a hot, charnel wind, stinking of burning. To Mariet, the girl was an unusual traveller, because all the ones she'd ever met before had been far older, and had had time to go mazy upon one of the cities.

'The sleeping lunatic lives beyond the mountains,' said the girl.

Mariet felt a spasm of irritation that the girl had been listening to her conversation. She wished she'd tried to sound more clever, and the realisation of that annoyed her even more. 'Be quiet,' she said waspishly.

'But it's true!' insisted the girl. 'I know, because I have been beyond the mountains myself.'

Mariet sneered. 'Oh, of course you have!' She disbelieved everything the girl had said since she'd arrived, simply because, to Mariet, none of it sounded at all plausible. The child was young for a traveller, true, but clearly already possessed the requisite self-delusion and bewildered lunacy. Mariet did not consider herself the owner of such attributes. 'Then all I've ever heard about the mountain ring is untrue!' she said, grinning at Odo. 'Everyone else I've spoken to, and all the books I've read, assert that nothing lies beyond it but chaos, abysmal murk, and formless ocean. How lucky we are to have the advantage of your knowledge to correct our dim views!'

The child had flushed a dark, purply-grey colour. Never had Mariet seen such an unattractive creature.

She seemed to be about fifteen years old, and should surely be on the brink of blossoming womanhood. Instead, it seemed she had jumped straight from childhood to dotage. There was something aged about her, something crabbed and bent.

'But I have been there! I have!' insisted the girl. 'I went there with my father, when he was alive.'

Odo attempted to defuse the situation. 'Come and sit upon my knee, child. Tell us all about it.'

Mariet uttered a groan of exasperation.

The child grimaced. 'No.'

Mariet wished she would move to another carriage. Her small but pungent presence had disrupted the atmosphere. Other than Odo and herself, the carriage was occupied only by a pair of catatonic discards, whose minds had clearly totally shattered a long time ago. Therefore, she and Odo had enjoyed a great deal of privacy before the advent of the girl. They did not know her name, and Mariet would not ask it.

'Go and play!' Mariet said in an angry voice, and then abruptly released a caw of cruel laughter. 'Go and play on the tracks!'

Odo laughed uncertainly and then gripped the arms of his chair.

'What? We are slowing down.'

Mariet groaned. 'Oh no! It makes me dizzy. I hate it.' She rubbed her brow, looked at the girl. 'If there is a city out there, you should disembark, seek asylum.' Her tone was not as abrasive as before; it was almost concerned.

The girl said nothing, her monkey face set in a defiant expression.

'We do not want you here,' Mariet said, resuming a more caustic approach. 'It can't be pleasant for you. Go somewhere you'll be wanted.'

'Leave her alone,' Odo said, rather timidly. 'She does no harm.'

There was nothing outside to indicate the train should stop; no station, no sidings, no simple flag to request a halt. There was only Ays, who stood with his luggage beside the half-buried rails, a hopeful expression on his face and his arm dithering in the air, wondering whether he had the power to halt the gigantic machine that was approaching. But whatever agency controlled the train was benign, because it seethed to a stop beside him, panting and flapping, an astounding, dynamic beast of shining paintwork, enormous spoked wheels, blade-like skis, and clawed sails. Ays stared at this heaving monstrosity for a moment or two before it uttered a solitary moan which seemed to speak of impatience. Afraid it might sweep off again without him, Ays grabbed hold of a chrome bar and stepped up on to the balcony of the nearest carriage: number three.

Inside, Mariet covered her face with a ripped black fan. 'More company?' she complained, and directed a poisonous glance at the nameless girl through one of the holes in the fan.

Ays walked into the carriage at that moment and the first thing he saw was a huge, black-rimmed eye, framed by torn black lace. He remembered something, but the memory was so fleeting he didn't have time to identify it. Giving the other occupants only a cursory glance, Ays was convinced the carriage was full of people, all of whom were staring at him. He sneaked into a window seat and presently the train lifted her skeins and courted the wind once more. A featureless landscape flashed past.

After a few minutes, Ays felt courageous enough to inspect the other occupants of the carriage. Contrary to what he'd first perceived there were only five passengers beside himself, and two of those appeared to be asleep. Where were they going, these people? he wondered. Why were they here? Were they asking themselves the same questions about him?

Mariet wanted to ignore the intruder, but eventually her natural curiosity overcame her desire for aloofness, and she peered over the scroll-work at the top of her seat and said, 'Who are you and what are you doing here?'

Ays was taken aback by the curt tone of these questions, and blurted, 'I was wondering the same of you.'

Mariet shrugged, unsure whether to take offence and retaliate or admire the coolness of the remark. Again, curiosity swayed her decision and she rose from her seat to join Ays, her thin body swathed in a froth of shedding feathers and moth-eaten brocade.

He screwed up his nose. Mariet smelled disagreeably of moth-balls.

'What are we doing here?' Her sweeping arm encompassed all the other travellers in her question. 'We are waiting to see where we will end up.'

'Can you remember where you came from?' Ays ventured carefully.

Mariet frowned. 'Is it of consequence? I've come from so many places, I barely remember the details. What of you?'

'I come from Min, a city that flies,' he replied. 'Perhaps you have seen it?'

'I have seen large shadows moving across the land,' Mariet said, 'but have always believed them to be clouds.' She smiled secretively. 'Could they really be cities?'

'There is only one that I know of,' Ays said. 'But perhaps there are others.'

‘And why have you left the flying city?’ Mariet wanted to know.

‘I am looking for something,’ he told her, in the cool, musical voice he generally used for inviting death into a room.

Mariet laughed. ‘Might as well look for one grain of sand out there in a hurricane!’

Ays shrugged, unoffended. ‘True. It does seem a huge task, and doomed to failure. I scarcely know where to begin, but I have to believe the hand of my goddess will guide me.’ He paused, remembering Mariet’s looming eye through the hole in her fan. ‘I’ve already been given a couple of clues.’

‘How fortunate,’ she said, and then told Ays her name. He repaid the compliment.

‘That,’ said Mariet, gesturing, ‘is Odo the jeweller. Those two shapes over there are Discards; they have no names, and barely any life to tell the truth. Once, no doubt, they succumbed to the calenture and flung themselves from their native cities. Now, they are burned out.’ She shuddered.

‘And the girl?’ enquired Ays. He was keenly aware of her huge black eyes staring at him round one of the seats.

Mariet pulled a sour face. ‘An ill wind blew her to us.’

‘I am Leeth,’ said the girl, coming out into the aisle and approaching Ays’ seat.

His instinct was to recoil, because the girl continued to stare at him intently. Inexplicably, he feared she would utter some harrowing and revealing words, which could end his search before it had begun; kill it. But the girl said nothing; only her eyes stared out from her bleak face, old before they should be.

As for Leeth herself, seeing Ays for the first time was like throwing open bedroom curtains one morning after a dreadful stormy night and discovering summer has come with the dawn. She had never seen such a beautiful man. Her instant attraction to him eclipsed all considerations of whether she herself was attractive to him. Her love for Ays was instantaneously kindled, and at once obsessive. She was drawn to him irresistibly, in the way that the cruellest forms of love sometimes affect a human heart. She succumbed to the disease of love, relinquished her flesh to its devouring infection, opened her mind to its gnawing abscesses and sores. But then, she saw only light and wanted to bask in it. For the first time since her father had died, the horror of being left alone slid silently from her mind, although she did not realise it.

Leeth sat beside Ays and he smiled at her coolly; manifesting an aloofness that, on the face of a beloved, is devastating.

Ays wondered if it was possible to acquire food upon the train. Nobody else seemed to have any with them, and for this reason he was loth to bring out something from his own supply. He was sure that Mariet at least would demand to share his meal, and the staring girl who had sat down beside him had a distinctly hungry look about her. Perhaps he could eat something while everyone else was asleep? He sat for what seemed like several hours, and soon his stomach began to complain. Odo drank steadily from a waisted purple glass bottle, occasionally offering it to Mariet who fastidiously extended a black glass flute for him to fill. Leeth read a book bound in a flaking leather cover, her eyes continually straying to Ays' face or hands. None of the other passengers appeared to get hungry, but then Ays was used to eating often and sparingly, the way of the Minnians. Occasionally Leeth chewed the skin around her fingernails. In the dusty shadows further down the carriage where the windows were shrouded in ancient, faded, red velvet curtains, the two shapes Mariet referred to as Discards remained unmoving. Ays began to wonder whether they were in fact dead. It seemed that, after their initial overtures of friendship, Ays' fellow travellers were prepared to leave him alone, perhaps until he felt ready to initiate conversation himself. He realised he had very quickly become a part of their group; accepted. Was this a good sign? Ays wasn't sure.

So now I am here, what do I do? Ays cradled his heavy luggage on his lap, blinking out of the window and watching the reflections of his fellow passengers in the glass. He felt tense, excited, unable to relax and think about his position. Where would the train take him? Of course, he had heard legends of the wind-trains, how they were full of lunatics and pilgrims and suicides, pelting mindlessly across the flat-lands on a never-ending journey of speed and nepenthe. Was he one of these now? A dispossessed, a refutee, a raving crack-brain who had renounced the security of his home city, cut loose like a discarded root bladder into the wind?

Think about the clues, he told himself.

A wind melody, a figure in the sand, an eye through ragged lace.

Were they clues enough?

In order to appease his hunger, he discreetly removed a jar of hela powder from his pocket, and in the shadow of the window curtains, snorted a generous pinch up his nostrils. Leeth twitched beside him; she had noticed something, obviously, but was politely refraining from peering too closely. The budding tendrils growing against Ays' body seemed to writhe slightly, send out a further spray of growth. The hela would numb his desire for food for a while, but he could not exist upon hela alone. He leaned back and surrendered himself to the experience of the drug; his whole body throbbed deliciously as if it was sobbing. Time seemed to decelerate, loop back on itself. He remembered the last of his recipients in Min, the man who, through design or accident, had propelled him from the city. He found himself wishing he'd been able to talk with the man before he'd been ill, asked his name. Anything.

Ays' stomach began to complain loudly, which perhaps inspired Leeth to put down her book and stand up. Her rusty black garments scraped audibly against the sticky carpeted floor. 'I can hear your belly!' she said, as if in disgust.

Ays stared at her with dull eyes. It was almost painful to behold the girl, she was so unpleasant to look at. Not ugly, but uncomfortably conformed. He could not put his finger on the exact fault.

'If you go further up the train, there is a cheer carriage,' she said. 'They have hot drinks and pies there.'

'I have no money,' Ays replied, although reluctantly grateful for the information.

Leeth shook her narrow head. 'You can barter,' she said. 'It is the accepted way. Who, on these trains, would carry the same currency, if any?'

Ays wondered whether he possessed anything he could bear to barter with. His scant jewellery? His clothes? The two books that Umbilana had given him? No. Perhaps the hela. Perhaps.

'They will take anything, generally,' Leeth continued helpfully. She hesitated. 'May I come with you . . . if you go?'

Ays stood up and heaved his basket frame on to his back. 'Yes.' He wondered when the girl had last eaten, and whether this was a thinly disguised request for charity.

'You can leave that here!' Mariet announced from a few seats further down, pointing at Ays' luggage. 'Odo and I are not thieves! Anyway, we can keep an eye on your belongings.'

'Thank you,' he replied, politely but dubiously, and lowered his baggage to the seat.

'Could you bring me a small onion loaf, seeing as you're going?' Mariet asked. She was now smoking a brilliant green cigarette in a shiny black holder, the smoke of which was beginning to fill the carriage with stinging fumes.

'I am not that rich,' Ays said with what he hoped passed for an engaging smile.

'The food upon this monstrosity is cheap,' Mariet declared. 'Most of it is scavenged from the refuse pipes of passing cities anyway. It gets recycled in the carriages behind the cranks.'

Leeth led the way out of the carriage.

'Who works upon this train?' Ays asked aloud, but really only of himself. 'Who controls it?'

'Nomads, of course,' Leeth replied, with a hint of scathe. 'These trains are like vast organisms and the passengers are parasites in their bodies. My father told me that.'

'How long have you been travelling?'

Leeth shrugged, looking backwards as she bounced from side to side along the corridor ahead. 'For ever. My father is dead.'

'Aren't you afraid?'

'No. There is nothing to fear.'

Nothing but privation, loneliness, physical danger from unknown threats in this unknown world. Ays felt strangely comforted by the fearless presence of Leeth. He could feel his panicked senses calming down deep within him. It had nothing to do with hela.

Chapter Seven
Sunset

A tired red sun dipped behind the sharp mountains that cradled Thermidore. Somewhere, a bell was tolling, or perhaps Casmeer imagined that. The air was balmy, red-tinted, as he sat in his roof garden. The roche of his wife courted the ruddy hues of the sinking sun. Casmeer felt unnerved. He did not feel alone. A perfume of flowers drifted up from the empty street below; a ghost fragrance, surely.

When he went in to write up his chronicles, he found that the previous night's entry was stained, as if dampened by dripping tears. That too was strange. Who could have read his words, for he was sure he hadn't dripped tears upon the page himself? The house shifted, as if spirits were turning within the walls. Suddenly, there was a great commotion outside on the roof garden; a crash and a series of wailing howls. Casmeer hurried outside to find a plumosite caught in one of his nets again. Angrily, he picked up a long-handled hook which he used for arranging the nets and struck at the creature. It cried out in pain, and then uttered a sad sound that was unnervingly human in timbre. It hung passively in the net, one long arm hanging down, twitching. Usually, the plumosites roared and struggled until they were dead. This was uncommon behaviour.

Casmeer leaned on the hook and stared at the plumosite. It was small, and lacked the usual spiked ruff around the head; a female. Not many of them came raiding, a duty fulfilled mainly by males. The plumosite blinked at Casmeer, whimpering. He was surprised to find his heart was moved, but then he was not naturally a cruel man. The plumosite looked at him with owl-like eyes. He thought he saw a dim intelligence there, and an unspoken plea for mercy. Perhaps it had been a mistake to invent a primitive culture for the creatures? Now he was anthropomorphising, which was surely unwise. If he moved to free the beast, it would undoubtedly attack him with claws and beak. He reached out with the hook and poked it; the plumosite cringed and whined.

Hidden among an array of tall pots in which grew domesticated trees with wide leaves was a wooden cage which had been part of one of Casmeer's earlier experiments with plumosite deterrents. He pondered for a moment or two, glancing at the cage and then back at the captured beast. Then he unhooked the net from its frames, which elicited a frantic, yelping struggle from the plumosite. Casmeer dragged the net, with protesting occupant, over to the cage and, using the hook, managed to push it inside and then secure the door. The plumosite stared at him miserably, and then slowly began to extricate itself from the net. After that, it defecated in a corner of the cage, before gripping the bars in long, hairy fingers and sitting down to stare at its captor with solemn eyes.

Casmeer went indoors and fetched a crust of bread, the remains of an earlier meal. This, he tossed between the bars. The plumosite looked at the crust, but did not touch it. Patting the bars of the cage, it seemed to be seeking a way to free itself. An episode of violent rage followed this exploration as the plumosite hurled itself against the bars, screaming wildly like a maddened woman. That was the moment when Casmeer began thinking of the creature in terms of its sex. Eventually, the plumosite's fury abated into weary despair and she lay down, stretched out upon the floor of the cage and put her long arms over her head, her leathery wings drooping listlessly. Casmeer thought she might be weeping, but chided himself for such romantic thoughts.

The night came down softly in a veil of dew. Casmeer sat in his chair on the roof garden, getting cold, staring at his captive. Eventually, weariness stole over him and he went indoors to go to bed.

In the morning, he went outside to investigate the occupant of the cage, and found the crust of bread had gone. He half expected the plumosite to be dead, but she was sitting with her back to him, gripping the bars of the cage, staring out at the city.

He fetched her some breakfast.

Chapter Eight
Forgotten Pilgrims

Finnigin drifted on the layered winds. Birds passed by below him. He kicked his feet into the air and one of his boots flew off. Below him, low hills undulated towards a green, greasy-looking lake. He could see the canopied tiers of a terranaut camp and waved, but no one looked up to see him. Pilot-stones glistened right up to the water's edge. It was feasible the terranauts were planning to lure a city into the lake itself, where its perambulatory mechanisms – wheels, punch-sticks, crawlers, magnetic repellents, skis – would find it difficult to manoeuvre. Finnigin's group had once passed a dead city lolling in the brackish water of an inland sea. It had been deserted; its people either all dead, or driven to dementia and flight. Finnigin and a few friends had climbed up the rotting rigging hanging from the city's cracked underside. They had walked the leaning streets, sifted through rubble, but it had been picked clean by earlier scavengers. Leaders of cities, murderers of cities. Finnigin had been told that sometimes the sacrifice was necessary, but no one had ever explained why.

Finnigin drifted. He rested his cheek against one of the ropes, and wondered who built the cities, who first constructed the tiny skittish hamlets that somehow evolved into the monstrous constructions that crawled across the land. Terranauts had no sense of history, and the people who inhabited the cities were concerned solely with their own. It was only the outcasts, the fugitives from civilisation, those who rode the wind-trains perhaps, who cared to question. But did the questioning come before or after the escape? Was it an awakening to the bizarreness of the world that instigated their flight, or was curiosity a consequence of their running away? Finnigin wondered if he was the first terranaut to consider these things. He drifted.

Night fell, and a myriad dots of light, of all colours, punctuated the invisible land below. The night above was starless; a smooth, dark purple sky. No moons were present. Finnigin was a black silhouette against the purple. He was cold, and had eaten nearly all of the food Varian had given him. More worrying was that his water had run out. Thirst was starting to take a hold of his throat.

Once he lowered himself to the ground to seek shelter and food, the vegetable root bladder would be unusable. He would have to continue his journey on foot or find another method of transport. How far was he from the mountains now? He'd hoped the vegetable bladder would take him all the way there. He knew he was safe in the sky, where his only enemies were the gaunt spectres of hunger and thirst, the slow killers, or the demon of ice who could freeze his blood. On the ground, it would be different. Hunger, thirst and cold could still stalk him, but they would be augmented by an army of worse predators; other humans, animals of fang and claw, poisonous areas of land. Finnigin had few weapons; just his nails and his teeth, his kicking feet, a short, sharp knife or two. Still, he couldn't stay aloft for ever. He had realised that part of his emergence into manhood meant he should suffer at least some privation.

Sighing in resignation, Finnigin leaned back and tweaked the cords of his root bladder. Air exhaled in an earthy-smelling puff, and slowly the bladder descended. As the earth grew bigger beneath him, the lights of the land faded from Finnigin's sight. Nearer to the ground, the root bladder increased its speed dramatically and propelled him forwards swiftly, dropping into a dense fog. Finnigin felt as if he was flying through a rushing void. There did not seem to be any cities near, and the night was silent and occluded, like the inside of a thick bag.

Landing in a bone-shaking heap, he disentangled himself from his harness, removing one or two straps that some instinct advised him might come in useful later. He shivered like a skinny dog in the night air. A whine escaped his throat. It seemed pointless to try and travel further now. Perhaps the morning would bring a clear sky, the sight of an approaching city. Shaking with cold, Finnigin curled up on the rocky ground, sleeping only fitfully until the dawn.

He awoke wracked with pain and the realisation that he had, at last, reached the end of the world he was familiar with. Behind him, the flat-lands – yellow in this area – seemed to stretch forever, with no hint of hill or trench. Before him hung a pinky-grey, dusty haze; the veil through which he would pass into a new land. The foothills to the mountains, he was sure, would lie beyond the haze. Shards of sharp rocks dug into his bare foot, which was thankfully numb from cold, but his other, booted foot had a sore on the heel which had almost reached the limits of tolerability.

Finnigin experienced a strange, unsettling, though not wholly unpleasant, thrill at the sight of the dirty mist before him. His roving terranaut blood somehow sensed the enormity of the land unseen in front of him, and intuited its alienness and novelty. He paused and leaned into the mist to sniff it, hoping to gather some clue as to what might lie concealed within it. Surprisingly, for all its dirty greyness, the mist smelled of fresh water. And there were sounds coming out of it; muted, irritable voices, and a muffled tocking, as of one porous rock striking another. Finnigin wondered for a moment or two whether these sounds might signify threat but, he reminded himself, such thoughts were for cowardly, hide-bound city-dwellers, not terranauts.

He stepped into the mist and, once immersed in it, found it wasn't quite as thick as it appeared. The ground could clearly be seen, and it was alive with scintillant sparkles. Finnigin was surprised. They were pilot-stones, thousands of fragments of pilot-stones. Uttering a soft cry of recognition, he squatted down, hands outstretched to touch the stones.

A voice squawked abruptly out of the mist ahead. 'No! Interloper! The pattern must not be broken!' A slender staff slammed down and caught the end of Finnigin's fingers. Yelping, he snatched his hand away and leapt up, adopting an attitude of defence.

He saw a striding, flapping figure approaching, who appeared to be further away than was possible for him to hit Finnigin's fingertips with the staff. 'Fool! Fool!' the stranger cried. 'Are you mazed or ignorant, or both?'

'Absolutely neither!' Finnigin declared, inserting his stinging fingers into his mouth.

The figure before him was tall and slender, wrapped in dust-coloured robes that were patterned with flaking scorch-marks, runes and other occult symbols. His face was hidden by a voluminous hood.

Finnigin gestured at the ground. 'Those are pilot-stones!' He wanted to say that if he wished to touch them, he would, for pilot-stones were the property of terranauts, no one else, but the words refused to come out. He realised he must be afraid.

His words, however, obviously struck a chord with the stranger, who straightened up and folded his arms. 'So,' he said in a hard tone, nodding to himself, 'we have another terranaut amongst us.'

'Not exactly,' Finnigin replied hurriedly. 'I am merely passing through on my way to the mountains.'

The man laughed. 'You think so? Most people who pass this way end their journey here.'

Finnigin disliked the direction this exchange was taking. 'Then I shall go another way,' he said carefully, and began to retrace his steps.

The stranger came after him. 'Don't misunderstand me,' he said hurriedly. 'What I meant was that only a *stupid* person would end their journey here. Someone who is not a terranaut; the credulous, the city-spat. There is no danger to *you* here.'

'I have to continue my journey,' said Finnigin, refusing to stop walking.

The stranger touched him with his staff, or more accurately placed his staff across Finnigin's chest as a barrier. He was forced to stop.

The stranger glanced down at Finnigin's feet, one of which was now blue with cold. 'I have met many of your kind,' he said, 'all of them passing into the mountains. I know of your journeys of youth. Now, you are heading the wrong way.' He smiled. 'Come and share food with me before you begin the climb. I can point you in the right direction.'

'What is the charge for food?' Finnigin demanded. His resolve was weakened by the offer. This person made him feel on edge, threatened, but his belly was too empty to pay attention to such feelings.

The stranger shrugged. 'There is no charge. I am not

avaricious. If I were, I wouldn't be living in this forsaken spot.'

'I can't stay long.' Finnigin hoped he wasn't making a mistake.

'Well, I have little food,' the stranger replied. 'Follow me.' He turned hastily with a flutter of cloth. 'Let your feet remain faithful to the pattern beneath them. It is best not to risk invoking dire fortune.'

Looking down, Finnigin could see that the tiny pilot-stones were set in a convoluted pattern which was a curling pathway. He followed. He had no better option.

Finnigin had already decided that this mysterious stranger would live in a tent, a warren of black swinging fabric which would match his attire, but his abode was a crumbling edifice of rough-hewn stones, stuck together by moss and mud, with grass sprouting from the cracks. They had followed an almost invisible path within the complexities of the pilot-stone pattern; twisting and turning, this way and that. Finnigin had seen indistinct shapes through the mist; squat buildings that appeared to have been hastily erected, gaunt wooden gantries whose purpose was not obvious, and shadowy, gesticulating hunched figures, who appeared to be pointing at things on the ground.

'Never mind them,' said the stranger, looking neither to left nor right.

'What is this place?' Finnigin asked.

The stranger was opening the door to his residence. Soon they would be inside, and the question had not been answered. Finnigin lingered at the threshold. 'What is this place?' The room beyond was bare, the light dim.

'Why won't you come inside? Are you afraid?' The stranger laughed and threw his cloak and hood on to the floor. 'What is there to be afraid of? You have travelled this far without harm!'

'You don't know how far I've travelled!' Finnigin said tetchily. The room made him feel uncomfortable. There was an untidy heap of coal in one corner, but no sign of a fire or even a hearth. The air smelled damp and earthy, and it was very cold.

'You are not unique,' said the stranger. 'There have been many like you before, and many will follow. It is the way of your people. Perhaps you should look upon this place as the start of your journey?'

'But I want to know where I am.'

'Come in. Sit down. And I will tell you.'

Finnigin left the light of the threshold and ventured into the poky dimness of the room. There was no furniture, only a muddle of strewn items on the floor. He sat down upon a pile of cloth which might have been garments or thin blankets.

The stranger squatted down opposite him and shook his head. He had the most astounding head of hair. It was so long it spread out on the filthy floor around his hips, shining as if with a light of its own; honey gold. 'I have bread to eat,' he said, and rummaged in a muddle of pans and dirt-encrusted plates at his side. The loaf he held out for Finnigin's inspection appeared stale and covered with soot.

'I cannot eat that,' Finnigin said.

'As you like.' The stranger thoughtfully broke off a piece of the bread and popped it into his mouth, talking while he chewed it. 'Like all young terranauts, you are a template for a adult, without the details filled in. Sometimes I wonder how any of you survive in the world!' He peered at Finnigin closely.

Finnigin felt uncomfortable under this scrutiny. 'Have you anything else to eat?' He did not have much hope.

'Not at the moment. At sunfall we collect manna outside, which we have to eat at once or else it fades away. It is a sweet fuzz which falls from the sky, and can sustain a person indefinitely. Still, I tire of the taste of it. A traveller gave me this bread. I'm making it last.'

Finnigin thought he detected an odour of madness. It could not possibly benefit him to remain in this place. 'Then perhaps I should go now?'

'Ah!' said the stranger, raising a hand. 'Impossible. You have agreed to spend time with me. That is a contract between us.'

'It isn't. If you do not have food, there is no contract between us.'

The stranger frowned. 'Oh please, don't leave yet. You don't know how much I suffer from ennui! Visitors are so few here. Are you thirsty? I have water. Do you want that?'

Finnigin sighed. 'Let me look at it,' he said sourly. The stranger pawed around the rubbish until he found a covered pail which he offered to Finnigin. Finnigin lifted aside the lead-weighted, torn muslin cover and sniffed the contents. They smelled pure and cold and clean, and tasted like fresh spring-water. Not until he'd begun to drink did he realise how thirsty he'd been.

'So, what do you want with me?' he asked, putting down the pail.

The stranger shrugged. 'Want? Want with you . . .?' There was no further reply. 'Nothing . . .' His voice tailed away.

Sighing, Finnigin looked around himself. The light coming in through the single sack-clothed window was dim and brownish. The only colour in the room was the bright gold of the stranger's hair. Finnigin covertly examined his host in order to take in more details. It was obvious the stranger was no ordinary man, perhaps even less ordinary than Varian. He was ethereal, almost insubstantial; this setting was entirely unsuitable for such a creature. He had the voice of a young man, but his face was almost female; the mouth, nostrils and eyes all slanting in a regular perspective towards a point between ear and temple, giving an overall impression of weirdness. Finnigin considered that his host might not even be human. In his short life, he had seen many strange things hanging from the underbellies of the cities, or flitting and crawling in between them.

The stranger seemed to become aware of Finnigin's scrutiny and with some effort pulled himself to a level of alertness and communication. 'I have talked to many terranauts, and the first question I always ask them is this: how much do you know about your world?'

Finnigin thought that a pointless question. 'Enough to get by,' he replied primly, 'like anyone.'

The stranger smiled languorously and shook his head. 'No, you are wrong. Not like anyone.' He leaned forward. 'I keep an eye open for wanderers, young terranauts like yourself. There are many people here, most of whom it would be quite unnecessary for you to run into. They might even be obstructive to you.' He lifted his hands in a graceful gesture before allowing them to drift back to rest on his thighs. 'This is the Shrine of All Quests.'

Finnigin looked around himself and wrinkled his nose. 'Oh.' He failed to see how such a dreadful shack could be a shrine.

'Not this building in particular, but this area,' said the stranger.

'So?'

The stranger rolled his eyes, seemingly in mild impatience. 'Doesn't that mean anything to you?'

'Should it?'

The stranger sighed. 'I am Valnisi, one of the few people here who are truly awake.'

Finnigin was beginning to fidget. What was he doing here being talked at in this way? He got to his feet, intending to leave the shabby building and its peculiar occupant at once, and continue his journey on foot. He'd wasted enough time. If only he hadn't lost one of his boots. 'Well, thank you for the water . . .'

'Wait!' Valnisi leapt to his feet and grabbed hold of Finnigin's arm. 'I haven't finished with you yet.'

'But I have finished with you.' Finnigin tried to pull his arm away.

'No!' Without warning, Valnisi's hand shot out and cuffed Finnigin hard across the side of his head, causing a single comet of light to explode before his eyes. Finnigin's legs buckled from the force of the blow. He uttered a yowl of displeasure and struck out, but his clawed hand was caught fast in swift retaliation. Valnisi's face hung close to his own, the slanted eyes wide and staring; the thin-lipped mouth grinning. 'Be still, I mean you no harm!' Valnisi hissed. 'You must listen to me!'

Finnigin tried to squirm away, wary of provoking him further. The man had incredible strength for one so slim. 'I've done you no harm!' Finnigin babbled. 'Let me go!' It occurred to him in that instant that Valnisi could probably kill him if he wanted to.

'Let you go?' Valnisi laughed, a high-pitched tinkling sound. 'But you've been so rude, after I've offered you my hospitality! Have you no gratitude?'

Finnigin realised it would be useless to argue. His only hope lay in escape. He lunged forward to bite Valnisi's face, simultaneously raising his knee to strike his opponent in the groin, but before his attack could make contact, Valnisi deftly tripped him up. Seconds later, Finnigin was pinned against the ground.

'I'll listen to you! I'll listen!' Finnigin cried. He let his body go limp in an attitude of submission.

'That's better,' said Valnisi. He took hold of Finnigin's shoulders, banged his head once against the ground, and then stood up, brushing down his robe. 'How unsavoury to have to resort to violence,' he said.

Finnigin said nothing; his head was swimming.

Valnisi sat down again in a cross-legged position, between Finnigin and the door, and continued to talk as if the hostile exchange had not taken place. 'Anyway, as I was telling you, this place is the Shrine of All Quests. It is peopled by exiles, by runaways from the cities, by those who have heard the voices of calling and have followed, by the fearful and disillusioned . . .' His voice trailed away, his eyes glazed, as he appeared to lapse into a kind of trance.

Finnigin sat up and rubbed his wrists, gingerly felt the back of his head. Could he make a run for it now?

Valnisi shuddered and became animated once more. 'They are a sad and pitiful bunch here! Believe me, should you talk to them, they will only tell you that this is the edge of the world, that you should abandon your journey or retrace your steps. They will tell you that only danger and ruin haunt the crags beyond our stones, but they are wrong.'

'I am going to the mountains,' said Finnigin wearily. 'Then I shall return to the flat-lands and be an adult among my people.' He hoped this was the truth and that his future was not destined to be cut short on the filthy floor of Valnisi's dwelling.

'Of course,' said Valnisi, 'but I feel it is only fair to warn you of what might happen very shortly. Some have been persuaded to stay here, perhaps against their will.'

There was a short silence, during which Finnigin mustered the courage to speak. 'Thank you for your warning.' He hesitated. 'Can I go now?'

Valnisi stared at him stonily for a few moments

before uttering a sound of despair and throwing up his hands. 'Oh, why do I bother? Every time one of you comes this way, I try to talk, to communicate, but to no avail. I believe the future of the world is in the hands of terranauts, but they are all empty of thought and initiative. Why do you plant the stones that guide the cities? Do you know?'

'We just do!' Finnigin said.

'Have you no curiosity?'

'I want to go now!'

Valnisi sighed and rubbed his face with his hands. His fingers were very long and dirty. He nodded. 'Yes. Go.'

Without further remarks, Finnigin stood up, picked up his backpack, and left the building hastily before Valnisi could change his mind. Outside, the mist was full of moving shapes, muffled voices. Ignoring any pattern in the stones beneath his feet, Finnigin moved off in the direction he felt must lead towards the mountains. He felt as if he was about to weep; his heart hammered erratically in his chest. Valnisi was insane! What a lucky escape! Finnigin was sure that only blind chance had decreed Valnisi should let him go. Events could so easily have taken a different, more lethal, course.

Presently, an unusual outline loomed up out of the mist before him. As he drew nearer, Finnigin saw that it was an enormous cage of wood and metal. Closer inspection revealed that there was a young woman squatting inside, stuffing something into her mouth. Finnigin approached, more with caution than curiosity. The episode with Valnisi had shaken him badly. Why was this girl shut up in a cage? Was she a criminal, or another mazy-mind? The girl looked up once she realised she was being observed, but made no overtures of communication. Finnigin leaned close to the bars.

She was eating shards of crystal, shards of pilot-stone, her mouth crunching steadily. The sight of it made him feel slightly sick, although he wasn't sure why. The girl stared back at Finnigin for a moment or two and then smiled widely. Blood dribbled from her mouth. Finnigin turned away in disgust; he had an irrational feeling the blood was not her own. The sooner he left this place, the better.

Further on, he came across a group of elderly women, all muffled in thick dark shawls, sitting around a circle of stones. A fire burned in the centre, but there were no flames, only a dense white smoke. Finnigin could smell water again. Could this smoking fire be the source of the dense mist? He had no desire to find out, and made to hurry past. Unfortunately, one of the women spotted him and called out, 'Hoy, you! Halt!'

Finnigin's instinct was to run, but he had no idea where he was, and could end up running into trouble. 'I beg your pardon, madam,' he said, in the most polite voice he could muster.

The woman pointed a gnarled finger at him. 'Where do you think you are going?' Her face was seamed with dirt, her hair a ragged, dirty mat around her shoulders. Finnigin thought her face resembled a stone gargoyle he'd once seen upon one of the cities; malevolent and cunning. Clearly, politeness was in order. He bowed slightly.

'To the mountains, madam.'

At these words, all the women glanced at one another and started to laugh conspiratorially. 'You cannot!' one of them said, a crone more terrifying in countenance than the first speaker.

'Why not?' Finnigin asked, with deference.

'You would be a fool to try!' another woman announced urgently. She seemed younger than the other two, and had a small animal curled up on her lap.

Finnigin had never seen an animal like it; a creature of scales and spines.

'Can you explain why?' he asked.

The first woman gestured abruptly. 'Come here, sonny. We won't bite you!'

The other women began to cackle, which the speaker silenced with an angry flap of her arm.

Warily, Finnigin took a few steps towards them.

'You would be deranged to try, because beyond this place all movement ceases,' the first speaker explained. 'The flat-lands are dynamic and while you are there, you are flesh. What lies beyond is static, and should you attempt to venture there, you will be turned to stone!'

Finnigin sighed. Had he really expected useful information? 'Well, thank you for your advice, but I must be getting along. Excuse me.' He began to walk away.

'Have you no fear?' cried one of the women in horror. 'It would be a crime for one so fair as you to turn to stone!'

Finnigin smiled politely. 'I know only what I have to do, and at this moment that is to go into the mountains.'

'Gah!' spat the woman, nodding to her companions. 'He has been talking to *her*, hasn't he! More fool him for listening.'

Her associates mumbled their agreement.

'The mazy-woman in the cage?' Finnigin asked. 'I've not talked to her. I don't think she can speak.'

'Not her!' said one of the women scornfully. 'Not Babooshpet. The other one, the other mad harridan.'

'I've only met someone called Valnisi,' Finnigin said, suddenly feeling more warm towards his erstwhile host. 'As a matter of fact, it was he who warned me about people trying to stop me going into the mountains.'

'Yes, Valnisi would, the insane bitch!'

'Valnisi is a woman?' Finnigin had not anticipated that, although perhaps the clues had been there to see.

'No, not a woman,' said the first speaker, 'she is an unman, an unperson, or a multiperson, but anyway, the terminology is irrelevant. Whatever she is, she speaks rubbish!'

'What she said to me was correct. You *are* trying to stop me, aren't you?'

The crone uttered a snort, folded her arms. 'If she believes what she says, then why does she stay here?'

'Mmm,' murmured another, 'but for all her ways, it is said that androgynes have the second sight.'

'Then she might know something we don't,' offered a third.

'Yet she has not braved the still country herself!' argued the first, in the loudest voice.

'Valnisi has the voice of a man,' said Finnigin. He had been searching his memory for clues. 'She has the strength of a man.'

'Aye,' said the first speaker. 'She has everything that a man has, including nonsensical ideas, and everything that a woman has too.'

'I must admit she was a trifle . . . strange,' Finnigin said.

The women all nodded, muttering, 'Aye!'

The first speaker grinned at him. 'Well, there we have it! Now, will you join us here? There is much we have to discuss, and I've no doubt your young, agile mind will contribute happily to our debate!'

'No thank you,' Finnigin replied. 'It's very kind of you to ask, but I have business of my own to attend to.'

The woman shrugged. 'As you like! Don't say we didn't warn you.'

As Finnigin turned away, he half expected the women to assault him in an attempt to curtail his journey, but it seemed they had lost all interest in him and had returned to their discussion. For a moment, he stood in the mist, hesitating. Then, he headed back towards Valnisi's dwelling of stone and moss. The woman in the cage made a strange, wheezing sound at him as he passed her.

Inside his home, Valnisi was still sitting in the position Finnigin had left him in, his face a blank mask of loss.

Finnigin threw his bags down on to the floor. Now, he did not fear Valnisi. Strange how a snippet of information could change his feelings like that. 'Someone has just told me what you are,' he said.

Valnisi looked up at Finnigin and blinked. His face was beautiful; weirdly malevolent, but still beautiful. 'I knew that would happen,' he said. 'Just as I knew you would return. Some things are interesting even to people who don't have a sense of curiosity.'

Finnigin wondered how many of his people had passed this way. How many of them had encountered Valnisi? He sat down. 'On this journey, I know I am supposed to see things, and remember them. So show me. Show me how you are both man and woman.'

Valnisi shook his head. 'No. But will you listen to me now?'

'Perhaps it would be useful.'

'There is something strange about our world,' Valnisi said. 'I don't even know what I'm doing here. I feel I don't belong, yet here I am, without a past, and to all intents and purposes without a future. I feel in my soul that I am a creature used to luxury and warmth and riches. How did I get here? Are these memories false? Perhaps I am dead in another world to end up here? None of it seems real, the people especially.'

'Are you expecting explanations from me?' Finnigin asked, remembering what Valnisi had said before about questioning terranauts.

Valnisi shrugged. 'Aren't you supposed to know the secrets of the pilot-stones?'

'I can't see what that's got to do with it. All I know is this. People live on the cities, and those who become calentured, or too curious for their own good, climb down and either wander pointlessly around until they die or become adept at living on the land. Some eventually find themselves a new city, more to their tastes; others attach themselves to terranaut troupes – although we barely tolerate them – but clearly a lot of wanderers end up here, of whom you must be one. Unexpected events occur when the paths of two cities cross. You must know that. Something must have happened to you once.' Finnigin paused and frowned.

'What is wrong?' Valnisi asked.

Finnigin shook his head. 'I don't know. I have never said these obvious things out loud before, and can't see why I have done now.'

'Nobody asked you before.'

Finnigin sighed. 'Perhaps that is the reason. Still, I can't have told you anything you've not heard from someone else.'

Valnisi smiled wistfully. 'That is true.'

'Perhaps you should leave here, climb up on to a city, look around it? If you don't like it, move on. You will find a city that suits you eventually.'

'I've heard that before too. Strangely, I have no urge to do it, although I can see it makes sense. Some perverse part of me is contented staying put and watching what goes on in this sad little pocket of mist and confusion.'

'Then you are truly mazy,' Finnigin said. He did not like the sound of Valnisi's existence and would certainly not put up with it himself.

'Oh, do not scorn me!' Valnisi replied. 'I can remember having been out into the flat-lands at some time, but I have returned.' He smiled. 'After all, this is the best place to catch terranauts.'

'Catch us for what?'

'To talk to you, to squeeze your knowledge from you. I know you all have the knowledge, but I'm not yet convinced you're aware of it.'

'It seems a fruitless thing to do,' Finnigin said. 'There must be much more to be learned away from this place. Your friends out there talk about being turned to stone in the mountains, but you might as well be stone people here. Your life is true stasis.'

'So the bright fledgling first stretches its wings,' murmured Valnisi, apparently to himself. 'In that, I have a function it seems.'

He looked Finnigin in the eye. 'I find the terranauts a fascinating breed. You are not afraid of the open spaces, but you appear to be dim and shallow creatures. This, I feel, is a deceit. It can be no coincidence that the only terranauts who pass this way are the young, on journeys of experience. Young men, young women, blank and pure as a new page. What happens afterwards? Are the older terranauts different?'

'I can't answer that until I'm older myself,' Finnigin said. 'Oh, my head is aching. You've made me think too much.' He rubbed his eyes and glanced at Valnisi slyly. 'So then, tell me what it is like to be both a man and a woman?'

Valnisi exhaled a painful sigh. 'In the company of men, I feel like a woman; I feel alien to them. They are lumpish and without intuition or finer feeling. In the company of women, I feel like a man; they intimidate me, therefore I have to feel physically stronger than them. It is all I have. Some parts of me have been lost, I think, some exquisite parts of my soul which would have elevated me above either gender.'

'What of the woman who is confined in a cage

outside?' Finnigin asked. 'Did you put her there in a moment of intimidated strength?'

Valnisi actually flushed. 'No! Babooshpet is a crystal-eater, therefore she must be confined. We found her wandering about the Shrine some months ago, eating the markings of our pathways. It is a disgusting habit. When she bites the stones, they bleed. It is their fire being released, I think.'

'Perhaps you are right to have confined her then,' Finnigin said. 'Pilot-stones should definitely not be eaten!' He frowned. 'But why do you keep feeding them to her?'

'That is simple,' Valnisi said. 'Without them she would die, and we are not killers. We take the coarsest stones from the stream that flows out of the mountain, and feed them to her. That way, we avoid her consuming more precious specimens, which must be used to construct our pathways around the shrine.'

'You are part of this silly life,' Finnigin decided. 'I want to sleep now. I will sleep until the manna falls. Then I shall eat and leave here.'

'As you like,' replied Valnisi.

Finnigin curled up on the floor, aching with exhaustion. He began to dream even before he fell asleep. He saw Varian come into the shack and stand over him. Finnigin was lying on his back, staring up into a face that stared down at him with an unreadable expression. He felt that even though Varian seemed to be fifty feet tall, he could reach out and touch that still face.

'I cannot imagine you reaching me,' Varian said.

Finnigin tried to and found that Varian's imagination was correct. He simply clutched at air.

'Are you following me?' Finnigin asked.

'More than that.'

'Why?'

'I must take that question from your mouth.'
'You don't make sense.'
'Yet. Keep talking. It is fascinating.'
'I can't think of anything to say.'
Varian laughed. 'You're wrong. It's just that *I* can't.'
Finnigin realised he was alone, drifting on the shores of sleep. What a strange dream. He was sure he would meet Varian again.

In the morning, Finnigin walked out of Valnisi's house, the owner of which was nowhere about. The ground outside was covered in a floating, furry stuff, like mounds of downy seeds. Deducing this must be the manna, Finnigin scooped it up and stuffed it into his mouth as he walked along. The taste was sickly sweet, with a rancid aftertaste, but he could feel it filling his belly for all its insubstantiality. Valnisi did not appear to wish his guest farewell, but Finnigin was not a person for goodbyes in any case.

He passed the cage of Babooshpet. She was not eating crystal, but rocking and humming to herself. The top of her cage was covered in a fine mat of manna, which she ignored. She looked up at Finnigin as he passed. She was a young woman, and her eyes were full of haunted sadness. She was filthy, her clothes ragged, her hair tangled with dirt and grease; and yet, for all her unprepossessing appearance, Finnigin felt there was a strangely ethereal quality to the girl. It was nothing at all like Valnisi's presence, and yet entirely similar. Peculiar, thought Finnigin. He had never performed an act of premeditated kindness, or recognised a spirit of charity in himself. He did not know why he was compelled to knock the pegs from the locks of Babooshpet's cage. Perhaps she lacked the intelligence to open the unlocked bars, but still he did it. Then, he walked on.

There was still a group of people sitting around the smoking fire as he passed. 'I should damp the smoke if I were you!' he called. 'Then you might see where you are.'

Finnigin walked until he came to a slabbed pavement. Up ahead, there was a dark shape moving on the ground. As he drew closer, he could see that it was a woman on hands and knees scrubbing the stone. She knelt upright as he walked past to watch him, but said nothing. Finnigin walked into the mist.

Soon, the fog began to thin and he was presented with a rising landscape of black, tortured rocks, between which a narrow pathway wound. There were many huge lumps of stone by the wayside, some of which resembled shocked figures looking back over their shoulders in horror. Finnigin walked past them but did not ignore them, as once he might. He took note of their posture and did not look back, for in that gesture, rather than walking into the mountains, might reside the curse of being turned to stone.

Casmeer

Casmeer left his captive plumosite ignoring the breakfast he had pushed through the bars, sure that when he returned she would have devoured it. He felt very energetic and looked forward to stepping out into the empty city streets. For the first time in weeks he had decided to go prowling, seek more of the enigmatic secrets of Thermidore; a new myth in the stone.

As he walked, he considered how his new-found activity – what he could only refer to as his story-telling – had become an obsession, subsuming the need to collate the sub-texts of the city itself. He was excited by the characters he'd created, and once he'd finished writing about them, was eager to lie in bed and continue his fantasies in his head. These, he felt reluctant to write down. He thought of intimacy, understanding, alliance. The terranaut and the Priest of Hands were aspects of himself, his inner younger self. He yearned to embrace them, not for any carnal gratification, but simply to become one with parts of his character which he felt had become lost or estranged. Ays and Finnigin walked bravely into the unknown; he himself cowered behind city walls, afraid of the land beyond. He was fond of his creations, and felt jealous for them. He knew it would be difficult to equip them with lovers, and realised it was no accident that the two women he had invented were based upon a dour, distant spinster, and a wild animal.

He found himself in the area of Thermidore that was known as the Dower Gates. Here, the grand façades of theatres and opera houses rose against the sky, facing one another across the wide expanse of marbled plazas where once street entertainers had danced, sung and mimed for the entertainment of passing crowds. Now, only dead weeds and seed-pods danced across the stones, their music the low flute of the wind. There were no roches in this area.

Casmeer went into the theatre called The Piramonte, the most expensive auditorium in the city. Here, the ingenious and celebrated plays of the most esteemed playwrights had been enacted upon the great stage. Casmeer himself had brought his wife to watch *Toramilia and the Bee-Keeper*; a tragedy. He had saved his earnings carefully and been frugal with materials in order to pay for the outing. Theatres had always excited him, and even now a ghost of that feeling was kindled in his breast as he stepped from the foyer up the wide, sweeping staircase, towards the circle. In the old days, he had only ever been able to afford a seat in the stalls.

The dry air of the mountains had preserved the majority of the fittings, and Casmeer was able to sit down upon a faded plush seat and gaze at the empty stage. The curtains hung in rags and glass from a domed roof had shattered inwards to litter the boards where once famous actors and actresses had trodden.

Who has written the script to *my* life? Casmeer thought.

In moments of reverie, he sometimes wondered whether he himself was but the subject of a lonely person's writing, as Ays and Finnigin were his.

Chapter Nine
Frenepolis

From the air, the cities had not looked so enormous as they did from the ground. *Whiteknuckle Rush* sometimes skimmed right underneath the overhanging weight of a passing city, close to its gigantic wheels, sticks and skis. In the darkness of these times, Ays could feel the oppressive weight of the colossus above bearing down on him; it was as if he could sense every busy mind oblivious above, the wealth of human activity; death, happiness, marriage, betrayal, murder, scandal, celebration and birth. All of this: above. He: a mote upon a silverfish hurrying below.

Mariet seemed to be sensitive to Ays' moods. 'Don't worry about the depression,' she said one time, as the train slithered beneath the seemingly endless bulk of a city rim. 'It gets to everyone. It's the humours, you see, coming down from above. Gets into your heart and your mind, oppresses. Happens to everyone.'

At first Ays wondered whether the train passed so close to the mighty wheels and struts of death to engage in some kind of fate-defying dare with itself, but soon realised it was because the unseen individuals who serviced the train collected refuse, and anything else they could scavenge, from every city they passed.

Ays knew that he could not ride the *Whiteknuckle Rush* for ever. He realised that in some ways he was hiding upon the train, turning his face away from the unknown, the possible dangers beyond the carriages. He could understand why so many people spent their lives travelling this way; it was probably the safest thing to do, once off a city. Still, he wondered about Odo and Mariet and Leeth – especially Leeth. How could someone so young be alone in the world? Surely, some charitable soul should have taken her in, or at least seen her safely established upon one of the cities. However, it was obvious Leeth was no ordinary girl; she seemed wizened, both physically and spiritually. Ays questioned Mariet about the girl. Shouldn't they encourage her to seek sanctuary on one of the cities?

Mariet only pulled a sour face at his concern. 'My dear boy, the world is awash with floundering souls. It is a terrible place. The girl is just one of them. You'd best harden your heart, otherwise in the not too distant future, your chagrin at the injustice of life will drive you to idiocy and unfathomable despair!' She indicated the motionless Discards whose only activities were scant visits to the cheer carriage and the privy. 'Look at them. They have given up, lost all hope.'

'For some good reason, no doubt,' he commented. The Discards made him feel uneasy. Heavy hoods hid their faces and often he had the uncomfortable feeling there was nothing there to hide.

Mariet shook her head. 'Sometimes it takes only a trifle for a person to end up that way. Even stepping down from your home city for a few scant moments can numb the brain. Once lost, a home city can never be found again.' She sighed. 'It is terrible. Still, why waste precious energy worrying about others?' She narrowed her eyes at Leeth who had been observing Ays and Mariet for some minutes from further up the carriage. 'I can't imagine any good citizen wanting to take that sinister little creature into their homes. She would undoubtedly taint their fortunes.'

Ays had already learned the futility of arguing Leeth's case with Mariet. He himself felt sorry for the girl. For some reason she had taken a shine to him, perhaps glamourised by his boyish good looks and the fact that he alone was disposed to talk to her in a friendly manner. Ays had to admit most of the other passengers he'd met upon the train were solitary individuals, often repellent both in manner and appearance. Carriage three furnished the best company, he supposed, and for all Mariet's erratic ways she reminded him of Umbilana, which offered a perhaps dangerous measure of comfort and familiarity. For this reason, as the days passed, Ays began to confront the inevitable. He would shortly have to leave the train behind, step off into the world, start looking for the things he was still unaware he needed to find.

Needing to speak his thoughts, he confessed some of his feelings to Mariet. 'I will have to disembark soon,' he said.

She appeared surprised by this remark. 'But whatever for?' She had to fan herself rapidly, as if Ays' words invoked bad luck, and her fan of shedding lace was protection against them.

Ays smiled. For a moment he ached with sadness for Mariet, stately and fading like a capsized and abandoned wind-yacht. 'I can see how it would be easy for someone to live out their days on this train,' he replied. 'I think you can lose track of time here, and become frightened of the outside.' He risked touching Mariet's hand and sensed her moment of hesitation as she considered withdrawing from his touch. Her fingers lay stiff beneath his own.

Mariet flapped the fan a few more times in front of her face, and gazed out of the window. 'Well, it is your life,' she said primly. 'Still, I would miss your company.

I think you are an intelligent young man.' She leaned forward confidentially. 'Odo, I'm afraid, lacks the capacity for intellectual debate, and the girl – well, she discomfits me. As for the Discards, it is beyond me to penetrate their torpor.' She paused. 'What will you do when you've left us, I wonder? Death lurks in many forms between the cities.'

'I am searching for something,' he told her.

Mariet rolled her eyes. 'Ha! Well, believe me, you have little chance of finding it, whatever it is. Nothing remains the same out there.' She waved her arm in the direction of the window. 'The thing you are searching for has undoubtedly undergone several changes since you lost it.'

'It's not something that I've lost exactly,' said Ays. 'I suppose I am searching for the city where I was born. After all, I'm not so old, the place must still be around.' He frowned unintentionally. 'It has to be.'

'Don't be so sure!' Mariet's face assumed an almost frightened cast, as if echoing Ays' expression, but it lasted for only a few moments before a more composed mask reasserted itself.

'What do you mean?' Ays asked.

'Cities can die.' This came from Leeth who had sidled up to sit beside him.

To his surprise, Mariet did not make a sharp refutation of Leeth's words. 'The child is right!' she snapped, taking out one of her vile green cigarettes from her tasselled purse.

'Cities can die?' Ays could only repeat what he had heard. For a split second, he was presented with the horrific image of Min tumbling from the sky.

'Yes.' Mariet screwed up her face and shook her head as she inhaled the first lungful of smoke from her cigarette. A thin, very black, rancid cloud drifted before her face. 'Yes. Yes. If you must know, that is the reason I am here on this train.'

'I don't understand . . .' Ays said. 'How can a city die?' He could not imagine one of the massive, slowly moving storehouses of life and activity ever diminishing and expiring.

'Ah!' said Odo, who had been roused from a post-prandial snooze by Mariet's raised voice. 'There are doubtless a thousand reasons! I myself have seen at least three cities falter and stumble in their progress; like lame mules. It is an astounding sight! Some of them recover, and I have to say that those I witnessed recovered their momentum, but it is not always the case.' He stood up and strolled across the aisle to join the others. 'Cities, you see, are like humankind. They are born, grow, become great and fulfil their potential, or else, in the case of failures, remain as straggling haphazard creations throughout their lifespan. Then, they die. They are dynamic things, the cities. If they did not live, their people would perish; the relationship between human and city soul is crucial to the well-being of both.'

'That is astounding!' Ays said. He considered. 'But then, I suppose the way I used to feel about Min supports your theory.' He shrugged. 'Still, here I am, surviving and sane upon the ground, and Min flies on somewhere else.' He smiled. 'I am sure I'll see its shadow again one day.'

'You hope,' Mariet said tartly.

'What happened to your city?' Ays asked her.

Mariet regarded him in a measured fashion for a few moments. 'To be honest, I rarely like to speak of it,' she said, and then leaned forward to squeeze Ays' arm. 'However, I feel I can be open with you.'

'I would very much like to hear the tale,' he said, and settled back in his seat. Leeth moved a little closer to him.

'Very well,' Mariet replied, and lit another cigarette. She closed her eyes and inhaled deeply before beginning to speak. 'I was born on Ossiter, a city of bone-white spires.' She sighed. 'How lovely were the ivory towers at dawn and dusk, how they caught the light! I wish you could have seen them.

'Our city grew like an animal without skin; beautiful bones towards the stars. And our lives were clean and scoured, our garments pale, our children silent and thoughtful, but smiling. Ossiter was ancient and regular; I could trace my ancestry back through twenty-four generations. The lintel of my great-great-grandmother's house was the mantelpiece over the fireplace in my mother's salon.' Mariet sighed again. 'Old and stately, no tremor to shake it, no social chaos. Everything smooth. And then, one day, Ossiter shuddered. We all felt it. Had it been an aberration in the setting of the stones we followed? Some kind of topological bump? Perhaps. Perhaps. Engineers swarmed down the rigging that hung from the city rails. They examined the great cogs, the crawler treads, the stickles. Everything appeared well-oiled and efficient. And so it was. Until the evening. Then . . .' Mariet leaned back against her seat and closed her eyes. She seemed quite overcome by emotion.

'Then?' Ays prompted gently.

Mariet blinked rapidly, as if waking up. 'Then it stopped moving,' she replied baldly.

Ays uttered a nervous laugh of disbelief. 'But how? Why? What had happened to the stones?'

'A double row of pilot-stones stretched out before us. The city simply refused to follow the trail any more.'

'But that's impossible!'

Mariet shook her head. 'Not at all. As soon as the city stopped moving, crazies came creeping out of the landscape to investigate. From them, we learned that these things happened now and again. Cities died. They advised us to leave straight away. It was terrible. For a day or two, the town governors had the engineers working day and night to get the mechanisms working again. We all believed it was a temporary fault, and law-makers drove the scavengers from our streets. But then, on the third day, the city gave a great groan and listed to the side.

'Buildings fell, delicate buildings that had stood for hundreds upon hundreds of years. Houses and farm terraces and people and animals fell off the side of the city in their thousands. Fires started. We all . . . fled.'

A hush filled the air of carriage three. Ays' skin had gone numb with dread. Listening to Mariet's fatalistic flat voice, it became easy to imagine the same thing happening to Min, except there would be no chance for its inhabitants to flee the dead bulk. No. If Min should suddenly halt in its flight, all would be dashed to pieces upon the ground. It was a dreadful thing to picture. Ays experienced a pang of relief that he'd left the city before that could happen. Then, he tried to pull himself together, to remember how Min had felt, so vital and dynamic around him. It could never fall; never. The philosopher scientists who had hoisted Min aloft via magnetism and repulsion must have thought of that eventuality and no doubt guarded against it. Perhaps, because Min flew, it was immune to death? Perhaps that was why its founders had lifted it from the ground?

'Do you think that every city dies eventually, or just some of them?' he enquired. 'Odo has already said they are like people – some stronger than others. Perhaps only the weak ones die?'

Mariet made an outraged sound. 'Ossiter was not a weak city!' she cried. 'Old, yes, but never weak!' Then she gave a theatrical shrug and took a draw off her cigarette. 'Oh, who knows? The terranauts? I doubt it! They are stupid!' Her voice became brittle, apparently uncaring. 'New cities are born, so old ones must die. That seems logical to me.'

'How are new ones born?' Ays asked.

'Nobody knows,' Odo replied. Then he laughed. 'If you're really interested, all I can suggest is that you find an infant hamlet and go and ask the people who live on it!'

Mariet shook her head. 'I've visited such places. The people are witless, undeveloped souls. They can't answer because they don't have the intelligence. It's all a mystery.' She nodded at Ays. 'But I hope you can see now why your search is probably pointless.'

Ays shrugged. 'Well, as I said, I'm not so old. If my parents' city was around when I was born, then there's a good chance it still is. I don't believe I was compelled to leave Min for no reason.'

'They all say that!' Mariet said sourly.

Odo nodded. 'As you've just heard, a city can die in days. Anyway, how do you know your parents weren't travellers themselves?'

'Just a feeling,' Ays said.

Mariet expelled a harsh sound of mockery. 'Oh, my lovely boy, I wish you wouldn't say such things! It makes me so terribly afraid you'll end up like them!' She stabbed her fan in the direction of the Discards.

Leeth reached out to touch Ays' hand, whispering, 'I think you're right.'

He squeezed her small fingers briefly, before pulling away from her.

'Just wait until you climb up on to one of those places!' Mariet said scathingly. 'They think *we're* mazy! Ha! Just you wait! It's an insane life to be city-bound. I'm glad Ossiter died. I'd probably be dead myself by now if I'd lived out my life there. Don't you realise that the only people who ever question how the world might work are those who leave the cities? City-dwellers are asleep; mindless. Only the dispossessed have spirit and mettle. The cities move, yes, but their societies are absurdly static. Nothing changes. It's stultifying!'

'Min was – *is* – not like that,' Ays said.

'Well, it flies, doesn't it? Probably something to do with that,' Mariet conceded.

Ays sighed and leant his face against the carriage window. 'I miss my home,' he said.

'Then you shouldn't have left!' Mariet replied. 'What's the point of moaning about it? Scant chance you'll ever find it again now! Go forward, get on with your life.'

'Like you?' Ays couldn't help saying. 'All you've done is sit on this train and watch life outside go by. You've just exchanged one static society for another.'

'You have no understanding,' Mariet said airily. 'You're only a boy.'

Ays turned away from her, longing to reveal that he might only be young, but that he'd handled death in his time: it came to his hand and let him feed it. Instead, realising it would probably open up an unwanted discussion, he turned his attention to Leeth and smiled, knowing that paying attention to her always irritated Mariet. 'Are you hungry?' he asked the girl. 'Shall we go to the cheer car?'

'I'm thirsty,' Leeth replied. 'I would like a mint broth.' Ays stood up.

'Give me some of that hela stuff!' Mariet demanded abruptly. The atmosphere of the train had caused the hela in Ays' coat to enjoy an unnatural spurt of growth and he had been sharing it with his fellow passengers because he couldn't keep it all. He had already explained to them that the drug could kill, and that the safe dosage varied from person to person, but Mariet and Odo seemed prepared to take the risk. Hela's effects, after all, were wonderfully euphoric. Ays had a pocket full of ready-rolled portions, one of which he now offered to Mariet. Leeth pulled a disagreeable face. She'd made it plain she disapproved of hela-taking.

As Ays and Leeth stood up, Mariet poked Leeth in the arm. 'I want a word with you,' she said. 'Catch Ays up in a minute.'

Leeth was surprised because Mariet had never asked to speak to her before. Surprise kindled curiosity. She sat down again. 'All right.'

'Go away, Odo, this is women's talk,' Mariet said. Grumbling, Odo stood up and moved a few seats down the carriage.

'What is it?' Leeth asked.

Mariet put down the small lump of Ays' rolled hela on the seat beside her. She lit another cigarette and blew smoke above Leeth's head in a thin spume. 'When he leaves, go with him,' she said abruptly.

Leeth frowned. 'Are you talking about Ays?'

'You know I am.'

Leeth smiled acidly. 'Are you that desperate to be rid of me?'

Mariet bared her teeth. 'Perhaps.' She took a deep breath, exhaled it slowly, folded her arms. 'You are young. Too young to be trapped on this train.'

'I'm not trapped.'

'We all think that.'

Leeth nodded gently. She had her own opinions about Mariet, and felt she understood the woman's weaknesses. She could almost smell Mariet's fear of the world outside, and she knew Mariet was aware of this perceptiveness. She might be weak, but she wasn't stupid. Leeth supposed this recognition of

Mariet's fears was partly why the older woman was so sharp with her.

'Don't end up like the other sad people on the *Rush*,' Mariet said. 'Get off while you can. I think you've aged before your time, young woman. You need to rediscover your youth, and Ays would be an ideal person to help you with that. I know for a fact he won't be with us much longer.'

Leeth's heart suddenly felt cold and heavy in her chest. The thought of Ays leaving without her was devastating. 'He might not want me to go with him.'

Mariet laughed harshly. 'Don't be a fool! He's male. You can make him do what you like.'

Leeth was not convinced. 'I shall think about what you've said.' She stood up.

Mariet blinked once and nodded. 'Do that. Quickly. Don't miss an opportunity. Be brave.'

Leeth hesitated. 'Thank you, Mariet.'

She sneered, and picked up the packet of hela. 'You're welcome!'

Wide corridors ran down each side of the train, walled by windows that could be opened to the elements in clement climates. People often sat there in wicker chairs among dead, but perfectly preserved, parlour palms. They sipped various beverages and either huddled together in groups to converse politely and ignore the flashing scenery outside, or else lurk among the stiff leaves alone, staring out through the glass with ravaged faces.

Leeth caught up with Ays as he was queuing at the cheer car's counter. A very fat woman moved slowly behind the counter attending to the demands of a rather fractious tea-maker, which hissed and groaned as she tweaked its taps and valves.

'What did Mariet want?' Ays asked.

Leeth shrugged. 'It was strange. I think she had a pang of conscience and wanted to be nice to me.'

Ays laughed. 'That doesn't sound like Mariet!'

'No,' Leeth agreed. 'It doesn't.'

She was about to say more, perhaps introduce the subject of what Mariet had actually spoken about, when the train suddenly lurched, causing her to bump into Ays. Instinctively, she reached out for him, shivering with pleasure at the unexpected contact. He was as solid as stone. The carriage filled with a screaming, grating sound, as halt mechanisms fought with the train's momentum.

'What's going on?' Ays asked in alarm, steadying himself against the counter. Behind it, the large woman still moved with slow grace, unperturbed by the jerking movement of the train.

'We're stopping,' said Leeth.

'Why?' Ays freed himself from her grasp and went to peer out of the windows. They had come to a leafy, grassy terrain, and the bulky outline of a city could be seen in the eastern distance.

'Someone must want to get on or off,' Leeth said.

'I can't see anyone,' he said, straining.

Leeth took a deep breath. 'Ays, do you want to get off now?'

He turned and looked at her. He was silent for a moment and then said, 'Strangely enough, I have been thinking about it.'

'Then perhaps this stop is for you . . .'

Ays smiled. 'What? Don't be ridiculous. I've said nothing to anybody.'

Leeth lifted her hands in an eloquent gesture. 'You might not have to. The train stops and starts as it pleases.'

'Of course it does!' He laughed sarcastically.

'Let's go together,' Leeth blurted out.

Ays regarded her thoughtfully. 'You and me? I didn't realise you wanted to get off the train as well.'

Leeth shrugged. 'Well . . . I don't want to stay on it for ever. We could travel together for a while. It's always safer to travel in groups.'

'A group of two!' Ays grinned, glanced outside, and then back at Leeth. 'Very well. I'll go back and collect my bags. Do you suppose the train will wait that long before starting off again?'

'If this is your stop it will.'

Ays began to hurry back towards carriage three, and Leeth followed him. 'So, am I coming with you?'

Ays considered. Surely it could do no harm. The flat-lands were an unknown territory to him, and Leeth was a more experienced traveller than himself. 'Well, we can see how we get on,' he said. 'If it doesn't work out, we can always separate.'

'Yes. That's a good idea.' Leeth's heart took flight within her breast. Already images of intimacy, laughter, companionship were winging across her mind. She felt like weeping with joy. 'I don't have much to carry, just a small bag.'

Ays nodded. 'Let's go and gather our belongings, then. We'd better hurry.'

In carriage three, Mariet observed their preparations for departure in silence, her face slack. Clearly she had dosed herself with most of the hela Ays had given her. He cast her an anxious glance. Was she strong enough to take that?

'Goodbye,' he said, too brightly, as he slung his bags over his shoulders. 'We've decided to get off now, while the train has stopped.'

Mariet listlessly raised a hand. 'Enjoy it,' she murmured in a slurred voice.

The train gave a whistle. 'Hurry,' said Leeth.

Ays glanced back at Mariet, but Leeth was tugging his arm. 'Goodbye,' he said again, as Leeth pulled him from the carriage.

'Have you visited a city before, Leeth?' Ays asked as they stood with the wind of the departing train in their hair.

It was late-afternoon, and the air was warm and calm. In the distance, perhaps coming from the city, a mournful, low-throated whistle sounded. They had begun to walk towards the hazy outline. The city might have been moving away from them, but the movement was so slow, it would hardly make any difference, or a need for haste.

Ays shuddered. Another sharp reminder, but no clear memory. 'You are shivering,' Leeth said, daring to hook her thin bony fingers around his elbow. She felt that his assenting to travel with her had already initiated a closer relationship.

As she took hold of his arm, Ays was thinking: I do not want a dependant. I mustn't encourage her too much. She was there to be exploited for her wider knowledge of the land, nothing more.

'*Why* are you shivering?' Leeth asked. 'It's not that cold.'

'A thought,' he replied. 'A memory. That's all.'

'A thought of a woman?' Leeth's voice was arch.

'No, I am not thinking of a woman,' he said, coolly.

'Oh,' said Leeth. 'A man then?'

'No, no one. I don't ever think of anyone in that way!' Ays was surprised to realise he had spoken the truth. Was that unusual? It was almost as if his former lovers had never existed. He could hardly remember their faces, and there was no tug of loss in his heart as he thought of them. How long had he been away from Min? How could he have lost track of time so quickly?

'Then you aren't running away from anyone?' Leeth asked impertinently.

'No, of course not!' Ays snapped, and then added, more as a voiced thought than a real question, 'Do people ever do that?' What extravagance of emotion could drive a person into the arms of dispossession?

Leeth nodded knowledgeably. 'Of course. All the time. Mariet Crane, for example.'

Ays glanced down at the girl in surprise, and then shook his head to dispute her words. 'I think you're wrong there. Mariet told us how she lost her home city.'

Leeth wrinkled her nose. 'She said that, but I don't think she was really talking about a city. I think she's running from a broken heart. She left it behind her somewhere, but she can still hear it cracking.'

Ays laughed, even though his skin prickled. 'How do you know this?'

Leeth shrugged. 'You get to recognise the signs.'

It seemed the inhabitants of the approaching city threw little away because there was so much rubbish hanging from its vast belly, which was caught in nets and wrapped in canvas, dangling and wobbling as the cranks and punch-sticks struck the earth below, feeling blindly for the pilot-stone path.

Ays was surprised, if not a little alarmed, by the sheer bulk of the city. It seemed impossible that it could travel across the land without disintegrating, or its own mass causing inner collapse. Ahead of the giant, oiled punch-sticks, a myriad of waving reticulated feelers nosed along the path, perhaps picking up items of interest. Leeth said that people operated the feelers from within cabins situated among the hanging nets.

'I have never seen anything like it,' said Ays, which was an understatement.

'Come along,' Leeth replied, with authority. 'There will be a visitor's chute or rope-drop somewhere near.'

Walking under the shadow of the city, Ays felt as if it would suddenly lurch forward and crush him to death. There was an almost deafening sound of machinery at work, and a subliminal groaning, as if each step the city took caused it untold pain. As they drew nearer, he could see that there were many people swarming up and down the rigging that depended from the city. They all wore leather harnesses with heavy clips attached, presumably so that they could cling to precarious areas of the mechanisms in order to carry out repairs and services He expected Leeth to address one of these people, but the girl did not. Neither did she pay attention to the first dangling walkway that jutted temptingly towards them at calf-height.

'Here?' asked Ays, who was anxious to climb aloft and escape the oppressive bulk of the city's underbelly.

The girl shook her head. 'No. That would only take us to one of the service areas.'

'How can you tell?'

'It is too wide to be for the use of travellers.'

Eventually, Leeth's unspecified requirements were satisfied, and she gestured for Ays to follow her up a hairy rope-ladder.

He balked. 'Surely that is not for travellers to use!' he protested. He had been hoping for something more upon the lines of a conveyor belt walkway.

'Believe me, this is the best route,' Leeth said patiently. 'It is a residents' rope, and will therefore lead directly to one of the more public areas. Routes designed specifically for travellers, whom city-dwellers despise anyway, will probably lead only to a knot of hawkers and expensive accommodation.' She began to ascend the ladder with a monkey's agility. Encumbered by his baggage, Ays followed less nimbly. He was gasping with nervousness, remembering how his own people in Min had regarded travellers: crazies, misfits, people to be wary of. Would he be treated badly in this place? Surely the ground cities would be more used to strangers than Min was – but as he'd learned on the train, nobody with any sense left the city of their birth. At best, he would be viewed with suspicion.

Breathless and red-faced, Ays and Leeth emerged from a narrow opening into a busy street, crawling out between hurrying feet. Even though a couple of men in smart uniforms stood on duty by the chute-mouth, nobody paid Ays and Leeth any attention.

Ays was astounded at how the presence of the city claimed him immediately. It was not like climbing aboard a moving series of platforms, but stepping into another world. The flat-lands might not exist. The city had a distinctive smell which reminded Ays of the fluid Umbilana used to season her wood. In fact, the bulk of this place was built of wood which perhaps explained the aroma. The buildings were complex and multi-storied, with designs that implied an advanced architecture had been employed, yet their wooden frames were tied together with what appeared to be tar-covered rope. Ays wondered whether that was a fashionable affectation. He couldn't believe the citizens didn't possess the technology for more sophisticated joinery.

A market was in progress, and many neat stalls lined the alley into which Ays and Leeth had emerged. Clearly, the city possessed fertile farming terraces, for the stalls were piled with glossy, colourful fruit and plump vegetables. Fat fowl hung from hooks at the front of butchers' booths, their wings still feathered, their bodies denuded. Affluent-looking people thronged the streets, most with shopping-buckets attached to their backs. And yet, Ays immediately sensed something unusual about the scene before him. Wide-hipped women swathed in shawls surveyed the produce upon the stalls. Rosy-cheeked vendors smiled obligingly and wrapped their purchases. Teenagers skipped in groups of two or three among the adults, daring to steal from the stalls, being chased away by outraged vendors. However, despite this apparent bustle, there was a kind of stilted unreality about the scene, something almost mechanical. Was it simply because this culture was alien to him? Ays wondered. Would it be a mistake for him to measure everything by Minnian standards? The people in this place seemed larger than life, like animated portraits. The hubbub held the regular discipline of a structured dance.

'Where do we go?' he asked, feeling small within the swirling crowd.

'I don't know!' Leeth answered. 'How could I? I'm as much a stranger to this place as you are!'

'I thought you were an expert,' Ays said waspishly. He felt sure his visit here would be wasted. There was nothing of his past here, he was certain of it. At least, he strongly hoped there wasn't.

Leeth sauntered over to one of the market stalls, and picked up a fruit which to Ays looked like an unnaturally red koopi, one of Min's own strains. 'We are travellers,' she announced baldly to the proprietor, causing Ays to cringe. He himself would have endeavoured to avoid that confession.

The stall-keeper gave Leeth a narrow glance, but then ignored her. She opened her mouth to speak again, but Ays stepped forwards and dragged her back.

'Don't say anything else!' he said.

'We need to eat,' Leeth said, pulling away from him. 'Therefore we should learn the local bartering system as quickly as possible.'

'True, but I feel we need to be more careful, more subtle.'

Leeth shrugged. 'As you like. I'll watch *you* do it.'

Ays sighed, shouldered his baggage and set off up the alley, Leeth following behind. The further he ventured into the city's heart, the more uneasy he became. It was as if he and the girl were invisible to the city's inhabitants.

There was one bizarre moment when someone came and tried to thrust what appeared to be a sack of vegetables into Ays' arms. Apparently surprised by his confusion, the man announced in a hiss, 'More practice is needed!' Then, looking furtively to left and right, he ran off into the crowd, taking his sack with him.

'This place is indeed peculiar!' Ays decided.

Leeth shrugged. 'No more than any other. I expect your own city would seem bizarre to strangers.'

'Hardly!' he snapped. 'We are a balanced and rational society.' He sighed. 'It's worrying that I might find Min is the only place pervaded by such sanity.'

'You shouldn't become disheartened,' Leeth said. 'You have set yourself an impossible task, but it would be best to try and enjoy it.'

'Hummph!' Ays grumbled. 'I'm hungry.'

'I have been thinking of that,' Leeth said. 'And it has occurred to me that since the locals seem disposed to ignore us, we might as well simply help ourselves to something to eat.'

'Steal?'

'Why not? At worst, it would open up a conversation of some kind.' With that, she sauntered over to a nearby sausage-vendor and removed a string of fat, orange meats from the counter.

As she moved away, the stall-holder cleared his throat and said, with what appeared to be some indecision, 'Excuse me, but I don't believe I was scheduled for a thief today.'

Leeth turned round. 'Then there is a change to your schedule,' she replied swiftly.

The man's face darkened. 'By whose authority?'

'Those who make the schedules,' she answered confidently. Ays was awed by her nerve, but it quickly became clear Leeth's audacity had not been sufficient to carry out her plan.

'You are an external!' roared the stall-holder, pointing an aggrieved finger at Leeth. 'Crew! Crew!'

At once a group of individuals wearing brown overalls appeared as if from nowhere, carrying thick sheaves of papers on clipboards. Hammers and packets of nails hung from their belts, items which Ays supposed might easily be used as weapons.

'What is this disturbance?' a woman asked, obviously in charge.

'My performance has been interrupted,' explained the stall-holder, 'by this girl. She is clearly an external! How has this happened? Is your vigilance so sloppy?'

'Is this true?' the woman asked Leeth.

She shrugged. Ays walked up behind her and put his hands on the girl's shoulders. Perhaps his own, more diplomatic, methods would be useful now. 'We are strangers to this city,' he explained in a soft, soothing voice, 'and have obviously violated some code or another. For this, we apologise.'

'She is a thief to boot!' added the stall-holder.

By this time, Ays would have expected bystanders to have gathered to watch what was going on, but save for this small pocket of disturbance, everyone else carried on with their daily business without giving the situation a glance.

'Travellers?' said the crew-woman.

'Yes,' Ays admitted with chagrin. The woman's cold tone was not lost on him.

She tucked her charcoal back into the top of her clipboard. 'Ah, I see. You should have entered Frenepolis by the Visitors' Chute on Breadmarket Boulevard. All visitors are required to undertake a short period of coaching before being issued with scripts for their stay. You have transgressed, but I am not a harsh woman, therefore I shall act as if your transgression was committed in ignorance. If you will accompany me now to a short-term college, I can get you settled in.'

'I'm afraid I don't understand what you mean,' Ays said. 'Would you be kind enough to explain?'

'All shall be revealed at the proper moment,' answered the woman. 'Please don't make any more fuss. Enough ad-libbing has occurred in this locality for the day as it is!' She smiled. 'Come along.'

She gestured through the crowd, and her colleagues shuffled forward to surround Leeth and Ays. They had no choice but to go where they were directed.

'I am worried about this,' Ays hissed to Leeth. 'What are they going to do with us? Short-term college? Scripts? What is going on?'

'At a guess, I'd say these people live a pre-defined existence,' Leeth answered. 'Though I expect there's more to it than that.'

They emerged from the low, uniform buildings of the trading district into an area where wider streets were bordered by tall, pale structures with imposing façades. Here, there was evidence of more complex methods of building, although still no sign of any stone or brick. Men and women in stiff, formal clothes, their faces expressionless, walked aimlessly up and down the sidewalks, which were boarded with polished planks. Muted music filled the air; light, stringed instruments performing a frothy unchallenging piece. Here Ays noticed that many overall-clad individuals could be seen flitting between the buildings, carrying timber, clothes, baskets, pushing trolleys laden with boxes, consulting clipboards. Their activities seemed furtive, as if they wanted to remain inconspicuous. Somewhere a bell began to toll, and the ladies and gentlemen walking the streets seemed to wake up, turn their heads and walk in a different direction.

'I am Marvane Clamp,' the woman in charge told Ays and Leeth, as they neared the end of a long tidy street with a park running down one side. White-painted residences opposite were fronted with delicate black wrought iron railings. 'I am an assistant director.'

'What is this city called again?' Leeth asked.

'Frenepolis,' Marvane Clamp replied. 'It has been in production for a thousand years.'

'I have never been anywhere like it!' Ays declared, which Marvane Clamp appeared to take as a compliment.

'Life is always busy for production crew,' she said, 'but never dull! Here we are. Down this street, if you please.'

They turned into a darker lane, where high buildings leaned towards one another overhead. Here, the atmosphere seemed palpably less constrained. Ays felt himself relax.

'I'm not sure what you require of us,' he said. 'Perhaps it would be best if we simply left your city by the nearest exit?'

Marvane Clamp shook her head. 'Oh no! I couldn't let you do that! Let you miss your chance for a part in the great production? That would be too cruel. You must put that unfortunate event in the market behind you. Anyway, all visitors are required to offer six months' performance as a fee for entering the city.'

'Six months!' Ays glanced in despair at Leeth. 'And how long is a month in Frenepolis?'

'That can vary from city to city,' Leeth replied. She didn't seem bothered by their situation, which Ays found incomprehensible. To his mind, they were being imprisoned and labour demanded from them. How could Leeth take that with such equanimity?

Marvane Clamp conducted them through the narrow doorway of a high, thin building which was approached by a flight of worn steps. There was a place above the door where a name had once been carved, but for some reason it had been crudely hacked away. Marvane Clamp noticed Ays' appraisal.

'This area has long been scheduled for re-design,' she said, waving a disapproving hand around her, 'but The Writers have been excelling themselves for decades with magnificent new plots, so scenery in the less-frequented and external zones has been neglected.'

Inside the building, a receptionist sat on duty behind a high counter. She was frowning in concentration at a notebook, her mouth moving silently to the words she read.

'Millie!' called Marvane Clamp.

The girl looked up, hesitated for a few moments, and then struck a dramatic posture, one hand arched against her breast. 'What is this?' she demanded. 'More lunatics? Have you no care, Mistress?' She put her other hand, which was trembling, to her brow, her face a mask of anguish. Ays was astounded by her behaviour. It seemed altogether too overstated for the occasion.

'Ah, but I am a lone girl!' cried the receptionist. 'Without protection. Am I to be hostess to an edifice of murdering lackwits?' She held out her hands. 'Look, my fingers drip blood from the last excursion!' She pulled a tragic face.

Ays glanced questioningly at Leeth, who merely shrugged.

Marvane Clamp walked forwards, rubbing her hands together. 'Well done, Millie!' she said unctuously. 'Although I believe the last word should have been "incursion".'

The girl reddened and glanced down at the sheaf of notes on the counter. 'Oh dear!'

'But still, the delivery was good, if a little melodramatic.' Marvane Clamp indicated Ays and Leeth. 'Two newcomers. I'll leave them in your capable hands!' She turned to Ays. 'Because you arrived in one of my zones, I shall take responsibility for your coaching.'

'Coaching in what?' he asked.

'Your part in the production.'

Ays shook his head with a smile that signified displeasure. 'Er . . . no. We have no part in your *production*. We really haven't the time to get involved – interesting though it undoubtedly is.'

Marvane Clamp ignored his remarks. 'I'm sure you'll settle in quickly! Anyway, goodbye for now. I'll see you later.' She hurried out of the door before Ays could say anything more.

He glanced down at Leeth's sombre face. 'The life in this city is not real,' he declared.

Leeth, as usual, simply shrugged.

The receptionist cleared her throat in a pointed manner. 'If you'd just register in the book,' she said in a loud voice, 'I can find you accommodation in one of the dormitories.'

'What we'd most like to do is leave,' Ays said, putting his back-pack down on the floor. His shoulders were aching.

'But we want something to eat,' Leeth said.

'It won't take you long to earn credits for that,' Millie said brightly. 'As for leaving, perhaps Mistress Clamp didn't explain, but all visitors have to take part in the city-life for a while before they can move on.'

'So we are prisoners?' Ays said, looking round at the door.

'Not at all!' Millie declared. 'There are wonderful benefits to be gained. I myself have decided to stay here once my probationary period is over. Travelling is a non-life. To be accepted by one of the cities is every traveller's secret dream, and in Frenepolis the realisation of that dream is easier than in other places. There is so little discrimination, you see.'

'So you were a traveller too, then?' Ays said. 'In that case, explain to me what is going on here.'

'Of course. Life in Frenepolis is a dance of moods and feelings which is part of a carefully crafted pattern, all of it written by a conclave of imaginators who are elected to the position. The citizens act out the parts that have been written for them, and in that way the life of the city is regulated.'

'It is disgusting!' Ays said. 'No freedom!'

Millie shook her head. 'You are wrong. The citizens of Frenepolis enjoy more liberty than most. Unless it has been written into their script, they are free from the fear of crimes against their person. They can feel secure in the knowledge that nothing unexpected will ever happen to them.'

'I've never heard of anything so ridiculous!' Ays said.

'It must require a lot of learning,' Leeth added.

Millie shrugged. 'Apparently it becomes a habit eventually, and therefore easier.'

Ays shook his head in amazement. 'So you were acting out a part when we came in just then?'

The receptionist nodded. 'Yes, well, I was practising. It wasn't a real part, as such.' She brightened. 'We could act it out together, if you like? There are other parts which you could take.'

'No, thank you,' said Ays.

'Oh, well, perhaps later. Will you sign this book now?' Sighing, Ays picked up the pen on the desk and scrawled his name with a flourish. Millie wrote a number beside it. Leeth stood on tiptoe and slowly wrote her name in a deliberate hand.

As he watched her, a thought came to Ays. 'What of the children?' he asked the receptionist.

'I beg your pardon?' Millie frowned.

'The children here in the city,' Ays explained. 'They can't possibly get young children to act out prescribed parts all the time. Doesn't that interfere with the city script?'

'You'll have to discuss such things with Mistress Clamp,' Millie replied.

'But haven't you wondered about it?'

'No, why should I?' Millie grinned. 'I haven't got any children. Later this week. I've been given the part of a shopper in the market. I can't wait! No lines, of course, but I get to visit the museum later.'

'How exciting for you!' Ays couldn't help sneering.

From the engraving on the front of the Register, Ays and Leeth learned they were in a place called Minction College. As Millie conducted them up a wide, stone stairway, which echoed dismally as they walked, she explained that Gustav Minction had been an eminent performer of the third century, and it had been he who'd initiated the practice of training visitors to take temporary parts in the city-life, rather than throwing any interlopers off the city rim. This scrippet of information alerted Ays to the possibility that it might well be dangerous entering certain cities. He was angry with himself that he had not thought of this before. Neither, apparently, had Leeth, who'd blithely led the way up to Frenepolis. There must be some way they could discern in advance whether a city was friendly to strangers or not.

Minction College seemed little more than a vast empty warehouse. Its panelled walls were painted a flat grey, its cellings were high and arched, and crossed by a confusing network of wooden rafters. The lighting was stark and unflattering. Ays did not relish the thought of having to live there for six months. There must be some way they could escape. It would be sensible to go along with the charade for a while, until he and Leeth could get their bearings, but Ays did not intend to stay the stipulated six months.

Millie, chattering excitedly about life in Frenepolis, apparently oblivious to the cold reception of her audience, led the way into a vast, draughty dormitory. Rows of uncomfortable-looking beds lined a wall, opposite which floor-to-ceiling windows did little to conserve the meagre heat. A single log-burning stove burned inadequately at the far end of the room. It seemed that only a few of the beds were currently being used, all of these being nearest the stove.

'Leave your belongings on one of the beds,' Millie said with a friendly smile. 'Then I'll take you to one of the workshops. You have plenty of time before supper to earn a meal.'

Ays did not want to be parted from his baggage. 'I'd rather take my things with me.'

Millie frowned in disappointment. 'Oh, I'm sorry, you can't do that. They'd only get under people's feet and Master Fabricious, the head designer, is most particular about things like that.'

'Look, we are here against our will!' Ays began, but Leeth interrupted, laying a small hand on his arm.

'I'm sure our things will be safe here,' she said.

Ays glanced down at her, took in the meaningful

glance, and capitulated. 'Oh, very well! But I'm not happy about this!'

The workshops were located behind Minction College. Here, it appeared the costumes for the city drama were created. Naturally, most of the clothing was functional and ordinary, but Ays saw a few splendid gowns, with gored sleeves and festoons of pearls, hanging on a far wall. He wondered what parts had been written for the eventual recipients of those costumes.

Millie introduced the newcomers to Master Fabricious, who was plainly a person obsessed with pettifoggery, to whom Ays took an instant dislike.

'You can sweep the floor,' he said dourly. To Ays, the floor already appeared spotless. Still, at least the work seemed undemanding. He and Leeth began sweeping at one end of the workshop, until Master Fabricious separated them for talking. Sweeping alone, Ays pondered how Frenepolis could possibly work as a society. Was the entire city one vast stage set? If so, did it mean that no one owned any property, or indeed any personal belongings? How could a team of writers constantly come up with interweaving storylines for the population of a whole city? And what of the children? He still had not seen any. And perhaps the most perplexing question: *why* had the citizens of Frenepolis elected to live in this way? Ays sighed. Having the usual absurd lack of curiosity about other societies, he had never thought to read works on the subject in the library on Min. Now, he had an uneasy feeling that the most sane and ordered people he'd encounter on his journey would be those he'd met on the *Whiteknuckle Rush*.

Meanwhile, Leeth analysed every transaction which had taken place between herself and Ays since they'd left the train. Did he like her? Were there any hopeful signs? He was a prickly sort of person, which might prove difficult upon the cities. She herself had learned it was best to be compliant in a strange city, until enough information had been gathered about how it functioned, what drives and desires inspired its people. Ays had embarrassed her with Marvane and Millie, and such behaviour could also be dangerous. Her father had coached her carefully about how to behave in alien locales, and Ays had already broken every rule she'd ever learned. Perhaps she could talk to him later, perhaps he would listen?

She looked across to where he swept, light from a high window falling on to his golden hair. If only he wasn't so beautiful; she ached to touch him. She'd been so lonely since her father had died, and often frightened, even though she had steeled herself to cope with both conditions. Her life had been lived from day to day, her expectations never extending beyond the next meal. She'd had vague, romantic dreams about finding something, which she supposed must have been love, but meeting Ays had shocked her. She was astonished at how powerful the emotion was when it hit you, and how debilitating it could feel. You are at its mercy, she thought, and it has no pity. She felt a person should never have to fall in love with someone who did not return the feeling utterly. She had no idea how Ays felt about her. Perhaps he thought she was too young, or found her unattractive? Her heart began to beat faster. What could she do about it? She wished she'd been able to talk to Mariet concerning these things. Mariet had loved, and loved bitterly, Leeth was convinced of that. She would have been able to speak plainly about the matter, offer advice and insight. What a pity the train had stopped so soon after Mariet had opened up a channel of communication between them, but maybe that was inevitable.

Oblivious of Leeth's covert scrutiny, Ays concentrated on observing the people at work around him, whom he presumed were outsiders like Leeth and himself. There were only six people – four men and two women – all of whom had a downcast, despondent appearance. As citiless individuals, they were undoubtedly outcasts or dispossessed, so perhaps, like Millie, they were grateful for what Frenepolis had to offer them? Ays tried to catch someone's eye, but they appeared too engrossed in their work. He cursed his situation. If it hadn't been for his own folly, he could be at home now, in Min. The city might be flying into a beautiful sunset. He could be idling at the rim, courting attention for his status. Now? He was a nobody, homeless and fundless, and clearly trapped. What would happen if he simply put down his broom and walked out of this place? He observed Master Fabricious, who was working on some papers at the back of the workshop in a raised, glass-walled booth. Occasionally, as if aware of Ays' attention, he cast a dour glance in his direction. Was violence written into the Master's script for the day? It seemed unlikely that those who had to work with externals – who must often be an unpredictable force – could possibly live to prescribed roles.

Surprisingly, perhaps because Ays had been thinking so hard, the time passed relatively quickly. A klaxon sounded and, as one, the people around him tidied away their work. Leeth came over. 'We might as well head back to Minction,' she said.

Ays sighed. 'I don't want to, and I wish we didn't have to. I wish we could leave this place immediately.' His stomach gave a timely growl. 'However . . .'

'We can't leave yet,' Leeth said. 'We have to eat and then get our bearings; see which way the stones point.'

Ays pulled a sour face. 'I suppose you're right.' He sighed heavily.

Together Ays and Leeth left the workshop and headed across the alley towards Minction. Other workers streamed past them in a hurry, most absorbed in their own thoughts.

'Aren't you at all interested in experiencing Frenepolis?' Leeth asked. 'My father liked to immerse himself in every city he encountered. He liked to become part of them for a while, simply because he knew it was only a temporary arrangement. Why are you in such a rush to leave?'

Ays stuck his hands into his pockets, and then removed them promptly, recognising the gesture as defensive. 'Everyone is different,' he answered lamely. 'I don't want to be forced into performing menial tasks.' He rubbed his chin thoughtfully. 'Those officials on the entry chute . . . I expect they wouldn't be so lax about people trying to *leave*.'

Leeth laughed. 'Planning a grand escape already?'

Ays objected to her tone, and reminded himself she was only a child and such behaviour should not be tolerated. 'I am not your father,' he snapped. 'I see things differently. I am going to leave as soon as I can, with the least inconvenience.'

If he'd hoped his remark about her father would make Leeth flinch, he was disappointed. She merely wrinkled her nose, as if to consider his words. 'Well, you'd be wise to play along with Mistress Clamp and her team for now, I think. You have to understand a city's system in order to wriggle through it. My father told me much about it.'

Ays rolled his eyes impatiently. 'I am surprised!'

Leeth gave him a measuring glance. 'You have too much hot blood,' she declared. 'What we should do is gather information, and then decide what to do.'

'Gathering information might take six Frenepolitan months!'

Leeth shook her head. 'That's unlikely. A displacement might happen. Anything. People are people. I don't believe everyone in this city obeys the rules, or observes tradition. If we bear that in mind, the right people will gravitate towards us.'

She spoke with confidence, but Ays was unsure. 'I hope you're right.'

In the dingy hostel reception, Millie was no longer on duty, and had been replaced by a thin, sour-looking young man with lank colourless hair. Leeth asked him where they might get something to eat, and he pointed dispiritedly to a door further down the hall. Without further exchanges Leeth and Ays followed his directions.

The food was plain but well-cooked and plentiful, served in a wide, echoing hall where a few scrubbed tables clustered anxiously in the middle of an open space. Individuals who were obviously practising the role of eccentric cooks paraded around enthusing loudly about their creations. About eight other people were sitting there eating. Leeth chose which table they should join, and Ays was happy to let the girl take the lead. He was beginning to feel rather tired. They joined a man and a woman who were talking quietly together. They were both dressed in russet brown coveralls, and both had long brown hair that was tied back at the neck. They had pleasant, attractive faces and astoundingly clear skin. Ays wondered whether he and Leeth were interrupting something, but the couple looked up without hostility as the newcomers sat down.

Before any words could be exchanged, a waitress in blue swooped down upon them, bearing a tray which contained a plate of freshly sliced new bread, a jug of water, steamed plum potatoes and a platter of fowl and fried leeks. Napkins appeared from her sleeves like a conjuror's scarves and were deposited with a flourish upon the diners' laps. The waitress chattered in an animated fashion, grimacing and rolling her eyes; she seemed quite excited about something, but it was impossible to divine exactly what, owing to the fact she appeared to be speaking in an unknown tongue. Ays already knew that each city tended to have certain words that were peculiar to their native vocabulary, but on the whole the people of the flat-lands spoke the same language.

The woman sitting opposite Ays smiled and said, 'Pay no attention. Dirabella here is inventing her own language as she speaks. She is what might be termed a natural.'

Ays smiled back, and leaned away from the table so that Dirabella could distribute the food.

His mouth began to water. The fowl and leeks smelled delicious. 'I can safely assert this is the most welcome aspect of Frenepolis' hospitality,' he said somewhat dryly, helping himself to a slice of bread.

'That, more than anything, must be the sign of a traveller,' said the woman opposite.

Ays shrugged and pulled a rueful face. 'Apart from this meal, how I wish I was travelling at this very moment!'

The woman nodded and took a sip of water. 'Frenepolis is not to everybody's taste, I agree.'

'Is it to yours?' Ays enquired, taking a forkful of meat.

'All cities are to our taste,' answered the man. 'We consider ourselves to be scholars of cities.'

'We visit and experience as many as we can,' added the woman.

'So you'll be staying here the full six months?'

They nodded, grinning cheerfully. 'Of course. We find it most interesting.'

Ays introduced himself and Leeth – who had become strangely sullen – and the couple told him their names were Nalinia and Brukish Tammer.

'We are brother and sister,' Brukish explained, 'and lucky enough to have a grandmother who encouraged our inquisitiveness as children. When we reached the age of eighteen, we both decided that the life of one city alone was not enough for us. We wanted to explore.'

'Like your father,' Ays said to Leeth, who did not respond. Ays had the absurd feeling she was jealous of his talking to the Tammers.

'How long have you been here?' Ays asked the Tammers, to cover a rather strained silence.

Both spoke at once, 'A few weeks,' before smiling at each other and shaking their heads.

'We tend to do that,' Nalinia said.

'Answer in tandem,' continued Brukish.

'One thing that intrigues me about this place,' Ays told them, 'is that there are no young children around. Obviously infants can't possibly be trained to follow a script, not until they are older. How do the Frenepolitans get around this . . . *problem*?' He did not bother to hide the sinister innuendo in his voice.

'Well, this is an interesting point,' began Nalinia.

'Once which intrigued us both as well,' finished Brukish. 'The citizens are rather prickly about it, and at first we concocted all kinds of nefarious reasons for their reaction to our questions.'

'The fact is,' said Nalinia, 'the Frenepolitans are unnerved by their children, simply because they are . . . unscriptable, for several years. The moment an infant is delivered from its mother's womb, it is transferred to a communal nursery until it is old enough to be indoctrinated in the ways of the city.'

'Childhood must be a terrible experience here then?' Ays suggested.

Nalinia shrugged. 'I don't think we can judge them too harshly. There are institutions for the young where very highly paid and privilege-endowed staff take care of and educate them. I've caught glimpses through the railings of the parkland, teeming with large, tame animals, through which the children run.'

'It is difficult for outsiders to determine whether the youngsters of Frenepolis are happy or not,' Brukish said, 'owing to the fact that externals are prohibited from speaking to them, for obvious reasons. The citizens do not want young, chaotic minds seeded with ideas of rebellion against the system!'

'We tried to visit a youngsters' centre when we first arrived,' Nalinia said, 'because by speaking to the children of a city, you generally get the most honest information about it and its cultures. However, it was made plain to us that we would not be allowed to do that here.'

Ays shuddered. 'I find this place bizarre,' he said. 'How can people live such regulated lives? How can they shun spontaneity?' He was thinking of Min; of the children who hung in nets from the spires, catching birds.

'Well, we have considered that,' said Nalinia. 'And although it's not made obvious, it's clear that the citizens have periods of "resting", when they retreat from city life. I believe they must only stick to their scripts when in public. I like to think that, in private, they must live ordinary, spontaneous lives like anyone else, fitting in around the performances that are required of them in public. Frenepolis seems unusual, perhaps, but then each city on the flat-lands boasts its own peculiarities. I take it you haven't visited many?'

'I am new to travelling,' Ays replied.

Leeth, who had remained silent throughout, cast him a bleak glance.

After the meal, Ays and Leeth walked up to their dormitory with the Tammers. Ays felt angry with Leeth because her sullenness bordered on rudeness, and her pinched expression made her look even less agreeable than usual. Surely the Tammers must be wondering what he was doing with such a peculiar companion? He shuddered to think they might assume Leeth was his sister.

Leeth was silent because Nalinia Tammer was so bright and attractive. Looking at this other woman, Leeth wondered how she'd ever dared to entertain the thought that Ays might find her desirable. Nalinia was obviously much more his type. Also, Ays had virtually ignored her throughout the meal. She longed to be witty, utter clever remarks, make everyone laugh, but the more she yearned to do that, the more her tongue seemed to thicken in her mouth. Everything she thought of to say sounded childish and stupid. Why does it have to feel like this? she wondered sadly.

As they passed through the reception area, a tall man who was standing at the counter turned round to stare at them. For a moment, Ays was convinced he recognised the man, and almost raised his hand in greeting. Then he realised he was looking at a stranger. The man was dressed in a long dark cloak, and his face was shadowed by a wide-brimmed hat in which reposed a single, magnificent blue feather. There was something about his stance that commanded attention, as if whatever the shadows concealed was of high quality.

'Who is that?' Ays asked Nalinia.

'I've no idea,' she replied, and then laughed, linking her arm through her brother's. 'I wish I had!'

Brukish joined in with her merriment, as if proud of her flirtatious remark. At the sound of laughter, the stranger turned away abruptly in frank irritation. Ays felt briefly breathless, as if something of importance had occurred. Bizarre. He wanted strongly to walk past the Blue Feather Man, laughing with the Tammers in a condescending manner, and cast the man a disdainful glance. The reaction was odd. Under normal circumstances, when someone impressed him in any way, he would simply want to speak to them.

The dormitory was mostly empty, which the Tammers explained was because Minction boasted a bar where residents could drink in the evenings. One or two beds were occupied by individuals who appeared to be asleep. Brukish busied himself preparing a milky beverage on the stove, while Ays sat down with Nalinia on her bed. She undid her hair ribbon and scratched her head. Ays considered that both the Tammers were very attractive people, and so healthy. Obviously the travelling life suited them very well. Leeth had slunk off to her own bed and now lay on top of it fully clothed, her back to the others.

Nalinia leaned towards Ays and murmured to him confidentially, nodding her head in Leeth's direction. 'She seems a sombre little thing.'

Ays nodded. 'She is.' He paused and then blurted, 'I've just sort of acquired her!'

Nalinia laughed. 'What an odd remark! What do you mean?' Ays explained about the *Whiteknuckle Rush* and how he'd met the girl. 'I think she's a little strange because her father is dead. Often, it seems as if she's an adult in a child's body.' He sighed. 'I must admit I find her hard to cope with at times. I get the feeling she wants something from me, but I'm not sure I want to give it.'

Nalinia looked at Leeth's rigid back speculatively, and accepted a mug of steaming liquid from Brukish who had come to join them.

'You say Leeth has visited many cities before?' Nalinia asked. Brukish sat down on the floor in front of them.

Ays shrugged. 'I'm not sure. She seems confident, but there are gaps in her knowledge. It's difficult to tell how much of what she says is truth or fantasy. I wish we hadn't boarded Frenepolis, but I trusted her judgement.' He pulled a face. 'I'll know better now.'

'Don't be too hard on her,' Brukish said. 'Believe me, Frenepolis is a friendly culture compared with some. As a traveller, you have to develop a special sense about cities.'

'How?' Ays asked, and then smiled. 'I hope it doesn't require years of experience, because I need to learn quickly.'

'Oh, it's quite simple, really,' Brukish said. 'A lot can be learned from how a city appears from outside. If it's bristling with armaments, or fortified, only a fool would blithely approach it. The majority of cities tend to expose criminals in one or two cages, or other contraptions, from their underbellies, but those that are overflowing with such devices are undoubtedly harsh places to live, and best avoided by the discerning traveller. Frenepolis has a modest count! Also, a good crowd moving around the mechanisms is an encouraging sign. Look out for cities that have residents jumping on and off collecting stuff as they move; they are generally lenient cultures. We felt fairly comfortable about climbing up here.'

'The harder it is to enter a city, the less likely it is to be a pleasant experience once you're on it,' Nalinia said. 'Frenepolis likes strangers because they're useful; it rarely abuses them, as long as they stick to the system. Personally, I find the idea of being fed and housed quite agreeable, and am prepared to give a little labour in return. The Frenepolitans are also very fair about letting people leave after six months – we've seen that.'

'Have you ever been in danger in any of the cities you've visited?' Ays enquired. He thought it important to pick up one or two tips about that.

Brukish screwed up his face in consideration. 'Not danger exactly, because we've deliberately avoided cities that somehow didn't feel right to us.' He smiled in recollection. 'On some cities, travellers are treated as scum, in others with deference. Reactions to our arrival have therefore varied: the people have believed us to be calentured, mazy, to be parasites, and in a few cases we've even been called mystics and have been treated accordingly. As I said, you just have to develop a sense for it.'

'When we're between cities, and we spot one on the horizon, we simply stand still and open ourselves up to any emanations it might be giving off,' Nalinia said. 'Also, if there are terranauts about, they can sometimes be bribed into giving information, not all of which is correct, however. Again, that is something else you have to cultivate a faculty for.'

Ays sighed and shook his head. 'It seems I have a lot to learn, but thank you for your advice' He glanced bleakly at Leeth. 'I'm lucky to have met you both so soon.'

Before he went to sleep that night, Ays covertly unstrung a few strands of hela from his coat lining and, lying on his bed, thoughtfully chewed them. What was it inside him that made him want to protest furiously about the restrictions Frenepolis had foisted on him, rather than accept events as an interesting education in city culture? He wished he could be more like the

Tammers who appeared so casual and confident. Why was he compelled to keep moving? He wasn't even sure exactly what it was he was looking for.

There are no clues for me here, he thought. He was afraid that if the few nebulous memories he'd coaxed into life weren't augmented soon, his recall of them would disappear. He yearned to experience that feeling of recognition again, and in a mild, euphoric haze replayed the moments in the wind orchestra and when he'd first entered the train. Perhaps he should include the moment at the reception tonight when he'd seen the tall Blue Feather Man; a silhouette in darkness, a suggestion of a man? Had that been the same? There was something chillingly familiar about the stranger, and with a sudden twist of his gut, Ays recognised the source of that feeling. The figure lurking at the wind orchestra . . . he was convinced it was the same person he'd seen in reception that evening. Surely that was impossible. And how could be so positive about the recognition? On both occasions, he'd hardly more than glimpsed the man. Come morning, Ays decided he would make enquiries concerning the man's identity.

Early in the morning, a gong banged downstairs and Ays woke up to find the dormitory had filled up with residents while he'd slept, all of whom were now yawning and stretching into the new day. Apart from himself, Leeth and the Tammers, the other travellers were middle-aged, and their faces bore the lines of experience and, in some cases, privation. Ays noticed that a few kept themselves morosely apart from the others, reminding him of the glum workers in Master Fabricious' studio.

Leeth seemed to have woken up in a better mood, or had at least resigned herself to the fact that Ays was not her sole property, for she smiled thinly at the Tammers when they suggested the four of them should go down to breakfast together. Ays kept his senses alert, but there was no sign of the man he'd seen in reception the previous evening.

Marvane Clamp turned up just after Ays and Leeth had begun eating.

'Settled in? Good!' she announced, beaming at everyone, clipboard in hand. 'I'll run you through an induction sequence today.' She seemed to look forward eagerly to the proposal.

Ays glared at her sourly, chewing porridge, while Leeth chirped up unexpectedly, 'Will we be able to have a look round the city?'

Mistress Clamp smiled. 'That could be arranged, although you must understand that it's vital you remain invisible, unobtrusive.'

Leeth nodded vigorously, grinning; an ordinary young girl on the brink of adventure. 'Yes, I understand.'

'I see you've met the Tammers,' Marvane Clamp said to Ays as they walked out of Minction. 'Nice people. I do hope you've got over your rather *angry* mood of yesterday.'

'I'm not angry today,' Ays replied coldly, 'but I still object to being forced to do things I don't want to.' He wondered then whether the Tammers had been briefed to feed him the information they'd given him.

'Ours is a fair arrangement,' Marvane Clamp said testily. 'I can't understand why you think you're being mistreated.'

Ays decided not to argue. He would do as Leeth had suggested the day before: watch, and listen.

Mistress Clamp led the way up a dark, narrow street. There was a feeling of being back-stage, that great activity was taking place in the brighter, wider avenues beyond the ancient buildings. Leeth tagged along behind, humming to herself. Ays did not speak to her. He had secreted a rolled-up wad of hela beneath his tongue, whose effects he hoped would lessen his resentment.

As they passed the lolling, shadowed portico of a drab, abandoned building, Ays caught a movement in the corner of his eyes. The shadows in the portico had moved! He jumped reflexively, feeling his spine stiffen, and a furtive figure seemed to flicker away from the shadows, round an alley corner. The figure was cloaked in black. Ays stopped walking and stood staring at the place where it had stood.

Marvane Clamp turned round and looked at him enquiringly. 'Is something the matter?'

'I thought I saw . . .' Ays shook his head. 'Nothing.' It might have been the influence of the hela, playing tricks upon his mind.

'A ghost,' whispered Leeth, her eyes shining darkly.

'There are no ghosts in Frenepolis,' Marvane Clamp said primly. 'We have no parts for them. This is an enlightened society.'

'I take it you have scant experience of other cities, then,' Ays said scathingly.

Marvane Clamp only laughed and gave him a withering, contemptuous glance. Of course, she would believe that only fools and lackwits left their home cities to visit others.

The induction centre was a small, octagonal building made of thin boards, huddled beneath the back of a huge, panelled façade which Mistress Clamp explained sported a grand portico at the front, where certain ceremonial functions were acted out. 'The interior to that building is situated somewhere else,' she said. Ays could not bother to query this, although he presumed he was expected to show an interest.

There were no other inductees in the centre which

consisted of a single, eight-walled room whose interior was surprisingly warm and peaceful. Ays immediately picked up an impression of an army of itinerant predecessors who'd been brought to this place before him. The tables and chairs, worn and stained, emanated the strains of a thousand souls. Ays swallowed the wad of hela.

Marvane Clamp started placing coloured beads on a dough-board near the back of the room, which she clearly intended to use to illustrate her words.

She cleared her throat, and began to speak in an important manner. 'As you can imagine, there is much behind the scenes work in this city, and those of us who are not actors perform a perhaps more valuable function. As visitors, you will be allocated minor parts from time to time during your stay, but mostly you will be needed in the backstage departments.'

'By that, I suppose you mean your factories, farms and such like,' Ays said.

Marvane Clamp smiled toothily. 'Not necessarily. All of life requires a part, an actor, but sometimes things need repairing, accidents happen.' She shrugged. 'I'm sure you can appreciate this. Do you have any manual skills?'

Ays smiled languorously and leaned back against a table. 'I invoke death,' he said. 'Is that any use to you?'

Marvane Clamp gave him a narrow stare. 'Facetiousness has its place I'll agree,' she said, 'but please try to confine humorous remarks to appropriate situations.'

'I am completely serious,' Ays said. He held out his hands. 'On my home city, I used my hands to stroke life from the bodies of the sick. It is what I am trained for.'

Marvane Clamp expressed a shudder. 'Well, that's very interesting, but hardly of use in an enlightened society like ours. We have no heathen ways. So, can you use a hammer and nails?'

Most of the morning passed with Ays and Leeth listening to Mistress Clamp list their duties for the next few days. Essentially, they'd be cleaning up in Master Fabricious' studio, although they would be allowed to try out for minor parts in the city life if they wanted to. Ays was quite tempted to agree to this, just so he'd be able to cause a little havoc. As Marvane droned on, he found his mind drifting, specifically to the event in the reception the previous evening, the possible reappearance of the tall man in the shadows that morning.

When Marvane called an end to the induction, he decided to question her. 'Last evening there was a tall, dark man in the reception area. Very distinctive in appearance, wearing a cloak and hat. I thought I recognised him. Do you know who he is?'

Marvane Clamp frowned, although she was obviously trying to place the man. 'I can't think of anyone,' she said, 'but then I don't know everyone on the casting list in Frenepolis.'

'Perhaps he was another un-citizen, like ourselves?' Ays suggested.

Marvane shook her head. 'No, I would have heard. I deal with most accessions. He must have been an official, although I can't think who. Are you sure of your details?'

'Quite sure,' Ays replied shortly. 'Obviously you don't know everyone in the city.'

'Naturally not,' answered Marvane Clamp, 'but generally I know everyone who visits the reception at Minction. Perhaps you'd better point him out to me if you see him again.'

'I will.'

'This is a nonsensical place,' Ays said to Leeth as they walked through a park area later in the day. Nearby, a group of masked individuals danced in time to the beat of castanets and tubular bells. An audience sat watching them in mild contemplation. Nothing about the scene seemed natural; even the applause was too regular.

Marvane Clamp had left Ays and Leeth at the gates to the park, with a modest packed lunch which they had eaten already. She had also issued the express instruction that they were not to bother anybody, and should report back to the induction centre within an hour. The park boasted several large clock-towers that marked the hours with trumpets and bells; it was unlikely Ays and Leeth would forget their appointment.

'Frenepolis is no more nonsensical than any other city,' Leeth said in an irritatingly high-handed voice. 'It has its own ways, that's all, which we should respect.'

Ays looked around at the wide expanse of parkland devoid of children. 'But how could a society have developed like this? How did it start? Presumably the Frenepolitans led unscripted lives at one time.'

'Frenepolis undoubtedly developed the way all cities do – at random,' Leeth replied.

Attempting to suppress the spasm of annoyance her smug tone provoked, Ays wondered how long they would remain companions. 'I want to leave here!' he snapped. 'Frenepolis is not part of me at all. I'm wasting my time here.'

Leeth shrugged her narrow shoulders. 'You are all hurry-hurry,' she said. 'I myself would like to observe this city. You approved of that in your new friends, the Tammers. Why can't you emulate their approach? You might learn more.'

Ays strove to keep the anger from his voice, reminding himself he was only arguing with a child. 'There is nothing here to interest me. I am bored by it all.'

Leeth gave an infuriating giggle. 'Are you? Then

what about the mysterious man you were so keen to question Marvane about?'

Ays narrowed his eyes. 'I am looking for clues to my origins,' he answered icily, 'as you well know.'

Leeth shrugged again, but made no comment. She sometimes wondered just how assiduously Ays was sticking to his professed search for a vanished childhood. Something about his interest in this mysterious man had alerted her instincts. She wished she'd paid more attention when they'd passed him in the hall last evening.' All she could remember was a tall, dark shape; no details.

Suddenly, Ays gasped and motioned for Leeth to stop. 'What is it?' asked the girl sharply.

Ays' eyes had begun to water. He could smell hela strongly, as if the fronds in his coat had suddenly burst forth with unnatural new growth. The sky had taken on a subtle, brownish tinge. 'A shift is coming!' he hissed.

'How can you tell?' Leeth's voice was scornful.

Ays smiled at her without warmth. 'Believe me, I can.' An impetuous idea came to him, filling him with what felt like a pure streak of golden energy – perhaps a hela flashback? Recklessly, he grabbed hold of Leeth's arm. 'We must hurry back to the hostel at once.'

'What for?' she protested, trying to remove her arm from his grip. 'We promised Marvane we'd be back at the centre soon.'

'I don't give a found stone for that!' Ays said. 'Come on.' He dragged Leeth roughly towards the gates, a show of strength which appeared to subdue her for she followed passively enough.

The shift was thrumming through Ays' fibres. He could almost feel the abstract configuration of the pilot-stones ahead of the city, which would conjure the shift, although he couldn't guess exactly how close it was. He wondered how the inhabitants of Frenepolis commonly reacted to shifts. On Min, people preferred to remain still if they could, to avoid unpleasant physical manifestations. He hoped the same behaviour would prevail here. In the stasis which should follow the shift, he intended to leave the city.

'What's the matter with you?' Leeth asked in a shaking voice as Ays dragged her along the streets that led back to Minction. 'What are you going to do?'

There was something in her voice that Ays found repellent; something too doting and languorous. He gave her arm a brief, hard jerk. Her body shook like a rag-doll's, bonelessly.

'I'm going to get out of here!' he said, through gritted teeth.

'During a shift?' Leeth squeaked. 'Are you mad? It's too dangerous.'

Ays laughed. 'You are quite the little expert on some things, my dear child, but on this, I'm afraid my expertise outstrips yours.' He paused and let go of her. 'Still, I don't have to drag you with me. You can stay if you like.'

'And how will you manage without me?' Leeth countered quickly.

Ays pulled a sour face. 'Enter cities by the correct entrances, perhaps, and avoid circumstances such as the one we're in now?'

'What do you know about shifts that I don't?' Leeth had begun to head towards Minction once more, of her own accord. Ays followed, smiling to himself.

'It was part of my profession back on Min. I can sense them easier than most, and judge their puissance. Each shift feels different and possesses different properties. You just have to feel your way through them. It can be quite exhilarating.'

'Shifts are the terranauts' revenge on city-dwellers,'

Leeth said darkly. 'Terranauts like to cause disorder.'

Ays pulled a sour face. 'What are you gabbling about? Sounds like superstitious rubbish to me. The terranauts are integral to the cities and their peoples. The concept of terranauts desiring revenge on the cities, and having a lust for disorder, is ridiculous.'

Leeth shook her head. 'Ays, you don't know everything. My father studied the terranauts. What is the point of creating shifts? Time and space blurs and jiggles; things change. It's tiresome for city-dwellers, unnecessary.'

'You can't be sure of that,' Ays snapped. 'Perhaps, without displacements, the cities could not move properly? How can we know for sure? Anyway, shifts are not that bad. If you relax into them, the sensations can be pleasant, and I, for one, find the small changes that are left behind them refreshing.'

Leeth could not be persuaded. 'Think what you like. My father believed the terranauts' motives for stone-planting and displacement-mongering were ultimately sinister.'

Ays sighed. 'And without the stones, would the cities live? Ah, I can't be bothered to argue with you. Perhaps we can put these theories to a terranaut face to face once we're off this appalling pile? There are usually a few hanging around the area when there's a shift.'

Millie was on duty in reception when Ays and Leeth came into the lobby carrying their belongings.

'What are you doing?' Millie demanded, consternation in her voice. 'Shouldn't you be at the induction centre with Mistress Clamp?'

'Come along,' Ays said, dragging Leeth past the desk.

'Where are you going?' Millie sprang out from behind the counter and somehow managed to leap in front of Ays and Leeth, thereby blocking their path to the door.

'Please don't try to detain us,' Ays said in a low, clear voice. 'I am not averse to using physical force.'

'I'm only trying to stop you leaving for your own good!' Millie said plaintively. 'You won't get past the gates, not without a certificate!'

'Then you shall probably see us back here soon,' Ays said. 'Excuse me!'

'I'll never see you again,' Millie said. 'You'll be taken to the torturers, and they are prima donnas of their craft, believe me!'

Leeth uttered an anguished cry. Ays hesitated. He wondered whether Millie would alert her superiors to their escape. If the shift wasn't immediately imminent, that might cause problems, and he had no desire to experience the excesses of the torturers. Letting go of Leeth's arm, he transferred his grip to Millie's shoulders. The girl went limp in his arms and moaned.

'Take us to the rim!' Ays commanded.

'The what?'

'The edge of the city, the rim!'

'What . . . what for?'

'Just do it!'

'Oh, you will be punished horribly! I can't bear to think of it.'

'Save your sensitive soul!' Ays snarled. 'I have no use for its vapours.'

Perhaps the inhabitants of Frenepolis imagined the sight of a wilting female being man-handled swiftly through the streets was part of some secret script and not to be heeded. Perhaps it was Ays' determination, manifesting as belief in a role, that got them through.

The rim of Frenepolis was safeguarded by an iron, spiked fence, three times the height of a tall man.

'Do you intend to climb this and throw yourselves over?' Millie enquired. She had regained some equilibrium since Ays had released his hold. 'You will be ground to a pulp under the crawlers and stampers.'

Ays ignored her and peered through the bars. Virtually below them, he could perceive a spreading irregular swirl of pilot-stones, over a hundred feet across. Shift must be imminent. Glancing to left and right, he noticed that lookouts in the spy-towers along the rim had also spotted the irregularity. There was a great deal of activity and pointing, although it was clear the populace had not been informed. How stupid these ground-dwellers were. Minnians would have realised a displacement was impending by now.

'What is happening?' Millie moaned.

'A displacement,' said Leeth authoritatively, standing hands in pocket and dour-faced a few paces back from the fence.

Ays could see a few moving dots in the distance, probably terranauts. 'Where is the nearest exit to the city?' he demanded.

Millie stuttered helplessly. 'I . . . I don't know. I don't know this area yet.'

'There will be many exits around the rim,' Leeth said laconically. 'Probably under the spy-towers.'

'That's good,' Ays said. 'We can wait outside one of them.' He started dragging Millie towards the nearest tower.

'Let me go now!' she cried. 'I don't want to be blamed for whatever it is you're going to do!'

'I'm sorry to involve you,' Ays said, 'but in desperate times, a few jewels are sometimes ground to dust.'

Almost as if the city was eager to experience the bizarre configuration of the stones, Ays could feel it accelerate its pace beneath them. At the same time, sensing the change in rhythm, the population realised what was about to happen. All around Ays and Leeth, people fled, presumably to their homes. Roles were dropped like paper masks; survival instinct took over. Underneath the city, stampers churned, crawlers burned rubber; clouds rushed by in tattered wisps above. Frenepolis wheezed towards its assignation with the stone circle, whether to experience pleasure or torment, Ays could not guess, but he could feel the soundless moan of the city as it was dragged forward against its will or even the power of its mechanisms. *Are* the terranauts malign to arrange events like this? he wondered. It seemed clear to him now how some cities might die. Too much of this kind of thing must damage their mechanisms. The air around them began to shimmer and images were broken up like those reflected in a disturbed pool. 'Hold on to me!' Ays ordered Leeth, and his voice seemed to hang like chunks of something brittle on the air. The door to the tower was vibrating so fast, Ays could see a dozen images of its handle.

Closing his eyes to dispel the illusion, he groped his way towards it, only to encounter what felt like a dozen handles beneath his hand. Taking a deep breath, he turned one of them, and felt a dozen doors give way. Inside, it was impossible to see clearly. The tower had been transformed into a vibrating gyration, but the shape of a spiral wooden staircase could be glimpsed at its centre, swirling like a vortex.

'There!' Ays screamed, and his voice was a banner of sound on the air, trailing out.

'No!' Leeth answered in terror, her voice slowed down, drawn out, as low in timbre as a man's. 'We'll be sucked down, taken under the mechanisms!'

'Go!' Ays pushed the girl forward, still hanging on to her coat.

Somehow they found their way on to the stair and

struggled down it. 'Just think down!' Ays hissed at Leeth. 'Down, down.'

They emerged into a maelstrom of pounding activity, and a sour, oil-filled wind buffeted their lungs. The machinery that propelled the city was flashing gold, brown, metallic blue and red. Leeth clung to the rail of the stairs, sobbing in fear.

Ays had wound his legs around a wooden strut and held on to the girl with all his strength. 'We won't jump, don't worry!' he shouted. He closed his eyes and let the hot, metallic wind blow over him. The power of the punching mechanisms, the grinding moan of the tortured city was exhilarating. Through the blur, he noticed many other figures dangling off the rigging and struts, hanging precariously, given to the wind, their free arms drooping down. If he concentrated, he could hear them yelling. 'Terranauts,' he said. Leeth did not hear him. Then, one figure in particular caught his eye: a man, hanging loosely from an unstable strut, his long cloak flapping, his hair whipping forward from beneath a wide-brimmed hat. Ays' flesh prickled from the scrutiny of those unseen eyes. It was the man from reception last night. Ays noticed the long blue feather which shimmered and tossed upon the stranger's hat.

'The Blue Feather Man,' he murmured to Leeth. 'Look.'

Leeth only hid her face against Ays' side. She didn't want to look at anything; her world was too unsafe. Still, she was grateful to be able to hold on so tightly to the one she adored.

Ays felt sure the man would swing across to them soon. What would he say? In his heart, Ays prepared himself, scripted questions. Was it you at the wind orchestra, you in the shadows this morning? Why?

Chapter Ten
The Mountains, the Crystal Eater

Finnigin's feet were hurting. He had walked all day, up and up, following a tortuous, niggling path into the mountains. The wind cut into his body in precise swathes, his clothes seemed insubstantial, so he almost flung them away and ran naked, gasping into the chill, to die. Finnigin put aside such fancies. He had ridden the brisk air above the flat-lands, tasted it, let it burn his lungs. This earth-bound air was no more powerful, only different. He wished he'd not lost one of his boots.

As a weary, crimson sun sank behind the mountains, Finnigin began to feel hungry. He did not need a great deal of food to sustain him, but when the urge came, it must be obeyed. He surveyed his surroundings. Nothing grew between the harsh rocks, and yet he knew many of his kind had made this journey before him, and it was doubtful any of them would have been adequately prepared for the barrenness of the surroundings. He sat down upon one of the smoother rocks, and allowed himself a sigh. Then, he heard a noise and glanced back down the path. A ragged shape was clambering up towards him, virtually on hands and knees. He squinted, shaded his eyes, and a sharp, brown face came into view. It was the mazy-woman, Babooshpet. She had followed him.

'What do you want?' he demanded, when the girl had almost caught up with him.

She stopped climbing, and put her head on one side to regard him warily, like some kind of wild animal. Finnigin wondered whether it had been a good idea after all to release her from the cage.

'What do you want?' he repeated standing up, favouring his sore foot, and when he received no obvious response, waved his arms and said, 'Shoo!'

The girl drew her upper body back, her face alarmed, but other than that made no move to retreat.

Finnigin sat down again, resolved to ignore the nuisance of Babooshpet. Perhaps she had fixed on him because he'd been the agent of her release, and she anticipated further compassionate responses? In that case, she would be disappointed. He had more immediate concerns to fret about. His stomach was empty and his foot was sore. Eventually, the night would come down, perhaps with mordant fingers of frost, and the foot might well be lost to their bite. It was not a pleasant prospect. For the first time, Finnigin cursed his lack of foresight. He should have brought food with him. He eyed Babooshpet.

'Well, it seems you cannot speak, which is a shame. Perhaps you might be able to tell me where I could find something to eat? Soon, you will be watching over a starveling corpse!'

Babooshpet, for all her silence, appeared to understand his words. Her face brightened and she scampered past him up the path, pausing after only a few yards to beckon him on. Reluctantly, Finnigin limped towards her. Babooshpet was heaving on a heavy black rock which looked strangely damp. Finnigin stood to watch her exertions, but offered no help. Eventually, the girl managed to pull the rock free from its bed of soil. Beneath it a faintly heaving mat of dark slime was revealed. Babooshpet made urgent gestures at the slime, her eyes appealing to Finnigin for understanding.

'You are suggesting I eat that?' He made a grimace. 'You are too mazed to be considered an asset!' He began to walk painfully up the steep path once more. Babooshpet uttered a wordless cry and grabbed hold of his coat. Finnigin turned on her with a snarl, but she let him go and held up her hands to show she was no threat. Then she tapped her nose and turned back to the slime. Picking up a dripping handful, she kneaded it into a dense ball and then pantomimed putting it into her mouth.

Finnigin laughed. 'You eat it first, then I might consider it!'

Babooshpet shook her head but held out the slime-ball to Finnigin with thrusting movements of her hand, accompanied by soft grunts. With her other hand, she rubbed her belly while licking her lips and grimacing a kind of smile.

'I am not convinced,' he said, but gingerly took the slime-ball off her and held it to his nose. He expected an earthy reek, or something worse, but the slime smelled savoury and yeasty. Babooshpet nodded encouragement vigorously. Finnigin put out his tongue and tasted the ball. It was very salt, but not too disagreeable. He bit off a small lump and chewed it. The texture was like that of ripe, soft cheese, if a little gritty.

'If you have poisoned me, I shall kill you as I die!' Finnigin said, biting off more of the slime-ball.

Babooshpet shrugged and removed a shard of crystal from the pocket of her ragged dress, which she proceeded to nibble at. So their first meal was shared.

Babooshpet knew where to find water, food and shelter. Soon after she'd located the edible slime, she disappeared off into the jagged crags at a pace which Finnigin thought to mean he'd seen the last of her. But after a few minutes she returned, her hands full of a leathery, red lichen. With grunts and gestures, she conveyed that Finnigin should sit down. More food? She chewed and stretched part of the lichen, forming a cord, and then bound Finnigin's bare foot with what was left of the sheet, finally tying it firmly in place with the damp cord.

'A shoe! You are clever!' Finnigin said. The lichen-leather boot effectively reduced the discomfort of the stones beneath his feet. He could now proceed with greater speed.

Babooshpet either lagged behind him a few paces or else scouted ahead, but seemed loth to walk close to Finnigin. He wondered why she had followed him and what she intended to occur between them. He was sure she was completely aware of what she was doing. She wanted to accompany him, but because she could not, or would not, speak, was unable to tell him why. He pondered what her history might be and how she had come to be caged at the Shrine of All Quests. Was she dangerous? Her actions so far indicated otherwise, but he could not safely be sure of that. If her mind was addled, she was no doubt prone to unpredictable behaviour. He resolved to treat her with caution.

As the sun sank, Babooshpet pulled Finnigin's coat and led him to a shallow cave away from the path, which she pushed him into. Finnigin protested, but was put on edge by the girl's frantic, emphatic gestures for him to stay put. He was further unnerved when she lifted her dress and squatted before him to defecate on to the rock. The smell was pungent and acrid, perhaps a result of her bizarre diet. Throughout the day, she had continued to nibble on shards of crystal. It could hardly provide proper sustenance, which was perhaps why she looked so thin and peaky. After her voiding ritual, the results of which she made no attempt to cover or disperse, she came to sit close to Finnigin in the shelter of the rock.

Finnigin, now filled with repugnance for the girl, could hardly enjoy her proximity. She ignored him and stared at the small pile of faeces with intense concentration. Silent, tense moments drew out. Finnigin had to fight an urge to flee, worried that Babooshpet might try to attack him if he moved. He noticed her fingernails were long and ragged and appeared to be very sharp. Her teeth too were formidable weapons, as if the crystal-eating had honed them. If anything, her teeth appeared to be the healthiest part of her body, for they were very white and clean. This close, he could see that her bare forearms, poking from the tattered sleeves of her dress, were corded with muscles. He had seen her lift the heavy rock earlier, so had no doubt she was stronger than was usual in a girl of her size.

The silence lengthened. Finnigin became convinced Babooshpet was waiting for something. Presently, a snuffling sound could be heard from among the rocks some distance away. Finnigin peered out into the dusk and noticed a glint of ruby light, two dots. Eyes. Soon, a troupe of spined, pig-like animals with long tusks began to approach them, their tails held high. The leader, a female, uttered angry, high-pitched squeals, and stamped with her forelegs on the rock. Her troupe arranged themselves behind her in neat formation, their spines erect. Beside Finnigin, Babooshpet exhaled a sound like a low purr. The leading animal uttered a sharp exclamation which was clearly a command for a smaller male behind her suddenly rushed forth.

Finnigin yelped and backed against the rock in terror. The animals were bigger than he thought, their size accentuated by the rigid spines. Babooshpet gripped his arm, digging her nails into his skin through his coat. She hissed in a way to suggest he should be silent.

The spined pig charged towards them, but suddenly, and quite comically, leapt into the air and came to a halt, wiggling its fringe of coarse eyebrows in surprise. Its lips curled back in an ugly snarl, but it became clear to Finnigin that it would not broach the boundary marked by Babooshpet's faeces. The girl turned a knowing look to him, implying triumph, hurt that he should have doubted her actions, and another indefinable, wistful quality, as if she yearned for understanding. Finnigin smiled at her uncertainly.

'It seems I was lucky to meet you,' he said. He should have realised before this that there would be a threat of predators in the high ground. On the flatlands, the majority of wild animals never attacked humans, but there were songs his people sang that immortalised events when individuals had been killed by creatures straying from the mountains.

They had an uncomfortable night, Finnigin disturbed from an uneasy sleep continually by threatening noises from the dark. Babooshpet leaned against him and snored, although occasionally she would wake up and stare in complete alertness into the night. Sometimes she would make a gruff, dog-like sound, before settling back to sleep.

In the morning, Babooshpet found more edible slime for Finnigin's breakfast and scrabbled in the dirt beneath another rock to provide a murky pool of brackish water for him to drink from. While he stole off among the rocks to relieve himself, she quite happily squatted to urinate in front of him, scratching herself without modesty. Finnigin regarded her shrewdly. If she was in any way physically attractive, Babooshpet negated her attractions with her crude personal habits. She was a creature of mystery, true, but not in the usual feminine sense.

'Don't you wonder where I'm going?' Finnigin said as he and Babooshpet set off along the uphill path once more. 'The answer is, I don't know that myself!' He stopped and looked back down the path. Babooshpet glanced at him enquiringly. 'If there are people in the mountains, why don't they come down to the flatlands?' Finnigin wondered aloud. 'The path is marked by cairns so it must have been used regularly at one time.'

Babooshpet patted his arm.

'What?'

She made a gesture with her hands, raising her arms above her head, stretching up. Then, she grimaced and shook her head, clasping her hands together.

'I don't understand. Are you trying to tell me something?'

Babooshpet rolled her eyes, tossed her head, and flapped a dismissive hand at him, as if in disparagement at his lack of intelligence.

After several days' travel, during which time Babooshpet displayed an astounding sense of survival and competence in the hostile surroundings, they arrived at a place where Finnigin believed the end of his journey was signalled. They had slept under another shallow overhang, only to wake to a magnificent, if terrifying, vista. The path stopped dead against a dizzying wall of rock that seemed to stretch up to the sky, unmarked by any foothold or blemish. Finnigin could hardly take it in, it was so massive. The meaning of Babooshpet's earlier gestures became clear. Here was an impassable obstacle.

'How far does this stretch?' he asked. Babooshpet made an all-encompassing gesture.

'It surrounds the flat-lands?'

She nodded.

Finnigin sighed. 'Then I either walk around it until I have circled the flat-lands, or turn back. I wonder what my predecessors did? Leeara said he went into the mountains. Did he scale that cliff?

He could not perceive any way in which he could ascend the rock wall. It was so smooth it appeared to have been made by unnatural means, and he thought he could discern faint but massive geometric markings in the stone. Who could possess the ability to construct such an edifice?

Babooshpet tapped Finnigin's arm and then touched her nose; a gesture he had come to recognise as meaning she had a plan of some sort.

'Can we get over the wall?' he asked.

She smiled slyly, her face set in a secretive expression. She held a finger to one of her eyes and then pointed up at the rock. Watch. Finnigin sat down on the ground.

After a short wait, Babooshpet hissed and pointed upwards. Finnigin could see nothing at first, but then perceived a small dot which appeared to be falling from a great height. It approached with speed, becoming larger and larger in his sight, until it was revealed to be a winged giant. The swooping figure was humanoid in shape, although its sex was indeterminate. Its feathered wings were of enormous span, and its body was swathed in purple, fluttering robes; its hair a flying, golden nimbus around its head. For a moment, Finnigin wondered whether he was looking at a supernatural creature, but although its body was perfectly formed and its garments clearly well-made, its face was a horror: a gargoyle mask of mindless ferocity, with grimacing mouth, black tongue protruding, and blind-looking, milky-red eyes. Its hands and feet sported great, hooked claws; it was clearly a predator of some kind.

As the creature caught sight of Finnigin and Babooshpet, it uttered a low, booming sound and glided towards them, talons outstretched. Finnigin screamed and flattened himself against the ground. Babooshpet pushed him away, scoring his face on the rock. There was a scuffle, and Finnigin was showered in a hot liquid that had a foul stink. Then, there was a series of agonising sounds – howls and wordless shouts of rage, pain and fear. Finnigin rolled over and opened his eyes in time to see Babooshpet being borne aloft in the claws of the giant. He screamed her name, feeling as if his heart would stop. Babooshpet had sacrificed her life to save him. He must run! Tottering to his feet, Finnigin looked around himself in frantic terror. His clothes were drenched in the reeking liquid which he supposed had been exuded by the winged creature.

After a few minutes of blindly running back down the path, Finnigin was frozen into immobility by the sound of the winged giant's call, somewhere overhead, behind him. He ran faster, but presently a looming shape overtook him, feet outstretched. The toes were as long as fingers, and clearly as agile. Uttering a triumphant moan, the giant lifted its wings and extended its feet. Strong talons pierced Finnigin's coat on his shoulders and back, fixing into the flesh beneath. With a sickening jerk, he was lifted from his feet, so that he was no longer running on rock, but air. Death! he screamed in his head. I am come to death!

The grimacing giant bore his struggles, uttering a few mews of what might have been irritation, and adjusted its hold to attain a firmer grip. It circled round a few times and then headed upwards towards the rock wall, Finnigin dangling helplessly from its clawed feet. In his terror, he had begun to weep. He believed he had come to the end of his journey and his life, but oh how abruptly and unjustly! What would his death be like? Would he be dismembered in motiveless cruelty, or eaten alive? Perhaps, if he was lucky, he would die of fright beforehand, or be able to free himself from the creature's grip and be dashed to pieces on the rocks below? That might be the best option; at least death would be quick. His eyes shut tight to blot out the sickening sight of the receding ground, he attempted to claw at the leathery skin of the giant's legs above his head. The creature ignored his attack; his fingernails could make no impression on its flesh, his fists no impact. Then, suddenly, Finnigin was falling through air. Even though he was afraid to, he opened his eyes, expecting to see the ground rushing towards him, to see the agency of his annihilation in sharp rocks and stones. But what he saw was a nest of branches, fur and long bones, which appeared to be rushing towards him. He flailed his arms and legs, but made a soft landing amid a huddle of dark shapes. The first thing he saw was the face of Babooshpet; she was alive.

Finnigin uttered a sound of despair, and moved towards her. Her face was set in a grim expression, looking out from what appeared to be a hood of bloody skin, which was hanging over her brow. As Finnigin huddled up against her, she threw something wet and stinking over his body, and then wrapped an arm about his waist, holding him tightly.

Above them, the monstrous giant paced the rim of its nest, occasionally extending an enormous hand to prod Finnigin and Babooshpet with a taloned finger. Finnigin buried his face against Babooshpet's skinny flank, becoming aware of a familiar, unpleasant smell. Gradually, as it became apparent the giant was not going to launch an instant attack, Finnigin dared to examine his surroundings. The first thing he saw was what appeared to be a couple of skinned carcasses lying near his feet, which were smeared with a substance that resembled faeces. Uttering a soft cry of revulsion, he drew up his limbs, prompting Babooshpet to dig her fingernails into his body. It was only then that Finnigin appraised what Babooshpet had covered them both with; she was wearing a disgusting cloak of tattered flayed skin, strands of silky cloth still adhering to its flesh. With churning gorge, Finnigin realised that he too was cloaked with a similar grisly robe. He retched uncontrollably, which only induced a smile upon the face of Babooshpet. Slyly, she extended a bloody fist and uncurled the fingers to display a sharp shard of reddened crystal.

Later, when Finnigin was able to review the sickening events with a rational mind, he realised that, while the winged giant was occupied in pursuing him, Babooshpet must have quickly killed its offspring in the nest. Finnigin was astounded, not just by the speed of her handiwork and her apparent ability to defecate to order, whenever she needed the substance as a tool of survival, but because of her calm resourcefulness in accomplishing such a dangerous feat. Still, the trick appeared to have worked. The giant evidently believed the skinned carcasses belonged to its prey, whereas Finnigin and Babooshpet, wearing the skins, were regarded as its young. But how long would the deception work? The creature wasn't simply an animal. Finnigin doubted it would accept them as its young for any length of time.

The giant was now making sounds of consternation and leaned forward to push Finnigin and Babooshpet towards the bodies of its young. Babooshpet obligingly wriggled over to the meat and leaned down to tear at it with her sharp teeth. Finnigin hunched beside her. The stench was disgusting, not just because of Babooshpet's faeces, but the flesh of the dead creatures themselves. Babooshpet reached out and grabbed Finnigin's hair. He understood the gesture, but there was no way he was going to put shit-smeared raw meat into his mouth. He would just have to pretend to do so, and hope the parent would be deceived by his pantomime.

Presently, the giant lifted its wings and climbed down ponderously into the nest. Then, it settled itself down and attempted to gather Babooshpet and Finnigin to its broad body. A third eyelid slid across its milky eyes. Clearly, it was preparing to sleep.

'What are we going to do?' Finnigin whispered to Babooshpet. She reached out and touched his face, touched his eyes, his mouth. Be patient, trust me, wait.

Finnigin could not feel panic, although he supposed he should. The day sank down towards evening, strange calls reverberated through the crown of the rocks. His skin itched as if the blood of the slaughtered giants was caustic. All he could smell was the stench of carrion and excrement. Once he had danced before the fire of farewell, neither welcoming nor dreading his coming journey. If he'd been able to imagine what would happen to him, would he have headed off towards the mountains so carelessly? Now, his fate rested in the fearless hands of Babooshpet, the girl who dared the impossible, the perilous. We shall cross the mountains, she'd gestured, and so they had, cowering now in the nest of a fearsome beast.

At dawn, the giant screamed and stretched its wings. An answering cry came from somewhere nearby, then another and another. The giant lifted from the nest in a graceful movement, that seemed impossible for so cumbersome a creature, and the sky became black with a hundred others of its kind. Finnigin opened his eyes which were sticky and sore. His flesh burned upon his body; a heat sickness that permeated to the core of his being. Even opening his eyes was an action almost too strenuous to accomplish. His whole being was a shout of agony. He felt he could do nothing but lie there shuddering in the nest until the giant discovered he was a fake, or death overcame him from other causes.

But Babooshpet had been waiting for this moment. Once the flock had swept, screeching, into the sky, she dragged Finnigin over the side of the nest. He saw, blearily, that they were on a kind of plateau, high above the world, which was teeming with nests identical to the one they'd just left. There were also signs of human activity – to Finnigin, a blessed relief. Enormous gantries had been erected across the plateau, some with canvas tents attached. Finnigin could not guess what their purpose might be, and it was of course equally possible that they had been built by the winged giants rather than people. Finnigin felt as if he'd been poisoned. His sight had become fuzzy, and odd spurts of colour flashed across his vision. Babooshpet either ignored, or did not recognise, his condition and dragged him across the smooth rocks without consideration for his weakness. Young giants in other nests began to scream and bark as they passed, at which Babooshpet hissed aggressively. Occasionally, she'd lift a rock and throw it at one of the nests.

Presently, they came to a place where rough steps had been cut into the stone. Finnigin, by this time, had begun to hallucinate. He saw strange shapes gliding around him; tall people in shining robes. He saw, as if through a heat haze, a landscape of towering spires, flashing in a sun that shone from no sky he knew. In his ears there was a ringing sound that might have been bells or voices chanting. And there was a tall, indistinct shape that wore a familiar aura.

'Varian,' Finnigin murmured, slipping to his knees. Babooshpet made an anguished sound and pulled on his arms. The figure of Varian hovered just beyond reach. He appeared to be floating several inches above the ground, and even as Finnigin tried to focus on the image, it faded, away, receding in his sight to a point of darkness, then nothing. Finnigin wondered whether he was about to die. He could hardly feel Babooshpet's hard fingers digging into his arm. She led him down and down relentlessly.

Eventually, she paused and stripped the animal skin from his back. He shuddered to an intense cold, and realised his meagre pack of belongings was lost. Babooshpet was speaking, perhaps to him, surely to him. But no, what was he thinking of? She could not speak. Simply part of his dream, then.

'Folks will keep trying, they will keep trying!'

And then he felt strong, human arms lifting him up from the rock. It was not Babooshpet.

The Quarriers lived in a settlement of round stone dwellings with thatched roofs that huddled together in a dark, barren valley on the other side of the cliffs. It seemed that, although they could hardly be described as being used to people climbing over the barrier, it was not unknown to them. Living so close to the winged giants, they had of course developed methods to deal with their toxins, and skilfully applied themselves to soothing Finnigin's pain. For several days, he floated on the hot waters of a tidal fever; in moments of lucidity he hallucinated wildly – haunted by images of Varian. In the depths of his sickness, his mind became as occluded as a pit of boiling mud, and he saw and felt nothing. Gradually, the poisons released their hold on his body, and the ebbings and flowings within him became solely those of emotion. Sometimes he wept in grief, sometimes he lay in a tranquil serenity. Time passed like a hooded woman beyond the narrow window of his room.

The people who'd taken him in were the Contamures, a sprawling family of some eight or ten individuals, not all of whom were related by blood. They lived in a large circular dwelling which resembled a maze. A spiralling labyrinth of corridors gave access to a multitude of small rooms. A single, large room at the centre of the building was the family meeting place, where meals were eaten and the rituals connected with birth, marriage and death were performed.

As a race, the Quarriers were thick-set and short-limbed, although to Finnigin their arms were perhaps a shade too long for natural appearance. As a startling contrast to their rather graceless physiques, their faces were unusually well-sculpted; rarely had Finnigin seen such beauty of countenance, except among his own people. The faces of the Quarriers, however, were still and composed; rarely given to spontaneous smiles. This was in strict contrast to the typical terranaut face which lent itself to a wry, audacious mobility. Sometimes, Finnigin thought he perceived an almost wistful quality to the Quarriers' expressions, but it was possible he was seeing something he hoped to find, and therefore saw.

As Finnigin lay recovering in a lumpy bed, various members of the Contamure family would come to sit with him, and those who were given to story-telling passed the time by relating tales of the many methods by which lunatic travellers from the Flat-lands sought to gain access to the mountain realm. They described complicated flying machines that inevitably crashed – smashed bodies were found often among the crags. People also contrived contraptions of ropes and hooks in order to haul themselves up the sheer rock face, only to be despatched by the semi-sentient, swooping predators, which the Quarriers called Lamitrices, that lived among the rocks. Finnigin and Babooshpet were not the first to trick the predators into giving them a ride, although not all attempts had been as successful as theirs.

'Perhaps you should invent a safe method and sell transport?' Finnigin suggested, a remark which drew dark looks from all present.

'Those that live beyond, live beyond,' someone said. 'The Louring is there for a good reason. We know.'

The Quarriers, though dour and humourless and hardly cheerful company, were nevertheless a considerate people. They were happy to minister to Finnigin's needs, treated Babooshpet with the wary respect others might reserve for an unpredictable, large pet (something part feral, maybe), and were not overly curious. Terranauts? Yes, they knew of them, and had met quite a few. Terranauts often came into the mountains when they were wandering, but generally they used the safer access far distant, through the Mouth of Anghia. This, it was explained, was a gateway that led to an underground maze, which if successfully negotiated delivered any travellers into the Valley of Dourn. Finnigin experienced a spasm of frustrated regret which he couldn't help but direct at Babooshpet. Had he been travelling alone, he would have elected to walk beside the rock wall, which would eventually have led him to the safe route. Now, he was clawed and weak from the after-effects of fever which the Quarriers told him must be the result of being soaked in Lamitrice blood.

'You senseless creature!' he yelled at Babooshpet who was squatting against the wall of his room, a position she had rarely changed since they'd arrived. She stared back as if uncomprehending, although by now Finnigin was aware that she understood him perfectly well.

The Quarriers, as their title suggested, mined the sombre, black cliffs of Overhang. They spoke of green jewels that spilled from fissures in the rocks, gems whose colour changed with the phases of the moon, metals that had no name and which were either soft or hard depending on the time of day. The products of their labours, they said, were taken over the mountains by ox-train, to be sold in the splendid, solitary cities of the crags, with names as fabulous as the legends that enshrouded them: Gleaming Fisk, Karaganzinad, Oubrahani, Phaxteriniad. At dusk, the Quarriers sang about these places. Sad, plaintive melodies lingered on the clear air of the mountains and hung like mist between the brooding shadows, eventually to dissipate into the blood-red sunset that flung gouts of ruby light on to the thatched roofs. Finnigin thought the Contamures might be interested to hear about the moving cities of the Flat-lands, but it seemed they feared the lands beyond the Louring, for whenever he spoke of them, they made quick, flicking genuflexions against malediction, and turned away.

What is beyond is beyond.

Finnigin knew that soon he would have to move on, and contemplated whether he should leave Babooshpet behind. He appreciated her resourcefulness, and the fact that she had saved his life – even though in some respects she had been the one to put him in danger in the first place. But although she might be useful to him, he felt it would be better for her to stay with the Contamures. They seemed to be fond of her, for all her peculiar habits and less than appealing appearance. One day she ate some of the Contamures' jewel-haul, which caused sad faces, but nobody seemed particularly angry about it.

His hosts insisted on giving him new clothes – thick, sensible attire far better suited to mountain travel than his own ruined garments – and a stout pair of boots that laced to the knee. They knew he wanted to leave, and told him to be sure to visit Gleaming Fisk, Karaganzinad, Oubrahani or Phaxteriniad if he passed by them.

'How will I know them?' Finnigin asked. 'Some of the cities might be hostile to strangers.'

'You will know Gleaming Fisk,' said Mama Contamure, 'by the lake that surrounds her, whose surface is as still and silver as a mirror. You will know Karaganzinad by his amethyst domes, his twisting spires. You will know Oubrahani by his bells, and Phaxteriniad you will know by . . .' She pursed her lips and nodded secretively. 'You will know her, that is all.'

'Phaxteriniad is a woman of mystery then,' Finnigin said wryly, which provoked no answering smile from Mama Contamure. 'What makes a city male or female?'

Mama Contamure shrugged. 'Who knows? It has always been so. Before I was born anyhow.' She seemed to have no curiosity about the matter.

Finnigin planned to leave in the morning. That evening, the Contamures held a sedate celebration to wish him goodbye, which was attended by members of other families who sat around the walls drinking beer and not speaking to anyone. Finnigin had already spoken with Mama Contamure concerning Babooshpet's future, and the woman agreed it would be best if the girl remained in the settlement when Finnigin left.

'She needs to learn to be civilised,' Mama Contamure decided. 'She needs a chance at life, poor mite.'

Finnigin said nothing to Babooshpet about this decision, for he sensed she would have preferred to continue travelling with him rather than learn to be a modest, genteel young woman with the Contamures. He hardened his heart, however, and ignored her sad, unblinking stare, which she maintained throughout the evening. She had that strange, ethereal air about her again, the one he'd sensed when he'd released her from the cage. He was sure that, with the help of the Contamures, she would exorcise the memory of whatever dreadful series of events in the past had so debased her, and emerge as a woman of poise and power. There was certainly something special about Babooshpet, for all her rather disgusting personal habits.

At sunrise, Finnigin washed and dressed slowly as a kind of pre-journey ritual. He ate fastidiously of the meal Mama Contamure's youngest sons prepared for him and then robed himself in the heavy woollen coat they'd given him. Food wrapped in waxed paper, and water skins, had been put into an ox-skin bag, along with a quilted blanket-bag which was waterproofed.

'I cannot repay your kindness,' he said fervently to the Contamures.

'It is nothing,' they replied, unabashed. 'Anyone would do it.'

I don't think I would, Finnigin thought, but kept his sentiments unvoiced.

Outside, there was no sign of Babooshpet. The sun was creeping up between the crags, and the sound of low horns being blown could be heard – a secret language between the Quarriers, which indicated the state of readiness of the rocks to be mined and shaped. Taking up the stout, gnarled staff, which was another gift from the Contamures, Finnigin began to walk away from the settlement. No one came out to send him off; goodbyes had been conducted the previous evening. It was as if he'd already left them.

Once out of the settlement, the path became a series of shallow wide steps that led upwards between two enormous pikes of quartz-veined obsidian. These sentinels to the settlement were named Outspar and Luxlox. That was where any legend began and ended. A more imaginative people might have invented histories for the noble stones, or even carved them in some way. The Quarriers simply named what they saw, plainly and without fuss.

Finnigin now had weapons in his bag. He'd been told of the most dangerous predators in the mountains, and was thankful to discover there were only a few and most of them cowardly beasts at that. More dangerous were the rhukahas – swashbuckling bandits who tormented, raped and robbed lone travellers, who stole children from mountain settlements and sent them back to ransack their families' homes later on.

Finnigin walked with an easy stride. He was well-rested, well-fed and well-armed, and the booming sound of the Quarriers' horns, the echoing clang of their tools resounding against far rocks, made him feel secure. He looked upon the incidents with Babooshpet as a caustic but perhaps necessary induction into his manhood. He doubted he'd ever see her again.

Casmeer

Casmeer had a terrible dream. In it, he was deranged. He dreamed of running through the streets of Thermidore, shouting incoherently, feeling consciousness slip from his mind. He could not keep still, his flesh itched and seemed to crawl upon his body. The windows of the empty buildings were full of peering faces. He saw blood running in hollow veins through the decaying roches which smelled of carrion meat. Long-armed plumosites carrying staves goaded him through the streets. His captive female was borne aloft by a group of her fellows on a gilded palanquin. She wore a garment of gold gauze, and pointed at him with a jewelled sceptre, yelling, 'Punish him! Punish the crack-brain!'

Casmeer woke with a start and sat up in his bed. A long mirror on the opposite wall framed his startled reflection. For a moment he saw himself as Finnigin; long, tangled hair falling down over his chest, his eyes large and dark. He looked young, his leanness that of youth rather than a meagre diet. At that moment he yearned for company, for another body to hold, to become real in the grip of warm arms.

He fell back on to the bed. Never. Never. He wished he were made of stone, and did not have to feel anything. Why had the curse of Thermidore spared him?

Chapter Eleven
The Terranauts

In the dizzying aftermath of the shift, Ays dropped down from the underbelly of Frenepolis, to stand with pounding head and swirling vision upon ground that seemed to writhe and curl beneath his feet. Leeth, clinging to his coat like a baby, buried her face against his body, her breath coming in ragged gasps. Dizzily, Ays squatted down and shook his head, until the world realigned itself into recognisable shapes. He and Leeth were being showered by a spatter of thin, brown oil that was spurting from a ruptured conduit somewhere above them in the city's guts. It smelled briny: a smell of the sea that Ays had neither seen nor sensed.

Frenepolis had heaved itself to a shuddering halt, its perambulatory mechanisms making grating and grinding sounds of complaint and strain. The city had been drawn by a double line of pilot-stones along a dry valley, of several cities' width, between gently sloping hills which were oases of green in a landscape of yellow dust. Small deer with striped hides and monkey-like paws were stripping the hill-side shrubs of leaves, occasionally glancing round with bulging black eyes at the enormous city that had come to dominate the wide valley floor and throw its gargantuan shadow upon the hills.

Frenepolitans were already swarming down the

underbelly rigging to inspect the city's machinery; voices were harsh. Nobody took any notice of Ays and Leeth huddled together in a pool of oil beneath them. The terranauts who, hanging with bravado from the city's guts, had ridden the unpredictability of shift, had scattered. Pilot-stones glittered dangerously in a pale sunlight. There was no sign of the Blue Feather Man.

Presently, Leeth's voice, shrill and quavering with fear, penetrated Ays' reeling senses: 'Don't ever do that again!' The girl let go of his coat and stood back to look down at him. Her white face was pinched with anger and fright. Ays blinked at her, laughed nervously and stood up.

'I'll do whatever's needed – whenever,' he said.

'We could have . . . could have died, or worse!' Leeth squeaked.

'No,' said Ays huskily, 'the shifts aren't as terrible as you think.' His flesh was aching, and it felt as if there was a taut wire clamped across the interior of his skull that was being wound tighter, until his head would explode. The stress of the shift had stimulated his need for hela.

Leeth watched with a deep frown while Ays fumbled inside his coat with shaking fingers and unpeeled a frond of hela.

'That's disgusting!' she announced, curling back her upper lip.

Ays had to admit the lining of his coat had become unpleasantly rancid and seething, smothered as it was by rampant crawling shoots of pallid fungus. 'Want some?' He offered Leeth a limp frond.

She made a sound of repugnance and turned away.

Ays shrugged and threw back his head to lower the hela frond into his open mouth. It tasted yeasty and salt upon his tongue and swiftly extended tender fingers of manipulation into his mind. After a few moments he felt strong and sure enough to take stock of his surroundings.

Where one of the hill-slopes levelled out, halfway to the softly rounded summit, there was a jumble of makeshift dwellings which Ays recognised as being a terranaut camp. Now was the time for him to make contact, with the thrill of riding the shift so recently in his blood, his head filled with the courageous swirl of hela. Without saying anything to Leeth, he began to walk towards the camp, anxious to be free of the hanging shadow of Frenepolis above him. Leeth made no remarks or enquiries but followed him sulkily, her feet scuffing the yellow dust of the valley floor.

It was a longer walk to the hills than it appeared, and by the time Ays and Leeth were picking their way between thorny ground-shrubs on the lower banks, their legs were covered with fine dust. Leeth announced she was thirsty. Ays ignored her complaint.

'Where are we going?' she demanded.

Ays sighed. 'Where do you think?' He glanced up to where dark-clad people could be seen moving between the tents and huts.

Leeth hastened to catch up with her companion. 'You can't go there. It's a terranaut camp.'

'I realise that.'

'They won't talk to us, or if they do, it'll be nonsense.'

'You have experience of terranauts too, then,' Ays remarked scathingly, spitting out a small wad of spent hela pulp. He made a mocking sound. 'You and your father!'

'My father knew a lot about terranauts,' Leeth responded primly. 'He knew they were untrustworthy. He told me. They are reckless and immoral. Life means nothing to them.'

Ays laughed again. 'How refreshing they will be after the dim Frenepolitans!'

The terranaut camp was a haphazard jumble of tents, waxed-card huts, covered carts and small geodesic domes, which stood in a state of utter temporariness beside a large, stagnant-looking pool that was collared by a flat, oily colony of ambulatory slimes. Tall, dark-clothed individuals were walking around the jumble of buildings, or else sitting in conspiratorial huddles between them. Ays walked towards them, Leeth following without enthusiasm.

The terranauts paid no attention to the approach of strangers, and their groups exuded an enclosed, discouraging air. Ays was unsure what reaction he'd get if he simply walked up to someone and spoke to them. Hostility? Welcome? Ignorance? Still, he had no desire to reveal his indecision to Leeth, and eventually approached a lone terranaut who was painting with a feather on a width of thin brown silk that had been stretched on to a wooden frame. The woman, though seated, appeared tall; her knees up around her ears, the long toes of her bare, brown feet gripping the short, fragrant grass beneath her. Her face too was long, the features almost pointed, and her hair was bound up in twigs around her head. Ays half expected to hear her dust-coloured clothes rustling like dead leaves as she moved. Her lean arms were scored with what appeared to be inked ritual scars. Ays stood behind her, watching her deft, nonsensical, but deliberate feather-strokes. She was humming to herself, her chin resting upon her hand, which was draped over a raised knee. Ays was entranced by the woman; she appeared too exquisitely bizarre to be real. He had imagined meeting a terranaut many times; now, he was nervous of speaking. Whatever words came from his mouth would be too ordinary to be of interest to this creature. She was perhaps just about old enough to be his mother.

After a few moments, she seemed to become aware of Ays' presence, or at least decided to pay attention to him. She stopped painting, her hand hovering over her work. A single splash of black ink fell on to the silk and spread out to obliterate a sequence of tiny, precise lines. The woman seemed oblivious of the accident. She turned her head to look over her shoulder. It was impossible to read her expression.

'I am a traveller,' Ays said.

The woman's expression did not change, although Ays thought her concentration had sharpened. Had he spoken the right words to breach her privacy? Encouraged by the fact she hadn't evinced any hostile behaviour, he squatted down beside her and leaned forward to examine her painting. He was acutely conscious of her scrutiny, and her silence was so profound it hurt his ears, but that might have been an effect of the hela. He was still aware of the small, dense presence of Leeth, but only dimly. It was as if she was hovering on the edge of an unseen boundary that enclosed himself and the terranaut woman; a frontier Leeth was powerless to cross.

Ays sensed it would be pointless to comment upon the woman's work. 'I am in your debt,' he said.

At these words, the woman bared her teeth in what might have been a smile. Ays decided to believe that it was.

'I was trapped upon the city, imprisoned. The shift you caused allowed me to escape.'

The woman sniffed. 'You have hela,' she announced suddenly in a clipped, husky voice. 'I can smell it.'

It seemed Ays had turned the key that gave access to communication. He looked into the woman's eyes. They had yellow irises that were rimmed with black, but their expression contained no emotion he recognised. The eyes of an animal. He nodded at her. 'I have. Do you want some?'

The woman put her head on one side. 'Trading, are you?'

Ays did not want to miss an opportunity to ingratiate himself. 'Naturally.'

The woman nodded to herself, and then stood up, gesturing stiffly. 'Come.' Without waiting to see whether Ays would follow she began to lope towards one of the terranaut dwellings.

The invisible frontier dissolved. Ays stood looking down at Leeth. 'You'd best come with me,' he said.

The girl looked frightened, scared of losing him. She did not complain.

The dwellings of the terranauts were eclectic in origin; no two were the same. The tall woman led Ays and Leeth towards a roughly circular construction that was part tent, part cottage. The wooden frame of the building appeared flimsy, as if it could easily be dismantled in a hurry. Inside, the light was dim and stripy, owing to the fact that the roof was slatted, covered by several bolts of cloth that were rolled back to let in the sun. Thick smoke curled in the uneven beams, obscuring the shapes of a large group of terranauts who were seated haphazardly upon the floor.

Standing in the shadows of the threshold, Leeth stiffened by Ays' side and even reached to take hold of his hand. The woman who'd led them there paused in the centre of the room to look back at them, her skin striated with light. She was the only person standing, although none of her troupe paid her, or her visitors, any attention.

Ays, emboldened by the hela in his blood, shook himself loose from Leeth's damp grip and followed the terranaut woman to a gap in the crowd, where both of them sat down. Leeth did not follow them but leaned sullenly against the door-frame, almost invisible in the smoky shadows.

'Your sister?' the woman asked, jerking her head in the direction of Leeth.

'No!' Ays said, opening his coat. How could anyone believe that swarthy Leeth was his sister?

The woman gazed with slitted eyes at the lush, yet foetid, flowering of hela that grew against the heat of Ays' body. 'Companion, then?' A certain tone to her voice, rich in innuendo, made Ays' flesh crawl.

He peeled a few strands of hela from his coat. 'In a way. The girl's alone in the world, that's all. We're both travellers, and company's welcome in our situation.' He shrugged. 'Smoke? You have a pipe?'

The woman nodded, reached inside the pocket of her trousers and handed Ays an elaborately carved pipe of yellowed bone.

He held it up to a beam of light. 'This looks so old,' he said in admiration.

The woman nodded again. 'Old enough. Handed down. Bestowments, renderments, oddments like that. You know.'

'Not really,' Ays said candidly. He carefully packed the damp hela into the pipe bowl. 'But I suppose I'm out searching for a similar kind of thing: bestowments handed down.'

'Oh?' The woman raised one brow and then lowered it, with a shrug. 'Well, you're a land-loper, a gadling. You people have mazed reasons for roaming.'

Ays found some of her jargon confusing, but answered carefully, 'And you don't?'

The woman threw back her head and laughed silently.

A little discomfited, Ays asked politely, 'Have you a

light?' And the woman produced a lighter made of exquisitely worked filigreed metal.

'Is this a bestowment too?' Ays asked as he lit the pipe. The woman sniffed, but did not reply. As a fresh tide of hela smoke infected his body, Ays became aware of a pent-up energy thrumming from the terranaut woman's skin. It was as if she might burst into unpredictable action at any moment. None of the other terranauts in the building bothered to look at Ays, even though he was a stranger. Ays examined them covertly as he sucked on the pipe and noticed that many of them were embracing intimately. Sexes were indeterminate. Perhaps he shouldn't have brought Leeth in here? Then he rebuked himself for such conservative feelings. Leeth kept reminding him how experienced she was. Perhaps her father had brought her into situations like this before? She was not Ays' responsibility.

Pleasantly euphoric, he told his new companion his name. 'I am Ays. My name is Ays.'

She looked back at him quizzically. 'Is that supposed to mean something? Is it that you want my name too?'

Ays shrugged awkwardly. 'I'd like to be able to call you something,' he said. 'It's friendly, isn't it?'

The woman grinned. 'If you say so. Call me Oon.'

'Here, Oon.' Ays handed her the pipe, from which the woman inhaled appreciatively.

'This is very droit,' she croaked, exhaling spent smoke between her teeth.

Ays hoped that meant the hela was good. 'As you saw, I grow my own.'

'Yes, I did notice.' She awarded him a lascivious glance. 'So, you're curious about me, then? Landlopers are always curious about us.' She laughed, a deep masculine laugh, implying the very commonness of the situation.

Ays decided to be circumspect. 'Well, it would be

fair to say I'm more interested in you than the Frenepolitans, whose company I've recently departed.' He smiled. 'Since leaving my own city, I've come to appreciate people who are . . . unconstrained.'

Oon's expression abruptly darkened. 'I don't want your history!' she snapped. 'Not interested.'

'I'm not giving it,' he replied smoothly. 'That was just an observation.'

They smoked in silence for a while, the pipe passing back and forth between them. Leeth still stood by the entrance flap, her face dark with a turmoil of emotions.

'That child is stray and nonsuch,' Oon remarked.

'She is an odd little creature,' Ays agreed. 'Still, she's travelled more than I have. Her knowledge, such as it is, has helped me to a degree.'

Oon nodded. 'Such folk can be useful.'

There was another silence, during which Ays became tense. It was as if the hela permeating every cell of his body had suddenly taken a tighter grip upon him. He felt squeezed of breath. Perhaps it was some subtle emanation from Oon affecting him. She was certainly more stray and nonsuch than any person Ays had met before.

Oon noticed his nervous scrutiny of her. She didn't seem at all perturbed by his presence. In fact, she seemed very much in command of the situation. Again, she uttered a deep, gravelly laugh. 'Look at you! Ha!'

'What is it?' he asked, wishing he could regain control of his senses. It was difficult not to leap to his feet and flee the building.

Oon rubbed her nose. 'I know what you want, what you've come here for.' She leaned close, baring her teeth in a manic grin. 'You want one of our women, or a man.'

Ays laughed in embarrassment, but was brave enough not to flinch away from her. 'No, I don't think so.'

Oon leaned back and made a disparaging gesture. 'Nasery flummery!' she declared. 'You can't fool me! It's what all gadlings want.' She pantomimed a preening gesture. 'After all, we are so beautiful, and of course we magic the cities about. Everyone wants us. You might as well be frank.'

Ays hesitated, his eyes narrow in the smoke. 'I can assure you I'm not looking for dalliances, but I suppose I am interested in someone. It's not a carnal curiosity though.'

'Means nothing to me,' said Oon.

Ays persisted. 'On Frenepolis, there was . . . there was a man. He seemed to have some interest in me, and I can't help wondering what. I think he might be one of yours.'

Oon laughed. 'Of course.'

'I bumped into him a couple of times. Seemed like he had something on his mind.'

'That's one way of looking at it!'

Ays did not feel the conversation was progressing in the direction he'd planned. 'Did you have any people in the city before the shift?'

Oon grimaced. 'How should I know!'

'As I said, I think this man has some interest in me.'

'Then he's not one of ours!'

'That's not very flattering.'

'Then don't expect it.'

Ays made an exasperated noise. 'I'm wasting my time.' He made to stand up, but Oon pulled him back.

'Don't get that way. Let me give you a girl. One of my carelings.'

'What's in it for you?' Ays demanded.

She shrugged. 'Nothing. I'm being helpful.'

'This is too abrupt,' Ays said. 'Too sudden.' He thought of his erstwhile profession, the languorous gestures to invoke death and peace. An impulse came.

'Can I travel with your people for a while?'

Oon smiled. 'That's your business. No one will chase you off with a pike.' Her smile widened. 'And you have good hela.'

By the door flap, Leeth observed Ays with the terranaut woman, discomfort building steadily within her. Ays seemed so at ease with other women, while with her, he was often terse and awkward. She loathed the way he regularly doped himself with hela. Surely it was bad for him. The look in his eyes, in the height of a hela strike, was terrifying; so undirected and selfish.

She herself would not have contacted the terranauts. She knew them to be capricious, and often dangerous. She felt they would use Ays and herself, or do something unpleasant to them. Her father had always told her to keep away from terranauts. Her body still ached from the effects of the shift; a condition that did not seem to bother Ays. She wondered whether he was brave, or simply wanton. Would she sleep alone this coming night?

Her thoughts tumbled swiftly, each more painful than the last. When Ays and the terranaut woman turned to look at her, she felt sick. I should run, she thought, while I still can.

There were several other travellers attached to the troupe, although they were mostly ignored by the terranauts who were clearly intent on keeping their famous secrets hidden. Anyone who tried to observe the planting of the stones was roughly pushed away with jibes and insults. The troupe referred to themselves as the Roughrovers, which might have been a family title or a nick-name.

Land-loper and gadling were mildly insulting terms in terranaut jargon. Their attitude to travellers was: 'You want to be like us, but you haven't a hope.' Still, they tolerated hangers-on, and seemed to enjoy the reverence they received from their followers. Oon had advised Ays to seek temporary accommodation with one of the other gadlings, which had prompted him to introduce himself to them as soon as he left Oon's dwelling. He took Leeth with him. She was refusing to speak, but at least conjured some maternal sympathy in the hearts of the female land-lopers. The travellers carried their own tents, or make-shift, easily assembled dwellings, and Ays easily managed to scrounge accommodation for Leeth and himself with an older woman named Beulah who asked no questions, was mostly mute, but otherwise quite hospitable.

Most evenings the land-lopers sat together around a fire outside their tents, emulating terranaut behaviour and hoping to attract the interest of a terranaut who was feeling a need for entertainment. Here were travellers who had seen so much more of the flat-lands than anyone Ays had yet met; people who had dared to explore the cities that the Tammers would naturally have avoided. He learned about the fortress cities, ruled by tyrants; fleet, predatory pirate cities that somehow managed to follow lines of stones that led them swiftly to helpless undefended cities, so that the pirates could loot and plunder with ease. There was a city where women lived alone, using travellers to father their children, and exposing unwanted sons in cages from the city's belly for raptor birds to devour. So too were there corroded cities of rust, with few inhabitants, that somehow managed to lumber on with a minimum of maintenance. Ays particularly liked the story of the derelict ghost city that still glided to the unheard tune of the pilot-stones, but whose streets were empty of life.

At night, forced into close proximity by the paucity of space in Beulah's wickyup, Leeth clung to Ays fiercely, often haunted by the fear that he'd use the cover of darkness to run away from her. She was relieved that he never moved to pull away from her, although he always slept with his arms beneath his head, and would not touch her himself.

Food was mostly scavenged as the Roughrovers moved along, although quite often the troupe would come across refuse dumps expelled by a passing city. Usually these piles of rubbish contained vegetable matter which had rooted or sprouted, and therefore burgeoned with wild strains of domestic legumes and seeds. Also rodents and other scavengers populated the dumps and could be killed for meat.

Oon made no effort to sustain her acquaintance with Ays, although he himself pursued the friendship, simply because he could not deny the fascination the terranauts held for him. None of them but Oon deigned to acknowledge his existence. She was not enthusiastic about his company, but was happy to accept any offer of hela, which meant she'd hardly ever walk away from him without speaking. Occasionally, when she was in a particularly charitable mood, Oon would let him talk to her. Ays would ask questions to which she might respond, 'Who cares?' or 'What does it matter?' Ays knew Oon was toying with him – a game she clearly derived great pleasure from – and tried to stem the annoyance this invoked. The majority of land-lopers were intrigued by the terranauts' supposed powers and secrets, and obviously attached themselves to terranaut groups in an attempt to penetrate the mysteries. But although the terranauts occasionally took lovers who were gadlings, and sometimes socialised with them, they certainly enjoyed preserving their own mystery; they had no respect for outsiders.

Ays had hoped to catch a glimpse of the man he had seen in Frenepolis, but was disappointed. He once mentioned this to Oon, who did not respond with the sarcasm Ays expected. 'He is the "one" for you?' she asked. In some strange way, the question seemed fearful.

Ays smiled and shook his head. 'I do not think so. In some ways, I feel he is only a symbol.' He tapped his head. 'Or hela-born!'

Oon appeared to ignore his response. 'The world is full of mysterious people,' she said, flinging out an arm. 'But only a fraction of those would be of interest to you. A different fraction of them would be of interest to me. But within those fractions, there is undoubtedly a "one" for both of us. If we are lucky, we will never find them.'

'If we are lucky? Why?'

It seemed the hela had mellowed Oon's reserve. 'Isn't that obvious? The "one" is the beloved, the adored, enshrined. They are the star that guides us. Should we be unfortunate enough to become acquainted with this paragon, we will discover their irritating personal habits, selfishness, or unpleasant moods. The dream is shattered.' She shrugged. 'The situation speaks for itself. Who wants to travel beneath a sky devoid of stars?'

'I have never thought of it,' Ays said. He believed if there was a 'one' lurking in his future, he would run from them madly.

'Few do,' Oon said carelessly. 'They seek their god-men or god-women, and kill them through familiarity. It is a kind of hunt. Yes. The object of it being the destruction of that which you desire. Hmm.' She took a long draw of hela smoke.

'I am not looking for anyone,' Ays said. 'Not in that way.' He paused, remembering Oon didn't like him talking about himself.

'You don't know what you are searching for yet,' she

said, surprising him. 'Perhaps you will only recognise it when you find it?' She laughed harshly. 'Perhaps it is death?'

Since Ays had developed a friendship with Oon, Leeth seemed to withdraw from him, thus reinforcing his view that she was a jealous creature. It occurred to him that Leeth might have been searching for another father figure, someone to care about her, if not for her. Now, she walked alone, her small face sullen and tight. Ays felt a pang of guilt about this, and tried to chivvy the girl along, but Leeth did not respond.

Silently, she suffered from the weight of her love for Ays. It seemed like a strangling python which had wrapped her in a suffocating embrace and whose coils were too thick and too numerous to escape.

Ays sensed a peculiar quality to the atmosphere among the terranauts. They seemed to live every day as if it was their last, subject to a brutal vitality, a careless disregard for conventional behaviour. Yet this mood was tinged by a kind of wistfulness, like a thin song in the great vault of the night. Oon spoke of solitary stars. Thinking about this, Ays shivered and felt the cold wind of history pass over him. He felt as if he was on the brink of a vast understanding, he could almost feel its intense shine within his mind, and yet the meaning evaded him. The scintillant ideas burst like shimmering bubbles of glass even as his imagination encountered them.

The Roughrovers travelled slowly, tumbling over the land, planting their stones in the arcane way they never divulged. They would put up their camp in one place for several days in order to make a special arrangement of the stones before moving on to a new territory.

Active stone-planters moved ahead of the troupe, their activities shielded from prying eyes by the bodies of their fellows and the vehicles and animals they used to transport their belongings from place to place. The terranauts owned a sizeable herd of pack-beasts, but no two belonged to the same species. Like their dwellings, the animals of the terranauts were diverse. Neither did any of the vehicles, mostly carts and wagons, appear to have been constructed by the same hand; design and embellishments differed widely.

Land-lopers who'd attached themselves to the Roughrovers were expected to follow behind the terranauts, although sometimes Oon allowed Ays and Leeth to ride with her on the back of a wagon, their legs dangling over the end boards.

'Does anyone ever unplant the stones?' Ays once enquired of Oon. He had asked her few direct questions about her people, expecting a rebuff, but hoped this particular query breached no boundary of propriety.

Oon gave him a speculative glance. 'Who knows?' she said.

'Your people, I expect,' Ays replied, rather impatiently.

'If that is so, it is nothing to do with land-lopers,' Oon replied.

'I might be a terranaut myself,' Ays said. 'You never know.'

Oon inspected him carefully. 'You said you were a gadling, a dispossessed city-dweller.'

'I said no such thing!' Ays retorted. 'You never want to hear about me. I don't know my origins. That's partly why I'm land-loping!'

Oon sniffed. 'Well, if you are a terranaut, there's very little evidence of it!'

One morning, as the Roughrovers were setting about dismantling their camp, Ays experienced another significant event; the first since he'd seen Mariet Crane on the *Whiteknuckle Rush*. One of the land-lopers travelling with the terranauts became victim to a kind of insanity, which was perhaps the result of some slumbering neural disease. As he cavorted and shrilled and ran, high-kicking, into an area of corrosive salt, the terranauts gathered to watch from a ridge. The man spoke in tongues, waved his arms around, his face alternately a mask of spiritual joy and horrific despair. Finally, he fell face down into the salt-mud and the terranauts turned away. Ays caught the glance of Oon, who shrugged at him. There were no words, and in that instant Ays felt he had divined the exact reason why his parents had abandoned him on Min. His mother or his father had lived through a moment such as the one he'd just experienced, of this he was sure. Then, as abruptly as it had come, the knowledge and its attendant feeling of enlightenment left him entirely.

Later, when the troupe stopped for the night, Ays went to sit with Oon outside her dwelling. He offered her some hela and, as she smoked in languorous silence, said to her; 'I have lost sight of the reason for my journey. Do I want to return to Min? I'm not sure.'

Oon listened quietly, blowing hela smoke rings. She no longer told Ays to be silent when he spoke about himself, which might be viewed as progress within the relationship. Then, she extended one long-fingered hand and gently stroked his face. 'Why look for reasons?' she asked. 'Why not just live?' She leaned over and kissed him on the mouth, a caress that might have been taken further had Leeth not at that moment marched towards them through the dwellings. Ays felt a spasm of annoyance at her appearance; it was almost as if she'd sensed Oon had touched him and had come to prevent it. He wondered whether he should order her away, but Oon had already withdrawn from him, hugging her knees beside him. She looked neither disappointed nor frustrated by Leeth's arrival, but smiled quite pleasantly at the girl.

Leeth appeared not to notice that anything had been going on, and even looked Ays directly in the eye – the first time she'd done so since they'd joined the terranauts. 'My father died the way that man did this morning,' she announced. 'He had the calenture.'

Ays suspected she'd been rehearsing the words, looking for an excuse to intrude on his conversation with Oon. Normally, she kept her distance when he and Oon were smoking together.

'Insanity,' Oon said. 'He died of a mazy mind.'

Leeth sat down between them, her legs stuck out straight from her dusty, black skirt. 'No, it isn't madness as such,' she said. 'It's just a disease. It can be cured, I think, but you have to find the city that has the knowledge.'

Ays made an irritated sound. 'Leeth is the headwater of all wisdom,' he said in a scornful voice.

She went red in the face. 'It's true,' she said angrily.

Oon uttered her deep, resonant laugh. 'Ah, what a wayward world we inhabit!' she remarked. 'We should all decamp to the mountains where the cities do not run about.' She reached out and cupped the back of Leeth's neck in a gesture of affection. Leeth glanced at Ays smugly.

He forced himself to grin back at the girl. 'There is nothing in the mountains, and beyond them lies chaos,' he said.

'You don't . . .' Leeth began, but Ays snapped, 'Oh, be quiet! You don't know everything!'

Oon raised an eyebrow at him, but she withdrew her hand from Leeth's neck.

Ays glanced at Oon sharply. 'Anyway, the cities only run about because the terranauts make them. If it's inconvenient to you, why not stop the process?'

Oon shrugged her shoulders. 'Because if we stopped the pattern of the stones, the cities would die. They are made to be dynamic. It would require a different kind of construction for people to stay put, and I suspect they wouldn't be able to stand it. As you might have noticed, even land-lopers keep moving.' She sighed. 'Ah, our vocation can be a burden at times!'

Ays had not known Oon to be so open before. 'You mean the terranauts have no choice but to guide the cities?'

Oon looked at him coldly. 'I never said such a thing!' She laughed. 'Ays, I do believe you might have terranaut blood in your veins after all! You beguile me into revealing too much and no ordinary gadling could do that!'

He digested this information. 'It is an intriguing possibility,' he said with a smile.

One morning, Ays awoke early with a full bladder and left Beulah's wickyup to relieve himself outside. The terranauts had camped in the open on a vast, grassy prairie which was teeming with herd animals. Vast spikes of rock dominated the empty landscape, so convoluted in form they appeared to have been carved by human hands. To east and west on the dusty horizon the bulk of looming cities could be seen. The rising sun flashed off something shiny among the spiky pinnacles of the eastern city. Ays heard a mournful sound, the alarm horns being blown on the one of the cities. Ays wondered whether the Roughrovers planned for the two cities to collide. As he idly contemplated this thought, a voice broke into his reverie.

'You are right, but it will not be the Roughrovers who are responsible for what will happen.'

There was a movement behind him and Ays turned round quickly, hurriedly relacing his trousers which were still hanging open. Behind him stood the Blue Feather Man, or else someone who looked very much like him. The sense of recognition was overwhelming, prompting Ays to think, I know this man. I know him.

All he could say was: 'What?'

A trick of the dawn light rendered the man's eyes a glowing band across his face. His mouth was smiling, but it seemed a mouth used to sadness. 'You heard me, as I heard you.'

'I said nothing!' Ays replied. He realised, with some surprise, he was not afraid. Perhaps he should be? 'Who are you? What do you want?'

The man did not answer at first, but simply continued to smile. His expression was sinister, as if his mind was on matters other than pleasantries. 'We have met before,' he admitted. 'I'm disappointed you don't remember.'

Ays' flesh went momentarily cold. 'The wind orchestra,' he said. 'It *was* you, wasn't it?'

The man shrugged. 'Perhaps.'

Ays forced himself to laugh. 'Have you followed me? Why?' He paused and then added, 'There is nothing I can give you.'

The man pulled a face of disgust. 'No,' he said, and sighed through his nose, as if in impatience. 'I am as yet undecided. You have not developed as I'd thought, or perhaps . . .' He paused. 'Perhaps you are evolving yourself?'

Ays felt as if he'd taken too deep a lungful of hela smoke. The man's words somehow unfixed him in time and space. He felt momentarily unreal, as if his very existence depended on the next words this stranger would utter. He had to make a noise, take some action, to dispel the terrifying sensation. Bending down, he picked up a stone from the ground and threw it at the man's face. 'Leave me alone!' He could not tell whether the stone had found its target or not.

The man narrowed his eyes. 'Time to make a move,' he said, and then turned sharply to hurry off among the rag-taggle dwellings of the terranauts.

Ays wanted to shout 'Wait!' but by the time he'd mustered the breath, it was too late.

Time to make a move. Had he been referring to himself when he'd said that? Ays did not mention having seen the man to Leeth or Oon. He was not sure whether he really had or not.

The Roughrovers seemed to anticipate that an unusual event was destined to occur involving the approaching cities, for they did not strike camp as had been planned the previous evening. Instead, they sat beside their carts and dwellings for the next three days, their attention riveted on the cities that were drawing closer to one another. The land-lopers, all of whom had once lived on a city, were skittish and bad-tempered at the prospect of something calamitous occurring. Some actually left the troupe and headed off alone. Fortunately, Beulah was not one of them.

During the three days' wait, Ays hung around Oon, hoping she might once again make a romantic move towards him. Oon, however, seemed preoccupied with her own thoughts and only took notice of Ays when he was handing her a pipe of hela. A young male terranaut brought her food on two occasions. Oon smiled at him and caressed him. Ays wrestled with an unfamiliar sensation of jealousy. He became impatient with Oon's languid expectancy of what might occur and demanded: 'What is going to happen when those two cities make contact? You must know!'

'Something,' she replied, nodding.

There was no evidence of another terranaut troupe

being in the vicinity. In fact, the Roughrovers had not crossed the path of another troupe since Ays had travelled with them. 'Then who is manipulating the stones?' he demanded. 'Oh, don't be silent, Oon! It can't possibly hurt you to tell me!'

She actually flinched away from the urgency in his voice. 'I've no idea! Don't shout at me!'

'I don't want to watch it, whatever happens!' Ays cried.

Oon stared at him coldly. 'Then go! No one's forcing you to hang around!'

They eyed one another in mutual hostility for a few moments, and then Oon sighed, running her fingers through her hair which was loose around her shoulders. 'Oh, calm down!' she said. 'Sit here. Reveal the inner delights of your coat.'

'Do you like me?' Ays blurted, the words spilling out of him, despite his concern for dignity.

Oon smiled at him in perplexity. 'Does it matter whether I do or not?'

It was as if she was encased in glass. Ays felt he could not reach her. He sat down beside her and unstrung a few strands of hela from his coat. 'I've no dried fronds left,' he said. 'Will you eat it fresh?'

Oon wrinkled her nose at him. 'I suppose so,' she replied. 'We need something to pass the time.'

During the afternoon, inhabitants from both approaching cities could be seen running backwards and forwards, presumably exchanging messages. An air of panic seemed to hang over the cities. Ays found it too painful to watch and took shelter in Beulah's wickyup, eating hela until he was delirious. Still, despite these precautions, at sundown a terrible noise perforated his delirious sleep, and he knew the two cities had collided. At first it was a scraping, cracking sound, and then a great pounding came, like thunder. Beneath the awesome lament of the cities was an under-song of human terror. Ays felt sick, assaulted by images of Min hurtling to the ground, bodies falling from her terraces as she plummeted down. He realised he had heard murder; the cities would die. What would happen to their inhabitants? It was too horrible to think about. Very few people were suited to the land-loping life. Most, faced with the prospect of a citiless future, would simply sit down and wait to die. Others, more courageous, might set off with the hope of joining another community. Some would lose their minds and become dangerous.

In the late evening, Oon came to him. He was too intoxicated by hela to do anything but cling to her lean body. He felt her kiss his hair, heard her say, 'I will miss you, Ays.'

In the morning, she was gone from his side, perhaps had never been there but in his imagination? Beulah and Leeth bundled him into Oon's wagon, and he did not open his eyes until many miles had passed. He never saw the dying hulks of the collision, and no one else told him what they'd seen.

Casmeer

One evening, they came for her. Casmeer was inside, working on an illustration for his book: two cities colliding, bodies falling from their tiers. He was alerted by a strange, crooning sound, and raised his head from his work. The sound was coming from the roof garden. Was his captive singing to herself? The song had a sad, beautiful melody.

Cautiously, Casmeer mounted the stairs that led to the attic giving access to the roof garden. What he saw from the doorway astounded him. A group of two dozen or so male plumosites had congregated on the roof garden. They had not come to plunder Elini's roche, however. Silently, they sat in stillness around the female plumosite's cage. She was standing upright against the bars, her wings spread out into the corners of the cage. Her dirty white fur gleamed in the starlight, as if she was surrounded by a nimbus of light. Her head was thrown back, and she sang a wordless lament. She seemed like an exotic priestess, invoking a dark and hidden god. She sang like the sole survivor of a massacre. Casmeer felt tears gather in his eyes. The song seemed to encompass all his own feelings of loneliness and pain.

Presently, the males began to chant a soft accompaniment to the song, their deep voices rising and falling in a complicated rhythm. Casmeer himself experienced an urge to join in with the song, add his voice to theirs. Eventually, the compulsion became too overwhelming, and he uttered a soft, perfect moan.

The plumosites all fell silent and turned their heads towards him, but there was no aggression in their posture.

Above them all, a star fell from the sky, a single blister of light. Distantly, another plumosite called; a single, sharp bark. Casmeer walked forward, and the plumosites did not move. He went to the cage and undid the latches.

'Go free,' he said, 'as *she* did.' He was weeping now; he could not help it.

At first the female plumosite did not move, and then she pushed past him. At once, the males began to hoot and jump around. The female leapt onto the low wall that surrounded the garden, and emitted a high-pitched scream. Then she flung herself over the side and her troupe quickly followed her. Casmeer listened to their receding howls as they sped across the rooftops.

He remembered all the plumosites he'd killed, and was filled with a deep sense of repugnance and guilt. How could he have been so brutish? Only a senseless barbarian would destroy other living creatures in such a way. The plumosites had never threatened him; they'd only yearned for the bright stones of the roches. How could they understand what the roches had once been?

Casmeer thought of the female he had held captive, her astounding majesty as she'd stood there singing in her cramped prison. He thought of the attentive company of males. Why hadn't they freed her? Surely, they possessed the ability. Perhaps the song, and his subsequent behaviour, had been part of a subtle plumosite plan? He could not tell.

But he would write about it.

Chapter Twelve
The Baroque King

The mountains were so bleak, Finnigin wondered how any creatures managed to survive in their realm. The only plants he saw were tough-stemmed rangy creepers; the trees, withered convolutions of ancient bark, whose leaves were small and dry. And the mountains of Overhang themselves dominated the world, obliterating the sky with their passionless black peaks, their razor-edged precipices. Wide-winged creatures soared the white sky; small patches of infinity glimpsed between the crowding cliffs. Finnigin was afraid the creatures might be Lamitrices, but they never came down into the shadowed regions of the gullies and canyons. Perhaps there were people living higher up among the crags? An easier, more radiant, prey.

The first few days of Finnigin's passage into Overhang were remarkable only because of his night-fears. He heard many alarming noises in the dark – screams that sounded human; heavy hammering; slow, furtive steps nearby – but even though the sounds tortured his sleep, kept him in a state of anxious alertness, they were never concluded, made whole, by sighted things. He realised there was another world going about its business around him but he was never drawn into it, never a witness to its tragedies and celebrations.

One morning, when Finnigin crawled out from a hole

in the rock beside the path, he found blood splashed upon the ground, and some fibres that might have been hair. Whatever had happened there had not awoken him, although early in the night he'd lain there listening to what sounded like a girls' chorus singing wistfully some distance away, their frail voices carried to his ears on the night breeze.

The discovery of the splashes of blood signalled a change in routine.

Finnigin attempted to begin his day as usual, eating frugally of the supplies donated by the Contamures. But as he breakfasted, his eyes were drawn back continually to the bright gout of red nearby, even though the sight adversely affected his appetite. Something sinister had happened, so close to him, something silent. He was unable to eat more than a few mouthfuls before a desire to flee the scene overcame his hunger.

The pathways he'd followed since leaving the settlement of the Quarriers had all been dark and shadowed gullies between high walls of rock. To him, they were like empty veins and arteries in the body of a fossilised giant. That day the silence of Overhang seemed more oppressive than usual; his footsteps were absorbed by it. The weather was overcast and grey, which meant less light than usual filtered down to the gully floors. The path Finnigin followed was narrow and tortuous; he was forever faced by blind corners, around which anything might lurk in waiting for unsuspecting travellers. The only sign of life was a profusion of thick, dusty spiders' webs spun between spiky niches on the rock wall, but even they seemed long devoid of inhabitants. The sight of these conjured a horrifying, insistent image in Finnigin's brain; that of rounding a corner and falling headlong into an enormous web that blocked the path, where something half human and half arachnoid would come rustling towards him, fanged and bright-eyed. He became conscious of the rapid beating of his heart, a shortness of breath. He was afraid. The thought of splendid cities – Gleaming Fisk and the others – seemed fantastic, improbable. Overhang was a realm of the dead, and paradoxically only death lived there. Finnigin could not dispel the illusion that his own life was draining away from him. He would even have been grateful to bump into a Lamitrice at that point. As an affirmation of life, even a predator is a welcome sight. But not all predators are monstrous in form.

When a clot of blurry shapes fell down upon Finnigin from shadowed crevices in the rock, when the sound of their yelping cries broke the silence, his first feeling was that of relief. The figures moved quickly like animals, their clothing sombre but embellished by bright jewels and shining gouts of coloured sashes. Finnigin called out to them as they circled him, held out his arms to them in a gesture of welcome. In return, they laughed and prodded him with long, pointed sticks. They were mostly of short stature, male and female, and spoke together in a chittering patois. Finnigin offered the only information he thought might help him: 'I am a terranaut.'

At these words, one of the crowd, a woman, came forward and pushed the end of her stick into his hair. Finnigin's head was forced backwards. 'Don't look for privileges, grigo. You are a commodity, that's all. Show us your purse.' Her voice was heavily accented, although she spoke Finnigin's language clearly.

'I have no purse,' he said. 'I have nothing.'

'You have meat!' came a voice, which prompted a round of gibbering laughter.

The woman frowned and held up her hand for silence. 'Terranaut,' she said, 'we shall take you to the Pursang Rodarigo.' She performed an ornate bow. 'He is the lord of these Crags, and will decide your fate.'

Her companions all began hooting and jabbing their weapons into the sky. Then, with a flurry of rapid movements, they jumped up into the rocks like gazelles, and dispersed. Only the woman and a single companion remained. She lifted her hand to her brow, palm outwards. 'I am Bustamonte,' she said. 'Sagamore of this domain and to Lord Rodarigo himself.'

'I am Finnigin.'

The woman inclined her head. She seemed a creature devoid of humour, her face set, her hair drawn back severely into a bloom of coloured scarves. Her nostrils were pierced by several metal rings, some of which were strung with tiny jewels. 'If you please Pursang Rodarigo, he will let you live. He has entertained terranauts before.' She turned, with a peremptory gesture for Finnigin to follow her, and took a more conventional route along the gully path.

Finnigin was encouraged by the woman's words, and blessed the star of his birth that he'd been born a terranaut. It seemed to grant him entrance to areas where an ordinary city-dweller would never be allowed.

Sagamore Bustamonte did not deign to speak to Finnigin as she led him to the enclave of her people, but her companion, a youth, walked behind him, occasionally jabbing his buttocks with a stick, which Finnigin thought a wholly unnecessary goad. He was so glad to come upon other people, there was little chance of him trying to evade them, and anyway, they seemed friendly enough.

Bustamonte led the way into a narrow corridor of rock which branched away from the main path. It was lit inside by burning torches, and the walls had been smoothed out in a rough fashion and decorated with crude paintings. Two women on guard by the entrance bared their teeth at Finnigin in lewd fashion which he ignored. He was, after all, being taken to the Pursang; a title which seemed to indicate a person of rank. Finnigin reminded himself he was a terranaut, and therefore transcended the company of underlings.

After a short journey, the corridor opened out into an enormous quarry which was occupied by a great number of flat-roofed buildings. The buildings themselves seemed ancient, almost weathered away, but the roofs, doorways and windows were clearly recent additions. There seemed to be a great deal of activity taking place which mostly involved the hewing of stone.

'You are miners,' Finnigin said conversationally to Bustamonte.

She gave him a hard glance. 'Well, I've not heard that one before! To most we are rhukahas – a term they see as abuse, but which we have adopted with some affection. We cut into the stone only to expand the Pursang's domain.'

'Rhukahas,' Finnigin said, trying to recall what he'd heard about them from the Contamures.

'Our main commerce is banditry,' Bustamonte continued in a prim voice. 'We see it as an art.'

Finnigin made no comment. He followed the Sagamore into the mud-tracked streets below. The enclave still seemed to be in a state of construction, as if the rhukahas had only recently taken command of the quarry. Finnigin commented on this to Bustamonte.

'The mountains are littered with derelict cities and settlements,' she said. 'We use them, and improve them, as and when we see fit. Sometimes the Pursang will get a divine message, and we move on to fulfil its dictates. We have been here two seasons, although in this area the distinction between the seasons is not always clear.'

'Where do you come from?' Finnigin asked. 'Originally, I mean.'

The Sagamore shrugged. 'I was raised as a child in the city of Oubrahani.'

'I have heard of it!' Finnigin cried. 'It has something to do with bells.'

The Sagamore cast him a sidelong glance. 'That is true,' she said. 'Occasionally I go back there to hear the monodies of the bells.' She sighed. 'Ah, I remember them now: the sonorous hum of Old Cumballa, the single clear note of Leocadia's Lament!' She paused. 'Still, they will always be there, and I have other prey to stalk at present.'

'Is Oubrahani near here?' Finnigin asked. 'Or, for that matter, Gleaming Fisk, Phaxteriniad or Karaganzinad?'

Sagamore Bustamonte laughed. 'You sound like a mountain guide! I'm not even sure all of those cities exist. Gleaming Fisk is far away, Oubrahani a moon's ride. As for the others – well – look for them upon the tongues of story-tellers.' She squinted up at the quarry walls. 'This is a desolate area. Life has in the main left it.'

'Pickings must be meagre for you, then, regarding travellers,' Finnigin observed.

The Sagamore looked at him sharply, sensing sarcasm. 'The Pursang is a vessel for the ineffable spirit of the god Harkh, from whom he regularly receives messages. He received divine instructions to remain in this place for a turn of four seasons.'

Finnigin was unsure whether he detected cynicism in the Sagamore's voice or not. 'Harkh? I've never heard of that name.'

'Harkh revealed Himself to the Pursang when Rodarigo was a boy. Harkh is Rodarigo's private deity. Therefore it is unlikely you would know of Him. We are His only followers. At the moment.'

Finnigin nodded. 'I see. Still, this is a harsh place to live.'

The Sagamore lifted her chin. 'We manage. Living here will make us appreciate the luxuries of regularly frequented highways when we return to plunder their travellers.'

They had entered the centre of the settlement. Finnigin abandoned conversation with Bustamonte in order to inspect his surroundings. He noticed that several buildings had been completely restored, and decorated with stone gargoyles. Others, however, were surrounded by robes of canvas, as if important architectural surgery was being conducted behind them. The streets were paved haphazardly with wide slabs, but mostly there was mud underfoot. The rhukahas favoured the use of oxen as pack animals, although Finnigin saw one or two important-looking individuals riding through the streets on large deer, crowned with long, ridged horns that were oiled to a gleaming amber.

'The Pursang will be interested to see you,' Bustamonte said. 'He is fascinated by your people.'

'I am eager to meet him too,' Finnigin said politely. Suddenly, he felt mature.

The Pursang lived in a sprawling, mostly two-storied building at the centre of the enclave. Windows were narrow and tall, overshadowed by flat eaves. The Sagamore's troupe must have hurried back to inform the Pursang to expect a visitor because two heavily armed women, large in stature, were waiting to take Finnigin into the Pursang's presence. It seemed the majority of the armed guard were female, but they appeared far stronger than the average man of Finnigin's acquaintance.

Finnigin and the Sagamore were escorted by the

guards down a cluttered corridor, lined by untidy heaps of artefacts – weaponry, clothes, ornaments, statues, pieces of furniture – which Bustamonte explained were the spoils of Rodarigo's exploits. Eventually, they entered a high-ceilinged room in the centre of the house.

Never in his life had Finnigin entered the presence of an individual with power, certainly not the kind of power that Rodarigo favoured. Therefore, the sight that met him in the Chamber of Audience impressed him greatly. He had no way of discerning the difference between true regality and a parody.

Rodarigo, self-styled Lord of the Crags, Pursang of his people, stood upright upon the seat of an ancient, carved wooden throne. His serviceable leather clothes were adorned with a multitude of bejewelled sashes; his chest was heavy with a riot of golden chains, ropes of pearls and amethysts, beads of amber. His long, oily hair was festooned with brooches, pendant earrings, and hat-pins. His skin gleamed sallow in the light of burning oil, and his eyes were heavily outlined in black. Three swords, of different shapes, hung from his belt. At his side, on a moth-eaten tapestried couch, reclined the most splendid female Finnigin had ever seen. She was neither small nor slim, but her sheer bulk was fabulous, and she gave off an air of voluptuousness and grace. Where Rodarigo's skin was olive, hers was an aching white. Her face was square, full-meated but without flabbiness, and her hair was an explosion of dense black around her head and shoulders. She gazed upon Finnigin with slitted, black eyes, stroking with a languid hand a small, tawny-furred animal that quivered against her thighs.

'Your Magnificences!' bawled one of the guards. 'We present to you a terranaut, found lost among the walkways of your Esteemed Domain.'

'Is this the only booty of the day, Scentally?' enquired the Pursang in a delicate voice. His face was fine-boned and should have appeared handsome, but there was something repellent about him that had little to do with appearances.

The guard stepped forward and bowed. 'My lord, the booty of the day is meagre in quantity, but rich in quality. Observe the beauty of this youth.'

The Sagamore Bustamonte stepped forward and, performing a hurried, formal genuflexion, interrupted. 'He is also very talkative.'

The Pursang nodded and sat down upon his throne, his left leg thrown over one of the chair arms. 'Good! That is excellent news.' He glanced at the large woman reclining beside him. 'My beloved, are you in a mood for questioning this terranaut stripling?'

The woman rolled her eyes, and fluttered a lazy hand before her face. 'La! A probe or two won't hurt, although I confess to feeling a mite weary this day.' She lifted her great body into a more upright position in a fluid, lissom motion, and fixed Finnigin with a stern stare.

The Pursang made an expansive gesture. 'Then please begin. Servers, ale if you please! Questioning is thirsty work!'

At his command, a flurry of movement erupted from the shadows behind the throne, and the guard Rodarigo had called Scentally grabbed Finnigin's arm and pushed him forwards. Finnigin was about to protest at this rough treatment, which he saw as wholly unnecessary, when Scentally kicked the backs of his knees, sending him helpless to the floor. Finnigin, rather dazed and confused, heard a high-pitched titter ring out somewhere to the side, but otherwise there was silence in the chamber.

The questioning was delayed for a few moments

whilst a scantily clad girl, assisted by a naked youth wearing a metal collar, poured ale for the Pursang and his lady. Finnigin observed strange markings upon the flesh of the servitors which he thought must be ritual scars of some sort. But they were so long and livid! Clearly, these people must have brutish rites.

Rodarigo's lady made a great fuss of sampling her cup of ale, grimacing in distaste and ordering more. The servitors hastened to obey her, every contour of their bodies proclaiming fear. Finnigin wondered why. The Pursang and his consort were clearly genteel individuals, of the type he had often seen promenading along the streets of flat-land cities he had visited, but to whom, of course, he had never spoken.

Eventually, satisfied and composed, the lady put down her cup and nodded to Bustamonte who cleared her throat.

'Captive,' said the Sagamore to Finnigin. *Captive*? he thought.

'You are about to be interrogated by the Pursang Rodarigo and the Pursanga Pashtarina. Answer every question with truth, speak clearly, do not stutter, dribble or falter. Do you understand these directives?'

'Yes, of course, but . . .'

'Silence!' commanded Bustamonte. She took two steps backwards and inclined her head to the Pursang and Pursanga.

Pashtarina smiled at Finnigin, which he took as encouragement. If he gave a good account of himself now, he could undoubtedly look forward to a few days' respite from the road, in comfort and hospitality.

'So then,' began the Pursanga, in a rich voice, 'what have we here? One so young, yet without doubt well-versed in the arcana of his people?'

Finnigin was unsure whether Pashtarina's words represented true questions or merely a few lines of opening conversation. Remaining on his knees, he straightened his spine and bowed his head. 'My lady, I am a terranaut on his first journey.'

'How fearless you young terranauts are!' declared Pashtarina. 'Sent out alone as you are, with so very little experience of life! Still, you must be hardy enough to take it.' She leaned back a little upon her cushions and stroked the exposed part of her grand snowy bosom with a perfect hand whose fingers were blistered with glittering rings. 'Now then, be so good as to share some of your mystery with us.'

'My lady, I can tell you of the flat-lands beyond the mountain ring. I can tell you of the vast cities . . .'

'Silence!' boomed Bustamonte.

Pashtarina made a small grimace of distaste, while Rodarigo fidgeted in impatience upon his throne.

'My dear boy, we require from you only one sparkling grain of knowledge. It is this: we know the flat-lands to be an inhospitable realm, seething with lunatics and lackwits. We know also it is a place without wealth, and as such below our interest. However, one thing that does intrigue us, and which we would dearly like to understand, is how your people guide the cities. What is the secret of the stones?'

Finnigin stared in silence. Not just because someone who was not of terranaut blood had dared to probe the hidden knowledge, but also because, even had he wanted to, he could not answer. Still, he remembered Bustamonte's words and spoke clearly and truthfully. 'My lady, I am not the master of such information. I do not yet know the secrets. Only our elders are aware of such truths.'

The Pursanga grimaced. 'You expect us to believe that?' she cawed in a harsh voice quite at odds with her earlier mellifluous tones.

'It is the truth,' Finnigin replied.

'But why do your people engage so seriously in this planting of stones and dragging of cities?' demanded Rodarigo, coming to life upon his throne. 'What is the purpose?'

'I don't know.'

The Pursang and Pursanga exchanged a glance, and then Rodarigo made a gesture. At once there was a surge of movement behind Finnigin and within moments he was thrown to his face upon the stone floor, cracking his nose sharply upon the flags. As blood began to ooze from his nostrils, he felt his coat being torn from his body. He protested, but his complaints only emerged as a bubbling warble; his mouth had filled with blood. His arms were jerked painfully in their sockets, his head hit the floor once more, and then his shirt was ripped from his back.

Finnigin tried to rise, utter pleas, but his imprecations were ignored. One moment, it felt as if a booted foot was placed between his shoulders, the next as if a charging animal had jumped on to his body with sharp hooves. The breath was pushed from his lungs and pain became his whole experience. Gasping for breath, he attempted to drag himself away, but another blow came and another. The sounds they made were terrible; a slap, a churning, a dull thud. Then, silence. Finnigin was weeping uncontrollably, terrified he had been cut in half and was living his last moments. What had he done wrong. *What?*

He heard the Pursanga's voice, and it seemed to come from far away. When he opened his eyes, he could not see for the boiling silver specks before his vision.

'Now then, terranaut, let us begin again. What is the power of the stones, and how might we use it?'

Finnigin could only utter a weak cry.

'Lift him!' ordered the Pursang.

Rough hands grabbed Finnigin beneath his arms, and he was hauled to his knees. Someone grabbed his hair and forced his head back. It felt as if his back was on fire. Through a red mist, he could see the Pursang and Pursanga looking at him intently. They seemed to be excited, pleased. Finnigin was beyond comprehending what this might signify, but his guts reacted instinctively: he vomited on to the floor.

Rodrigo jumped up and stepped down from the throne with light, dancing steps. The ornaments in his hair swung, catching the light of the lamps. He paused beyond the circumference of Finnigin's vomit. 'My Lord Harkh tells me that my people need power,' he said, extending a fisted hand. 'Everyone needs power, and you have the knowledge of it. If you would live, speak!'

'We . . . we have no power,' Finnigin managed to gasp.

'No power?' cried the Pursang. 'No power?'

'No power?' echoed Pashtarina in outrage. 'A race who can lure gigantic cities, cities that in essence should not possess the ability to move at all, has no power? The concept is derisory!'

The Pursang cupped Finnigin's chin with a thoughtful hand. 'Listen, boy, I can have you lashed until your heart can be seen beating through your ribs. I can have your entire body whipped until you are nothing but a pulsing pile of bloody bones. I can have spikes driven through your groin, your eyes washed with acidic banes. In short, I can do whatever I like with you, should you displease me. In your position, I would see the wisdom of communication.'

'My knowledge is limited,' Finnigin said weakly, 'but I want to live. I will tell you whatever I can . . .' He felt as if consciousness was held to his body by a thread, and that should he lose it, it would not return. If only these people would ask him a question he could answer!

'Where do you obtain the pilot-stones?' demanded the Pursang.

'Every year, certain of our elders depart the troupe and return with a new stock of stones which others break into smaller pieces.'

'Where do your elders go to fetch the stones?'

Finnigin shook his head and moaned. 'I don't . . .' Suddenly, a spark of cunning ignited in his brain; it was an urge to survive. 'There . . . there is supposed to be a place where giant winged beings nest among the mountains. The stones are traded for with them.'

'What do you trade?'

'City . . . city produce.'

Rodarigo nodded and retreated to his throne. Pashtarina took up the questioning.

'And how is the power of the stones accessed? Once we have them, how do we use them?'

'They . . . they have to be charged with intention.'

'What does that mean?'

'I cannot explain. I would have to show you.'

'Then do!'

'I can't . . . not like this. I need to be strong.' Pashtarina made a noise of annoyance and leaned over to consult with her consort.

While they debated, Finnigin hung limply in the grip of his guards. Looking down, he could see that he was kneeling in a pool of blood that had been smeared across the flagstones by his scrabbling feet. The front of his clothes were wet and red. Soon, he was sure, he would die.

'Terranaut!' commanded the Pursang. 'My lady and I have discussed your remarks. They are in truth quite different to any we have gleaned from other terranauts who have come to visit us, but perhaps this presages we at last have a measure of truth. Your predecessors were less sage than yourself. They died protesting they knew nothing. You are a sensible boy, and for this we are inclined to let you live. However, we shall send emissaries into the crags to seek out the winged beings you spoke of. You will advise us of what produce to take in order that they will trade pilot-stones. When the emissaries return, and should they have acquired stones, you will instruct certain of our people in their use.'

Finnigin uttered a groan.

'Yes, you might well feel grateful. People have perished for less insubordination than you exhibited! You are well-favoured in appearance, which also induces us to be lenient in our treatment of you.' The Pursang addressed Scentally. 'Take him away. Allow him a little salve, and let Scaphander and Pleurice attend to him. When he can speak coherently, bring us word.'

Finnigin lost consciousness as he was carried away, for movement caused terrible pain in his body. He was awoken rudely by a bucket of water being thrown over his head, and found he was lying on his belly in a bed of soiled straw. He was too afraid and hurt to move, but could see a pair of booted feet standing close to his head. This figure leaned down and offered him a battered metal cup of water. The benefactor was Scentally. Beyond her, kneeling down and staring at him with round, hysterical eyes, were the young girl and youth who had waited upon the Pursang and his consort. The girl held a ceramic pot between her knees; the boy was hugging his skinny chest with trembling arms. As far as Finnigin could make out, they were in a small, stone-walled cell, with meagre daylight coming down from a source somewhere overhead.

Finnigin raised his head painfully and tried to sip

sideways from the cup. The water tasted metallic, almost poisonous. He slumped back down with a groaning sigh.

'Get on with it!' said Scentally, and the two servitors quickly crawled forward.

The guard grunted and stalked away. A door banged and Finnigin heard the sound of a key being turned.

The girl and youth were making soft sounds of consternation, and touched him diffidently with gentle fingers. They whispered to one another, and Finnigin could not catch their words.

'What is happening?' he sobbed. 'Speak to me!'

'Lie still,' said the girl. 'I will try not to hurt you.'

The servitors were named Pleurice and Scaphander. As they attended to Finnigin's hurts, they distracted him from his pain by telling him about themselves. 'As children we lived in Oubrahani,' said the girl, Pleurice. 'But one day, travelling with our nurse to our grandmother's summer palace in Twall Tar, we were set upon by the rhukahas. All our guardians were killed, and we were taken captive.'

'Ever since, we have been slaves to the Pursang and Pursanga,' said Scaphander.

'I don't understand,' moaned Finnigin. 'At first, the Pursang and his lady seemed so gracious and courteous. Why have they treated me this way? What did I do to displease them so?'

The servitors laughed at his words. 'Gracious? Courteous? You are a fool! They are rogues, cut-throats, bred from filth, aping the ways of the lords and ladies of splendid cities, whom they envy greatly. Their wealth is filched, their people are all criminals cast out from lawful societies, or else bred from slaves. Rodarigo is an addled crack-brain, and Pashtarina a heartless slut.'

'Why don't you run away?' Finnigin asked.

'We would be killed,' Scaphander answered. 'We can only wait for the day when the royal guard of Oubrahani flushes the scoundrels out and rescues us.'

'Will that ever happen?'

'We have to believe so,' Pleurice replied with sad softness.

'The Sagamore is from Oubrahani,' Finnigin said. 'Why won't she help you?'

Pleurice stroked Finnigin's hair. 'Poor boy, he's talking nonsense.'

'He doesn't understand,' Scaphander told her, and then addressed Finnigin himself. 'There is scum in every city. Some of it floats far.'

Finnigin was not called to the Pursang and Pursanga's presence for several days, during which time he recovered much of his strength. He was fed, if not well at least adequately, and Pleurice and Scaphander did all they could to ease his suffering. He confessed he had lied to the Pursang, a remark which prompted a swift response from Scaphander.

'No, do not tell us!' he cried.

'But . . .'

'No. They will lash us, as they did you, if they think we know anything.'

So Finnigin could only keep his thoughts to himself. He felt he was capable of giving directions in a convincing manner as to how to find the winged giants and also what to take to trade, but from there on his plans were of course unclear. He could only hope the Lamitrices would destroy any rhukaha emissaries, and in the meantime he might formulate a way to escape the enclave. Surely there was more than one exit from the quarry? Scaphander and Pleurice were unclear on this matter. They knew of warrens leading into the mountains, but were ignorant of whether they led to the surface again or not.

The Sagamore Bustamonte came to visit him regularly, more so than was perhaps necessary. Finnigin felt they were mutually intrigued. One day, she announced that he could accompany her on a walk around the enclave if he wished to. The Pursang obviously trusted her implicitly.

There was a squat alehouse in the middle of the enclave where Bustamonte and Finnigin finished their walk and sat together outside to converse and share a jug of ale. It was hard for Finnigin to equate the pleasant experiences of the day with his previous treatment. Bustamonte was obviously an accomplished woman, and Finnigin couldn't help wondering why she had chosen the life of a rhukaha. He did not believe she shared Rodarigo's passion for Harkh.

'Mine is a sordid tale,' she said, with a vague gesture of her arms. 'Deaths, marriages, a change of circumstance.'

'What do you mean?' Finnigin asked, hoping she wouldn't repent of her frankness.

'My father died, my mother remarried. A new man in the house. Need I say more?'

'Well, I'd like you to.'

Bustamonte rolled her eyes. 'In short, this brute became trustee of my inheritance, and the oppressor of my spirit. His physical attentions I parried with difficulty. I am sure my mother knew of his behaviour, but then, we had never been close. I think she'd always been jealous of me, because of the love my father had for me, and she saw her new husband's treatment of me as a fitting punishment for the pain I'd caused her.' She shrugged. 'I ran away eventually. My step-father had arranged for me to marry one of his friends who, while not repellent in appearance, and certainly very rich, was undeniably a cruel and possessive man. I wanted none of it, so I fled. The rhukahas were happy to let me join them when they learned of my pedigree. As you've probably gathered, our honoured leaders are easily impressed by what they think is blue blood.'

Finnigin was warmed by this last, frank remark. It meant that Bustamonte respected his discretion.

Eventually, the Pursang sent Scentally to fetch Finnigin. He followed the guard, breathless with nerves, running over in his head the script he had concocted for this encounter.

The Pursang received him in an ornately tapestried room whose stone floor was thick with splendid rugs and furs. Highly polished darkwood furniture and heaps of spoils cluttered the space. The Pursang sat in a chair before a huge fire which made the air in the room hot and unbreathable. It stank of must and old fur, of unwashed flesh and stale food.

The Pursang glanced up in a staged manner as Finnigin approached him. 'Ah, you are recovered,' he said, as if Finnigin had suffered a minor fever.

'Quite well,' he responded, hoping he could talk in a convincing manner to this demented man.

'What beautiful hair you have! I once had a shirt woven from hair such as yours. It was cut from the heads of seven virgin sisters, and was as soft as silk.'

'A garment fit for a king,' Finnigin responded.

'Yes,' Rodarigo agreed. 'It felt that way.' He stood up. 'Now, to our business.' He indicated the way to a table beneath a curtained window where a large, tattered map was spread out, weighted with bowls of burning oil. The oil was rancid, which contributed to the unsavoury odours of the room.

'Here is a map of Overhang,' said the Pursang, pointing. 'But it is incomplete. Still, I hope it will serve to reveal the whereabouts of the stone-traders.'

'I will have to study it,' Finnigin said carefully.

'Of course.'

As Finnigin leaned over the map, his eyes blind with panic, the Pursang put a hand on the back of his neck and stroked his hair. Finnigin's mind fell into chaos. He could think of nothing to say.

'Well?' enquired the Pursang after a few moments. 'What are your conclusions?' Fortunately, he stepped away to help himself to a measure of ale, and Finnigin was able to compose himself.

'Hmm, it is difficult to tell. I passed by the settlement of the traders on my way into the mountains, but I have no map myself. I suppose I'll have to rely on intuition and memory.'

'I'm sure both are of peak calibre,' said the Pursang. 'You are a terranaut, after all.'

With a shaking finger, Finnigin pointed at random to a place on the map, hoping it was a considerable distance away from Rodarigo's territory. 'These formations seem familiar.'

Rodarigo leaned close to inspect the map. Finnigin wanted to recoil from the smell of the Pursang's breath, which was rank with the reek of inferior culinary herbs. 'Oh? Near to Twall Tar? That's a good distance off. Are you sure you came that way? There are impassable rock slides – here and here – and I fail to see how you managed to find your way from there to the walkway Bustamonte found you on.'

'Just a moment. Let me look again.' Finnigin frowned, and then spoke carefully. 'Perhaps my orientation is wrong? Would you be kind enough to point out the position of this enclave? That way I can perhaps retrace my steps.'

'Here!' Rodarigo stabbed the map with a dirty fingernail.

'Ah, yes! Now, I see my mistake. This part here is obviously where the traders live.'

Rodarigo nodded. 'That seems feasible. We avoid that area because it has been claimed by the ordure-heap ruckster known as Toomtwellier the Glee. A knave of the first order, unworthy of the title rhukaha. He fails to acknowledge the Ineffable Power of Harkh, or my true sovereignty of this district, which of course extends far, and encompasses the very frontier of Overhang.'

'Well, that is the place then.'

Finnigin stood up and found himself face to face with the Pursang, who was uncomfortably close. 'How timid you are! How you tremble! Do not be in awe of my person. We have privacy here. Let us be nothing more than man and youth. Forget the trappings of power!' The Pursang threw out an arm in an expansive gesture. 'Come, don't be shy. Sit at my feet by the fire, and tell me what temptations might be attractive to the stone traders in order for them to exchange their wares.'

With extreme trepidation, Finnigin walked gingerly to the fire and sat down on the rugs.

'I regret having to chastise you earlier,' said the Pursang, sitting down, 'but sometimes a man in my position has to commit himself to unsavoury actions. Believe me, it is a duty that I far from relish. Still, that is past, and you have commended yourself via your tractable behaviour.'

'Thank you,' Finnigin murmured uncomfortably.

'So, to the trade. What do you recommend?'

Finnigin glanced round the chamber. 'Well! any bright trinkets you might have lying around. They especially like gold, but the value of the items is not as important as their appearance.'

'Oh, well, we have plenty of that sort of material,' said the Pursang. 'What is the value of the stones?'

'That varies,' Finnigin replied. 'Each trade is a very different experience.'

The Pursang stuck out his lower lip and nodded. 'Hmm, I shall have to make sure I send an individual astute in bartering! Perhaps Bustamonte? She is quick and clever with words.'

Finnigin's heart became heavy. He wanted to cry out: 'No, not her!' but realised he must not speak. His own survival depended on the efficacy of his lies.

The Pursang extended his legs which were encased in ancient leather. 'You have no idea how possessing the power of the stones will ease my rule! Not only do I have to put up with irritations caused by militia from nearby cities, but also the predatoriness of scoundrels who wrongly use the title rhukaha. Harkh has convinced me that the power of the stones can be used for operations other than coaxing cities to move about. He has told me that they can affect the structure of the mountains themselves, so that I might realign the rocks to my convenience. For example, I could cause an upheaval beneath Oubrahani, or a volcano to erupt around the site of Toomtwellier's harem stable.'

Finnigin was sure the pilot-stones could never conjure such effects, but kept his silence. It was all academic anyway, since Rodarigo had no chance of obtaining any stones.

'Now!' said the Pursang, lacing his fingers together, 'Business is concluded. I would honour you, young terranaut, so lie down passively while I acquaint myself with the exquisite contours of your flesh.'

Finnigin froze. 'What? But . . .' He attempted to rise, but the Pursang grabbed hold of a fistful of his hair.

'Don't be coy!' he said. 'Oh dear, of course, you are still in pain. Might I suggest you adopt a comfortable position and lie upon your belly? I will essay to avoid your wounds.'

★ ★ ★

The emissaries, of course, did not return. Weeks passed, Finnigin existing in a delirious haze of anxiety and exhaustion. Nightly, he was summoned to the Pursang's bed which was an experience he found distasteful in the extreme, if only for the ghastly odours that permeated the blankets and cushions. After gratifying his needs with Finnigin's body, Rodarigo liked to tell the terranaut about his life's work. Banditry he saw as an intrinsic part of the human condition.

'Everyone is part bandit,' he said, 'but some of us have to perform the function for humanity as a whole. It maintains balance, you see. Where would be the pleasure of accruing wealth without the attendant terror of losing it, hmm?'

Finnigin agreed, thinking it best not to argue by stating the obvious. He believed greed, rather than altruism, was Rodarigo's driving force.

The Pursang's relationship with the Pursanga intrigued Finnigin. It appeared to be platonic because they never, to his knowledge, made love, or even touched. Like Bustamonte, Pashtarina must have a story to tell. Perhaps one day Finnigin would hear it? During the day, having been informed of Finnigin's delights by her consort, the Pursanga demanded Finnigin's attentions. She believed that the bodies of men were carriers of a malign disease which caused women to age, so would not countenance Finnigin having intercourse with her which in some ways disappointed him because he wondered what it would be like to ride the splendid mountains of her flesh. Instead, she required him to pleasure her with a vast assortment of erotic instruments which had been fashioned to her specific directions by craftsmen in joinery and metalwork. Before this ritual took place, however, she attached him to various contraptions she'd invented to elicit the sexual pleasure of men. Some were successful, others not. One or two were quite painful to experience.

Finnigin realised the futility of behaving badly in the Pursang and Pursanga's presence. For the time being, he must swallow his outrage at their initial treatment of him, and the casual manner in which they amused themselves with his body, and work on a way to regain his freedom. Co-operation, for now, could only assist his aims.

Occasionally he woke up from wistful dreams in which the mysterious figure of Varian figured prominently. Finnigin had to admit it seemed unlikely he'd ever seen Varian again, or penetrate the mystery of why the man had been interested in him. Surely the details of Varian's appearance should fade with time, and yet whenever he walked through Finnigin's dreams, he was as vivid and solid a character as in life. How can I miss a person I barely know? Finnigin wondered.

Whenever he got the opportunity, which was rarely, he tried to examine the boundaries of the quarry for exits. Unfortunately, during the times he was not attending to the Pursang and his consort, Scaphander or Pleurice were constantly in attendance, and although they were sympathetic to Finnigin's situation, were quite emphatic that they would not let him escape. They feared punishment, and were content to await passively in captivity until the day of their rescue. Finnigin could not share their serene and unshakeable faith, but all his patient attempts to fire them up into a lust for escape were met with quiet resistance. Once, he even tried to make a run for it, but Scaphander carried a small sling, and expertly brought him down with a stone. It took Finnigin some explaining later to make a convincing excuse to Rodarigo as to why he had a lump on his head.

His own fear of the Pursang and Pursanga diminished as the days passed because they clearly enjoyed his presence. Still, he could only dread the day when the Pursang realised something was amiss with the emissaries. That day came all too soon.

Rodarigo summoned Finnigin to his chamber in the afternoon. 'It has occurred to me that the traders should have returned by now,' he said. 'Have you any idea what might be causing the delay?'

Finnigin shrugged, his heart contracting suddenly as a swift memory of Bustamonte skidded across his mind. 'I'm afraid not. I suppose your emissaries wouldn't consider taking charge of the stones themselves? They are, after all, very powerful and precious things.'

Rodarigo clipped Finnigin round the ear, a blow which sent him crashing into a table. 'Don't ever suggest such a thing! My people are utterly faithful to me.'

'I beg your forgiveness,' Finnigin muttered, rubbing his ear. 'Perhaps more emissaries should be sent to investigate? I think the stone-traders sometimes make people wait until a certain phase of the sky occurs before they'll consider trading.'

Rodarigo fixed Finnigin with a penetrating stare. 'Hmm, that is a possibility. Harkh has in fact already suggested that I should consider venturing forth myself. You will accompany me.'

'Perhaps you should wait a few more days?' Finnigin said.

The next morning, a weak, torn and bloodied individual staggered into the enclave. To Finnigin's horror she was one of the emissaries.

She was carried into the presence of the Pursang and Pursanga and there gave account of what had happened to her and her companions. Finnigin, crouching beside

Rodarigo's throne, listened painfully to the description of the Lamitrices' reaction when the emissaries had boldly approached them speaking of trade. Needless to say, there had been no dialogue.

Rodarigo heeded the woman's desperate speech and sat in silent thought for a few moments. Then he addressed Finnigin.

'This is astounding news! Can you shed any light on why the traders behaved in this fashion?'

Finnigin shrugged helplessly. 'My lord, I have told you all I know. Only terranaut elders know all the secrets of the stones. Perhaps the emissaries should have performed some ritual of respect or introduction – which I haven't learned about? Other than that, I'm as puzzled by the traders' behaviour as you are.'

'Perhaps it was because the emissaries were not terranauts?' Pashtarina suggested.

Rodarigo nodded. 'That is true. Well, then, the solution is obvious. Finnigin must be the one to approach the winged giants concerning trade.' He grinned down at Finnigin who was mute with terror. 'You can leave tomorrow. A sizeable armed guard will escort you.'

Bustamonte, in all her womanhood and glory, was dead, torn to pieces by a Lamitrice who no doubt had been unable to believe its fortune when eight prime specimens of humanity had walked into its nest. Finnigin wondered whether he should feel responsible for the Sagamore's death. He, after all, had not warned her, or tried to sway the Pursang from sending her as an emissary. Still, it was too late to fret about all that now. In the morning, he himself would be on his way to a horrible death.

That night, Finnigin was tense and nervous in the Pursang's company.

'Harkh says you are afraid,' said Rodarigo with disapproval.

'Afraid? No!' Finnigin uttered a cackling laugh. 'I'm just thinking up a few plans. We already know that the traders are unpredictable.'

How could he possibly escape before morning?

When he heard Rodarigo praying aloud to Harkh, Finnigin was almost envious. How convenient to have a divine presence, imaginary or not, to come to daring's aid when it was needed. He spent the night despising Scaphander and Pleurice, who could have helped him but would not. He considered slipping away from the Pursang's bed, but whenever he as much as put a toe on the floor, Rodarigo woke up and complained of his restlessness.

Before dawn, a cacophony of unusual sounds roused Finnigin from restive dozing. Rodarigo sat up beside him, a frown on his face. 'What is that?'

Finnigin watched in silence as Rodarigo stalked to the window and threw wide the dusty drapes. It sounded as if a herd of wild animals was running amok outside. Rodarigo's body froze in an attitude of surprised outrage. Moments later, he was scrambling into his clothes, hopping to the door, half dressed, to issue frantic orders. He scanned the chamber for any available weapon.

'Well, what was it?' Finnigin asked, sitting up in the bed. Rodarigo seemed not to hear him, and ran out into the corridor beyond his chamber, shouting hoarsely.

Perplexed, Finnigin got out of bed and dressed himself in a leisurely manner, listening to the hysterical noises that came from outside. Then he went to the window.

The Pursang's enclave was being attacked. The plaza in front of the palace was a mêlée of struggling bodies, and the ground and the walls of nearby buildings were striped with blood. Some people already lay dead from the fighting, whilst others lay groaning or sought to crawl away from the scene. Finnigin felt strangely clear-headed and serene. It was, he decided, almost as if the hand of a benign deity was resting upon his brow at that moment. In the confusion, it would surely be easy for him to sneak away unseen.

He rooted around the artefacts and piles of clothing in Rodarigo's chamber and helped himself to items he thought would be of use. Of course, he had no food, but from what he'd heard the city of Oubrahani was not far distant. As luck would have it, he discovered a plate of rather wizened figs underneath a heap of embroidered robes. These he stuffed into a leather bag, along with the other things he'd decided to take with him. Donning a long leather coat of the Pursang's, which he'd often admired, Finnigin stepped out into the corridor. It was empty and silent. He decided it would be best to make his way to the rear entrance of the building, and from there somehow edge his way around the perimeter of the quarry, where massive boulders would provide ample cover, and see what was happening at the main gate of the enclave.

He passed a few cowering slaves, who winced as he looked at them, but other than them, the palace seemed deserted. His confidence growing, Finnigin marched smartly along the cluttered corridors, humming beneath his breath. He was therefore horrified when a huge shape suddenly plunged out of a doorway, grabbed him and dragged him into the room beyond. Finnigin was quite prepared to fight for his freedom at that point, and drew out a wickedly barbed knife which he'd found in a fruit bowl in the Pursang's room. It was only when his attacker cried, 'Finnigin, don't hurt me!'

that he realised it was Pashtarina who'd grabbed hold of him.

She drooped before him, her huge bulk shaking uncontrollably and bursting from the confines of a flimsy night-dress of pink silk. Her hair tumbled over her shoulders in a mat of astounding tangles. Finnigin was disappointed. He would not have expected Pashtarina to manifest fear. Rather, he would have thought she'd be out there in the thick of the fighting, swinging something like a giant rolling-pin, and felling the attackers as if they were tin soldiers.

'Finnigin, you must help me!' she cried.

He was confused. He had not expected anything like this. 'I can't,' he said. 'I'm leaving.'

'Of course you are. We must go together!'

'No, you're too conspicuous.'

Pashtarina reached out and grabbed Finnigin's shoulders. Her large white face was mottled with red, the flush of tears. 'Finn, my darling, I can't believe this! Can you really bear to abandon me here? Can you?'

'Yes. My back still smarts from the first caresses you and Rodarigo gave me. Let go of me.'

'Oh, Finnigin, don't be so mean-spirited as to harbour a grudge for that! Haven't we enjoyed happy hours together since?'

He shrugged. 'Well . . .'

The Pursanga shook him sharply. 'My beloved boy, you *must* assist me! I have my bags packed, and need someone to carry them for me. Also, I shall need the attentions of a valet upon the road.'

Finnigin could not free himself from the Pursanga's strong grip. 'Pashtarina, let me go. I am not your slave, and I'm going to use this opportunity to escape both you and your consort. Anyway, who exactly is attacking your people?'

The Pursanga seemed to recollect herself at the

mention of her enemies. Majestically, she heaved herself erect. 'Oubrahan scum!' she declared, thumping the palm of one hand with the fist of another. 'Finnigin, if they catch me, they will incarcerate me, or worse. Yes, worse.'

Finnigin couldn't help smiling. 'Well, you have been stealing their children, and no doubt their belongings as well. Didn't you think they'd come and attack you one day? I'm surprised the Pursang hadn't prepared for it.'

'Harkh has never spoken of it,' Pashtarina said darkly, daring Finnigin to make a facetious remark.

'A sad oversight,' he said. 'Oh, well, if I were you, my lady, I'd pretend to be someone else.'

'Impossible. Our servants will betray us.'

'Hmm. It's a pity you treated them badly, otherwise they might be more sympathetic. Still, it's too late to cry about that now.' He began to walk towards the door.

'You are a cruel and ungrateful boy!' Pashtarina shouted tearfully. 'Our warriors will have no chance against the Oubrahans. There are too many of them, and they are fired by a nauseating, righteous zeal! There is no escape for me. If I run, I shall be an undefended target. We need to leave together, so that one of us can cover our flight. See, I have crossbows over there with my luggage. If I remain here, the Oubrahans will take me prisoner and subject me to a multitude of humiliations! Oh, Finnigin, did I ever raise the lash to your flesh? No! How could I countermand Rodarigo's orders, who takes his commands directly from his personal god?'

The benign deity, who had been hovering around Finnigin's head since he'd awoken, made its presence felt again. There were things he could have said concerning the fact that it was Pashtarina's free choice to remain with the Pursang. He did not believe she was as helpless as she made out, only very lazy. Neither was he convinced she objected to maltreatment of the helpless. Still, she had taught him many things concerning pleasures – and pains – of the flesh, which he would carry with him forever. He paused and turned around. 'Lady, I think it pointless for me to try and make a run for it with you beside me, but if you surrender, and take me to the Oubrahans, I could perhaps speak in your favour. If there's one thing I've learned from dealing with Rodarigo, it's that I'm good at lying.'

Pashtarina considered these words, then shook her head. 'Scaphander and Pleurice will speak against me, and I think the Oubrahans will believe them rather than you.'

Finnigin nodded. 'True, but I could also say that I have been trying to escape since my capture, and Pleurice and Scaphander, being honest souls, would not deny they've deliberately tried to prevent that. I could then go on to explain that you and I had been planning to escape together in the near future.'

Pashtarina brooded over Finnigin's suggestions, and then visibly brightened. 'Yes! You could tell them that Rodarigo treated me badly, that I had no wish to be part of his filthy atrocities, but that I was afraid of him.'

Finnigin regarded her imposing figure with a critical eye. It would be difficult even for the most gullible person to believe Pashtarina was afraid of anything. 'Yes, you could say that. You could tell them all about your hard life. We'll need the Oubrahans to feel sorry for you. Shall we go?' He extended an arm, which Pashtarina daintily took. Together, they walked out into the corridor, she towering over her light-footed escort.

The fighting was all but over when Finnigin and Pashtarina emerged with stately tread into the daylight. At once, voices cried out and fingers pointed. A gang of Oubrahans, led by Scaphander and Pleurice, hurried towards them. Pashtarina held her head high, a regal figure, despite the fact she was dressed in her night-wear and her hair was in disarray.

'There!' shouted Pleurice. 'The devil's whore!'

'Say nothing,' Finnigin said, aware his own voice was shaking. Now that he could see the Oubrahans – all tall soldiers with unsympathetic faces – he wondered how feasible his plan had been. It seemed likely both he and the Pursanga would be despatched by sword without any explanations being asked for.

'Wait!' he cried, holding out his arms. 'I too am a captive!' He turned to Scaphander and Pleurice. 'Tell them!'

'You are a collaborator!' Scaphander spat. 'You soiled yourself with them!'

Finnigin was outraged by the injustice of Scaphander's remarks. Had he forgotten how Finnigin had urged him to escape?

The Oubrahans surged forward and grabbed hold of Finnigin and the Pursanga, ignoring all their protests.

Finnigin heard Pleurice shout: 'Behead them! Behead them!' Everything was struggling confusion, as Finnigin and Pashtarina tried to escape the implacable hands of the Oubrahans. They were dragged down into the plaza where Finnigin caught sight of the body of Rodarigo, minus its head, which lay nearby; the Pursang's last expression being that of horror. Pashtarina's anguished wail indicated she too had seen the head. Slipping in a slick of blood, Finnigin experienced the numbing dread that he was about to die. It seemed the feeling was becoming a familiar one.

An Oubrahan soldier forced him to his knees, against a litany of his crimes being chanted by Pleurice. 'Bestiality, heresy, conspiracy!' How had she come to hate him so much? It made no sense.

'You are wrong!' Finnigin cried. 'You are wrong.'

The Pursanga's voice was nothing more than a wordless howl. Just as the sword was about to fall, and Finnigin was floating in a disorientated state, hardly aware of proceedings, a strange, loud yet husky voice penetrated the hubbub. At the sound of it, all activity fell still.

'Stop!'

For a few moments nothing happened, and then Finnigin dared to raise his head. What he saw was surely the subtle presence he had felt around him all day: a slight figure clad in translucent gauze, with a halo of floating hair around its head. Surely a goddess.

'Stop!' The goddess glided forward, touching the drooping swords of the men with delicate hands. Her presence brought with it an overwhelming sense of peace. There was no sound but for the panting of the soldiers, the gasping of Finnigin and Pashtarina.

Then one of the soldiers spoke. 'Lady, this is no place for you. Retreat to the rock wall where we left you. I shall command an escort . . .'

'No!' The word was harsh, an abrupt rasp. Having uttered it, the goddess condensed into a girl. And with this transformation came recognition.

'Babooshpet!' Finnigin struggled to his feet. '*Are* you Babooshpet?'

The girl looked at him, her expression unreadable. Then she smiled, and Finnigin could see that her brilliant white teeth were broken and spiky.

'You could not speak,' he babbled. 'You could not speak . . .' What had happened to reality? a calm part of his mind wondered. What new surprises would this extraordinary day reveal to him?

Babooshpet ignored him and addressed the leading Oubrahan who appeared to be in charge. 'I know this person,' she said. 'You mustn't cut his head off.'

The Oubrahan bowed respectfully. 'My lady, he is part of the rogue's entourage. I cannot believe that you know him.'

'We travelled together before you found me,' she said. 'We became separated.'

'What she says is true!' Finnigin interrupted. 'I was taken by the rhukahas and forced into a terrible and disgusting slavery!' He heard an anguished noise from the Pursanga. 'Daily, I urged Scaphander and Pleurice to plan an escape with me, but they were too lily-livered to listen. They, more than I, were collaborators! If it hadn't been for the good Lady Pashtarina, who agreed to help me, I would have ended my own life in despair!'

Pleurice uttered a cry of fury. 'There is nothing good about that stinking trollop! I lost count of the number of times she had me beaten!'

'If you'd had a little more sense, you would have realised the Pursanga was as much a slave to Rodarigo as any of us,' Finnigin said scathingly.

'The boy speaks truly,' said Pashtarina in a honeyed voice, permeated by a convincing sadness. 'Oh, how I have suffered in this place!'

The Oubrahan commander glanced from Finnigin to Pashtarina to Pleurice and Scaphander. 'What do you say to this?' he enquired.

Scaphander shrugged. 'Finnigin was often trying to convince us to run away, but his plans were absurdly dangerous. It was obvious we couldn't succeed. My sister and I had faith that one day our people would find us. As it happens, we were right. Neither did we submit to gratifying the bestial desires of the Pursang and his whore.'

'You were never asked to!' Pashtarina couldn't resist exclaiming.

'Well, this matter needs a more minute appraisal, in

any case,' said the commander. 'I suggest we take these two back to the city and interrogate them.' He bowed to Babooshpet. 'As our glorious flameness has spoken, we cannot countenance executing these people.'

Finnigin looked at Babooshpet and caught her eye. She blinked slowly. Again, she had saved his life, but she had changed almost beyond recognition. What had happened to her since he'd last seen her at the Contamures?

Casmeer

Sometimes Casmeer woke up full of self-loathing, and today was one of those occasions. The sight of himself in the mirror opposite the bed was like a hot brand against the eyes. There was something too self-adulatory in the arrangement of the facial features, something too pompous about the position of the limbs. His hair was a conceit, like a harlot's; too decorative to be tolerated.

On these days, it was Casmeer's habit to throw a robe over the mirror and thus conceal the offensive image. He wasn't sure what provoked this particular mood of self-hatred, but presumed it was something to do with dreams that were forgotten by the waking mind but all too vivid in the subconscious. As it was, his reaction to his reflection was but a presentiment of a recollection he would experience later in the day.

As he ate his breakfast, he read over his notes of the past few days. He had a feeling something was brewing in Finnigin's story; something that involved himself and which he was unaware of yet on a conscious level. Still, re-reading the notes made him feel excited and shameful at the same time.

He went out into the roof garden, still chewing a

hunk of bread. There was no sign of any plumosites, which disappointed him. The sky that day was overcast. Perhaps rain would come? Casmeer liked the smell of the city after rain; it refreshed his mind through his senses, and the electric presence in the air that presaged thunder energised his flesh.

If it rains, I shall walk in it, he thought.

Later, with the brooding pressure of imminent storm still hanging in the air, Casmeer went out for his walk. The air was hot and humid; the calls of plumosites in the distance sounded hectic and enraged. Casmeer let his feet lead him, wandering without conscious thought.

Today, his body took him to a residential area that was quite close to Womber's Yard. He remembered, without emotional replay, that this was where his family had once lived, where he, his siblings and his cousins had been brought up.

The garden to his parents' house was of course overgrown, and the rear façade of the building had virtually crumbled away. Casmeer did not want to go inside, but he sat in the garden for a while as the first warriors of thunder practised their war chants in the west. He picked berries from a ground shrub which had grown over the step where he sat. His fingers were stained a dark purple. Looking at this stain reminded him of his cousin, Mercaster, the eldest son of his aunt's family. Casmeer and Mercaster had been the same age; spawned from identical sisters within a few days of each other. Both were dark in hair and fair of skin. Casmeer's mother's sister lived in a house a little way down the road, so the two women spent much time together as their first sons grew up. The children naturally became close. They fought a lot, but they loved one another. The love was painful and plaited with hate. Mercaster had been such an abiding presence in Casmeer's childhood. Now, he wondered how he'd survived the experience.

'They are so alike, it is incredible,' Casmeer's mother had once said, beaming in maternal joy as the two women viewed the boys tumbling like cubs together on the lawn behind the house.

'Yes, they could be twins,' said Casmeer's aunt.

Physically, the boys were very similar, but in their hearts they were not.

Mercaster was cunning and cruel; Casmeer was naive and gentle. Mercaster was brave, Casmeer cowered. Mercaster liked to inflict pain, Casmeer wanted caresses. They were, in fact, very different.

Often, their games together ended with Casmeer being hurt, which he had to lie about to his parents. 'I fell, I tripped, a branch hit me.' Once, Mercaster pinned him down on his back and knelt on his chest to inflict a series of agonising drumming pokes with stiff fingers to Casmeer's breast-bone. 'I am your dark brother,' said Mercaster, 'as you are the lighter side of me. Together, we make a whole.'

Mercaster had an aura which to Casmeer was purple, like berry-juice. It surrounded him always. He had died in his twenty-second year, murdered by a woman he had imprisoned and repeatedly raped. She had been more clever than he'd assumed; perhaps Mercaster's greatest fault was that he made grand assumptions based upon little evidence.

Casmeer had not mourned Mercaster's death and had contributed generously to the donation which his family felt driven to make to the victim of Mercaster's perverse obsessions. The woman had accepted the money with poor grace, and had accused Mercaster's mother of being responsible for her son's depravities. She had looked at Casmeer in a different way, almost with fear. He had wanted to say, 'I can tell what you're thinking, but no: we are very different.' He had said nothing in the event, but turned away, hid his face.

At the funeral, he'd met Elini. Strange, he thought, strange how events are linked.

Chapter Thirteen
God-riding

A species of creature that seemed to be part giant insect, part reptile, inhabited the flat-lands, scavenging amongst the detritus that the great cities left in their wakes. These creatures were known by many different names, but the terranauts called them slivellers. The creatures were composed of great plates of chitinous armour, in colour a dull grey, although disposed to pink along the underbelly. They possessed a multitude of segmented legs, and an array of horned feelers. Slivellers were placid creatures that fed only on vegetable matter, preferably decaying. They were also host to several species of parasite, one of them human. The terranauts referred rather scathingly to these people as sliv-sitters, or slivsits. They were a small, swarthy-skinned people whom Oon said had too many children, most of which died.

'If you are to travel this land in entirety,' said Oon to Ays, 'and experience all that is on offer, you must ride with the slivsits, for as long as your nose can bear it.'

Ays took offence at Oon's advice, mainly because he thought it meant she had become bored of him, or found him a nuisance, and wished he'd move on.

'What if I want to stay with the terranauts?' he snapped.

Oon gave him an enigmatic look. 'You wouldn't for long.'

'I have lost sight of my purpose!'

'I know. So why waste any more time?'

'You seem to care more about my search than I do now,' Ays remarked, not without sarcasm.

Oon shrugged. 'I hardly think so!'

Ays wished he did not feel disappointed that Oon displayed no concern. He thought with some affection of his old friends back on Min, who'd been sorry to see him go. The only person who cared about him now was Leeth, and her intensity often irritated him. Sometimes, when he looked up and caught sight of her dark, thin face, he wanted to slap her.

'You have a sense of responsibility towards that child?' Oon asked him once.

He shrugged. 'No, that is . . . Sometimes, I wish she hadn't left the train with me. At first, I thought I wouldn't be able to survive without her, but now . . .'

Oon made a mocking sound. 'As long as you are loyal to imposed ideals, you will remain . . .'

'Remain what?'

'Nothing.'

In a spurt of sudden anger, Ays resolved he would leave the terranauts as soon as a convenient opportunity presented itself.

'You are right,' he said firmly. 'It's time to make a change.'

If he hoped his words would inspire chagrin in Oon, he was wrong, but perhaps it was hard to tell what she was thinking?

As if the webs of destiny had been waiting for this conversation to take place, a sliveller was sighted later that day. It lurched into view over a gentle incline, alongside which the terranaut group was passing. Ays was astounded at the noise it made; a constant grating creak.

At the sight of the terranauts a group of people emerged like lice from between the sliveller's plates and hurried forward, intent on bartering.

Oon, travelling with Leeth and Ays on the back of a wagon, explained in a bored voice how the slivsits wove yarn, of exceedingly good quality but rather drab in colour, from a soft fuzz that grew from the underside of the plates. This they traded for anything that people were willing to exchange.

'Of course they want pilot-stones,' drawled Oon, 'but they'll never get them. We give them volcanic chard and clinker in return and they think themselves hard bargainers!' She laughed at the thought.

'Is the sliveller intelligent?' Ays asked.

'I wouldn't presume to judge,' Oon answered.

The creature was adorned with poles that appeared to have been stuck in between its segments. These were festooned with fluttering rags that might have been washing strung out to dry or else decoration of some kind. From this distance it was impossible to tell.

The slivsits were now haranguing a group of terranauts near the front of the troupe. They waved their arms in expansive gestures, while others held out their produce for inspection. The terranaut line had come to a halt.

'Want me to arrange an introduction?' Oon asked, as she and Ays gazed at the slivsits.

Ays gave her a hard look. 'What is it to you whether I stay or go?' A needle of martyrdom threaded the bones of his spine as she refused to answer. 'Yes, all right,' he said.

Oon put her fingers in her mouth and whistled shrilly. The slivsits responded immediately, a couple of them running towards the wagon in a bent-kneed, ducking gait, as if they were avoiding some low-flying hazard. A wizened man arrived first, his arms full of a floating, silky stuff. Ays looked at the man's own clothes; they were coarse and stiff. Clearly, the slivsits did not use their fabulous yarn themselves.

'Look, look!' exclaimed the slivsit. 'I'd swap my cleeks for a hank such as this.' He displayed the yarn to better effect. 'Observe the way it traps the light . . .'

'Yes, yes, beautiful,' said Oon impatiently. 'I'll give you this boy and this rather unattractive child in exchange for your hank.'

Ays made a spluttered protest, and Leeth whined in outrage. 'A joke,' Oon said with a careless gesture of her hand. 'Have you room for land-lopers upon your sliveller?'

The man shrugged. 'Anyone may enter among the plates,' he replied. 'If they are an irritant, they are expelled. The decision does not rest in our hands.'

'Well, there you are then,' said Oon, patting Ays on the back. 'Better gather up your belongings and jump down, before we move off.' She pushed Ays off the wagon quite roughly. 'It was nice meeting you.'

He was annoyed that Oon's casual farewell came as a surprise.

The smell of the sliveller hit the nose from several yards distant. Surprisingly, it was not altogether unpleasant, being salty sweet and musky, but so strong it made Ays want to gag. The slivsit who'd offered them the yarn told them his name was Bockstave, and that he was a member of the estimable family Raughty, residents of the beast.

Ays and Leeth gingerly followed Bockstave beneath the awning of a plate which had been propped open while the sliveller was being fed morsels it particularly enjoyed and was therefore stationary. Ays had had visions of people wedged tightly between the chitinous plates, but discovered there was more room beneath the sliveller's carapace than he'd imagined. The body of the beast was comparatively slim, and the undersides of its plates had been buttressed into position so as to provide a series of small rooms. The floor was made of plaited branches which were fixed to outer edges of the plates with large metal staples, and to the body of the sliveller itself with silver rings that pierced its hide. Dozens of bright eyes gleamed in the shadows; the women and children of the Raughtys who had not ventured outside to deal with the terranauts. All were clad in shapeless garments of rough-spun cloth, yet they worked upon wooden looms, weaving the sumptuous yarn harvested from the soft furze that grew on the undersides of the plates and against the sliveller's body. No one greeted the newcomers, but neither did they show any hostility, simply a cautious curiosity.

'Find a space as best you can,' Bockstave advised. 'We've entertained gadlings before, and we don't expect payment for our hospitality. However, an offer of help with the weaving would not go unappreciated.' With these words, he scurried back outside.

'It stinks in here!' Leeth hissed.

'Oh, be quiet!' Ays replied. 'You didn't like the terranauts, so don't complain now we've parted company with them.'

Leeth made a disgruntled sound and sat down upon the floor, complaining to herself that it was far from comfortable to sit on and that she could do with a cushion. Hearing her complaints, a slivsit child tiptoed forward and offered Leeth a folded blanket which she accepted with poor grace. Ays sighed and stood beside the opening, watching the slivsits conclude their business with the terranauts. He could see no sign of Oon.

Presently, the men swarmed back on board and the

opening was let down, so as to wrap the occupants of the beast in a moist, oily twilight. The remains of the food had been taken away from the sliveller's mouth-parts and it soon began to trundle forth once more in a gentle rocking motion. The movement and the smells made Ays drowsy, and before too long he fell asleep.

The slivsits kept a divine gelding in the innermost cavities of the beast. The boy was blind, pale, pawing at darkness, uttering gobbets of wisdom down the years. The hairy feelers of the beast, scrabbling through loose dirt, blind antennae nosing the earth, mirrored the blind groping of the gelded boy hidden among its parts.

Life aboard the beast was bizarre; the creature rocked from side to side, or undulated, but very soon the rhythm of it became compelling, needed. The Raughtys called the beast Beraftiel; they considered it to be a god, although they knew that a few generations forward, it would die and have to be burned and eaten. Then, a new god would have to be found, or the family would die out. Ays told them he had worshipped a living goddess too, although the Raughtys said that female beasts were too small to be lived in and therefore not divine. They comprehended no divinity that was not plated and segmented. Beraftiel gave them life; they farmed its lice and other parasites, milked its scent glands, for the liquor they produced was very nutritious. Ays found it too pungent and sweet; it seemed unnatural that the juice of the beast should be sweet. When Beraftiel scented a female in its path, it would trundle forward, uttering a beautiful fluting call, a bugling of love. Then pots, pans, mattresses, and all other living appointments would have to be tied down while the beast mounted his paramour. The people would copulate amongst themselves in honour of the blessed union of their god.

'Beasts do not make love,' Ays said.

'Gods do,' he was told.

The Raughtys did indeed have an abundance of children, as Oon had suggested, and it was also true that they were sickly creatures. Three died while Ays and Leeth lived upon Beraftiel. Ays wondered whether the sliveller itself was responsible for the poor health of its inhabitants; it provided food and shelter, but perhaps its liquors and perfumes were toxic?

The Raughtys made Beraftiel stop often so that they could trade with passing cities or terranaut groups. Beraftiel seemed, to Ays, a placid and gentle creature; it certainly didn't attempt to dispel its new inhabitants, and anything that could tolerate the irritant presence of Leeth had to be a temperate soul, Ays thought.

Leeth was getting worse. It was as if she needed and wanted something from Ays, but would not speak plainly about it, or even offer signals of a definite nature. He was sure it wasn't simply love or protection she was after, but something more profound which she was perhaps unable to define herself. Her feelings for him obviously ran deep, because she was waspish with him to the point of farce. He wasn't sure how old she was, but sometimes he caught her looking at him, as if she was cursing her lack of years. When he thought this, Ays shuddered. He couldn't imagine anyone less attractive than Leeth; her ugliness was on the inside, something damp and cold and dark. He was glad she was not yet a woman.

The Raughtys, on the other hand, were gregarious and friendly, if not overly intimate. There were perhaps thirty of them resident on Beraftiel, and half of those were under the age of ten. Ays soon came to realise that all slivsits died young, before reaching forty, and that Bockstave, whom at first he'd thought to be an old man, was only thirty-two. Still, despite their frail constitutions, they were patient and tolerant people.

Beraftiel had been halted so that the Raughtys could trade with a city that was passing nearby. The slivsits built a fire outside the beast, and the men and their older male children sat beside it to talk into the night. The blind gelding was brought out and decorated with garlands of plaited wild grass. He gibbered prophecies at the sky which the men appeared to pay little attention to. Ays joined them after having some difficulty leaving Leeth inside, even though he pointed out to her that it was considered a breach of etiquette for women to go outside. It was a relief to get away from her for a few hours; travelling on Beraftiel could often be claustrophobic.

Ays surreptitiously chewed on a wad of hela and gazed up at the bulk of the city. It was an astounding place; scintillant as if it had been carved from crystal. The evening breeze, winding through its towers, conjured a mournful, eerie music which reminded Ays of the wind orchestra. What had happened to his mysterious pursuer? Perhaps Ays had simply dreamed him up?

Bockstave settled down beside him, a jar of sliveller-juice in his hand. 'Ah, a splendid sight!' he said, nodding at the city.

'Yes . . . I would like to see every city. There seem to be no two the same, and each is more amazing than the last.'

Bockstave chuckled. 'Better seen from this vantage than from within!'

Ays nodded. 'Yes. I have seen many cities but have entered only one since leaving Min. The experience left a bitter taste.'

'True, true,' agreed Bockstave. 'The people of a city are the cells of its mind and tend to resent the intrusion of alien thoughts.'

'Unlike Beraftiel.'

Bockstave shrugged. 'Beraftiel is a tolerant Being, but He will not suffer dangerous souls.'

Ays laughed. 'I am almost ashamed to be so harmless!'

Bockstave shook his head. 'No, take pride in it! This world is full of strange characters, but no doubt you've encountered a few.'

'Not really. Perhaps I've been lucky?' Ays sighed and leaned back on straight arms. 'Sometimes, being alive feels like inhabiting a dream. Where do they all come from, these cities? What makes them come into being?'

'There are many theories about it,' Bockstave said. 'But there is one that I'm particularly fond of.'

'Tell me about it.'

Bockstave pulled his face into a sheepish grin. 'It is not the most likely . . .'

'I'd still like to hear it.'

'Well, there is a legend that at one time most of the flat-lands were covered by a salty sea. The first cities formed beneath the water, and were inhabited by fish that had hands instead of fins. Gradually, as the sun grew hotter, the waters receded, and the fish had to learn how to breathe air. Eventually, they had to contrive means whereby the cities, which were now crammed together in the ever-receding brine, could venture out on to the land. The first cities that crawled out of the water were encrusted with salt and shone in the moonlight, and blinded those with unblinkered eyes by day, so radiantly did they shine.'

Ays had closed his eyes, and through the agency of hela could easily visualise the sight. 'That is a lovely story,' he said. 'But it does not explain how new cities come into being now.'

'That's simple to answer,' Bockstave replied. 'When a city dies, and its inhabitants flee or become calentured, it breaks into a thousand parts, and each part takes with it a few mazed citizens of the original city. They have forgotten their pasts, forgotten everything they learned, so society has to begin again. Eventually, they rediscover science and engineering, and then the cities are expanded upon, until they become too big and die once more, only to spawn a thousand new ones. Not all the new cities survive, of course, otherwise the flat-lands would be covered in them.'

'And where do the terranauts fit into this theory?'

Bockstave shook his head and grinned. 'Ah, now I could tell you a dozen stories about them.'

'And which is your favourite?'

Bockstave shrugged. 'I simply believe the terranauts guide the cities because they always have done. It is the will of the slivellers. Everyone in the world has a part to play in the great drama of life.'

Ays gave Bockstave a sidelong glance, wondering if he was being serious or not. 'Do you really believe the story about how the cities came about?'

'Do you have a better explanation?'

'No. I would have to see it happen though.'

Bockstave laughed. 'Strangely, no one of an older culture ever does. It's one of the mysteries of life.' He stood up. 'Well, I'm for bed. Are you coming?'

'No, I'll stay here awhile.'

'Then goodnight.'

Ays closed his eyes and experienced the moonshine on his skin, picked up by the delicate senses of hela-rapture. Behind him, he could hear the soft gibberings of the gelding; a confused, saddening and lonely sound.

We are all calentured, Ays thought. All of us. This

whole world is nothing but the delusion of a fevered mind.

He opened his eyes, and the sight of the crystal city, in all its splendour, came at his sensitive pupils like a hail of spears.

'Mazed and addled,' he said aloud, 'but beautiful all the same.' Perhaps it was an effect of the hela, or the romantic mood of the evening, but sitting there basking in the radiance of the city, Ays felt strongly that there something – someone – just beyond the reach of his perceptions, someone who was waiting to approach him. He sensed a yearning in the cool, night air. 'Come forth!' he murmured, closing his eyes once more, and throwing back his head, so that his hair pooled on the ground behind him. 'Show yourself!'

Did he imagine the rustle of garments, the brief touch of fingers on his brow? He opened his eyes, expecting revelation, but there was no one there.

The men groomed and polished Beraftiel's plates as He moved along. With the use of cleeks, long-handled hooks, they bounded from segment to segment and removed detritus and parasites from between the plates. Ays offered to help because he liked to stand upon the beast's broad back and watch the countryside pass by. As time passed, he developed a fondness for Beraftiel, and came to sense His personality. It became easy to understand why the Raughtys worshipped Him. He was like a small city, providing most of what His inhabitants required, including an individual sense of community.

Leeth too developed a grudging tenderness for the beast and His inhabitants. At first, she'd found the women boring, and despised their fear of the outside, but with time, she realised she had been wrong to judge them so harshly. Their perceptions were simply different from hers. Ays still caused her a problem, and she knew she was driving him further away by her abrasive remarks and cool demeanour. Still, the frustration she felt because of his enduring indifference to her forced her into behaviour she knew was self-defeating. Sometimes, she thought about confiding in her new friends, but something prevented her from doing so. She did not fear ridicule, but felt the Raughty women, who were all naturally demonstrative, would decide to take the matter into their own hands, and try to force Ays to form a physical relationship with Leeth. The slivsit women shared all the men of the group between them, and fell in and out of love all the time, although there was never any jealousy among them. Leeth listened wistfully to their conversations. Once, someone asked her a direct question concerning Ays. 'We are like brother and sister,' she'd replied, and had turned away from the knowing looks and lewd titters that followed her disclosure.

Beraftiel was heading in an easterly direction which Bockstave said would eventually lead them to an inland sea where the beast could be anointed with brine and certain seasonal rituals would take place. Ays decided he would stay with the Raughtys until then, if only because he had never seen a sea. He did not bother to consult Leeth about it. She had struck up a friendship with a couple of the young women, and now appeared quite happy to help them with their weaving. Ays was naturally suspicious. He suspected Leeth would not be content to live the sheltered, quiet life of a Raughty woman, and guessed that she must have ulterior motives for being so co-operative with them. Once Ays overhead one of the women talking to Leeth about how to weave a love spell into the yarn she was working on. He wondered what Leeth had told them about him, and couldn't suppress a shudder.

Beraftiel, for reasons of His own, ventured beneath the canopy of a forest. The trees were widely spaced; thick-trunked with all their foliage very high overhead. The forest-floor was covered in a dark green lush grass that was starred with tiny white flowers and small, round, milky-white fruit. All were well nibbled by forest animals. Ancient large ferns clustered around the bottoms of the trees like feathery skirts, and the trunks were laddered with broad plates of fungus which the Raughtys sawed off and cooked like meat. The forest was silent at ground level, although the sounds of animals and birds could be heard overhead; a muted, distant song. Ays liked the forest, although it also made him feel edgy. It was so vast, the light in it so thick, like green wine. It seemed to breathe, to watch him. Beraftiel moved slowly, grazing on the flowers and fruits.

One evening, Ays climbed Beraftiel's plates and lay down alone on the beast's back, staring up at forest canopy until his eyes watered. A cold breath came down from the sky; the season was turning. Soon, it would be cold and the leaves would fall. Ays had taken to talking to Beraftiel, especially when he'd been chewing or smoking hela. It felt as if he was speaking into a space where his words were collected and *felt*. He was sure Beraftiel understood him, and sometimes, when he spoke, an idea would come into his head that he thought might come from the beast. The Raughtys were all convinced they could communicate telepathically with Beraftiel, but until recently Ays had discounted their claims as being nothing more than religious beliefs.

A sound came from below which at first Ays ignored. All the Raughtys were inside Beraftiel, but it was possible someone had come out to attend to something or simply walk through the forest for a while. Perhaps they would join him shortly? He looked forward to a few hours' pleasant conversation. Suddenly, Beraftiel fluted a sound of distress and came to an abrupt halt, rearing up on His first few segments. Ays found himself sliding to the ground. Raughty men immediately came hurrying out from inside to investigate the trouble. They rushed to Beraftiel's head to check He hadn't damaged himself while grazing. Ays picked himself up off the floor. Luckily, he hadn't landed awkwardly, although his shoulder had taken a painful knock.

'What's happening?' he asked one of the men.

'Some clenchpoop poked Beraftiel in the face!' he replied. Ays followed him to the knot of men who were gathered around Beraftiel's head. They were talking to a stranger, a tall man in a cloak and hat. For a moment, Ays' blood stilled in his body, because he thought it might be the Blue Feather Man, but it quickly became evident that this was someone else. The man took off his hat, which was decorated with an abundance of dyed feathers and colourful ribbons. He bowed, and Ays heard him say, 'Fineas Rigg at your service!' The man was grinning widely, in a way that suggested he was being condescending. He was handsome, with a look of the rogue about him. Ays immediately sensed danger, as perhaps had Beraftiel.

'What were you thinking of, poking our Lord in the face with that stick!' Bockstave said in a voice of outrage.

Fineas Rigg shrugged apologetically. 'I wanted to attract your attention, and the beast would not stop.'

'A simple tap upon the plates would have been sufficient to alert us,' another man said.

'Well, I'm sorry,' Fineas said. 'Please take pity on me. I have been travelling for days through this blighted wood, with nothing to eat, and now my water carrier is dry.'

'There is plenty to eat around here,' Bockstave said gruffly. 'Fungus, fruit, the spores of ferns.'

Fineas shrugged again. 'Plenty if you know what is and what is not poisonous.' He caught sight of Ays, who towered over the diminutive Raughtys. 'Ah, I see you have another visitor. Can I come aboard?' He indicated a small cart which was covered with a leather blanket. 'I have scant luggage, and won't take up much room.'

The Raughtys reluctantly agreed, because it was not in their nature to be inhospitable, but they were clearly unhappy about the situation. Ays wondered whether Beraftiel would expel Fineas Rigg. How would He do that?

Ays hung back while the Raughtys struggled to push the cart through one of the plate apertures. Fineas Rigg approached him. Ays had a horrible feeling of recognition which was nothing to do with appearances, or any kindling of memory. There was something else through which he and Rigg were akin, and Ays far from liked the thought of that.

Fineas Rigg must also have identified the recognition. He reached out and pinched one of Ays' eyebrows; an odd gesture. 'I feel we have much in common.'

Ays stepped back. 'I can't see how you can say that, considering we haven't yet become acquainted.'

Fineas raised an eyebrow and laughed. 'It's in your eyes, my friend, your eyes. I've no doubt it's in your breath too.' He put his hand in his pocket and removed a small packet, wrapped in waxed paper, which he held to Ays' nose.

'Hela,' said Ays.

Fineas Rigg lived by selling hela. His main customers were terranauts, all of whom had a tolerance for the drug, but he also traded with apothecaries on the cities who used the substance in certain of their philtres and medicines. Ays could not help but be intrigued by Rigg's profession. Until he'd left Min, he'd believed that hela was holy, and used only by the Minnian priests and priestesses. It was a shock to discover how widely it was used upon the ground.

'A dangerous mistress,' Fineas said, sniffing a pinch of powdered dried hela. They were nearing the edge of the forest, and Fineas had decided to spend most of his time with Ays, sitting on Beraftiel's back. Ays knew the Raughtys didn't like Rigg being inside the beast, so tolerated the man's presence outside for their sake, even though it curtailed his private communion sessions with Beraftiel. He had very mixed feelings about Fineas Rigg; in some ways he was interesting and attractive as a personality, in others he was seriously unpleasant, although Ays could never specify how exactly. Fineas was always polite and friendly.

'Where do you obtain the plant?' Ays asked.

'Aha!' said Fineas, tapping his nose. 'That is a secret, but rest assured that my family have cropped hela for centuries. We have secret farms at the foothills of the mountain ring, where the water is crystal clear and good for the harvest. If you ever found it, you would be killed before the scent of the flowers ever hit your nose.'

Ays grimaced. 'Then I shall avoid any farms at the foot of the mountains.'

'Don't worry, you'll never find them,' said Fineas airily. He leaned forward in a conspiratorial manner. 'Anyway, I have my own personal farm that I carry with me always.'

'Oh?' Ays felt a sudden need for caution sweep over him, so strongly he thought it might have come from Beraftiel.

'Yes. Look.' Fineas opened his coat, and Ays' first

thought was that the man grew hela as Ays did, in his coat lining. But Fineas was unlacing his shirt. He pulled it up out of his trousers and lifted it to his armpits to display his torso. 'Well, what do you think of that?'

Ays made a sound of astounded disgust. Fineas had hela growing all over his skin, burrowing into it, in fact. His flesh was discoloured and flaky. 'That looks . . . painful,' Ays said lamely.

Fineas shook his head. 'A little uncomfortable at times, but a swift snort of hela dust puts paid to any irritation.'

'Mmm.'

Fineas laughed. 'Don't look so sceptical, my young friend! Be thankful such as I exist, otherwise you wouldn't be able to buy your precious hela!'

'I suppose not.'

Two days later, Beraftiel left the cover of the trees and emerged into a greener landscape than that on the other side of the forest. The land sloped down gently towards a wide plain, dotted by spinneys of ancient trees. Here, a bright ribbon of light could be seen bisecting the land: a river. Cities of medium size had been drawn to it and several were stationary beside its banks, extending their aqueduct pipes into the water. Beraftiel was given a special meal in order to halt His progress, and the Raughtys all came out of the beast in order to ramble the countryside. Even the women and children emerged, yawning and stretching as if they'd been asleep. The men carried out panniers of food to eat in the open, while the women uncorked jars of alcoholic liquor, fermented from Beraftiel's essences. The divine gelding was guided out and helped to sit down on the grass. Leeth crouched like a black spider among the small Raughty women, her accusing eyes occasionally straying to where Ays stood alone. He realised he hadn't spoken to her for days, since he'd been forced into the company of Fineas Rigg. Perhaps Rigg's acquaintance did have its compensations after all?

Rigg came to stand beside Ays, and pantomimed a shudder. 'Time to move south very soon,' he said. 'Can't stand cold weather.'

'I've never noticed any difference between north and south,' Ays said.

Fineas gave him a narrow glance. 'Then you can't have travelled far.'

'My city never went to the mountains, but it ranged quite widely.' For some reason, he didn't want to explain that Min flew. He knew Fineas would ask lots of questions he couldn't answer. He realised he didn't really know exactly how big the flat-lands were, and wished he'd kept his mouth shut.

Fineas, however, dropped the subject, much to Ays' relief, although his next topic was hardly congenial. 'That girl's very strange,' he said, nodding towards Leeth.

'Each to their own,' Ays replied.

Fineas ignored the glacial tone to Ays' remark. 'How old is she?'

'I've no idea.'

Fineas rubbed his chin. 'She has a hot, dark air about her. It's frustrated virginity, you know.'

'That's disgusting!' Ays spluttered.

'Oh, why?' Fineas actually sounded surprised.

'Well,' Ays said awkwardly, gesturing, 'look at her! She's . . . well, I just don't like to think of her in that way.'

Fineas laughed. 'Myself, I like a little of the unusual!' He paused to consider. 'I might liven her life up a little.'

Ays felt sickened. 'She's only a child.'

'She's small, granted, but that's a budding woman, not a child.'

Ays was amazed anyone could think of Leeth as 'budding'. To him, she was dry and withered, used up before her time.

'Want to join me?' Fineas enquired.

'In what?' Ays snapped.

'Seducing the little creature.'

Ays shuddered. 'No.' He wondered whether he should try to protect Leeth from Fineas. For all she discomfited him, he couldn't help but feel a little responsible for her welfare, and Fineas was, to his mind, hardly a suitable first lover. Hopefully, Leeth would reject his advances.

'Suit yourself,' said Fineas nonchalantly. 'But observe. I'll show you how to make a woman bloom. I've no doubt the change will astound you.'

Ays made no comment, but watched carefully as Fineas sauntered over to the group of women, and bowed extravagantly to Leeth. She glanced over at Ays before responding. Receiving no signal from him obviously prompted her to smile up at Fineas, encouraging him to sit beside her. Ays turned away. He had no wish to observe Fineas at work, and the idea of Leeth as a sensual being was utterly repulsive to him.

Leeth herself had no particular interest in Fineas Rigg. She accepted he was attractive in a rakish sort of way, but she disliked the aura of cold callousness that seemed to surround him. Still, he lost no time in making it clear to her that he found her presentable, and would like to indulge in a little dalliance. His smooth words seemed to glide right over her head; their specious shapes meant nothing to her, yet she intuited the hot, grunting actions inside the dainty sounds. Ignoring his convoluted sentences of seduction, she thought to herself: Do I want this? Is it time? She looked over at Ays, who was now talking to Bockstave.

'What did you say to him?' she asked Fineas, interrupting him mid-sentence.

'What?' Fineas looked annoyed.

Leeth gestured at Ays. 'Did you tell him you liked me?'

Fineas shrugged. 'I suppose so. What does it matter? Are you after him?'

Leeth lowered her eyes. 'No. We are just companions. I thought he might object to you talking to me. He's like that: a bit over-protective.'

Fineas puffed up with male pride. 'I'm sure you're capable of protecting yourself, damsel Leeth.'

As evening came down, and the lights of the cities beside the river shone out into the twilight, the Raughtys built a fire around which the women danced to the tune of instruments played by the children. Ays went to sit with Bockstave and his sister Amily.

'Leeth seems to have found a friend,' said Amily.

Ays couldn't help but detect some censure of himself in her words. 'If it gives her a little pleasure,' he said, 'I hardly think we can interfere.'

Amily made a sound of disagreement. 'I'd want no daughter of mine near that man – he is a carrion lizard. Beraftiel has not been happy since he joined us.'

'Then why not ask him to leave?' Ays asked.

'It is not our place,' Bockstave replied. 'If Beraftiel wants him gone, He will emit an irritant at the place where Rigg sleeps. Living with us will then become unbearable, and he will have no choice but to leave.'

Ays thought of Fineas Rigg's personal hela farm, and decided it would take rather more than that to cause the man discomfort.

'I think you should say something to Leeth,' Amily announced, fixing Ays with a stern glance.

'Me? Why? I'm not her relative. We were only travelling together.'

'She is very fond of you, and will listen to your words.'

'I don't want that responsibility,' he replied stiffly. 'Neither have I any wish to encourage her attachment to me. I can't give her what she wants.'

'You are strange,' Amily said. 'You seem such a good-natured person. How can you be so hard on poor Leeth?'

'There is nothing worse than the adoration of a person you find unattractive,' Bockstave remarked.

Amily nodded thoughtfully. 'True, true, but it still seems sad for her.'

All three of them glanced to where Leeth sat with Fineas by the fire. He was playing with her hair, while she blinked at him in a hideous parody of girlish glee. At that moment, Ays wished he'd never have to set eyes on her again. He thought about how they had got on well together on the *Whiteknuckle Rush*; it hardly seemed as if Leeth was the same girl now. If only he'd been able to see into the future, he'd never have brought her with him.

Leeth knew the moment would come when Fineas Rigg would want her to slope off somewhere private with him. Although it seemed clear that Ays had little interest in the matter, Leeth knew she would have to gather all her courage in her hands and face him before anything happened with Rigg. Even if it only earned her the most crushing humiliation, she could not surrender herself to a man other than Ays, without knowing definitely that Ays would never want her. She watched him steadily from the corner of her eye while she dutifully giggled at Rigg's fatuous remarks. Drinking the Raughtys' liquor seemed to calm her nerves, give her strength. When Ays eventually stood up and went into a nearby clump of shrubs to relieve himself, Leeth made an excuse to Rigg, leapt up swiftly and crept up on Ays in the bushes.

When he saw her, Ays cried out in outrage. 'Go away! Can't you see what I'm doing?'

Leeth glanced behind herself and then moved closer, pulling the dense branches of a tall shrub across the path behind her. 'I want to . . . I *need* to talk to you,' she hissed. 'Please.'

'What about?' Ays adjusted his clothing and made to walk out of the trees.

Leeth grabbed his arm to stop him. 'That man, Fineas, he is paying me certain attentions.'

'So?' Ays' eyes were cold as a grey sky. If he had any interest in the matter, he had no intention of letting it show.

Leeth felt a panicking despair well up within her. Maybe she should run away now, before her defeat became more devastating, but her mouth, directed by her heart and loosened by liquor, ignored the advice of her common sense. 'Doesn't it bother you?'

Ays shrugged, and frowned. 'Why should it? Rigg and I are nothing to one another.'

At these words, Leeth felt her shame transform instantly to a burning anger. She was pleased when Ays took an involuntary step backwards.

'How dare you! You know perfectly well I wasn't talking about you and Rigg.'

Ays' eyes had widened. Leeth felt, without much satisfaction, that he was a little afraid of her.

'Well, if you were implying a relationship between you and me the idea is even less credible!'

Leeth gestured at him wildly, causing him to flinch. 'What is wrong with you?' she demanded. 'You wanted to be with me once, I know you did! You were happy to leave the *Rush* with me!'

'Leeth, we were friends,' Ays said. His voice had assumed a more conciliatory tone. 'It was never any more than that.'

'Liar!' she cried. The season of her emotions had turned again; now it was misery, drawing a mist of tears across her heart. She felt them brimming, about to break. Her voice was shaking. The confession, when it came, was irresistible; it had to be said. 'I love you. I was saving myself for you, and that is something so special! How dare you disregard such a precious thing!'

Is there anything worse, Leeth wondered, than facing a person you adore, weeping as you tell them of your feelings, and seeing only frozen winter in their eyes? Not even embarrassment. Just utter coldness.

Ays' voice was toneless. 'Leeth, I had no idea you felt that way. I am flattered, but . . .'

'But! But!' Leeth shook her head. 'I told myself that we were meant to meet, *meant*! And part of me still believes that.'

'You have a crush on me, Leeth, that's all,' Ays said in a chillingly cheerful voice. 'And I'm afraid your feelings aren't returned. Now, just calm down, and we'll forget we ever had this conversation. Come and sit with Bockstave, Amily and I. Fineas Rigg is untrustworthy and, I suspect, cruel. I can't be your man, Leeth, but I don't think Rigg should be either. Save yourself for someone special.'

Leeth uttered a strangled sound and turned away. She marched off, back towards Rigg, with the words, 'I'll do what I like!' Anger, misery and shame struggled in her breast like competing siblings; whichever one emerged victorious would grant her no comfort.

Ays watched her leave, astounded. He could see now what Fineas meant about Leeth's not being a child. Her size and her apparent naivety had perhaps disguised her true age.

'You'll regret it!' Ays called after her. He felt he had done all he could to dissuade her from impulsive action.

Before dawn, the Raughtys' party broke up and everyone wandered back into Beraftiel to sleep or make love. Ays went to the curtained cubby which had become his private space aboard the beast. Beside him, separated by only a width of fabric, he could hear Fineas Rigg uttering sweet words to Leeth and her soft responding giggles. He hoped that whatever carnal business they'd conducted was now concluded, but it seemed Leeth must have been waiting for Ays' return. He heard her say in a breathy voice: 'I'm ready now, Fineas.' And Rigg's response, 'Well, aren't you!' It sounded as if she'd consumed a vast amount of the Raughtys' liquor.

Ays considered going back outside and sleeping in the open air, but the pre-dawn air was chill and he had no idea what predators might be about. In annoyance he put his pillow over his head, but it was insufficient soundproofing to drown out the sound of Leeth's anxious mews, and Fineas Rigg's deep grunts. The curtain between them and Ays shook and occasionally a limb would come through and strike him on the side or the head.

'Oh, it hurts!' cried Leeth. The whole Raughty family must have been able to hear her. Ays turned on his side. If Leeth thought this was some kind of spiteful revenge, she was wrong. He pulled off a few strands of hela from his coat, more than he'd usually consume in one go, and chewed the lot. Fairly soon, the sounds of Leeth and her lover faded out of his consciousness, and he dreamed a dream of bright water and laughter. The shadow of the Blue Feather Man haunted the perimeter of the dream images; a watching shadow.

* * *

Beraftiel had clearly had enough of Fineas Rigg. The next morning, he complained of a rash on his arms which itched continually. Bockstave gave Ays a significant glance and smiled, indicating that soon they would see the last of Mr Rigg. Leeth hid behind her curtain and wouldn't come out, not even when her friends came to ask how she was. Beraftiel lumbered forward at a faster pace than usual, and filled the air with a bitter odour.

'What's wrong with the beast?' Fineas asked Bockstave.

'You,' was the terse reply. 'You might as well get down now and give us all peace of mind.'

Fineas laughed lightly, scratching his arm. 'Not likely! I need a ride to the river at least. You'll all have to put up with me until then, you and your great beast.'

At his words, Beraftiel emitted a puff of acrid scent which caused everyone to cough. Fineas Rigg pulled Leeth's curtain aside and sat down beside her in full view of everyone. She was sitting hunched up and miserable, her face more gaunt than usual. She would not look at anyone.

Leeth was caught in a stupefying numbness, unable to think about the previous evening. She felt she had done something very stupid, and that everyone knew about it. The thought of seeing Ays, whom she knew must have heard every squeak of her lovemaking with Rigg, made her stomach turn. How could she ever face him again? Her only desire, at that moment, was to disappear, to die.

Something evil seemed to have got into Fineas Rigg. He spent the entire day berating the Raughtys, kicking their possessions around and poking sharp objects into Beraftiel's body. Everyone looked on in painful silence, waiting for the beast to react. Ays felt that something terrible was about to happen, so great was his depression. Beraftiel had made the air almost unbreathable, so that certain of the plates had been propped open, a hazardous action during movement. Fineas Rigg discovered that the beast-juice was quite intoxicating to his system and demanded jugs of it to be brought to him, which he consumed with sloppy greediness.

'Leeth, my lovely Leeth!' he exclaimed, and laughed hysterically, reaching out to rip Leeth's dress down past her shoulders. Her skin was marked with dark contusions; either the result of Fineas' ardent caresses or else the effects of being rubbed by raw hela. 'Isn't she just so beautiful?' said Fineas Rigg. The entire community was silent, which seemed to enrage him.

'I want other women!' he shouted. 'Bring me your prettiest girl!'

'Bockstave, you must do something,' Ays said in a low voice. 'You can't let him behave like this!'

'Beraftiel will deal with it,' Bockstave answered patiently.

'So, will you let him abuse your women?'

'Beraftiel will not let it go that far!'

While they'd been talking, Fineas Rigg had continued to exhort the Raughtys with ever more outrageous demands. 'I want to see your ugliest boy ride the bones of my lovely Leeth! Bring him here now!'

Ays noticed that a dark, foaming liquid was emanating from Beraftiel's body around where Fineas and Leeth were sitting. Leeth looked stricken; terrified and humiliated. Fineas was now squeezing one of her small breasts. Her face was screwed up in pain, although she seemed too listless to move away from him. Ays could bear it no longer. He stepped in front of Rigg.

'Let her go.'

Rigg laughed up at Ays. 'If you want her, have her!'

He thrust Leeth away from him. 'She's a monster! I want beauty!' He stood up and shouldered past Ays, who hurried after him.

'You want nothing!' He grabbed Fineas Rigg's shoulder from behind. The Raughty women had rushed forward to drag Leeth away from the toxic pool dribbling from Beraftiel's flesh. She had started to weep.

Fineas Rigg swept round and punched Ays in the face. The blow was so unexpected, Ays crumpled to the ground, his head reeling. 'No one tells me what I want, or what to do!' Rigg adopted an aggressive stance. 'Is there anyone else who wants to try?'

The Raughty men looked on with sad faces. No one moved. A cunning gleam came into Fineas Rigg's eye. 'Ah, yes, I know what I shall have. I know exactly.' He ran down the length of the beast and pulled aside a patterned curtain. The Raughty women all began to shriek and the men stiffened into attitudes of horror. Uttering a cry of triumph, Fineas Rigg leaned forward and dragged a struggling figure from behind the curtain. It was the Raughtys' sacred eunuch.

'It is said a castrated boy is better than a woman!' declared Fineas Rigg.

Ays scrambled to his knees. The Raughtys, pacifists to the bone, would not fight Fineas Rigg. Ays was young, and not so strong as Rigg, but he couldn't countenance this outrage without trying to do something. He glanced around for a weapon, and picked up the first he came across: a saucepan.

Fineas Rigg had dragged the eunuch back down Beraftiel and was now systematically ripping off the boy's clothes while lunging forward occasionally to bite his throat. The Raughtys were all making pitiful noises of horror.

Ays leapt up and struck out with the saucepan, catching Fineas on the shoulder. He uttered a roar of rage, threw the eunuch away from him, and came for Ays with clawed hands. Ays stumbled backwards, holding out his arms to protect himself. Then Rigg paused and shook his head. 'No,' he said softly, folding his arms. 'I know how to deal with you.'

There was a moment's stasis, filled only with the suppressed whimpering of the Raughtys, the weeping of Leeth and the gasping of the eunuch. Ays realised Beraftiel had stopped moving. He could almost sense the beast listening to what was happening, planning what to do.

Fineas Rigg kicked Ays in the stomach and marched past him. He paused at the place where Ays kept his belongings. 'Your little friend is too talkative,' he said brightly, and picked up Ays' coat.

Ays struggled up, fighting against the pain in his belly, and threw himself forward to grab the coat, with a cry of 'No!'

Fineas Rigg stepped back daintily, wagging a finger at Ays. 'Ah, no, my dear boy, no. Watch this.' He grinned and then threw the coat into the spreading pool of Beraftiel's ooze. The fabric immediately began to smoke. Fineas jumped on to the coat and, as Ays watched in mute horror, performed a small jig. Then, he bowed. 'What jinks, what larks, what fun! Now, where was I?' His face hardened and he marched back towards the eunuch.

Ays could only stare in fascinated dread as his coat, his own hela farm, disintegrated in the caustic steam of Beraftiel's displeasure. Behind him, he heard the eunuch emit a groan of fear.

Then, the beast took action.

Afterwards, Ays would always remember the feeling that flooded through his mind, as Beraftiel suddenly reared up into a vertical column of rage and retaliation. The feeling was of love, of incomprehensible sorrow, of ending. Something vital had been irreparably damaged, something vital to Beraftiel's being.

Heat flashed out from the body of the beast, jets of stinking hot liquid spurted out, and then everything was aflame.

It was Leeth who dragged Ays from the conflagration, Leeth with her skirts smouldering, her hair singed, her face blackened. Beraftiel plunged and reared, his death throes violent and destructive, yet somehow Leeth found the strength to get herself and Ays away, thrown from one scalding plate to another as she dragged him outside. Once Ays was safe, she did not pause but put a corner of her skirt over her mouth, and plunged back into the conflagration – Beraftiel's shape now unrecognisable within the smoke and flames – to try and save others. Heat and smoke drove her back, but she managed to grab hold of the collar of a feebly moving figure who had crawled out of the smoke towards the light.

Lying panting on the ground, his vision blurred by sparkling dots of light, Ays felt the heat of Beraftiel's death scorch his skin. There were no cries to be heard from the Raughtys, and not one of them, but the for youth Leeth had hauled free, emerged from the smoke and flame.

Ays lay on his stomach on the grass, with Leeth kneeling over him, one hand on his shoulders. She was hiccuping with fear and shock, her whole body shaking. Nearby, the blackened body of the Raughty youth lay on its back, one hand twitching against the grass. For more than an hour, no one spoke or made significant movement. The sun sank down behind the forest, and the air turned cold.

Ays slowly pulled himself into a sitting position, and together he and Leeth stared in silence at the smoking ruin that only that morning had been a vibrant community. A charred coloured feather was borne on the breeze from Beraftiel's body; the only evidence that Fineas Rigg had ever existed.

'It's my fault,' Leeth murmured in husky voice. 'It's all my fault.'

Ays groaned. 'I can't comfort you,' he said. 'I can't.' In his heart, he couldn't really blame Leeth for Rigg's behaviour. She had simply been playing with fire, unaware of the consequences.

Leeth sighed deeply. 'I should die for what I've done.'

'What would another death accomplish?' Ays tried to stand, but the world swayed sickeningly before him. He tottered over to where the Raughty youth lay in the grass.

'Is he still alive?' Leeth asked, getting up.

Ays knelt down. He did not want to touch the boy's black, flaking skin. 'Yes . . .'

The Raughty boy's eyes opened as Leeth knelt down beside Ays. His mouth and his eyes were unnaturally red. Leeth felt sick. 'What can we do?' she asked Ays in desperation.

He sat back on his heels. 'I shall apply my craft,' he said. 'It's the least I can do.'

Leeth glanced at him sharply. 'No! No!' She extended her arms over the body. 'You can't do that. Kill him? No!'

Ays rubbed his filthy face wearily. 'The boy is in pain. Look at him! Why prolong the agony? I shall simply perform the ritual, and it will be over.'

'You have . . . you have no hela,' Leeth said.

Ays laced his fingers together and flexed them, cracking the knuckles. 'There are other ways. We are trained.'

Leeth shook her head. 'No, I can't allow this. I can't

sit here and watch you kill someone.' She stood up and turned her back. Her voice was agonised, sharp. 'How many times have you done this!' It was not a question.

'It will be an act of compassion . . .'

Leeth wheeled round. 'Will it? Has it ever been? You have no heart. You don't know what compassion is.'

She and Ays held each other's eyes for several long, awkward seconds. Then, Ays dropped his gaze. With one gentle finger, he touched the boy's face. 'Have you heard us?' he murmured. 'Have you heard this?' The boy made a sound. Ays closed his eyes briefly and nodded. 'Good. Listen to me. I am a Priest of Hands, and I am able to help you on your journey into death. Do you understand that?'

Again, a sound.

'I will ease your pain. I shall be with you. Now, you have to answer me clearly. Do you want my help?'

There was a moment's silence, and then a mournful, clear note came from the Raughty boy's ruined throat. His burned lips moved, and words came out. 'Help me . . .'

Leeth uttered a cry of sorrow, and put her hands over her mouth.

Ays threw back his head and blinked at the sky. Leeth saw his eyes were full of tears. 'Mother Darkness,' he said, 'come to us. Come to this far place . . .' His voice was as clear and as beautiful as a sacred bell in an empty wilderness.

Leeth wanted to turn away, but she could not. She watched Ays' hands hover over the body. He could not remove the clothes for they were burned into the flesh, but his hands, his long, mobile hands, fluttered like moths over the charred rags, luminous in the dusk, making slow, sinuous movements without touch. He had no music-maker, so he hummed a soft, tuneless melody as he worked. The sound of it made Leeth feel drowsy, removed all sense of reality from the scene. She felt she could see Ays gathering up a shining energy from the body, like gossamer yarn around his fingers. The evening was utter stillness around them, and Ays' hands, the hands of the Mother, closed around the boy's neck. It was so quick. Too quick. Such strength in such graceful hands.

Ays looked up at Leeth from where he knelt beside the body. His lovely face was puckered into a child's mask of misery.

'That is . . . this is the first time I've *truly* worked,' he said. Leeth hurried round to him, held him as he wept.

They had nothing to bury the body with, and it seemed pointless to cover it with handfuls of grass, so Leeth simply picked a few, straggling late flowers and laid them on the dead boy's breast. Ays had moved away, and had sat with his head in his hands for over an hour. Leeth had not disturbed him, honouring his time of privacy. She knelt beside him, quietly absorbed in her own thoughts. Something terrible had happened, yet she felt strangely cleansed and renewed. The sadness in her heart was a cloud over a rising light.

Ays made a movement, raised his head. 'We'll have to go to the river,' he said. 'To the cities.' He slowly got to his feet, and looked down at Leeth. She knelt with straight back, her hands laced in her lap, and seemed to him like a vision of death; too black, too ruined.

'I'm sorry, Ays,' she said. 'I'm sorry about everything, and especially about your coat. I shouldn't have told . . .'

'Don't say it,' Ays said wearily. 'Don't bother.'

Leeth stood up. 'I'll help you find more hela,' she suggested hopefully.

Ays checked his trouser pocket. 'It's not an immediate problem. I have a packet of dried fronds in here. If I'm careful, it will last a while.'

'Look at us!' Leeth cried, gesturing at her burned clothing. 'The city people will drive us away!'

Ays could not respond. He was beyond caring about anything. His body hurt, his skin was scorched, his friends were all dead. He had been grateful for Leeth's presence after he'd performed the death ritual with the Raughty boy, but his warm feelings had been all too brief. Now he resented the fact that the only person he had left was Leeth, the hated Leeth who loved him. Why did she have to be the only other person to survive? He wished she'd perished in the flames.

'Do you think we should check for . . . survivors?' Leeth asked.

Ays made a bitter sound. 'Go ahead!' He began to walk unsteadily down the slope towards the city lights. Had people watched Beraftiel and the Raughtys die from there?

Presently, Leeth ran down the slope and caught up with Ays. He glanced at her bleakly, aware that in some ways Fineas Rigg had been right. Leeth had been changed by her experiences; she would never be a child to Ays again.

Casmeer

This is getting too painful, Casmeer thought. It should not be this way. The stories were supposed to uplift him as he wrote them, allow him to experience a freedom he could not have in reality. Instead, the act of writing seemed to be an exorcism ground. He felt pain, so he had to write about pain. The story of Beraftiel made him wonder whether Elini could still experience physical sensation. Was she aware of what was happening when the plumosites attacked her and broke off pieces of her body? It was too terrible to think about. For a few agonising moments, Casmeer considered rushing up to the roof garden and smashing Elini's roche to pieces, just to be sure. Then, he calmed himself.

Later, he heard a noise from the roof garden and was drawn to it. To his surprise, he found his freed plumosite had returned. He presumed it was she, although there was no real proof. All plumosites looked very much alike to him, although he recognised females as being smaller than the males, and lacking a spiked ruff. The plumosite was sitting on the low wall, hooting a low tune.

'What do you want?' Casmeer asked.

The plumosite jumped in surprise, and lifted her wings in a scrabbling, inelegant attempt to regain her balance. Casmeer could not restrain the involuntary laugh that came to his lips.

'I have made you a great lady,' Casmeer said.

The plumosite looked at him warily. Perhaps she wanted food? Casmeer picked up a plate of rather over-ripe fruit which had stood just inside the door for several days. He proffered this to the plumosite, realising he didn't know whether her diet was carnivorous or not. She had eaten the scraps he'd given her while he'd held her prisoner, but that might have been because she was so hungry she'd have eaten anything. It seemed she had no intention of taking the fruit from him, so Casmeer put the plate down on the ground in front of him. He went to sit in his favourite chair, hoping the plumosite might approach.

'Your name is Babooshpet,' he told her, thinking, She is just an animal. She can't understand me. I am going mazy, alone like an old man with a pet mouse, talking to anything that moves.

Then, the plumosite whistled over her shoulder, and presently a group of three males furtively came up over the wall beside her. She made a fluting sound and one of the males dashed forward, making cringeing movements every time he glanced at Casmeer, who sat as still as he could in the chair. The male picked up the plate and ran back to the wall with it, offered it up to his female. She sorted through the fruit, and then selected one, with delicate claws. This, she put into her beak before leaping down off the wall. The males took what was left of the fruit and followed her.

The next day, Casmeer began collecting fruit on his walk around the city. He felt he had company now. Not friends yet, but other living souls who recognised him as alive.

Chapter Fourteen
Oubrahani

Finnigin and Pashterina were conveyed to Oubrahani in a covered cart, with only a dour Oubrahan guard for company. At first, Finnigin attempted to find out how Babooshpet had been adopted by the Oubrahans, but the guard only blinked at his questions as if they were were spoken in an alien tongue.

'Oubrahans,' said Pashtarina with disdain, 'are superstitious and secretive. It only takes one of them to come up with a wild idea and the whole lot surge towards it with outstretched arms.'

Finnigin told Pashtarina about how he'd met Babooshpet. 'Is it possible she was a captive Oubrahan too? Someone who'd strayed from the mountains?'

Pashtarina shrugged. 'Who knows? We live in strange times, and the mountains' cities are all populated by mooncalfs and gadwits. Rodarigo and I created our own community. We were honest about indulging ourselves, at least.'

Finnigin ventured a possibly dangerous question. 'Do you grieve for Rodarigo?'

Pashtarina gave him an arch glance. 'Grieve? Of course. Your question supposes I do not.'

'I did not mean to . . .'

Pashtarina waved a hand in a dismissive gesture. 'I shall miss my little dogs more, of course. I only hope some other people will come to inhabit our enclave and find and look after them.' She pulled a mournful face. 'Rodarigo and I were never much more than conspirators – hardly lovers.'

'How did you meet him?' Finnigin asked. 'Where did you live?'

Pashtarina smiled. 'Ah, how our stations have altered! Now, you can ask me intimate questions with aplomb, while my erstwhile subjects are chained in a line and trot miserably behind our wagon!' She pulled a sour face at the Oubrahan guard, who appeared to be totally uninterested in her story. 'I'm not sure I should speak frankly. Harkh knows how the information might be used against me.'

'Ah yes, Harkh,' Finnigin said. 'Do you believe in him?'

'Rodarigo did,' Pashtarina replied, 'and I think a god only has to have one believer in order to exist. Myself, I shun religion. Gods are functional only for their names being used in oaths. They lend a piquancy, a focus, to sharp remarks.'

Finnigin laughed. 'Will you ever tell me your story?'

Pashtarina leaned forward and patted his knee. 'My dear and lovely boy, if we swim through the maelstrom that the court of Oubrahan has waiting for us, I will reward and regale you with tales. Until then, we must hope and pray for just treatment.'

'Pray to Harkh?' Finnigin couldn't resist enquiring.

'To anyone divine who's listening,' Pashtarina replied.

Finnigin had confessed to her about the Lamitrices, afraid she'd be furious with him but half hopeful she'd approve. His instincts proved correct. She'd slapped his head, but laughed. 'If things had turned out differently, I've no doubt you'd have made a mark for yourself in rhukaha society.'

'Not if the Lamitrices had killed me first!'

Pashtarina had shaken her head. 'No, you'd have wriggled your way out of trouble, I'm sure. Rodarigo was fond of you. He wouldn't have got rid of you, whatever happened.'

Oubrahani, city of bells. It was heard long before it could be sighted.

'Listen, what a racket!' Pashtarina complained one night as she and Finnigin were attempting to sleep in the confined space of the wagon. The ex-Pursanga was in a particularly waspish mood, owing to the fact that the Oubrahans would not let her perform her toilet in private, and she feared that one or two of them had made disparaging remarks about her. 'They worship bony women,' she'd confided to Finnigin. 'They make me feel like a freak!'

Finnigin had hastened to reassure Pashtarina on that account. 'You are very beautiful,' he said, 'almost . . .' he struggled for suitable words, '. . . like a goddess, a vast and powerful goddess.'

Pashtarina had laughed at that, but it seemed to soothe her. Now, she and Finnigin lay awake, listening to the haunting song of far bells flinging an echoing lament through the gulleys and crags of Overhang.

'I think it sounds wondrous,' Finnigin said. 'It sounds like history.'

'You are a poetic boy,' declared Pashtarina. 'I shall miss you when you recommence your travels.'

'I'd almost forgotten about that,' Finnigin said. 'I wonder if I could go back to the flat-lands now? I'm not sure I want to go any further.'

'Nonsense!' Pashtarina poked him in the ribs. 'You've hardly seen anything yet.'

It warmed Finnigin that she seemed to care about his future. 'I have no doubt you are capable of making history yourself,' Pashtarina said.

'No more than you,' Finnigin replied.

'Then I am more qualified than most to spot the ability in you. Those bells sound angry!'

'Not angry, bewildered.'

Pashtarina grunted in mock impatience. 'As I said, poetic!' She hesitated. 'Finn, my lovely, I confess to feeling anxious. I'm not sure I'll ever have the opportunity to talk with you frankly about my life once we reach Oubrahani.'

Finnigin swiftly reached out to touch her hands. 'No, don't think that! Everything will be fine.'

Pashtarina smiled and shook her head. 'Dear boy, I wish I could believe you. No, I have been thinking, and there are certain things I want you to know. You asked me questions about myself, and I feel that you have a far-reaching future, while I do not. My future, I feel, is narrow, and I would like my story to be carried out into the world.'

'I wish you wouldn't talk like this,' Finnigin said. 'It sounds . . . final.'

'Perhaps it is? The truth is this. I was born in a quarrying settlement deep in the mountains, and there suffered greatly in my youth.'

'A hard life?' Finnigin tried to sound sympathetic. He liked Pashtarina, but felt nervous of witnessing an emotional display.

Again she shook her head. 'Not exactly.' She sighed. 'My sisters were all very beautiful girls, and so were their friends. They were cruel, as young people can be. They mocked me for my size, and I was made to feel very unattractive.'

'Stupid clenchpoops!' Finnigin exclaimed, embarrassed.

Pashtarina smiled. 'I think so too – now – but at the time it tortured me. Sometimes, my sisters incited small children to throw stones at me, telling me I was to be driven from the community. I believed them utterly, and would hide in some dark corner, sobbing, aching for a love I never had. As a young child, I wanted my sisters to like me and would do whatever they asked, so I might join their circle. They laughed and dared me to do dangerous tricks. Often I was bruised and dazed after an afternoon's play. My mother was a proud woman, and having ten children hardened her heart to demonstrative displays, I think. I always felt as if I was an embarrassment to her. She despaired of my ever finding a partner or rearing a family myself. I became a very closed and bitter creature. Anyway, when the rhukahas came and attacked our community, I wasn't sorry. I was glad to see our house burn, glad to see those preening, pretty women taken away to lives of subordination and slavery.' She frowned. 'Was that wicked? No, don't answer. I know it already. Still, Rodarigo was a very young man in those days, and was preparing to challenge the leadership of his group. He took a fancy to me, recognised something in me that would be useful, I suppose. He too felt like an outcast, but that was because he was insane, of course. Anyway, we became allies, and in the first days, when we were briefly lovers, vowed to build ourselves a little empire.

'Then, Rodarigo told me about Harkh. I was the first person he dared to speak with about such things. I encouraged him. It seemed the best thing to do. I knew his mind was mazy, but I was also able to direct his actions.' She threw back her head and grinned, her eyes focused on past triumphs. 'Ah, we cut a swathe, we did. We achieved our dreams . . .' Her face fell. 'I can't understand how the Oubrahans breached our defences. Someone must have betrayed us . . .' She shrugged. 'Ah well, that is my story, Finnigin. Remember it.'

He nodded gravely. 'For ever.'

Mid-morning, the following day, the party entered the city. Oubrahani was protected by high rock walls, and its buildings occupied every available flat space within. Some were indistinguishable from the natural stone. Finnigin and Pashtarina observed their surroundings from the back of the wagon, watched nervously by their guard who seemed to expect them to make a leap for freedom. The streets of the city were paved with glazed purple tiles and, where the roads widened into plazas, intricate mosaics of blue and gold were worked into these. Finnigin was awed by the soaring towers of black stone, the elaborate decorations in the masonry. Every building sported grimacing gargoyles, simpering saints or representations of fantastic beasts.

'Look how many churches there are!' Pashtarina cried, gesturing. 'One for each new religion their sophists have invented!'

Towering campaniles dominated every street corner, every square, and even the houses were crowned with scaled-down bell-towers.

'Bells, bells and more bells!' Pashtarina said. 'It's a wonder they aren't all deaf.'

The wagons came to a halt in a wide street, behind a line of buildings that had a military air. Here, their guard uttered a few words to the effect that Pashtarina and Finnigin should climb down to the street. To Finnigin, it was as if he were about to take part in a celebration, for the clamour of the bells made him feel as if something amazing was about to happen. He looked to see if Babooshpet was around, but it appeared the bulk of the party had headed off somewhere else; all that remained were the captives from the enclave and their guards. The rhukahas, of whom there were pitfully few, became almost hysterical when they caught sight of Pashtarina. The guards allowed her to speak a few words to them, in the hope of calming them down.

'I shall do all I can for you,' she said to her people in a confident manner, 'but for now I suggest co-operation.' As they were led away, she said to Finnigin, 'Poor fools. All is lost for them now.'

Finnigin and Pashtarina were escorted into one of the buildings, which was very dark inside and had a cold, official atmosphere. Guards led them down a stone corridor and directed them into a small, barely furnished room where they were given fresh water and some fruit and cheese. The offer of refreshment seemed a good omen.

Pashtarina sniffed, and examined the food. 'Well, this seems civilised enough!'

'What do you think they'll do with us?' Finnigin asked her, breaking off a chunk of cheese and nibbling it.

'I think that's mainly up to you, boy. The others, what's left of my people, will be sentenced to work in the Oubrahan mines, I expect, but I think you and I should essay to escape such a sentence.'

Finnigin could not imagine Pashtarina working down a mine. 'Well, the Oubrahans seem like a reasonable people.'

Pashtarina scowled, and bit aggressively into a piece of fruit, to talk with her mouth full. 'Don't be taken in. They're pious and haughty, though admittedly never outright cruel.' She swallowed and wiped her mouth with one hand. 'But they also believe strongly in repentance and privation to expiate sins. Religion is very strong here. They worship celibate gods who never have any fun and inflict the same lifestyle on their devotees. No doubt we'll be fed a plateful of religious claptrap and be expected to undergo some sort of uncomfortable rehabilitation. Such a prospect fills my proud heart with bile, but I can bite my tongue when the occasion merits it.' She took another mouthful of fruit.

'Can't you claim noble birth or something?' Finnigin suggested.

'Well, I can try,' Pashtarina replied, 'but in all honesty, my nobility is self-taught rather than inherited.'

'You can't tell,' Finnigin said.

Presently, the door opened and five elderly Oubrahans came into the room; two men and three women. All were tall in stature and wore dark maroon robes of soft material. Upon each thin breast reposed a splendid pendant of amethyst, hanging on a thick golden chain. Every face was set in a stern expression, as if carved from granite. Finnigin's spirits fell; he could see no signs of sympathy in these people.

'You are Finnigin?' one of the men enquired.

He stood up. 'Yes. Yes, I am.'

The man who'd spoken turned to address someone standing just outside the room. 'Is this the boy you're looking for?'

The group separated to let the interested party step forward. Finnigin expected to see Babooshpet, and was so surprised when he saw who it actually was that he felt his heart would stop beating.

'Varian!'

Varian walked into the room, his face expressionless. He was wearing his hat with the blue feather, and a long crushed velvet coat of deepest blue which was covered in intricate embroidery. His hands were heavy with enormous jewelled rings. Affluence seemed to roll off him in waves. He inspected Finnigin for a few long moments. 'Yes, Trondini, this is the one.'

Finnigin felt an uncontrollable grin spread across his face. 'Varian, I can't tell you how glad I am . . .'

'Silence!' Varian said, and turned to the man who'd addressed him. 'I thank you for your co-operation.'

The man named Trondini bowed slightly. 'No more than we are grateful for yours.'

Varian inclined his head. 'My pleasure. May I take this boy into my custody now?'

Trondini bowed. 'Whatever you wish, my lord.'

Finnigin could have wept with relief. First Babooshpet, and now Varian, had come to his aid. Surely this was incontrovertible proof that benevolent spirits existed and cared for the welfare of those under their vigilance. It seemed his life was charmed with good luck when he needed it.

'This way, Finnigin,' Varian said in a cold voice. 'Follow me.'

Finnigin grabbed hold of Pashtarina's arm. 'And my lady, Varian. We must take her with us.'

Varian shook his head. 'No! Now be quiet and follow me.'

'But . . .' Finnigin looked at Pashtarina in a moment of total indecision.

'Go!' said Pashtarina. 'But don't forget me.'

She and Finnigin hugged briefly before he followed Varian out of the room. A female Oubrahan guard, who'd been on duty outside the door, fell in behind them.

Finnigin attempted to speak excitedly to Varian, but every time he began to say something, the guard behind him poked him sharply in the back with the blunt end of her spear. Varian strode ahead, never looking back.

The three of them went out of the building and through several streets on foot, before reaching the portico to a large, four-storied house, approached by wide shallow steps. The front door opened on to the road, the front of the house was separated from the sidewalk only by a narrow iron railing. Here, the guard produced a key and mounted the steps ahead of Varian to open the door. Finnigin followed Varian inside, his heart racing.

'You really do have a house in every city!' he said.

In the hall, Varian turned and deigned to speak to him. 'I never lie,' he said. 'Marvrani, my cloak.' He handed the guard his outdoor garment, and his hat, which she hung up in a closet, before removing her helmet and scratching her scalp.

'I suppose you want refreshment,' she said.

Varian inclined his head. 'If you'd be so kind.'

She shrugged. 'Well, I'm thirsty myself.' With a toss of her hair, she disappeared into one of the dark corridors of the house.

'Thank you for rescuing me,' Finnigin said, once they were alone.

Varian smiled thinly. 'I've been watching your progress, and felt it time to intervene, otherwise a protracted and quite uneventful period would be spent here in Oubrahani. That would be far too tedious to observe!'

Finnigin couldn't believe Varian spoke the truth. How could he have watched him in the enclave? 'I'd like you to help Pashtarina too,' he said. 'We are friends.'

Varian yawned. 'Oh, she'll be all right. Quite capable of looking after herself . . . There is a bell in this city named after me, you know.'

'I'm not surprised.'

Varian led the way into a comfortable, if dim-lit, salon, where Marvrani brought a tray of wine and food. Her informal manner suggested she was not an

Oubrahan guard at all, but some confederate of Varian's. 'How long do we have to stay here?' she demanded. 'It's such a dank, dark place. You said we'd go to Karaganzinad.'

'A temporary change of plan,' Varian told her. 'Be patient.'

Marvrani restlessly paced the room, ignoring Finnigin completely. 'I want to wear fine gowns again, dress myself in jewels and feathers.' She gestured in distaste at her functional soldier's leathers which Finnigin thought suited her very well. She was a lithe individual.

'In time, in time,' Varian answered vaguely. 'I need to speak to Finnigin now. Alone.'

Marvrani directed a sour glance at Finnigin. 'He is no better than me, and in fact seems far less intriguing.'

'Let me be the judge of that,' Varian said in a toneless voice.

Marvrani growled in displeasure and slammed out of the room. 'Forgive her,' Varian said to Finnigin. 'She is disappointed to be here.'

Finnigin shrugged helplessly. 'I share her puzzlement. Exactly why are you so interested in me?'

Varian smiled and gestured with languid hands. 'I am a manipulative person, whom some might call evil because I like to interfere in people's lives.'

'My life seems to consist of a series of bizarre coincidences,' Finnigin said. 'If another acquaintance of mine hadn't miraculously been with the Oubrahans when they attacked the rhukahas, I'd be dead now.'

Varian laughed. 'I know. I know about the crystal-eater.'

Finnigin gave Varian a narrow glance, but decided not to ask any direct questions. He realised he must be learning to play the game. 'I must find out how she happened to be with the Oubrahans,' he said. 'The last time I saw her, she was as mute and wild as an animal.

Something very . . . strange must have occurred.'

Varian's smile widened. 'But of course. *I* happened to her. Babooshpet was tailor-made to be a flameness of the Oubrahans. They hold crystal-eaters in high regard, because of their prognosticative powers.'

Finnigin took note of how Varian had not been able to resist telling him how he'd been involved in the incident. Clearly, questioning Varian was not the way to obtain information. 'It was lucky for Babooshpet the Oubrahans came across her, then.'

Varian shrugged. 'Coincidence had nothing to do with it. Rodarigo's little band have been a splinter in the heel of Oubrahani for many years. All I had to do was suggest that an Oubrahan scouting party should make enquiries concerning the rhukahas at the Quarrier settlement. It was inevitable they'd come across the girl and claim her as a holy person.'

'She couldn't speak before.'

Varian leaned forward with an admonishing gesture. 'Finnigin, you are guilty of great presumption! Just because Babooshpet did not speak to you, did not necessarily mean she lacked the ability to do so.'

Finnigin shook his head. 'I do not believe you! I spent a long time in Babooshpet's company. She definitely could not speak. She was . . . *wild*.'

'You talk about her as if she was an animal.'

'Sometimes, it seemed as if she was. She was certainly feral. That's why I find the transformation she's undergone so hard to understand.'

Varian leaned back again. 'There are several ways of looking at the situation. Some might say the potential was there all the time, and a perceptive person would have seen it straight away. Others might add that the rituals the Oubrahans conducted to inaugurate her as their flameness affected her mind, enlightened her, and allowed her to perceive herself in a different way.'

'I wonder what had happened to her in the past that made her the way she was,' Finnigin said. 'I wonder what her childhood was like.'

Varian grinned. 'Quite! Poor Babooshpet.'

'You know so much about me and my acquaintances,' Finnigin said, carefully. 'It is as if you have eyes in every city – in every corner of the world.' He hoped this remark would prompt Varian to explain himself.

Varian shrugged. 'I have an effective network,' he said.

'Extremely effective! Why are you so interested in me? Are you just a bored man with too much money who needs to while away the long hours of an empty life by mystifying people? I would like to know.'

'I cannot begin to explain,' Varian said abruptly. 'It really would do you no good. There is a risk the knowledge would kill you. You might simply cease to exist.'

A tremor of shock coursed through Finnigin's body. Had that last remark been a threat or a warning? 'What is going to happen to me now?'

Varian stood up and walked to the table where Marvrani had left the tray. He poured himself a cup of dark red wine. 'Well, I've freed you from the Oubrahans,' he said, sipping his wine. 'So you can continue with your journey. You are lucky that I am present in your life, because, as in Zanymandias, I shall again conveniently equip you with supplies. What you do, and where you go, after leaving Oubrahani is your decision. I do not intend to try and influence that.'

'But you will be . . . near me,' Finnigin said, almost to himself. 'Watching me, or following me.' He looked up at Varian, unsure whether it would be better to appear helpless and bewildered or defiant.

'I cannot help it,' Varian answered shortly. 'May I refill your cup?'

Finningin held the cup out. 'I can't help wondering whether should I . . . end up in a bad situation again, you will come marching in to sort it out.'

Varian opened his mouth and laughed silently. 'Does the thought of that make you feel secure? Perhaps you should start praying to me, seeing as you believe I have so much influence over your life!'

Finnigin was stung by the laughter, and forgot he was being careful not to ask questions. 'Exactly who are you?' he demanded. 'Or should I be asking: *what* are you?'

'I am your . . . friend,' Varian answered airily. 'Now, I have business to attend to. May I suggest that today you study the maps in my library and plan your journey? We shall meet again later. Tomorrow, you must leave, so that Marvrani will stop fretting, and she and I can set off for Karaganzinad.'

'What if I don't want to go?' Finnigin snapped. 'What if I want to stay here with Pashtarina?'

Varian's eyes became narrow; mere damp, black slits. 'The erstwhile Pursanga is part of your history now, Finnigin. A concluded episode.'

He shook his head. 'No. She is my friend. I like her. I won't leave her here in trouble.'

Varian sighed. 'Why do you have to develop a sense of loyalty now? It is tiresome and unexpected.'

'I want to see her. Can't you bring her here?'

Varian shook his head. 'That would be undesirable, but as a concession I will arrange for you to visit her tomorrow, before you leave the city. It's clear you'll be intractable until you've reassured yourself of the woman's wellbeing.' Varian sat down again, and crossed his legs, nursing his cup of wine in both hands. Finnigin's eyes were drawn to the array of dark gems gleaming dully upon Varian's long fingers. Each jewel was the size of a small bird's egg.

'I would also like to see Babooshpet.'

Varian inhaled deeply in impatience. 'That might be more difficult. She is sacred to these people now. I doubt she'd be allowed here unchaperoned.'

'They address you as "my lord" here,' Finnigin said. 'Surely you can arrange anything you desire.'

Varian shook his head. 'There are limits. Anyway, to return to your own future. I think it's important for you to know that if you don't leave the city, the Oubrahans will inter you in a monastery, cut off your hair and teach you to be a good boy, in the manner they consider fit. You wouldn't enjoy that at all, believe me. You are used to living an eventful life, and the tedium of existence here would drive you insane.'

'How long are you going to meddle in my life?'

Varian smiled, widely and slowly. 'Finnigin, consider this essential truth: I *am* your life.'

The remark irritated Finnigin more than it frightened him. He was beginning to find Varian's behaviour tiresome. 'You might think you are,' he said, 'but I don't.'

'I am glad,' Varian responded smoothly. 'It would be so dull for me otherwise.'

Finnigin sat in the long, dark library of Varian's house with maps spread out on the table before him. He couldn't be bothered to examine them, but spent his time staring into the fire which sought to warm the draughty spaces of the room and throw a little cheerful light into what was otherwise a place less cheery than a tomb. Why did Varian live here? Surely, there were more comfortable houses in Oubrahani. Finnigin found the same thoughts rotating in his head. Who was Varian? Why was he interested in Finnigin? What would happen eventually? He felt that Varian was playing a very complicated game which he was enjoying immensely. It was unfair of him not to inform the other player – Finnigin – of the rules. Perhaps this sort of thing had happened to Leeara too? Perhaps it was an inevitable part of wandering? Terranauts influenced the movement of cities; people such as Varian influenced the movement of terranauts. Was that feasible? Finnigin wished Leeara was there to answer his questions.

In the late-afternoon, Marvrani stalked into the library and abruptly informed Finnigin he should go with her in order to prepare himself for dinner. 'We have guests,' she said. 'So clean yourself up a bit.'

She led Finnigin up some narrow back-stairs into a dim-lit corridor, carpeted in purple and black. Stained-glass windows filtered the dull evening light, to throw morose gouts of colour on to the floor.

'This is a miserable place,' Finnigin said. 'I imagined a city of bells would be more . . . lively.'

'I agree,' Marvrani said, looking back. 'I can't wait to leave.'

Finnigin increased his pace to catch up with her. 'How long have you . . . been with Varian?'

She gave him an arch glance. 'Long enough.'

'I don't suppose you can tell me anything about him?'

Marvrani seemed to find Finnigin's hopeless tone amusing. 'He is not cruel,' she said. 'You mustn't be afraid of him.'

'I'm not,' Finnigin said hotly. 'That wasn't what I meant. I'd like to know why I'm so important to him.'

Marvrani paused in front of a thick, wooden door, and put her hand upon the handle. 'He has never told me,' she said. 'And that's the truth. He has always kept things to himself . . .' She appeared to be confused, as if Finnigin's questions had thrown her into a state where she herself had begun to ask questions.

He risked an impertinent query. 'Are you in love with him?'

Marvrani glanced at him sharply and raised her eyebrows. 'Does that come into it? I don't know. I'm not sure anymore.' She opened the door. 'You'll find a bathroom in there, and clean clothes. I'll return later.' She left Finnigin standing alone in the corridor.

Bemused, he went into the room beyond. It was a bedroom, smelling of must, its chill only partly relieved by a fire roaring in a grate on the right-hand wall. The bathroom, which led off the left side of the room, was vast and echoing. Finnigin ran himself a bath and undressed in the bedroom, wondering whether he was still being watched. He bathed hurriedly and, wrapped in a towel, examined the clothes that had been left out for him on the bed: a vest and leggings of blue velvet, a long purple robe to be worn over the top, stiff velvet slippers. He felt ridiculous wearing these garments, as if he were a child dressing up in an old man's clothes. Perhaps that was intentional?

Presently, Marvrani knocked on the door and entered the room without waiting for a response. 'Ah, you're ready,' she said. She too was dressed in a formal manner, wearing a trailing black gown which revealed her long throat and strong shoulders. Her mass of dark, curling hair was held up in a black net, confined by jewelled pins.

'Who are the guests?' Finnigin asked, walking to the door.

'Your friend Babooshpet, and her escort,' Marvrani replied.

'Oh . . .' Finnigin was surprised. He hadn't expected Varian to indulge him concerning Babooshpet.

Marvrani led the way to an uncomfortable dining-room which was lit by candles that adorned the table in pewter sconces. There was no one else in the room.

Marvrani sat down next to the head of the table, and gestured for Finnigin to take a place opposite her.

'Where is everyone?' he asked, in a low voice.

'They'll be here soon,' Marvrani replied, shaking out a napkin and placing it on her lap.

Finnigin was about to ask another question when the door opened and Babooshpet came into the room, followed by an older woman who might possibly have been one of the people whom Finnigin had seen when he'd been waiting with Pashtarina earlier in the day. Finnigin wondered who had let them in, seeing as Marvrani was sitting there opposite him and he had seen no servants in the house. He couldn't imagine Varian condescending to open his own front door. Neither Babooshpet nor her companion wore coats, and both were dressed in the sombre, trailing garments typical of Oubrahan couture.

Marvrani stood up. 'Greetings. Please, take a seat.'

Babooshpet sat down next to Marvrani, the older woman next to Finnigin. He thought that in her youth the chaperone would have been a great beauty. Even now, in late middle age, she was still striking to look at. 'There is a nasty drizzle this evening,' she said.

'Yes,' said Marvrani. 'May I offer you an aperitif?' She picked up a tall, crystal decanter in which glowed a dark green liquid.

'Just a small one,' said the woman. She turned and looked at Finnigin, her head held gracefully upon a long neck. 'I am Leda,' she told him. 'Leda Affine.'

'How do you do?' Finnigin said lamely. He felt too nervous to look at Babooshpet. It was hard to believe she was the same person he'd travelled with, and the sight of her now was somehow disorientating. Still, he supposed, in some measure he was responsible for her good fortune. He risked a glance. Babooshpet was staring at him. Her hair was a pale nimbus around her head, her skin as white as if she'd never been outside. She smiled, revealing spiky teeth. Finnigin shrugged helplessly. He didn't know what to say to her.

The atmosphere in the room was stilted and formal. Leda spoke about the weather to Marvrani, who barely answered her. The company sipped a bitter, herbal aperitif. Finnigin was conscious that the three women and himself were waiting anxiously for Varian to make an appearance. He wondered who would serve the food. Perhaps there would be none, and they would all sit there, like figments of a dream, until one of them woke up?

'So, you are an old friend of our beloved flameness,' said Leda in a loud voice.

Finnigin presumed the remark must be addressed to himself. 'Yes,' he said. 'We were companions.'

'Finnigin set me free,' Babooshpet said. 'In many ways.' Her voice was strange; at once resonant and husky.

'How did I do that?' he asked. His question seemed to hang in the air over the middle of the table. He was unsure whether it would ever reach its target.

'You opened the cage,' Babooshpet eventually replied.

'But the person I set free is the not the person you are now,' Finnigin said. 'At least, I don't think she is.'

'I was never an animal,' Babooshpet said. 'You were wrong about that.'

Finnigin had the strange impression Babooshpet thought she was speaking to someone else entirely. The conversation seemed unreal; words glancing off one another without making sense, or being related. He felt very uncomfortable, as if should he remain in this company for much longer, something would be revealed to him that would drive him mad, or kill him. He would simply cease to exist.

'How did you know where Rodarigo's enclave was?' he asked, in a voice that sounded too loud, somehow too accusatory.

Babooshpet blinked at him. 'Well, Varian told us, of course. He told the guard when would be the best time to launch an attack, and where to apply the most force.'

'Did you know I was there?'

Babooshpet's face seemed to cloud over. 'He told me,' she said. 'I knew you were there.'

Finnigin turned to Marvrani. 'I feel strange,' he said. 'I feel . . . unwell.'

'Drink up,' said Marvrani brightly. 'You'll be fine.'

'He's not coming, is he?' Finnigin said. He had to grip the table-top in order to remain sitting upright.

Marvrani's necklace glittered in the candle-light. Her eyes seemed to be black jewels. 'Drink up.'

A clock on the wall behind Finnigin made a strange croaking sound. Marvrani stood up and walked to the door, which she opened. She returned to the table dragging a food trolley behind her. Finnigin poured himself more of the herbal liqueur. How had the food arrived at the door? Who had prepared it? He drank the measure of liquor in one gulp and poured another.

With extreme courtesy, Marvrani played hostess and wheeled the trolley around the table, dishing up a meal of cold food – salad and cured meats – to Leda and Finnigin. Babooshpet's plate remained empty, but then as she ate only crystal, her escort might have fed her earlier. She was staring at the crystal decanter in a intent manner. Perhaps she would pick it up and bite into it presently?

'Such a pity Lord Varian could not join us,' said Leda, tucking into her meal.

Finnigin stared at his plate. He felt hungry and nauseous at the same time.

'Eat something,' Marvrani said, pointing at him with her fork.

Finnigin picked up a sliver of ham, felt his stomach churn. 'Such a pity . . .' Leda began again.

'Yes,' interrupted Marvrani. 'But never mind. This meeting was for Babooshpet and Finnigin. They are old friends.'

Finnigin suddenly felt angry. He felt that Varian had manipulated this meeting, knowing full well it would be unpleasant for Finnigin. He remembered what Varian had said about Pashtarina, how she was a concluded episode of Finnigin's life. Although he still believed Varian was wrong about the Pursanga, he felt that Babooshpet certainly fell into the concluded category. There was something wrong about seeing her again now. It was as if they belonged to different worlds. He wished he could excuse himself.

'What is a flameness?' he blurted out. His voice seemed to come from a far corner of the room.

'A kind of religious mascot,' said Marvrani, which prompted a noise of disgruntlement from Leda.

'A flameness is a woman of great power who can see into the many futures of the world,' she said. 'We have not been blessed with such a wondrous person for over a hundred years.' She beamed at Babooshpet. 'Now is a time for rejoicing.'

'Indeed!' said Marvrani with a irreverent laugh.

Finnigin couldn't help smiling at her. Marvrani, it seemed, was the focus of the room. It was she who held everything together, who prevented reality from dissolving into a mass of swirling motes. Finnigin tried to get a grip of his imagination. Was he succumbing to a fever of some kind? His thoughts tonight were uncontrollably bizarre.

After the main course had been consumed, Marvrani dished out a cold custard. She allowed Finnigin to refuse a portion. In contrast, Leda consumed her dessert, and a second portion, with gusto. Leda alone seemed at ease. Babooshpet might have been in another room entirely, for all the contribution she made to the gathering.

'So tell us, my dear,' Marvrani said to Babooshpet, 'about the extraordinary details of your life.' Finnigin felt she had made the request for his benefit.

Babooshpet flicked a bright glance at Marvrani. 'What do you want to know?'

'Why you were in a cage at the Shrine of All Quests,' Finnigin said quickly.

Babooshpet shrugged. 'They did not understand me there. They were ignorant.' A slow radiance seemed to spread over her face, her eyes became unfocused. 'We, the crystal-eaters, have no cities. We travel. In the mountains, we come across the ruins of dead civilisations, and here we pluck the crystals from the very ground.'

'Don't you miss your people?' Finnigin interrupted.

Babooshpet shook her head. 'How can I? I am still with them, in one sense.' She rested her chin in her hands. 'One day I went for a walk among the rocks and came upon the Shrine. Everyone was sitting around talking, so I sat down with them to listen. They saw me nibble a crystal and began to shout at me. They saw me as an animal, and I became one. I became their vision of me.' She sighed, smiling gently, gazing into her own past.

'Then why didn't you start talking to me when I let you free?' Finnigin asked. 'I didn't see you as an animal.'

'Didn't you?' said Babooshpet.

Finnigin lowered his eyes. 'What changed you?'

Again, Babooshpet raised her slim shoulders in a shrug. 'When you left the Contamures, it seemed the world changed. I had been living in a mirage without realising it. On the morning you left, I woke up and the world seemed real. It was perhaps the first time I'd really woken up for a long time. I went to Mama Contamure and asked if she wanted me to do anything for her that morning. She just said, "Oh, found your voice, have you?" and then gave me some vegetables to clean. I probably would have stayed with the Quarriers if it hadn't been for Varian . . .' She glanced at Leda. 'Not that I don't appreciate my position now.'

'Why do you eat crystal?' Finnigin asked. 'How can you live on it?'

'You might as well ask me how I can breathe,' Babooshpet replied. 'It is just so.'

Finnigin would have asked more questions, but at that moment, Marvrani noticed that the custard bowl had been scraped clean. She stood up and spoke brusquely to Leda. 'Well, the meal is finished. It has been very interesting having you and the flameness here. No doubt your conveyance is now waiting at the steps. Thank you for coming.'

Leda looked suprised. She was still dabbing her mouth with a napkin, and perhaps thinking about the hot beverage which should surely have been the next course of the meal. Babooshpet appeared to have retreated back into herself, and was staring at the table.

'I'm afraid I shall have to hurry you out,' said Marvrani without the least embarrassment.

Leda stood up. 'Of course. I understand.'

Weakly, Finnigin crawled out of his seat and stood leaning against the table. Babooshpet stood up from the contemplation of her empty plate and walked towards the door.

Finnigin suddenly felt panicked that she was leaving, deeply aware she was about to walk out of his life for ever. 'Babooshpet,' he said, almost shouting, 'I never thanked you.'

She paused, turned, and smiled at him slowly. Then she came to stand in front of him. 'There is no need,' she murmured in a throaty voice. 'If anything, I should thank *you*.'

Finnigin shook his head, smiled a tight smile. 'I would be dead if you hadn't . . .' He looked at her intently. There was something not quite right about her appearance; she looked strangely insubstantial in the low light of the room. 'Are you all right?' Finnigin asked her.

She nodded. 'Yes. And you?'

'I think so.' He wondered how he appeared to her, whether he was presently as wraithlike as she was. Are we meant to be speaking to one another now? he thought.

Babooshpet wrinkled her brow in an expression of perplexity. 'Everything is . . . very odd at present, isn't it?'

Finnigin nodded. 'Very. I hope it will pass. Good luck, Babooshpet, I wish you the best in fortune and peace.'

'Thank you.' She leaned forward and kissed his cheek. He could not smell her breath, which was odd because she'd always had a very strong smell before. 'Goodbye, Finnigin. I wish you luck also.'

They briefly clasped hands and then Babooshpet glided unhurriedly from the room, without a backward glance. Leda inclined her head to Finnigin and departed at a smarter pace, with Marvrani behind her. He was left alone.

He listened to the erratic ticking of the clock behind him, looked at the cruel glinting of the tableware, experienced the vigilant stillness of the unfriendly room. Then Marvrani appeared in the doorway.

'It is time, Finnigin,' she said.

He looked at her. 'For what?'

'You will see him now.'

'Where?'

'He is waiting. Go to your room.' She turned away in a swish of gown, and by the time he'd reached the door, she'd disappeared down one of the corridors.

Varian was sitting in a chair beside the fire, in Finnigin's room. He was staring into the flames, his fingers steepled against his lips, his long legs thrust out into the hearth. The gems upon his fingers glittered darkly, and his tumbling hair gleamed like fluid. When Finnigin saw him there, he was aware of the force of Varian's attractiveness. It seemed to be dangerous, like a weapon or a lie. Finnigin marched into the room, conscious of how ridiculous he looked in the long robes, and said, 'Why did you do that to me?'

Varian looked up from his meditation of the flames. 'Do what?'

'Make me endure that dreadful evening! You knew what it would be like. That's why you didn't come!'

Varian smiled in a maddeningly serene fashion. 'Come and sit down,' he said. 'Calm yourself. I don't see why you should be angry. It was you who asked to see Babooshpet. I merely obliged you.'

'It was horrible!' Finnigin sat down on the floor, ignoring the chair on the other side of the hearth. He was surprised that no strategies of evasion had come into his mind. His honest feeling was that he wanted to lean against Varian's legs, like a dog needing the comfort of its master's hand. Rather than perform a series of social manoeuvres, he simply obeyed his instinct and sat down. The fact that he felt relaxed doing this surprised him greatly.

Varian reached out and touched Finnigin's head,

drew him close. 'Be at rest.' He seemed to be aware of Finnigin's needs.

'Strange things are happening to me,' he said. 'I feel so odd.'

'I'm sorry about that,' Varian said.

'I suppose it's your fault?' Finnigin pulled away from him to look him in the eye. Varian reached out and cupped Finnigin's chin in his hand.

'Probably. It is difficult to tell. I myself am suffering from disorientation. It is hard to distinguish reality from fantasy at times.' He stood up and leaned against the mantlepiece, with his back to Finnigin, his brow pressed against his hand. 'It is quite natural for you to be angry and bewildered, for I have made you independent,' he said. 'You are independent of me now, and yet . . . so much a part . . .'

'What are you talking about?' Finnigin asked. He got to his feet.

Varian turned round. His face was haggard, miserable. 'What's wrong?' Finnigin asked.

'I need to . . . I need to experience something,' Varian said. 'I feel it is very important, and perhaps part of your evolution. And yet, even though I am directing this scene and you are simply a component of it, I am nervous of speaking to you about it directly because I know you have autonomy.'

'I have no idea what you're talking about,' Finnigin said. He felt, in his heart, a little afraid.

Varian held out his arms. 'Embrace me, Finn. I need to feel that.'

Finnigin complied without hesitation. He was surprised at how quickly he complied. It also surprised him to find that Varian was, ultimately, a man of flesh and blood, with perhaps the same weaknesses.

Finnigin had always felt that some people are awkward to embrace; the contours of the bodies do not match. With Varian, it was as if they were two halves of a whole. Almost too comfortable. Varian seemed diffident, wary, and it was Finnigin who sought his mouth for a kiss. Varian tried to pull backwards with a cry of anguish, but Finnigin was persistent. 'Isn't this what you want, what you talked about?'

'Yes,' Varian said, 'but no. We are one another, Finn. I'm not sure what's happening here. I'm not sure why I need to do this.'

'Then just do it without thinking,' Finnigin said. 'In truth, I don't think this situation has occurred to me before.' He wondered whether that was a lie or not.

'My wife . . .' Varian muttered.

'Marvrani?'

Varian shook his head. 'No . . . no . . . that is . . . are you my wife, or are you me?'

'You are mazy,' said Finnigin. 'Be quiet.' He felt very powerful having a physical control over this man who had interfered in his life so adeptly. The control was that of seduction.

Lying in the cold bed, with Finnigin pressed against him, curious and eager, Varian suddenly exhaled a moaning cry. His hands went around Finnigin's throat, but did not exert any pressure. He pushed his knee between Finnigin's legs, and let his weight fall upon Finnigin's body. Finnigin felt he was very experienced in carnal affairs, and was therefore alarmed by what happened next. Varian put his hand flat on Finnigin's stomach and clawed the flesh. At that point, Finnigin felt as if he had fainted from the waist down. All sensation fled. Simultaneously, his mind flooded with an alien form of desire. He wanted something that he could not feel, and it was something he'd never wanted before, or would have been able to imagine. He did not feel as if he was himself any more.

The numbness left his body as swiftly as it had

arrived, and the sensations, when feeling returned, were the most invasive, terrifying and powerful he had ever experienced.

'What have you done to me?' he cried. 'You have gored me! I am dying!' His vision became starred with points of light. Enraptured, Varian moved forcefully inside Finnigin's body, in places where he should not be able to move.

Panicked, Finnigin reached down with his hand to explore their conjunction. His findings invoked a scream, and terror. He expected to find some terrible wound, blood. What he found was something else entirely. An image of Valnisi scampered across his mind, trailing ragged robes and hair; a laugh.

Woman, I am woman! Finnigin thought.

For a moment, he wondered whether he had always been so, and had somehow dreamed being male. Nothing seemed real any more; not his memories, nor the world he had travelled through. Reality was this: a bed, a lover, a body that should not be his. He was an observer of what was happening rather than a participant. There could be neither enjoyment nor disgust, only awareness.

Varian groaned and climaxed, to fall heavily on to Finnigin's chest. 'My love,' he murmured. 'So long . . .'

The dream ended there.

In the morning, Finnigin woke up alone. The bed was vast and cold around him. At first, he tried to remember a distressing dream he thought he'd had, and then a chill of remembrance sent his hands flying to examine his body. Nothing amiss. No physical change, no mutation. A nightmare, then. Nothing more. He wondered at what point he'd fallen asleep. Had he collapsed in the dining-room? The walk from there to the bedroom was indistinct, and perhaps had never happened. Last night, reality had been an elastic thing.

He climbed out of the bed into the chill room, and found his clothes, his old clothes, lying on the floor. In a daze, he dressed himself, and then after a visit to the bathroom, went in search of his hosts.

He found Marvrani in the dining-room, drinking tea and eating burnt, leathery toast. She was wearing her soldier's uniform. She offered breakfast to Finnigin and he ate dispiritedly.

'You look terrible,' said Marvrani, smiling over her tea-cup.

'Did I pass out last night?' Finnigin asked her.

She gave him an enigmatic stare. 'You were in rather a state. Perhaps you drank too much. That liqueur is rather potent, yet it tastes so sweet and harmless.'

'Where's Varian?'

'Not here.'

'Where then?'

Marvrani shrugged. 'How should I know? I don't keep a timetable of his movements.' She smiled. 'Anyway, cast Varian from your mind for now. I'm to take you to visit your other friend this morning.'

Finnigin nodded miserably. The idea of seeing Pashtarina now had little appeal. He felt like weeping.

'Cheer up,' said Marvrani. 'You'll soon be out of this gloomy city. And so will I. What a relief!'

'Marvrani?'

'Yes?'

Finnigin fixed her with what he hoped was an appealing look. 'Did I see Varian last night?'

'You were supposed to,' she answered. 'But as I didn't witness it firsthand, I can't really say whether you did or not.'

'You know what happened, don't you!'

Marvrani pulled a comical face, ducked her head from side to side. 'I can imagine.'

Finnigin doubted whether she could. He decided to abandon the conversation. Perhaps, once he'd left the city, things wouldn't seem so surreal? He was frightened of Varian now, and worse, helplessly enthralled. It would be best to put a distance between himself and Varian as soon as possible. Thinking of what seemed to have happened the previous night was like probing an infected tooth with his tongue. The recollection sent stabs of pain, shame, outrage, excitement and withering adoration throughout his mind and body.

The sun was shining that day, which improved the city's appearance, although the lack of trees and greenery still made it a dour and forbidding place. High buildings loomed oppressively over the narrow streets. Bells rang dolorously, and citizens moved gravely about their business. Finnigin and Marvrani walked in silence to the place where Pashtarina was confined.

The ex-Pursanga had been installed in a convent for rehabilitation. From the road, the place looked like a prison; featureless grey walls rearing up and up, unrelieved by window or balcony. A single gateway, barred by metal-studded wooden gates, appeared to be the only entrance.

A letter signed by Varian, which Marvrani proffered to an invisible presence behind the inspection hatch in the gates, gained them access to a hushed inner courtyard. They stood under an archway which was lit by oil lamps owing to the fact that sunlight was unable to find a way beneath the wide arch. Marvrani impatiently tapped her thighs with her fingers and shuffled from foot to foot, sighing, as they waited for someone to attend to their request.

Finnigin walked numbly to the frontier of sunlight, where the gateway opened out on to the courtyard which was lined by a gravel path and occupied in its centre by a small, well-kept lawn. It was the first greenery Finnigin could remember seeing in Oubrahani. There was no sign of any of the inmates. Diamond-paned windows that punctuated the far wall of the building blankly reflected the sun, although there was little sense of light or levity about the place. Finnigin glanced at the sky: heavy, purple clouds massed on the eastern horizon above the spires of the city, soon to obliterate the sun. Were there any places in this shunned landscape that bloomed with colour and life? He wanted to run away. He wanted to see Varian again.

Presently a woman wearing a severe habit of dark indigo emerged from an arched doorway and approached the visitors. She was smiling mildly as if she was slightly intoxicated, or simple-minded.

'We have sanction to speak with your latest arrival,' Marvrani said in a drawling voice, arms folded. 'Her name was Pashtarina.'

'Ah, you refer to Cousin Distrid,' said the woman in a smooth, cool voice. Her smile never faltered.

'Whoever,' said Marvrani.

The nun regarded Finnigin with a patient eye. 'This way, if you please.'

They were conducted into one of the cloisters where the weight of history oppressed the senses, oozing from the massive stone columns, soaring windows of multifaceted glass, and ornate candelabra. In a small stone cell, occupied only by a narrow bed and a wooden washstand, sat Pashtarina. Her bulk filled the tiny room. She was staring in disdain at the door as it opened, but when she caught sight of Finnigin, leapt up and surged forward to embrace him.

'Ah, my sweet morsel, you have come for me!'

He awkwardly returned the embrace. 'I am allowed to speak with you,' he said.

Pashtarina stood back, perhaps sensing the reserve in his voice. She looked at him with suspicion.

'Are you well?' Finnigin enquired.

Pashtarina raised her arms and shrugged. She was wearing a voluminous habit of purple cloth, her face hugged by a wimple. 'I am very well,' she answered.

'You may speak alone for a few minutes,' said the nun who'd taken Finnigin there. 'But only for that time.'

Pashtarina snarled silently at the closing door. 'These women are dry as sticks,' she said. 'I can't bear all the scraping and kowtowing.'

'But they are treating you well?'

Pashtarina sniffed. 'I suppose so. They keep telling me that, with their love, I can overcome my past. So sanctimonious. It turns my stomach!'

'But at least you are not in the mines.'

'Captivity is captivity,' Pashtarina said. 'An ordeal is an ordeal. So, who was your friend, and when are you going to get me out of here?'

'I don't think I can,' Finnigin confessed.

'What? But you must!'

Finnigin shook his head. 'The long and short of it is this: today, I have to leave the city, or find myself in a situation similar to yours. I have no influence over your future. The man who took me from you yesterday is called Varian. Believe me, I have tried to persuade him to help you, but to no avail.'

'Perhaps you haven't tried hard enough.' Pashtarina said in a flinty voice. 'Perhaps you are too wrapped up in your own good fortune?'

'No . . .'

'Then why are you here?'

'To say goodbye.'

Pashtarina made a strangled sound and swept around to face the window, her strong white hands gripping the bars that covered it. 'It pains me to think you have freedom while I do not. It was thoughtless of you to come here unless you could help me.'

'But it doesn't seem too bad for you here . . .'

'Ha! How long can I hold on to my real self in this place? It will be killed! I don't want to be what these people want me to be. I want to be free. I want my old life back!'

Finnigin was helpless against the anguish in Pashtarina's voice. He wished he hadn't come to see her, and thought about how he could get out quickly now, without further embarrassment and unpleasantness for either of them. He realised that his friendship with this woman had existed solely while they were experiencing the same things, bonded by a common captivity. Varian had been right. Pashtarina was a concluded episode. Did all friendships forged under such difficult circumstances share the possibility of ending so abruptly? It was confusing. He and Pashtarina stood in silence, she still pressed against the window. Finnigin was relieved when the door scraped open again, and the nun put her head inside.

'It is time for you to leave,' she said sweetly to Finnigin.

'Goodbye,' he said to Pashtarina's tense back.

She did not reply.

'I am instructed to equip you and send you from the city,' Marvrani said as they walked back to Varian's house.

'I want to speak to Varian.'

Marvrani sighed impatiently. 'Too late. He's not at home any more, neither did he express a wish to see you.'

Finnigin stopped walking, forcing Marvrani to turn and look at him. 'I want to know what's going on.'

'What's going on?' Marvrani struck a pose, hands on hips. 'You are an ingenuous little terranaut who is having a series of grubby adventures. I don't suppose your sordid history is anywhere near completion, and you will soon resume your scurrying and hurrying through Overhang. There: that's the end of it.' She obviously felt she had made her point and attempted to march off once more, but because Finnigin wouldn't follow her, was obliged to pause again. 'Oh, do stop stalling! The sooner I see the back of this place the better.'

At that moment a line of priests filed down the street. They were all dressed in maroon robes, chanting in a deep undertone and swinging ropes of hand-bells. Finnigin and Marvrani were pushed back against the wall of a building. Marvrani sighed heavily. 'Listen, don't bother trying to resist Varian. He is stronger than you. Let him amuse himself.'

'I don't understand his motives, or even his plans,' Finnigin said.

'That is his intention,' Marvrani replied, 'and please don't attempt to interrogate me. Your questions are tiresome, and anyway, I know no more than you do.'

'When will I see Varian again?'

'When he wants to see you. That is the truth. Now be quiet and hurry with me to the house. Those Oubrahan cubs who were rescued from Rodarigo are anxious to have you punished for your collaboration, and I know for a fact they are at this minute stating their case to their family – all of whom enjoy prominent positions in this city. Be sensible: get out of here.'

'Could I come to Karaganzinad with you and Varian?' Finnigin asked, without much hope. He was not looking foward to travelling through Overhang alone once more.

'Certainly not!'

'What about Babooshpet? Couldn't we get her to come with me again?' The suggestion had not been serious. He guessed Marvrani's response before she uttered it.

'No. Babooshpet is no longer your concern.'

Back at the house, Marvrani began strapping a laden back-pack on to his shoulders. Finnigin, bowing beneath its weight, asked again if he could see Varian.

'I told you, no!' Marvrani replied, buckling the straps. 'Keep still!'

'I shan't leave until I've seen him,' Finnigin said.

'He's gone,' Marvrani snapped. 'Will you just get that into your head? He's not with us at the moment.'

Ignoring any more pleas from Finnigin, Marvrani virtually frogmarched him from the house, and swiftly escorted him to the eastern gate of Oubrahani. She assured him the road beyond would lead him to another city, although she wasn't sure of its name. Gleaming Fisk seemed to mean nothing to her. She did not stay to watch him leave.

Finnigin walked beneath the shadow of the gate, and a vibrant tremor of air fluttered against his face. He paused and looked back. There was an intense atmosphere of expectancy, and something didn't sound right to him. Of course. For the first time since he'd entered the city, the bells were silent. Overhead came a grumbling roar; distant thunder. The blue-grey of the sky was fast becoming occluded by the purple clouds Finnigin had noticed earlier. Suddenly, without warning, it seemed as if every bell in the city began to toll. But it did not sound as if any human hands were involved. Finnigin retreated involuntarily from the violent cacophany. What was going on? As if on cue, doors to the buildings flew open and people ran out into the streets. The combined clamour of the bells condensed into a single pealing tone that made Finnigin's head ache. People ran along the pavements, hands above their heads; women spiralled in circles, tearing their hair; children gaped and writhed upon the streets; horses and beasts of burden galloped madly over anyone in their way; men fell upon each other with snarling mouths and clawing fists. Oubrahani, tolled from its effete splendour, had gone insane. Finnigin backed under the archway, his eyes round. Had Varian anything to do with this? He stumbled over something behind him and turned quickly to find a crumpled guard slouched against the wall, his nose and ears weeping blood.

'What is it?' Finnigin asked. 'What's happening?'

The guard groaned and raised a shaking hand, pointing out towards the mêlée. 'The fatal tone,' he gasped. 'The bells . . . the winds of disorder.' He moaned and slumped back against the stone.

Finnigin squatted down beside the guard's inert body and stared at the scene before him. People were slumping to the ground, to lie twitching and scratching in muddled heaps. The cry of the bells had condensed even further until it sounded like a single, crazed voice clanging out over the city.

Finnigin got to his feet. He felt as if he'd somehow stepped out of time. Whatever was going on, he was slipping between its events and effects. He was beyond it, outside of it. Slowly, he went back into the city.

The door to Varian's house was ajar. Dreamily, Finnigin mounted the steps and went inside. He expected to find it covered with dust, unused, withered corpses in every room. But the house was clean and silent; empty. Marvrani had already left it. Finnigin went from room to room, found nothing. Why had he come back here? What had he hoped to achieve, to find?

At last, he went into the parlour where Varian had spoken to him the day before. The hearth was cold; ashes had scattered, or blown, on to the carpet. Two large chairs stood before the hearth. One was tipped over, its legs pointing towards the door. The other . . . Finnigin froze. From where he was standing, he could see something draped over the arm of the chair. Something limp, white, dead. It was a human hand.

Tentatively, Finnigin edged forward until he could see who lay in the chair. At first, he supposed it was a mannequin, a life-size doll, for there was nothing remotely alive about the occupant of the chair. A mass of tangled red-brown hair fell over its face, spilled over its chest. It looked a discarded, crumpled thing. Summoning courage, Finnigin reached out and lifted the head by its hair. The skin of the face was waxy, but not made of wax. He couldn't put a name to what it might be made of. But one thing was certain: the face was his own.

Finnigin found himself outside on the street, his vision disturbed by swirling motes of light and shade. He thought he would faint and crouched down to put his head between his knees. What had he seen? He didn't know. What was its significance? He dared not think.

Around him, Oubrahani had fallen silent but for the mournful tolling of a single bell several streets away. The wind, dying down, fretted the hair and clothes of the people who lay comatose or dead upon the streets. Finnigin slowly rose and retraced his steps to the gate, his mind numb. He edged past the fallen bulk of a great black horse whose eyes rolled, whose heavy lips twitched, revealing long, yellow teeth. As Finnigin passed its head, the animal shuddered violently and then scrambled to its feet, shying away, its ears back. Instinctively, Finnigin reached out and grabbed the dangling reins. The horse had been lying on its owner who was crushed to death. Its hide was wet with blood that was not its own.

Now I have a horse, Finnigin thought. Another gift of Varian's?

The animal became malleable as it felt his hands upon the reins. It was a soldier's horse, well-trained, strong. He transferred his baggage to its back and secured it on the convenient leather loops that were attached to the back of the saddle. Then, he hopped around for a few moments, trying to mount the beast. It was so tall. Eventually, he scrambled aboard and felt the animal collect itself beneath him, like the ignition of a mighty engine. Finnigin had ridden animals before, but never one like this. When he applied pressure to its flanks, he expected the beast to shoot forward like a comet. Instead, it broke into a mincing, sideways trot, rolling its eyes at the fallen citizens around its fetlocks. After much goading and coaxing, Finnigin got it to take him to the gate.

Here, he miserably contemplated the lonely road leading into the shadows of looming crags and narrow, empty gullies. He knew that soon the silence of the mountains would swallow him and the bells of Oubrahani would be nothing more than memories.

The next journey, the next story, he thought.

The horse snorted and walked briskly out of the city.

Casmeer

The dreams of his wife had become more vivid. For hundreds of years, Casmeer's libido had lain dormant, but now, as if the act of writing had rekindled a forgotten lust, he was moved to enact his feelings upon his stories. He'd had no intention of doing that. Also, he felt as if the tales themselves were running away from him. He found it hard to keep them in line. In Oubrahani, he had barely managed it. He felt ashamed of what he had imagined; the plundering of Finnigin's body, the transformation of Finnigin's flesh. He was unsure what had prompted him to do that. In embracing Finnigin, he embraced his own youth. In melding with Finnigin, he became young, more vital. Elini lived in the character of Marvrani, yet she was distant from him; he could not touch her. It made him realise that in life they had been little more than companions. What Marvrani had said was true: he had always kept secrets from Elini.

Now Marvrani, freed from the restrictions of the individual who'd been the inspiration behind her creation, wanted a different life to the one Elini had adored; that of quiet domestication, the acquisition of expensive material things. Marvrani wanted adventure, glamour, danger. She was a stranger, and yet utterly familiar. Casmeer found this hard to understand. Why had he made Marvrani that way? Was it because he'd always wanted Elini to be more adventurous, or was it because, as he feared, Marvrani had a personality of her own, and would not bend to Casmeer's will?

When he felt sexually excited, Casmeer found, with some alarm, that he wanted to harm his characters, his self-children. He wanted to squeeze them, make them bleed. This, he despised in himself, but then considered that as the stories were fictions, it was acceptable for him to exorcise his feelings through them. He did not have to judge himself for lewd or wicked thoughts. Perhaps there was more of his cousin Mercaster in him that he'd thought?

Every night, he now read his stories to the plumosites who ate the fruit he'd gathered for them as he spoke. They were kind critics for they never left the roofgarden until he finished reading, and if they disliked the stories they'd probably throw the fruit at him. Casmeer tried not to believe that the plumosites could understand his words, but it was difficult not to. Too much time alone, he thought. I must stop imposing human characters on these animals. Then he'd smile and think to himself, Perhaps Babooshpet likes the character I have invented for her?

Chapter Fifteen
Living On Skin

Distances were deceptive. Although it had seemed that only a couple of hours' walk would get them to the river, Ays and Leeth continued on foot all night, and in the early morning had to skip from tussock to tussock across a marsh. From there, it was easy to see that the nearest city was a leviathan, the most enormous Ays had yet encountered. Thick aquaduct coils spilled from its guts, lying in unscaleable, segmented tangles across the ground. People, dwarfed by the city's bulk, were engaged in servicing activities among the coils. A group of terranauts stood up to their knees in the river, apparently washing pilot-stones in the flow.

Because Ays knew he'd got to be sparing with his supply of hela, the dawn brought with it an overwhelming desire to partake of a robust dose. He found his mouth watering with a longing to taste the acrid tang of fresh hela strands; his limbs shook. Leeth, who was attempting to be solicitous, treading carefully, said that she thought he was feeling the cold.

'You will have to get a new coat,' she decided.

'How?' Ays snapped. 'Steal one? Or risk entering that city and being trapped in whatever web their society weaves for travellers?'

'Why can't you grow hela on your body like . . .'

A swift, murderous glance from Ays silenced her

before she could finish the sentence. 'Hela does not grow naturally upon human skin,' he said coldly. 'It would require a protracted preparation, of which I lack the knowledge.'

'It was only a suggestion. Won't those terranauts have hela?'

Ays sighed. 'I need my own supply again, but that can only be achieved with a certain kind of spore. I have no currency to buy hela, and nothing with which to barter for it.' A cloud of gloom descended on his soul with these words. 'In short, I am in affliction.'

'Do you need the hela?' Leeth asked. 'I mean, really need it?'

'I have a feeling we'll both soon find out,' he said. 'I've taken hela since I was very young, and my body is used to it. I don't know what will happen should I stop taking it, but it seems obvious the effects will be very uncomfortable, if not debilitating.'

'I would hate to be slave to such a craving!' Leeth cried angrily. 'If I were you, I'd try to be rid of it.'

'It is an easy thing to speak such words.'

Picking their way among the tussocks and between drooping riverside trees, Ays and Leeth eventually came to the riverbank itself. To the left, the imposing bulk of the nearest city blotted out the landscape, and much of the sky; to the right, the river roiled lazily from what appeared to be some kind of village built on stilts, which plunged into the river-bed. Ays was intrigued. He'd never seen a static community before.

Leeth seemed to divine his thoughts. 'There are not many settlements this far from the foothills of the mountains. I wonder why these people have built here.'

'I think we should go and find out,' he said, pointing towards the village.

'That means we are doubling back upon ourselves,' Leeth replied.

'Does it matter? Do you have a set destination in mind?'

Leeth shrugged petulantly. There was a faintly coquettish air to her manner now, which, to Ays, rested grotesquely among her other attributes. Clearly, she had decided she was no longer a child, but a woman.

'Remember the words of the Tammers,' Ays said. 'We should make enquiries about the city before approaching it. Have you noticed the number of corpse-cages hanging from its belly?'

'In a city that size, you would expect to find more,' Leeth argued. 'Look at its spires and pennants; it is a beautiful place. It looks noble and ancient. My father would have said . . .'

'This is not the time to bring your father out of moth-balls,' Ays snapped. 'You haven't mentioned him for weeks, as if you'd conveniently shut him in his coffin. Now, you drag him out again.'

'Your words are in poor taste,' Leeth said, with a hint of indignant tearfulness. 'I have undergone a trauma.'

Ays made an exasperated sound and began walking towards the village of struts and platforms.

The sun rose slowly into the sky, and reflected off the river surface with such dazzling brilliance it confounded sight. By the time they reached the village, Ays' eyes were aching and streaming, and Leeth had wound a corner of her shawl across her brow as a shade.

'I have never seen anything so bright!' she said. 'It is like pure sunlight.'

Her words seemed to evoke a sleeping memory in Ays' mind which reared up with unexpected potency. 'Yes,' he murmured. 'Yes.' For a few moments he stood and stared at the shining water, his mouth hanging open. Leeth had to shake him.

'Are you all right?'

Ays shook his head, causing his temples to throb with pain. 'Yes, I'm fine.' He did not speak of the sensation that had gripped him; that of utter familiarity. Had he been here before? Surely, that was impossible. Leeth was smiling up at him in the fashion of a young girl at one with her body and the whole world. Ays considered that he should have found her bewitching, but he always saw something aged and haggard about Leeth that suffocated her youthful charm in its crib.

'Stop grimacing at me!' he snapped.

Leeth performed a couple of skipping steps. 'But I feel so . . .' she threw out her arms '. . . so alive! What a glorious day this is.'

'There is a chill from the north; the season's turning.' Ays suspected Leeth had never experienced the exhilaration of being alive in a dynamic world before. Had Fineas Rigg done that for her? It seemed an obscene thought. She appeared to have shrugged off the dreadful events of the previous couple of days. It could hardly be said that her whole being had bloomed, but a few buds had shot forth upon the dried twigs. Could it be, that with the proper attention, Leeth *could* become attractive and charming? Ays struggled to see that possibility, but gave up after a few minutes. Whether it was coloured by his personal opinions or not, his imagination simply couldn't stretch that far.

A group of women, wearing their voluminous skirts tucked up into their waist-bands, were standing in the river near its edge, handling nets and wicker cages. Ays and Leeth stood on the bank, hoping to catch their attention, but none of the women made any sign of having seen them.

'Churlish behaviour!' said Leeth. 'They are ignoring us.' Ays struggled with foreboding. Should they proceed towards the village or not? Leeth made the decision for him by stamping off up the bank, tossing her tangled black hair.

The river widened considerably in the place where the village stood, suggesting the inhabitants had perhaps increased its width themselves by excavation. The structures of the village appeared delicate, as if a strong storm could have tossed them all nonchalantly into the water. As they approached, Ays and Leeth could see that a large number of people were swimming around the struts of the village, calling to one another in cheerful voices, diving beneath the surface and jumping back up into the air. There was almost a festive atmosphere to the scene. Swallowing any misgivings, Ays approached an elderly man who was sitting on a small jetty that poked out into the river, dabbling his toes in the water. Ays was virtually blinded by the glare from the surface and had to rub his eyes as he spoke.

'Good day, sir. My companion and I are strangers to these parts, and we'd welcome any advice you could give us on how to secure lodging.'

The old man turned round, and blinked up at Ays. His eyes were a curious milky blue. 'Eh? Eh?' he said in a gruff voice. 'What is it you're wanting?'

'We suffered an accident recently, and have lost all our belongings. To be honest, we need to throw ourselves upon someone's charity in order to reorganise our lives.'

The old man nodded thoughtfully. 'Makes sense. My daughter might be able to help you. Can you swim?'

'Most certainly,' Ays replied, remembering with fondness the icy cool underground cisterns in Min where he'd sneaked off to as a young boy for illicit swims with his friends.

'I can't,' said Leeth, but both Ays and his newfound acquaintance ignored her.

'Help me up,' said the man. 'Oh, these old bones! The only time I'm comfy nowadays is Below.'

Ays offered the man his arm.

'I'm Tollink,' said the man, 'Max Tollink. And you?'

'Ays. Just Ays.'

'Traveller, ah! Gone are the days when I gadded across the land. I went beyond the forest, you know, in my youth. Saw the yellow lands, and a great many extraordinary sights.'

'That is where I have come from,' Ays said.

'Indeed?' Max Tollink grinned heartily, blinking his blind-looking eyes. 'Then we shall swap tales! Yes, I can guarantee you accommodation for a night at least!' He laughed, and patted Ays' arm.

'I have never come across a village that does not move,' he said coaxingly as they strolled up the bank.

'There are some, there are some,' Max replied. 'Though you'd have to travel far to visit them all. Most are situated at the mountains' skirt.'

'Who built them?' Ays asked. 'Exiles, fugitives?'

'Who knows?' Max answered. 'Radianti was established here hundreds of years ago by a woman who claimed the moving cities made her dizzy. She brought her children with her, and they erected the first platforms. Others joined the community over the years, the kind of people you spoke of, the dispossessed. But there is no brain fever here in Radianti; the water soothes the heart and mind, brings sanity and serenity. Radianti will outlive the eldest city, I'm sure. A settlement such as ours does not get tired and worn out, cannot fall to its knees and die. Also, the river sustains it. It brings balm to the most troubled soul.'

Ays glanced over his shoulder to catch sight of Leeth scuffing sullenly behind, very much in her former manner. When she noticed Ays looking, she lifted her chin, flicked her hair and attempted to walk with a more sprightly step. Ays looked away in distaste.

The Tollink family lived in a one-storey, but sprawling, series of rooms in the middle of the village. 'Do many cities come to the water to drink?' Ays asked, as they walked along the extremely narrow slatted streets of the village. Between the slats, the river could be seen glinting far below.

'Oh yes indeed!' declared Max. 'There are never less than three visible from Radianti. The more amenable terranauts who frequent this area are forever laying stones to drag the cities down to the water. It is an act of kindness on their part. Me, I've seen cities die of thirst in the yellow places. And you know, most terranauts are capricious rogues.'

'I've met a few. They seem unpredictable at best.'

'An astute judgment in one so young as yourself! Yes, this is the place for city-watchers.'

Ays gestured towards the huge leviathan. 'And what city is that? Do you know?'

'Salaganda,' said Max. 'It is an ancient crawler, and often appears along this stretch of the Skine. The nobles of that city have a taste for our crawfish pâté, and often send their retainers to buy it from us. They give us jewellery and beautiful metal ornaments as payment. Some say that once a year Salaganda scrapes her skirts along the edge of the mountain ring and excavates her riches from there. Others speak of a city that was once swallowed by the land, but whose whereabouts the Salagandans know of. It is said that there are vast tombs there, that the Salagandans plunder of booty.'

'Is it a place friendly to strangers?'

Max grimaced. 'Take this advice from me. Never enter a city when you have nothing upon your person that the citizens require. If you give them something they like or need, they will love you. Otherwise . . .' He shook his head. 'I have heard stories of all manner of difficulties.'

'Allow me to add to them later,' Ays said dryly.

Max put his head on one side as they approached an open doorway. 'Ah, here we are! I recognise the wind-chimes tinkling at the threshold.'

Ays had already guessed that Max' eyesight was bad, but was surprised to find that the rest of his family appeared to share the affliction. His daughter, Yemina, was a woman of maturity, yet carrying her first child at her hip. Her partner, Derrell, was younger than she, but both were dark-skinned, slender people who appeared more like brother and sister than husband and wife. Their eyes, a startling pale blue, were all the more unusual because of their swarthy colouring. In Radianti, husbands assumed the surname of their wives, and it seemed that Yemina was head of the family.

Max explained to his daughter how he had found Ays and Leeth on the river bank. 'Beds and meals!' he declared. 'The best we can offer!'

'Welcome,' said Yemina, moving forward to take hold of Ays' hands. She rubbed his palms with her thumbs. 'Ah, you are weary. You must come Below before we eat. We would not dream of denying guests the experience.'

'Below?'

'Into the spill, the Skine.'

'The river?'

'Mother of all life,' said Derrell.

'Actually, I could do with a rest first,' Ays ventured.

The Tollinks all shook their heads. 'Nonsense!' said Yemina. 'A dip will revive you. Come along!'

In the manner of all people who espouse particularly

strong religious convictions, the occupants of Radianti were eager to convert visitors to their faith. Yemina led the way down a series of wooden walkways and ladders to a shrine woven of flexible withes, at the centre of which was an opening that led beneath the water. Many other Radiantians were present, all of them disrobing before entering the water, or rubbing themselves down with switches of dried grass after having re-emerged. Ays thought that Max's family greeted the prospect of a quick swim with the same vigour and excitement that he'd once have reserved for the prospect of a long evening's drinking and hela-smoking with his friends. Leeth, who at first had tried to chatter animatedly with the Tollinks, had reverted, as if uncontrollably, to her habitual taciturn state.

She'd always harboured a fear of water, and the thought of lowering herself into the depths of the Skine appalled her. 'I will not be joining you,' she said to Ays.

'It would be rude not to,' he replied in a low voice. He was distinctly uncomfortable about having to take his clothes off in front of Leeth, feeling she'd glean more prurient pleasure from the situation than he'd like.

'I hate water,' she replied.

'Keep your voice down. Your words might be taken as heresy, and although these people are all sweet smiles at the moment, they might take a different view if they think we're blaspheming against their beliefs.'

'Is there a problem?' Yemina asked brightly. She had unselfconsciously stripped down and now stood naked before them.

'My companion is a little nervous of the water,' Ays said.

'Nervous? But why? The water is life itself.'

'I am afraid of drowning,' Leeth said primly.

Yemina laughed. 'Oh, Lady Skine won't drown you! Here, let my old dad take you in. He'll look after you! Come along, you two. Clothes off! The Lady is waiting.'

'Do as she says!' Ays ordered, with as much threat as he could put into his voice.

Leeth made an angry sound and turned her back on him to undo the buttons of her dress. Ays quickly threw off his clothes and sat down on the edge of the opening before Leeth could inspect him. Below, the water licked richly at the underside of the withes. It looked as black as ink, but its surface was shot with brilliant swathes of light. Perhaps it was magical?

Derrell sat down beside him and then eased his body with luxuriating pleasure into the water. 'Follow me. Sink down quickly.'

Ays slid into the water. It was cold and yet strangely comfortable. Derrell resurfaced and, stroking the water with his arms, grinned at Ays, who so far had kept his head in the air.

'What do you think?' Derrell asked, his pale eyes shining. Obviously, the villagers took great pleasure in the reactions of visitors to the water.

'It feels . . . very . . .' Ays baulked at using an inadequate word. He smiled. 'Wonderful.'

'Take a breath and hold my hand.'

Ays did as he was bid and allowed Derrell to take him below the surface. After a few moments, he opened his eyes. What he saw came as a surprise. There was a tangle of bodies swimming around him, but they were only vague shapes. The river was murky, full of floating debris, perhaps kicked up by the multitude of swimmers. His flesh was tingling in a pleasurable way, however. Derrell led him through the murk, until Ays thought his lungs would burst. Indicating as such by repeatedly squeezing Derrell's hand, Ays eventually headed for the surface and broke through into sunlight, where gouts of light seem to arc around their heads. He paddled breathlessly, yet felt undeniably invigorated.

'The surface is so bright, yet it's so muddy below,' he said. 'I expected clear water.'

Derrell was still grinning. 'Well, there are a host of religious explanations for it,' he said. 'Delightful tales for children. However, the more rational among us tend to believe the Magisteri from Salaganda who tell us the Skine is full of a microscopic animal that causes all of these effects. The animalcule undergoes a life-cycle that takes it through a sort of vitrified stage, when it clings to the surface of the river; that is what causes the shine. I've been told that my body is host to a swarm of these creatures, but the relationship, if it is parasitical, is beneficial to both parties. I enjoy health and happiness, and lose only clear sight.'

'Ah . . . I did wonder about that.'

Derrell lifted his shoulders. 'I can see perfectly well beneath the water. It is very odd and the Salagandans have been studying the phenomenon for generations. Skine crawfish are also held to have healing properties when eaten.'

'Your father-in-law mentioned the Salagandans were partial to them.'

Derrell nodded. 'Mm. Incidentally, please don't mention any of my theories in front of Yemina. The old man is sympathetic, but my wife espouses a more traditional view. There is some dissension in our household over the matter, so I tend to avoid the subject.'

'As you wish.' Ays hesitated. 'I hope my eyes aren't going to be affected by this dip.'

Derrell was quick to reassure him. 'If you bathed regularly for a month or two, you would become one with the water, which basically means your sight would be affected. At the same time, you would feel like a spring sunrise. However, as you're a traveller, poor sight might be an inconvenience. Still, don't worry yourself. A few days' pleasure in the river won't harm you, but will certainly be beneficial. You look as if you've had a hard time recently.'

'That is true,' said Ays. 'I promised to tell Max some tales later.'

'We love the stories of travellers,' said Derrell, 'seeing as we don't stray much from the Skine ourselves.'

Ays could see no sign of Leeth, and wondered if she was giving old Max any trouble. He imagined that her naked body would look like a skeleton of knobbly sticks covered with brown paper.

In fact, Leeth had been pleasantly surprised by her experience of Below. Max's hands were strong and sure, and she felt safe beside him. Her first anxious paddlings soon subsided into a languorous beat of limbs. She wondered why she'd ever feared death by drowning. Surely, even if the water filled her lungs now, the experience of dying could only be tranquil and comfortable.

Beneath the water, villagers joined hands and danced, their limbs pale and insubstantial in the fluid gloom. Max took Leeth down to the river-bed, where the water was very deep. Here, in ancient times, a squat underwater cathedral had been constructed. Max and Leeth swam beneath a series of arches. They passed a girl who swam in a web of hair, slowly tumbling in a series of devotional saltations, her eyes shining like pearls through the fusc.

When they broke through the surface, Leeth wept a few tears of joy.

'You needed that, didn't you?' said Max.

It made Leeth realise that a person didn't necessarily need eyes to see.

Yemina and Derrell prepared a meal of river fare: plump crawfish simmered in a sauce of blood-minnow butter; sauteéd deepwater weeds, mud potatoes and pickled carp berries. The meal was accompanied by a honey wine, fermented from the produce of riverbank bees. 'I haven't tasted anything so delicious since leaving Min,' Ays said, licking his fingers. He felt pleasantly drowsy now, cleansed, as if the Skine had tenderly flushed away all the horrors of Beraftiel's death. Even his hunger for hela had diminished, though he couldn't resist taking a pinch of his meagre supply before the meal was served. Even the sight of Leeth inexpertly and crassly flirting with Max, who clearly enjoyed the attention, couldn't mar his good humour. Perhaps Leeth was lucky Max was nearly blind.

Leeth liked Max. She was aware of his amorous roguishness, but saw no harm in indulging him. Ays, as usual, was aloof and sneering. She wondered why she loved him so much; there seemed little in him worthy of the emotion at times. In the hours following Beraftiel's death, she had felt close to him, and had believed their days of distance had gone for ever, but it hadn't taken long for Ays to recover his composure and erect his barriers once more. She reflected there was something vaguely inhuman about him.

'So, to tales!' Max said, as Derrell cleared away the platters, and Yemina went to investigate her wine-store. Ays watched as the family lightly glided around the room, avoiding obstacles either through familiarity or an extra sense. For people whose eyesight above the water was so poor, they were amazingly graceful.

'What do you want to hear about?' Ays asked.

'Everything!' Max declared. 'Begin with the beginning of your journey.'

'I can do better than that,' Ays said, realising he was full of a need to talk about himself. 'Let me begin by telling you about Min. It is a city that flies.'

'That flies? How extraordinary!' said Max, settling himself in his cushions with an arm around Leeth.

'Min flies over the yellow lands,' Ays said, 'beyond the forest. It follows the lines of power on the ground below, around and around. And there I was a Priest of Hands.'

The Tollinks listened to Ays' story, occasionally asking questions. He hesitated about mentioning hela, but decided he might as well be honest about it. Yemina made a sound of disapproval.

'How foul of your people to make children become addicts of the stuff!' she said. 'None of our people ever use it.'

'To me, it was a way of life,' he said. 'Still is.'

'Perhaps you should rid yourself of the habit? I'm sure the Mother would help you.'

Ays wondered whether he dared believe that was possible. Before, he would never have considered a life without hela. Now, with the threat of losing his supply, the thought did not seem quite so outrageous.

'Ays likes being addicted to hela,' Leeth announced. 'I suppose he thinks it makes him more interesting.'

He was gratified no one saw fit to respond to such a remark. 'It is strange there are so many Mothers,' he said dreamily. 'Mine was the Mother of Darkness, Mother Death, yet yours is the Mother of Life.'

'Ours is the true Mother,' Yemina said. 'There are no others.' She shook her head. 'What terrible things were done to you as a child!'

'Yemmy!' Derrell dared to caution his wife.

They exchanged significant looks, until Yemina

shrugged. 'Well, I can't help feeling for the lad.'

'The Skine is our Mother,' Derrell said, 'and she nurtures us. The plant mara hela is the Mother of the people of Min, and I've no doubt Ays believes Her effects to be beneficial.'

'It imparts certain knowledge,' Ays said warily, wondering why Derrell had chosen that moment to be contentious.

Yemina would not countenance such a suggestion. 'Derrell, you are full of wild ideas! It comes from mixing with those absurd Salagandans! They taint your mind with exotic theories.'

'They know about hela and its cult,' Derrell continued bravely, looking only at Ays. 'Salaganda regularly visits the Brine of Recondities, a vast sea near the mountain skirt, which is reputedly the birthplace of mara hela.'

'Really? I did not know there was one.'

'Derrell, will you stop wittering!' Yemina said.

'I've heard of it too,' said Max. 'The Brine is fed by six rivers, and during the summer and autumn is populated by water nomads who set up extensive floating markets. In winter the Brine freezes over entirely, and it is said that the ice traps all the words that were being spoken as the water froze. In spring, when the ice melts, the air is full of the ghosts of conversations. The hela spores breed beneath the ice, and turn it a russet colour. In spring it burgeons, and the sea is a mat of hela which can be gathered.'

'I've never heard of hela "breeding" in water,' Ays said.

'It is the Mother strain, or so I've heard,' Max replied. 'Salaganda, through the agency of its tame terranauts, will be crawling down to the Brine of Recondities once the leaves begin to fall. At the end of the season, the nomads sell off all their produce at very reasonable rates, and the Salagandans always have an eye for a bargain.'

Ays found he was being presented with a choice. He could endeavour to overcome his addiction, or seize a lift with the city and replenish his supply of hela.

'Sometimes, it is best not to desert your Mother,' Derrell said.

Ays looked at him sharply, but said nothing.

'And what of you, young Leeth?' Max asked to break the silence, squeezing her shoulder. Surely he could feel the bones grating together? 'Are you also an angel shorn of wings?'

'I was not born on Min, if that's what you mean,' she replied. 'My mother died when I was very young, and I've spent all of my life travelling with my father. That is, until he died too. Now, I am alone.'

'But for your friend, Ays.'

Leeth hesitated, her face a stormy sky of contrary emotions. 'We have not known each other long,' she managed to say.

Ays slept well, lying on a pallet in a small room, where the morning sunlight came in between the withes. Strangely, the air was not chill, even though the room was well-ventilated. Ays sniffed a pinch of hela and lay back with his arms behind his head. He dared not examine how much hela he had left. Perhaps he should attempt to go without the stuff for a whole day, just to see what happened to him? Radianti creaked about him, and the sound of gently lapping water lulled his senses. He heard bare feet padding by outside.

After an hour or so, Derrell came to see why Ays hadn't got out of bed. 'They are drawing up the aquaducts at Salaganda,' he said.

He sat up, clasping his knees. 'I've been thinking about whether I should enter the city,' he said.

'Perhaps travel with it to the sea you spoke of?'

'It would be a slow journey,' Derrell said.

'Until spring.' Ays sighed. 'I don't know what to do.'

Derrell paused, his face showing he was thinking hard about something. Then he spoke. 'If you stayed with us here, we could no doubt help you . . . overcome your problem. But I don't think you would be happy doing that.'

'I'd be free of hela but blind.' Ays gave a dismal laugh.

'You carry a great sadness,' Derrell said, shaking his head. 'It is as if you're driven to keep moving.'

'Sometimes I feel melancholy,' he agreed. 'I wonder why I ever left Min. My experiences have been educational, and for the most part lacking great discomfort. Still, the initial zeal that fired my imagination when I descended from Min has largely evaporated. The memories I sought are too few, and have no pattern for me to follow. I am sporadically accosted by a mysterious man, for which I have no explanation. I looked for a truth in my life, a harmony, but I have found only random chaos, unconnected events, spurious recollections. Now, I am soon to be without hela, and face an adjustment which might kill me.'

'Unless, of course, you managed to acquire a generous patron until you were able to replenish your supply.'

Ays accorded Derrell a suspicious glance. 'Correct me if I'm wrong, but you seem very keen for me to continue in my habits. What is it to you?'

'I will be honest. An acquaintance of mine called Massifer Oskovellier, who lives on Salaganda, requires an assistant to help him with certain explorations. He is studying the effects of mara hela upon the human frame, and I must admit you are amply qualified for the position of helping him in his studies. Massifer's father,

Explendian Oskovellier, is the one of the Gribnarchs of Salaganda. They are a very rich family.'

'Hmm, the proposition sounds interesting,' said Ays. 'But I feel quite strongly that I should go to the Brine of Recondities, and helping your friend would delay that. Unless, of course, I could acquire new spores from him.'

'If you were to be employed by Massifer, your requirements would be fulfilled on two counts. First, Salanganda itself is heading towards the Brine, and you could travel there in comfort, and second, I expect Massifer would be sympathetic to your situation and make sure you had an adequate supply of hela. He would not want his assistant to suffer.'

'This seems like massive good luck,' said Ays. 'Almost too good to be true. Why didn't you mention this last night?'

Derrell pulled a sour face. 'Yemina dislikes the Salagandans, Massifer and his revered father in particular. She feels they lead my thoughts astray from the contemplation of Mother Skine's omnipotence.'

'Ah, I can understand your reluctance to speak frankly in front of her. Perhaps you could arrange an interview for me with this Massifer?'

'I shall make haste to do so. Salaganda prepares to depart the area. I have already noticed the terranauts placing a new lurement of stones.' He squinted myopically at the pile of Ays' clothes which were all scorched and tattered. 'I think you'd better borrow a more respectable costume. I shall fetch you some of my garments; we are much of a size. Gather up your belongings. We shall go to Salaganda as soon as you are dressed.'

'Belongings? I have none, other than the rags of my clothes and a small packet of hela. You seem quite confident I shall be accepted for the post. I'd have thought your friend would have a multitude of individuals to choose from.'

Derrell paused at the door. 'That is not the case. The taking of mara hela is frowned upon in Salaganda. Massifer has to be discreet, and he can't afford to employ any old ragamuffin. You, with your genteel manners, will pass quite easily for an assistant scholar. Also, my recommendation alone will count much in your favour.'

Presently, Derrell returned with an armful of clothes for Ays to try on. While he'd waited, Ays had washed his face and combed his hair, using implements that had been left out for his convenience. He realised, with a cruel satisfaction, that he would now be leaving Leeth behind. Should he simply sneak off without saying anything to her, or seek her out to say goodbye? As if she sensed something was afoot, she presented herself at Ays' door, just as he was tying his bootlaces.

'Oh, you have new clothes,' she said lamely, one hand unconsciously touching her own faded old dress.

'Derrell was kind enough to offer me some,' Ays said. 'Anyway, I'm glad you're here.'

'Oh?' Leeth attempted to be arch, a parody which prompted him to shudder.

'Yes. I feel I should say farewell to you, seeing as we're now parting company.'

'What?' Leeth hurried into the room. 'If you're leaving, I'm coming with you!'

'I'm afraid that's impossible,' he said. 'I've acquired a position of employment upon Salaganda, and it does not allow for dependants.'

'You can't!' Leeth cried. 'We have been through so much together!'

'Haven't we! A series of calamities I hope to forget.'

Leeth was temporarily silenced, her chest heaving with shocked emotion. When she eventually spoke, her voice was unsteady. 'Ays, I beg you, don't leave me behind. I can't bear the thought of waking each day and not being able to see you! I know you have no feelings for me, but being near you is enough.'

Derrell, who was clearly becoming embarrassed by Leeth's confessions, cleared his throat purposefully and said loudly, 'Come along now, Ays. I can hear Salaganda's stampers running through their preliminary movements.'

Ays put on the russet brown jacket Derrell handed to him. 'I'm sorry, Leeth.'

She turned away.

'We shall look after her,' Derrell said. 'Old Max has taken a fancy to her.'

'I will not stay here!' Leeth cried, wheeling round. Her sallow face looked green with fury. 'No one speaks for my welfare but myself.' She ran out of the room.

'Young girls are prone to such displays,' Derrell said feebly.

Ays shook his head. 'Leeth has never been a young girl,' he said. 'Sometimes, I doubted she was even human.'

Avoiding any members of the Tollink family, Derrell led Ays hastily out of the village. Ahead, the riverbank was churned to mud by the Salagandan aquaducts, but now appeared empty since the pipes had been removed. Huge, coppery-coloured mechanisms were being tested; all ran with an efficient, oily smoothness; ancient machinery that had been kept in peak condition, lovingly repaired and serviced. Salaganda was so huge, Ays couldn't imagine how it could move. It covered the landscape for as far as he could see. There were no simple rope-ladders or narrow walkways depending from its belly, but a series of stairways, wide enough for two dozen people to ascend side by side. An engineer, who was lowering himself from the machinery by means of a seat-winch, waved at Derrell. 'Hoy there! If you have good craws in your bag, remember to leave a couple at my address!'

'Good day to you, Emling! How goes your work?'

'All is in order!' called the engineer. 'It'll soon be goodbye until the spring.'

'You seem to know quite a few Salagandans,' Ays remarked.

Derrell indicated the way to one of the stairways. 'Yes. There is a long tradition of trade between the city and Radianti; a relationship also enjoyed by the cities of Loomeden, Stars of Triumph and Homingdown.'

'The cities here keep quite a tight circuit then.'

'Look around you; this is fertile country. And the terranaut troupes in this area are notoriously lazy. As the forest grew, it isolated this patch of land and the cities from all others.'

They mounted the stairway and after a long climb entered a covered area, so that anyone on the stairs was not offended by the noisy, oily machinery of the city. Eventually, they emerged into the streets of Salaganda. Security seemed lax, and there was an air of great activity as the inhabitants greeted the prospect of renewed movement.

'This seems a city of riches,' Ays said in awe, gazing up at the tall buildings of creamy stone, the lush awnings, the terraced gardens.

'It is indeed!' agreed Derrell. 'This way. It isn't far to Massifer's house, and I'm anxious to disembark before the city begins its journey.'

They hurried through the opulent streets, and arrived at the gateway to an impressive manse. Here, liveried guards greeted Derrell as someone well known to them, and he and Ays were allowed ingress to the estate. Derrell marched directly to a modest side door and was there welcomed by a woman who carried the keys to the house. 'Derrell Tollink!' she declared. 'Another visit, even as the stampers pound? This must be urgent business!' She led them inside to a spacious back parlour, obviously her personal realm.

'I trust Master Massifer is at home?' Derrell said. 'I must see him immediately. Tell him it concerns his work. I have a candidate here for the position he is offering.'

'Of course!' said the housekeeper, glancing at Ays. 'I shall alert him to your arrival.' She activated a communication trumpet on the wall, and spoke into it importantly. 'Yes, yes, Derrell Tollink. He has a friend with him who is applying for the post you have.'

Ays heard a cultured voice coming from the trumpet. 'I shall be down at once.'

Covertly, Ays examined his surroundings. If the housekeeper's room was as opulent as this, it boded well for the guest rooms. The parlour was cluttered with ornate furniture, wall hangings, ornaments, plants and rugs. It smelled of a heady, flowery perfume.

Massifer Oskovellier came directly into the parlour, indicating an informal relationship with his staff. He looked approximately ten years older than Ays, and was of thin build, with a keen, alert face, long black hair which he wore in ringlets, and garments of a deep viridian hue. His hands were remarkable because of his overly large knuckles. He approached Ays and Derrell with his face set into a wolfish grin, rubbing his hands together. Ays was not sure how he should take such a voraciously gleeful advance.

'Derrell, my good friend!' he announced, in a voice which seemed too large and melodious for his meagre frame. 'From Mistress Pasker's remarks, I gather you've been working on my little problem.'

'Absolutely,' said Derrell, with some deference. 'This here is Ays. I've told him a little about your project and he is willing to work for you.'

'I was thinking of travelling to the Brine of Recondities,' Ays said.

Massifer's eyes held a twinkle. 'Aha!'

Ays suddenly felt as if his hela-taking was a grubby and unmentionable habit. He did not like the thought of colluding with Massifer, which was a ridiculous way to feel. 'In my home city, my vocation required me to make regular use of mara hela. It was a respected part of my profession. Now, I'm in the situation where I've lost my supply. It's an embarrassing circumstance, but I'd be happy to assist you with your work if you could help me overcome my difficulties.'

'With absolute pleasure!' announced Massifer. He turned to Derrell. 'Well, we shall meet again come spring.'

'I shall await the day with impatience,' Derrell said, bobbing a smart bow. Ays received the impression some kind of business deal had just been completed. Derrell collected himself. 'Well, I must be off with haste. I have no wish to shimmy down a rope or hire a more expensive method of departing this fair city!' He nodded at Ays. 'Good luck. I wish you well in your search.'

'Goodbye, and thank you,' Ays said. For some reason, a thread of uneasiness had entered his mind. As the door shut on Derrell's retreating figure, he felt as if it was imprisoning him inside.

'Well, well, well,' said Massifer cheerfully, still rubbing his extraordinary hands together. 'I don't stand on ceremony here, so we'll forego formal addresses. Mistress Pasker is not quite so lenient. Call her "mistress" and nothing else. Now, would you care to follow me? I'll show you to your accommodation.'

The manse of Oskovellier was large and Ays soon felt lost in it as Massifer led him through a maze of corridors. Massifer explained that his father had another palace nearer the city centre, where he was on hand to administer law and order when it was required. Ays had the impression the Gribnarch was an inflexible individual, and made a mental note to avoid him.

'You must not be awed if ever you come across any of my family about the house,' Massifer said. 'For all their elevated station in life, they are still creatures of flesh like yourself. I don't tolerate hoity-toitiness.'

Massifer used the attic floor as his workrooms, and Ays was given two chambers of his own there. From the small, gabled windows, he had a commendable view of the city. He envisaged being able to lie on his bed in hela-stupor gazing out over the towers; the prospect was pleasing. The appointments in the rooms were hardly lavish, but comfortable and well-worn. There was a sense of other people having lived there in the past. 'Has your last assistant been gone long?' Ays asked Massifer.

'What? Oh . . . A while. To be frank with you, we had a disagreement.'

'Oh, I'm sorry.' Ays wondered whether he should probe the subject further, but Massifer pre-empted his enquiries.

'Yes. It was a trivial matter that was expanded out of all proportion. Gawrina decided she knew how to conduct my experiments better than I did. I had to point out that she was wrong, and a bitter argument ensued. She left my employ some weeks ago. Right in the middle of an important experiment, I might add.'

'That must have been very inconvenient.'

'It was. I hope you will not be so careless of your duties.'

'Not at all. I have been brought up to be meticulous.'

'That is good news. Well, make yourself at home. Pasker will bring you a tray. I think we shall delay initiating any gruelling research until the morrow. I have preparatory work to attend to today. Might I suggest we meet up for dinner this evening? Then, I can show you round my workrooms.'

'Is there nothing I can help with today?'

Massifer made a nonchalant gesture. 'Not really. Explore the house, if you like. But refrain from leaving the grounds until I have equipped you with the proper costume and furnished you with papers. Salaganda does not tolerate vagrants, and I would hate you to find yourself in a humiliating situation.'

'I shall abide by your words,' said Ays. 'I'm very grateful for this opportunity.'

'No more than I. Later, we must discuss your history with regard to the hela frond.' Massifer cleared his throat delicately. 'Ahem, do you require anything for the day?'

'You mean hela? No . . . I have a modest supply.'

Massifer stroked his face. 'Ah! Well, until later then.'

Left alone, Ays explored his rooms. He opened all the cupboards and drawers, hoping to find some sign of a previous occupant, but discovered only a bent hairpin in the back of the armoire. The linen upon the bed was newly laundered, covered by a thick quilt which was also unstained and bright. To Ays, the only thing in the room that spoke of predecessors was the atmosphere. Perhaps he sensed an abiding vapour of peers, hela-takers like himself? Apart from the bedroom, there was a small sitting-room, furnished only with a table beneath the window, a small book-case on the opposite wall, which was empty, and a two-seater recliner before the fire-grate. Ays sat down upon the sofa and regarded the swept hearth. As winter drew on, he imagined he would sit here of an evening, perhaps reading in front of the fire. He sighed and spread out his arms along the back of his seat, allowing his head to drop back. Had he fallen into a bed of down, as it seemed, or a mattress of thistles, which would only come to prick him as time progressed? Something about his situation unnerved him, but he thought that might only be a fear of being cooped up, after having travelled around for so long. Massifer seemed an affable sort, but his mention of having argued with his previous assistant made Ays uneasy. He detected in his new employer a tendency towards mulishness. Therefore, he would not emulate the mistakes of his predecessor. He would be compliant, and keep his opinions to himself.

As Massifer had predicted, Mistress Pasker soon arrived with a tray, containing a tureen of hot soup and a plate of bread, accompanied by a moderate tankard of yellow ale. She stood tall behind the couch to observe Ays eating. 'Forgive me, but the lass here before you would not eat her food. Such a peaked little thing, she was. I used to stand over her at mealtimes to make sure she filled her stomach. I shall do the same with you.'

Ays smiled weakly and sipped the soup. 'This is very tasty.'

'Yes. Fresh made. All my victuals are fresh made. I might as well tell you a little about house routine. We have few staff here, because Master Massifer resents intrusions. Apart from myself, there are only two others who live in. The rest of the staff work shifts of four hours a day, to clean, attend to security, and so on. You'll be expected to take care of your own apartment, and I won't tolerate sloppiness.'

'That's fine by me. I prefer tidiness.'

Mistress Pasker nodded briskly. 'Good. You'll be fed

in your rooms when work intrudes, but other than that, come down to the staff dining-room for your meals. There's a bathroom down the corridor, and the only rooms that are off-limits are those that are locked.'

'I'd be more than happy to lend a hand whenever I can,' Ays said, attempting to find favour with this severe woman.

'That's kind of you, but you'll find Master Massifer keeps you busy.'

'You really don't have to waste time making sure I eat,' Ays said with a smile. 'I have a good appetite.'

'So did she to start with,' Mistress Pasker said darkly.

'What do you mean?' Ays asked in alarm.

'Just don't let your work get on top of you,' the woman replied. 'Take time to relax.'

'I intend to. Do you have a library in the house?'

'There's a big book room on the first floor. It's locked, but Grundle can let you in to borrow a volume.'

'Thank you. Where might I find this Grundle?'

Mistress Pasker folded her arms. 'After you've finished eating, I'll take you to her.'

After a visit to the library, where a dour young woman reluctantly handed over a novel, Ays spent the rest of the day looking round the house, marvelling at the sumptuous rooms, at the display of wealth. He saw nothing of Massifer, and when he turned the door handle of another room in the attic, which he supposed was one of Massifer's workrooms, found it locked. At sundown, just as Ays had settled down on the sofa to read the rather uninspiring book Grundle had given him, another member of staff knocked at the door and entered the room. This was a young man of haughty appearance, dressed in a smart uniform.

'I am Savalin, Master Massifer's valet,' he said in a cold voice. 'I am to escort you to the dining-room where the Master is waiting.'

As Ays followed the man downstairs, he reflected that the staff of the Oskovellier manse were hardly a congenial bunch. Pasker was starchy and disciplinarian; Grundle suspicious and grudging; Savalin condescending and scornful. Massifer, in comparison, was a ray of light.

He was already seated at the table when Ays entered the dining-room. As soon as Ays sat down, Mistress Pasker swept in, followed by Grundle pushing a trolley. Between them, they laid out the food, Pasker uttering sharp orders to the other woman in a tight undertone. Massifer sat quietly, drinking a glass of wine in a thoughtful manner, until the staff had left. Then, he offered Ays the decanter and initiated conversation.

'Well, are you comfortably settled in?'

'Quite comfortably,' Ays replied, pouring himself a generous measure of wine.

'Glad to hear it.' Massifer lifted the lid of a tureen. 'Ah, what do we have here? Engineer's Pie – a plain but hearty feast. Help yourself.'

Ays did so. 'So, what will my duties entail?'

Massifer leaned back in his chair. 'I must outline something of my work. The effects of mara hela upon the human body is a fascinating study. In its pure state, it invokes euphoria, second sight, heightened sensitivity, and in extreme doses, vivid hallucinations that are often prophetic.' He leaned forward and picked at his meal with a fork which he also used to gesture with in between mouthfuls of food. 'I have found that by mixing hela with other substances yet more wondrous effects can be achieved. Blending hela paste with mudbark shavings induces an effect whereby the user can virtually see with their skin, so sensitive do they become to outside stimuli. Similarly, raw hela chopped with cone mushroom affects the hearing. One subject claimed to be able to hear animals the size of peas scampering away from the city's stampers. Another could hear the stars conversing with one another.' He waved the fork vigorously. 'There are a multitude of permutations I have yet to try.'

'It sounds fascinating,' Ays said. 'Perhaps I should tell you a little about myself, and how the fronds are used on Min?'

Massifer nodded in interest throughout Ays' narrative. 'That too is fascinating,' he said, when Ays had finished speaking. 'The link between hela and death opens up a host of possibilities. Of course, the drug is highly toxic, and it takes a determined user to overcome the initial delinquencies of its effects. That brings me to another point which I feel I should mention: my experiments are not without their hazards. It is essential you are fully aware of this, although I insist on taking every possible precaution.'

'As long as nothing rash or reckless is attempted, I will be amenable,' Ays said carefully, hoping that wasn't too forward a remark.

'Your caution is understandable,' Massifer replied, 'indeed commendable. Some of my assistants have become over-enthusiastic in their research, with unfortunate consequences. I will show you my theses which catalogue the results of all my experiments. No doubt you will find the information useful.'

'Thank you. I look forward to beginning the experiments.' Ays felt he spoke with honesty. Massifer had been frank, and had not attempted to conceal the more perilous aspects of the work.

'There will also be a small stipend,' Massifer said. 'Obviously, it will only be useful here in Salaganda.'

'That is more than I hoped for. Accommodation and meals would have been enough.'

'You are a virtuous young man,' said Massifer. 'I'm

sure we shall work well together.' He raised his glass.

'So am I,' Ays said, and lifted his own glass to touch that of Massifer and thereby seal their contract.

After the meal, Massifer took Ays up to his work-rooms, and there showed him some of the equipment used in his experiments. There was a great deal of apparatus for the distillation of various herbal and fungal essences, contraptions used to test the senses of hela-takers, shelves and shelves of substances, and a humid hela-farm under glass. Ays found himself slavering as Massifer lifted the lid of the frame and a whiff of flourishing hela wafted out. 'Prime strain,' said Massifer. 'I gather spore at the Brine of Reconditties.'

Back in his own rooms, Ays lay on the bed and took a generous snort of his hela-dust. With eyes half-closed, he gazed out at the city; a microcosm of winking lights. From far away came the bleat of music, and from somewhere in the house a trill of female laughter. Ays wondered whether he'd hallucinated the sound. He couldn't imagine any of Massifer's female staff laughing with such abandon. Much to his annoyance, he found his thoughts drifting towards Leeth. Would she stay with the Tollinks? Ays attempted to banish such thoughts; Leeth was no longer his responsibility. Never had been, in fact. He must not think of her again.

Sleep came easily, and his dreams were vague and soothing.

In the morning, he was woken by a knock at the door. Savalin walked in carrying a flask of water and a glass. 'Master Massifer would prefer you to fast this morning,' he said. 'And please refrain from taking any of your drug. I have brought you water.'

'Er . . . thank you,' Ays said. Savalin did not move. 'Can you put it down over there?' Ays pointed at the chest of drawers.

'I'm instructed to escort you to the workrooms.'

Ays objected to the man's sneering expression. 'Put the water down over there, and wait outside,' he said sharply. 'I will be dressed in a moment.'

Reluctantly, Savalin withdrew.

Ays was apprehensive about not taking any hela, but supposed he must abide by Massifer's request. No doubt he would be given a measured amount of the drug later. He got out of bed and dressed himself in the shirt and trousers and soft slippers which had been left out for him the previous evening. Then, after drinking one glass of water, he left the room. Savalin was standing stiffly to attention just outside the door, manifesting a strained patience.

'There is little point in being coy,' he said brusquely. 'Over the next few months, we shall be forced into a certain amount of intimacy.'

'Excuse me?' Ays couldn't keep the shock from his voice.

'Put it this way. Some of the experiments will leave you quite senselessly intoxicated. Then, it will be my duty to bathe you, feed you, put you to bed, and so on. You must look on my services as being almost medical.'

Ays did not greet this information with any enthusiasm. 'I'm sure I'll be quite capable of attending to myself,' he said. 'I do not intend to be over-indulgent during the experiments.'

Savalin declined to comment.

Massifer greeted Ays eagerly. He was wearing a light green overall, and had tied back his ringlets in a business-like fashion. 'No food, no hela?' he asked, smiling benignly.

Ays confirmed that neither substance had passed his lips.

'Excellent! Now, before we begin, I must ask you to hand over your own supply of hela.' Massifer held up a finger. 'I don't mean to be impolite, but situations might arise when you'll crave a dose, which may be dangerous. Please trust me and put yourself in my hands. Allow me to regulate your dosage.'

Ays did not like the sound of that. 'Of course,' he said blandly. 'I'll go and fetch it.'

'Not necessary,' said Massifer, with equal smoothness. 'Savalin can fetch it. Just tell him where it is.'

'No, really . . .' Ays began.

'I insist,' said Massifer. 'Oh, come now, Ays, surely you don't suspect us of villainous intentions?' He smiled widely.

'No . . .' Ays sighed. 'The package is in the pocket of my old trousers.' He would have preferred to fetch it himself, just so he could have reserved a small portion in case of emergencies. Now, he was truly at Massifer's mercy.

'That's splendid!' said Massifer, rubbing his hands together. 'Today, we shall try a concoction of hela-dust and rubbed booby-grass.'

'I haven't heard of booby-grass,' said Ays dubiously. 'What is it?'

'Well, it is a fairly recently discovered herb. It is supposed to counteract the effects of any stimulant or intoxicant. In public houses on Salaganda, it is now being sold as a late-evening cure for overindulgence. It should be interesting to see whether it reduces or annuls the effects of hela.'

The dose was administered, and Ays was seated in a comfortable chair, his only task to report regularly on how he felt. 'I feel a tingling sensation, but I'm unsure whether that is simply anticipation or not.'

Massifer made marks upon a chart. 'Hmm.'

Half an hour later, Ays experienced a sudden spasm of heat in his belly. He was allowed to observe this symptom for only a moment before terrible urgency forced him to his feet. He ran to the bathroom with seconds to spare and suffered an explosive void.

Back in the workroom Massifer listened impassively. 'Hmm. That is one of booby-grass's less clement effects. Do you feel any hela-strike?'

Ays wrinkled his nose. 'To be honest, I'm not sure. But neither do I feel any withdrawal clutch.' He rubbed his belly and puffed out his cheeks in a gesture of acute pain. 'I wish you'd warned me of that, Massifer.'

'I regret I forgot about it. Still, no harm done. I shall just write up my report.'

'Can I look at one of your theses now?'

'Hmm?' Massifer looked up from the workbench where he was busy scribbling notes. 'Oh, later, Ays. I'm busy at present. Sit and relax and be alert for any twitch or flex of your body.'

The effects of the booby-grass gradually subsided, and by evening Ays was keen to explore the city. Massifer exhibited a certain reluctance about this, but eventually handed over a set of papers in a grudging manner. Ays read the papers and laughed in incredulity.

'These documents state that I am a criminal from off-city who is currently undergoing rehabilitation in your establishment.'

Massifer made a nonchalant gesture. 'Ignore the text; it is merely a means of bypassing regulations concerning the employment of off-citizens.'

'It also states that under no circumstances will I be allowed to roam the city unsupervised.'

Massifer turned to concentrate on rearranging articles on his workbench. 'Well, Grundle has a night off. She is more than happy to be your companion.'

'These are stringent restrictions, Massifer.'

He sighed. 'I know. I know. No more savoury to me than to you. Please look on it as a formality, nothing more.'

'No disrespect to Mistress Grundle, but I would have preferred to stroll the city streets alone this evening. Today has not been without its trials, and I could do with the relaxation. I'm not in the mood for conversation.'

'A temperament Grundle shares,' Massifer said, with a hint of tired impatience. 'I shall allow you a pinch of hela-dust before you depart. That should make no difference to our working tomorrow.'

'You are generous,' Ays said dryly. 'Am I to eat downstairs this evening?'

'Whatever you prefer. Pasker will bring you a tray if you crave solitude.'

Ays elected to eat alone and once the autumn dusk filled the sky with vivid colours, put on the coat he had been given and went downstairs. He wondered whether he dared to walk out of the house alone, but before he could endeavour to do so, Grundle emerged from a side doorway, wearing outdoor garments. She pulled on a pair of gloves, saying, 'We shall take a short promenade to the Pleasure Gardens. More than that will tire me. I've been buffing iron all afternoon.'

Ays made no response, but indicated the way to the door in a debonair gesture. Grundle marched forward, and Ays followed.

As they walked the wide avenues, Ays reflected that the stroll would have been enriched by the presence of a like-minded companion to whom he could have addressed his remarks concerning the wonders of Salaganda. Grundle walked along in silence, her head bowed, her mouth a grim line. She was worse than Leeth; at least the girl would have been full of opinions about what she saw. Ays stemmed the thought before it advanced any further. When curiosity overcame him, he asked the woman questions to which she was quick to respond, giving concise yet informative answers.

Ays' opinion of her mellowed; he sensed a wounded melancholy in her eyes.

Long blue shadows fell across the road, where light traffic moved slowly. Salaganda, because of its advanced age, possessed a seasoned technology. Long black and chrome automobiles cruised breathily along, which Grundle explained were fuelled by a distillation of plant essences, native to the area.

'See over there,' said Grundle, pointing. Ays saw a cluster of narrow, elaborate spires. 'That is the University and the seat of Magisteri. There, our scholars invent ever more fabulous marvels to enrich our lives.'

Ays glanced at her askance. Grundle's voice held no hint of wonder. Was that cynicism in her tone, or merely a customary flatness?

'Your city is very beautiful,' he said politely, 'and so clean! Neither is it cluttered by an excess of citizens.'

Grundle shrugged, and pulled her shawl more tightly together beneath her chin. 'The population is regulated,' she said. 'What need have we of people of low intelligence, when our machines carry out all the tasks of drudgery? What need have we of invalids and weaklings?'

'None whatsoever, I imagine,' Ays replied, 'but unfortunately nature is not so meticulous.'

Grundle shook her head. 'The Magisteri have conquered the mysteries of human breeding.' She paused in what Ays could only perceive as a significant manner. 'Master Massifer does much research for the University.'

'You must feel privileged, working for such an influential man.'

'It has its benefits,' Grundle agreed. She stopped walking, and put her head to one side in an attitude of attentiveness. 'Hmm, that is most odd.'

'What?' Ays looked around himself. The street,

brushed by the muted colours of dusk and empty of people, held a quality of absolute stillness.

Grundle shook her head. 'I must be imagining things. For the last few minutes, I've been convinced someone has followed us.'

Ays examined the shadows more urgently. 'I can see nothing.' He thought of the mysterious man he'd seen in Frenepolis and the terranaut camp. Was he still on Ays' trail?

'The information did not come to me by sight or sound,' Grundle said, 'but simply a feeling. I have very acute senses.' She sighed. 'Now, the feeling has gone away, but a moment ago I was quite certain.'

Presently, they returned to the house.

Debilitated by an agony of grief, Leeth accepted the Tollinks' offer of hospitality, and remained in their house once Ays had gone. Yemina attempted to counsel her about her feelings, but as with the Raughtys, Leeth shrank from discussing the way she felt. What more proof did she need that her affections for Ays were pointless and futile? She didn't need anyone else to tell her that. Still, she could not accept that she'd never see him again. At night, she lay awake thinking about him, imagining him turning to her with an expression of pleasure and welcome. The image was so realistic she refused to believe it couldn't be made to happen one day. Also, she couldn't help feeling that Ays would be in danger without her. This feeling was as irrational as her abiding love, but she could not rid herself of it. There was something furtive about Derrell Tollink that she mistrusted. Part of her dreaded that he had sent Ays into peril.

After a few days of solitude, Leeth came to a decision. She would follow Ays. Obviously, she couldn't tell the Tollinks about this because they would try to stop her. Yemina would point out the utter folly of such a plan, while she suspected Derrell might attempt to restrain her physically. Max wouldn't want her to leave for other reasons, none of which she had any intention of fulfilling. When she emerged from her room, to rejoin the family in their daily affairs, Leeth conducted careful enquiries. She asked Yemina where Ays had gone. 'Derrell got him a job on Salaganda,' she said. 'Do you know where?'

Yemina was obviously extremely surprised by this piece of news, a fact she sought to conceal. 'Why don't you ask him, my dear?' she replied, but her face had gone dark with suppressed anger.

Leeth found Derrell on the riverbank, engaged in net-casting with a group of women. He was surly and stone-faced when Leeth questioned him.

'It is none of your business where Ays has gone. If he'd wanted you to know, he'd have told you himself!'

Leeth despaired of finding anything out. However, that same night she overheard Yemina scolding Derrell severely.

'What kind of friend are you?' Yemina yelled. 'Do you think Ays will survive Oskovellier's vile torments?'

'You don't know what you're talking about,' Derrell replied sulkily.

'I know enough!' Yemina snapped. 'Enough to know Massifer Oskovellier is a rogue, and probably a murderer. I know what he gets up to, no matter how clever you think you are at concealing the facts from me.'

Leeth lay breathless in the darkness, in the adjoining room. Now she had a name to work with: Oskovellier.

The following morning, she arose before the Tollinks woke up and fled Radianti, in search of Salaganda.

Because the cities moved so slowly, it didn't take Leeth long to catch up with Salaganda. However, that was only the first obstacle to be overcome. Once she'd found it, nobody took any notice of her entreaties for entrance. There were plenty of engineers working on the city mechanisms, but they wouldn't extend a walkway for her. Leeth, however, was not so easily discouraged. She was quite prepared to sleep in the open every night and then run after the city each morning. She told herself that eventually the city would have to stop moving for a while, or else a shift would happen. Then, she'd have her chance to embark.

One night, as she lay sleeping, wrapped in a blanket she'd stolen from the Tollinks, someone spoke her name. She awoke immediately, and brandished the knife she always kept by her side as she slept.

'What do you want?' She saw figures standing over her, and imagined they must be bandits intent on robbing her.

'Put away your weapon.' The voice was female, cultured. Leeth sat up. She saw a man and woman, dressed in expensive furs. The man was standing farther back, and wore a wide-brimmed hat. The woman was dressed in leather armour, over which a cloak had been flung.

'What do you want?' Leeth repeated.

'To help you,' answered the woman.

Leeth did not trust them. 'Are you from the city?'

The woman shook her head. 'No. You must come with us.'

'Why?'

'It will be to your benefit.'

Leeth shook her head. 'I don't know you. I have no reason to go with you.'

The woman sighed. 'Please don't waste my time by being stupid. We are no threat to you, and mean you only kindness.' She paused. 'You were right about Derrell Tollink. He is not to be trusted.'

'Is this about Ays?' Leeth leapt to her feet, cast the blanket aside.

'Come with us,' said the man. Leeth looked at him carefully for the first time. He seemed familiar.

'Is Ays all right?'

There was a silence then the woman said, 'At the moment. Please, no more questions, just come with us.'

There was a narrow walkway hanging down from the belly of Salaganda, almost hidden between the great mechanisms. Leeth was sure it hadn't been there when she'd been trying to gain entrance before. The woman preceded her up the walkway, and the man followed her. She felt excited and nervous, but not afraid. This strange couple exuded no air of threat.

The walkway emerged on to a secluded side-street, bordered by shuttered shops.

'How did you know about me?' Leeth asked the woman.

She did not answer, so Leeth turned to the man. 'Do you know Ays? Why are you helping me?'

The man proved no more informative than the woman. He would not answer her at all.

'Are you hungry?' the woman asked.

Leeth shrugged. 'I suppose so.'

'Then we must feed you. Come, dawn is nearly with us, but I know of inns in this city that are open all night.'

The woman once again led the way along a maze of narrow streets, until the yellow gleam of the windows of a small inn illuminated the damp, cobbled alley ahead of them. What kind of inn, Leeth wondered with a tremour of unease, stays open all night? In her experience, most public houses closed for at least a few hours before morning.

The inn had no name posted upon the door, and the woman had to knock loudly to gain entrance. A thin, middle-aged man grudgingly allowed them in, and locked the door behind them. A few other patrons were seated in shadowed cubicles around the low-ceilinged saloon. The room was smoky and smelled strongly of stale alcohol. An emaciated girl, wearing only a skirt of feathers, leaned against the bar, a stained, wooden tray drooping from one hand.

Leeth's female escort addressed the pot-girl. 'A meal,' she said. 'Whatever you can provide.'

The girl listlessly pulled herself erect and wandered behind the bar, to disappear through a dirty beaded curtain.

Leeth's male escort went to sit in one of the cubicles. 'A salubrious choice of venue,' he remarked to his companion. The woman ushered Leeth over to the seats and pushed her down.

'It is discreet,' she said.

Leeth noticed there was a dried pool of blood on the table. She shuddered. 'Who are you?' she asked her companions.

The woman laughed. She was a very attractive creature; tall and dashing. 'Call me Panoplidia,' she said, grinning, and then gestured at the man. 'Him, you can address as Periculus.'

Leeth frowned. 'Do you know Ays?'

'In a manner of speaking,' said Panoplidia.

The pot-girl ambled over to their table and deposited in front of them three bowls of non-descript stew and three unmatched wooden spoons. Leeth noticed the girl's blue-white chest was seamed with dirt. Her hair hung lank with grease, and might once have been blonde. Periculus gave the girl a few coins which gleamed outrageously gold in the depressing squalor of the room. The sight did not bring much joy to the girl's face. She shambled off as lifelessly as she'd approached.

Leeth picked up a wooden spoon and began to eat her stew. It did not taste as bad as it looked, and once the first mouthful was taken, she realised how hungry she was. Her companions neither spoke nor ate. Leeth appraised them covertly. The man was very handsome, but from what she could see beneath the brim of his hat, his face was sad. The woman seemed much more approachable.

'Do you know where Ays is?' Leeth asked. 'Can you help me find him?'

Panoplidia and Periculus exchanged a glance. Panoplidia nodded, and her companion removed a heavy purse from his coat pocket and placed it carefully on the table.

'This is for you,' he said. 'I think you'll find it's all the help you'll need from us.'

Leeth stared at the purse for a few moments. Then she put down her spoon and picked up the purse. She knew without looking that it was full of money.

'Salagandan currency?' she asked, feeling absurdly mature and experienced.

Periculus nodded. 'Of course.'

'Buy yourself some winter clothes,' said Panoplidia, 'and secure yourself lodgings.'

'But Ays . . .' Leeth began.

Periculus interrupted her. 'You will find your friend through your own efforts.'

Leeth narrowed her eyes at him. 'What is your interest in this matter?'

Periculus smiled. 'We are altruists,' he said. 'When you discover your friend, I think you will understand why we have offered to help you.'

Panoplidia stood up. 'Come, we have lingered long enough.' Periculus nodded and manoeuvred out of the cubicle.

'Where are you going?' Leeth asked desperately. 'You're not going to leave me here, are you?'

'You will be fine,' said Panoplidia. 'At dawn, walk into the sun, and your feet will lead you to an area of Salaganda where it will be easy to find accommodation.'

'I must stay here until then?' Leeth glanced uncertainly around the inn. She felt it would be dangerous to sit there alone.

'Don't worry,' said Panoplidia. She gestured to her companion, and the pair of them headed for the door.

Leeth watched them leave in stunned silence. Am I dreaming? she thought. But she didn't wake up.

Over the next few months, in rare moments of lucidity, Ays wondered many times whether he had done the right thing in coming to work for Massifer Oskovellier. His times of doubt coincided with the hours when Massifer withheld doses of hela, in the name of accurate research. Often Ays would lie upon his bed, his body a multitude of nagging aches, his belly clenching, his head a mosaic of different exquisite pains, cursing Leeth aloud. She was wholly responsible for his having to put himself in this position. Through her imbecilic actions, she had not only murdered an entire family, and a noble beast, but had forced Ays into a position of weakness and dependability.

During the first few weeks, when hela had been denied only on three occasions, Ays had voiced his discontent to Massifer. 'I am not an animal,' he said, 'but a human being with intelligence. You cannot treat me like some kind of disposable rodent, on whom to exercise your caprices.'

Massifer patted his arm. 'My dear Ays, please don't think that way! I acknowlege our work will sometimes cause discomfort, but on these occasions, rest assured, you will be earning a bonus.'

'What use is that to me?' he said. 'I'm generally too weak and tired to venture out of the house. What do I have to spend money on? And as you pointed out, Salagandan currency will be useless to me once I leave the city.'

'But think of the important work we're accomplishing!' Massifer cried.

'If you had to suffer withdrawal clutch, I very much doubt whether you'd utter such heroic cries,' Ays said crossly. 'Anyway, I'm ignorant of the desired result of your work. It seems merely like curiosity to me.'

Massifer was quick to deny this. 'By no means! Mara hela is a wondrous substance. I, and my colleagues, have no doubt that the revelation of many secrets lies within its fronds.'

'What colleagues?' Ays asked. 'I haven't seen any.'

Despite Massifer's initial mention of family, Ays had yet to come across anyone unknown in the house.

'Scholars at the University,' Massifer said stiffly. 'I take my papers to regular meetings there, and read them aloud. Most are impressed by my findings.'

'I have yet to read your theses,' Ays said. 'You did promise I could do so.'

'All in good time,' Massifer said. 'I don't want your brain crowded with stuffy facts. You should spend your hours of relaxation reading gentle works of fiction.'

'Nothing could come gentler than the works of fiction in your library,' Ays said sarcastically.

'Well then, you have something to spend your money on!' Massifer declared brightly. 'Grundle can buy you more challenging works from the book market.'

Massifer seemed to have an answer for everything, which Ays assumed must be the result of being an academic. The experiments became more gruelling as time went on. Massifer decided to abandon the use of mixtures, and instead concentrated on the effects of varying doses of pure hela. Sometimes, Ays floated on what felt like the brink of death, so intoxicated was he with a massive dose Massifer had given him. Other times, suffering doubly because of withdrawal from a high dose, he would feel as if his organs were close to giving out, his heart on the verge of stopping, his lungs of inner collapse. During these times, Savalin ministered to Ays' needs in the manner he'd predicted. Far from objecting to this, Ays took some comfort from his presence and would ramble incoherently about his childhood or weep uncontrollably. Savalin was not over friendly, but neither was he cruel. He was a presence, which at times was all Ays needed to feel secure.

Once, in a moment of complete lucidity, Ays grabbed Savalin's arm and said, 'Tell me the truth: has anyone died in Massifer's employment?'

Savalin did not withdraw as Ays had expected. 'No,' he said. 'In all honesty, I can tell you that. Massifer will drive you to the very lip of doom, but will always pull you back at the last moment. His experiments seem ungoverned, but they are not. He has at least two dozen books of case notes. Believe me, he knows what he is doing.'

Ays flopped back on to his bed. 'I hope you're right . . . What time of year is it? Where are we?'

Savalin drew the curtains against a late-afternoon dusk. 'The year draws on,' he said. 'We still follow the river Skine downstream to the sea.'

Most of autumn passed unseen beyond Ays' window, but as a chill took hold of the air, he began to dream hopefully of the winter, and the Sea where he could replenish his spore supply and gain independence once more. Sensing that Massifer would not greet his departure happily, Ays refrained from mentioning his intentions. Let Massifer think he was wholly reliant on him; it could only expedite Ays' escape, if flight became necessary. He fantasised often about running away. If he could only be left alone in Massifer's largest workroom, where the hela-farm was, he could perhaps steal some spores and attempt to grow them. But he was never left alone. In the beginning, it might have been easier, but as the experiments progressed, and Ays involuntarily gave voice to his discontent, he was supervised more scrupulously. He remembered Yemina Tollink's advice about trying to give up the hela. Now, he believed that would be impossible.

The times he'd spent in withdrawal clutch had been the most horrific of his life. Delusions had thronged his mind, agonising pangs his body. It was as if he'd somehow become the hela, or it had a firm grip, like some hidden cancer, deep within his flesh, and it craved nourishment continually, which was the smoke, the dust, the juice of its own being, its mother. To think of a life without it was to think of the inner being, the hela-Ays, dying, and in its death throes, it would drag the human-Ays down with it, in a stranglehold too tenacious to evade. In moments of denial, the hela-Ays shunned food, demanding only its source, its prima materia. Then, Pasker would be on hand, to force the weak human-Ays to push food down his throat into a stomach that writhed in complaint and disgust. All food tasted like sand; what he desired was the yeasty earthiness of hela fronds against his tongue. Even plain water tasted foul at those times.

Sleep was terrifying during these episodes, and apart from terrible nightmares concerning death and decay, Ays often dreamed of the Blue Feather Man. No dialogue ever took place, but the man would be a silent sentinel at the edge of Ays' visions, a tall wafer of black among the rampaging colours of surreal vistas. Once Ays awoke, convinced the man was standing in a corner of the room. He could see the narrow wet gleam of half-closed eyes, blinking from an intense darkness. He cried out: 'Who are you? What do you want?' which prompted Savalin to come running. When the light was turned on, there was of course nothing in the corner.

One evening, as night lay thick across the city in a blanket of fog from the river, an unusual event occurred. Massifer was engaged in giving a series of talks at a convention at the University, so for a few days Ays had been allowed a regular amount of hela, and had thus been restored to a state of comparative health and tranquillity. On the occasions when he was in a normal state of mind, Grundle often came to spend a couple of hours with him, to play intellectual board games or discuss books. She refused to listen to his complaints about Massifer and the experiments, but was otherwise a reasonable companion, although her flights of thought were sometimes hard to follow.

On the evening of the event, she came to Ays' room after dinner, carrying a selection of new volumes which he had commissioned her to purchase from the book market. 'I must say I share your tastes,' she confided. 'Master Massifer and I have ever been at odds about the expansion of the library. It has done the collection good, having you here.'

Ays thought it best not to point out that the books were his rather than Massifer's, and in view of the often unpleasant experiences he had suffered at Massifer's hands, had no intention of leaving the books behind when he left, even if that meant simply dumping them on a stall in the market.

Grundle was excited about the new purchases. 'Look

at this,' she said reverently, handing Ays a volume bound in soft black leather, tooled with gold. 'D. Trupellier's new novel. It is destined to win prizes, I have no doubt.'

Ays flicked through the book. In actual fact, he disliked the pomposity of the literary writers of Salaganda, and often found their musings too rarified, their characters frankly unbelievable. 'You must read it before me,' he said, handing the book back to her.

Grundle wouldn't hear of it. 'No! I am eager to hear your opinions first.' She put the book down beside Ays on the sofa. 'Here I have Marnia Worster's last book, *Today, By Firelight*. It sounds fluffy, but isn't. Here . . .'

Before she could speak further, a terrific rumpus resounded through the house. 'Whatever is that?' Ays cried, jumping up and running to peer out of the window.

'Sounds like someone, or a party of someones, banging on the door,' said Grundle in indignation. 'Whoever would come here and act so uncivilly? None of Master Massifer's acquaintances, I'm sure!'

'I can't see anything,' said Ays, straining to look down. 'Shall we go and investigate?'

'It's nothing to do with us,' Grundle said primly. 'Savalin will see to it.'

'But whoever it was, the gate guards let them pass,' Ays continued. 'Do you suppose one of Massifer's friends or family is chafed with him?' The banging had now stopped, but Ays thought he could hear the distant sound of angry voices.

'I doubt that very much. Come and sit down again. I have more books to show you.'

Sighing, Ays was about to leave the window when he noticed someone had begun to walk down the drive. He pressed himself to the glass. The figure was familiar. At first, he thought it was his mysterious follower, then it seemed to shimmer until it looked like Leeth in her flapping, faded dress. No, it couldn't be. He shook his head, attempting to clear his vision. 'Come here,' he hissed urgently to Grundle.

Reluctantly, and grumbling, the woman stood up and came to stand beside him at the window.

'What do you see?' Ays asked her. 'Tell me what you see.'

'An off-city salesman, I expect,' Grundle said dismissively. 'They must have bribed the gate staff.'

'It is a girl,' Ays said. 'It is someone I know.'

'The person is shapeless, but it could be a female, I suppose,' Grundle conceded. 'However, I don't see how you could recognise a person from this distance.' The figure had disappeared beneath the trees.

'You are right,' Ays said with a sigh. He went to sit down again, and put his head in his hands. 'I'm losing all sense of reality.'

Nervously, Grundle cleared her throat and spoke brightly. 'Well, what have we here? Bortrum Clasp's great classic, *On the Shores of a Secret Sea*.' She opened the book. 'I shall read you a passage.'

Blinking, Ays lay back against the cushions, wondering if his sanity would survive until he reached his own secret sea.

The following day, Massifer returned to the house, full of self-congratulation and waving Certificates of Commendation. Ays and Savalin were in one of the workrooms, where Savalin was encouraging Ays to write about his impressions of the experiments. When Massifer burst in, crying, 'Ha, I showed them! Let anyone nitpick about my experiments now!' Savalin bustled forward and spoke a few, quiet urgent words in his master's ear.

'What?' Massifer responded irritably, and then

sighed. 'Very well, we must speak of the matter.' He looked up and the dark scowl faded from his face. 'Good day to you, Ays, you look radiant! I have business with Savalin. Back in a split.' The pair of them left the room.

For a few moments, Ays sat twisting his pen in his fingers, thinking wistfully how fortuitous it would be if he was currently sitting alone in the room with the hela-farm. Then, obeying an inner urge, he quietly got down from his stool and crept towards the door where he pressed his ear against the panels. Muffled voices came through. Most of it was unintelligible, but he heard Massifer utter a few sharp remarks, as if he was reprimanding his valet. The voices grew louder, as if the speakers were approaching the door.

'I'll hear no more of it!' Massifer said, and Ays just reached his stool in time before the door opened and Massifer came back in

'Ah, Ays!' boomed Massifer. 'I hope you've had a restful holiday. Today, work begins anew.'

Ays' heart fell. 'What do you have planned?'

'Well, an unusual new herb has been brought into the city by itinerant phylacterers, which they claim they found growing in the foothills of the mountains. It has remarkable properties.'

Ays pulled a sour face. 'Such as provoking irritable bowel, irascible stomach, hysterical head and vibrating eyeballs, no doubt.'

Massifer laughed. 'Ha, ha, ha, you are such a wit!' He held up a finger, one of his habits which Ays had grown to hate. 'No, ingestion of a tea made from the herb is said to create a talismanic aura, a circle of protection from both disease and acts of violence.'

Ays flinched as his imagination started screaming. 'And how do you propose to test the efficacy of the substance?'

Massifer darted to his workbench and leaned over to stare unnecessarily at an array of glass tubes. 'Well, I have cultures of certain plagues . . .'

Ays yelped and leapt from his stool which crashed sideways to the floor. 'No!' he roared. 'I am engaged for hela experiments, nothing more! I have complied with your every whim, at great discomfort to myself! But this is too much!'

Massifer straightened up with a pained expression and delicately put his hands over his ears. 'Oh, please don't bellow at me so! The herb is quite effective. I have seen it at work already.'

'Then why bother testing it further?'

Massifer rolled his eyes as if in exasperation at such a facile question. 'Because its effects need to be scientifically analysed, and noted. The University has engaged me for the task. It is a considerable honour. The seat of a Magister may be involved.'

'Much as I'd like to expedite your advancement, I can't help you with this,' Ays said.

Massifer tapped his lips thoughtfully with the pale, attenuated fingers of one hand. 'Hmm. Some might say you have no choice.'

'What are you suggesting?'

'Savalin!' Before Ays could act, the valet slid into the room and, at Massifer's direction, took Ays in an inescapable hold.

'Confine him in his room,' Massifer said. 'And no hela.' He turned away, ignoring Ays' frantic protests, and Savalin frogmarched Ays from the room.

Locked in his room, Ays roared furious complaints and hammered at the door. No one paid attention to him. After a while, he sat down upon his bed and wept frustrated tears. The day passed interminably.

By sundown, no food or water had been brought to him and the first teasing tweaks of withdrawal clutch had begun to worry at his belly. Ays groaned and turned upon his bed, alternately shouting expletives to the empty air, or sobbing into his pillow. Then, his head pounding, he lapsed into silence, hating himself for hoping that a display of amenability might magically conjure Savalin with a pouch of hela. If anything, since being in Massifer's house, Ays' addiction to the frond had intensified. His room filled with a dark blue gloom, and the air became chill. Were they now denying him heat as well? A network of hot water pipes beneath the floor had previously supplied warmth. Ays reached over the side of the bed and, as he'd thought, the floor was cold. Massifer, I will kill you for this, I swear it, Ays murmured to himself. He had begun to shake uncontrollably.

Some time in the middle of the night, while Ays wilted in the arms of a violent spasm of sweating, he heard the sounds of quick footsteps running across the roof above him. Back and forth, back and forth; the slates grated together with a silvery grinding sound. Rooftop ghosts, thought Ays deliriously. His sweat became cold, and it felt as if the mattress had turned into something massive and soft that was attempting to smother him. When he gazed at the blue square of the window, the air outside was full of floating motes. The breath in his lungs seemed as clean and chill as a blade of ice. Back and forth, back and forth, the footsteps scrabbled overhead. They became hypnotic; when they paused for a few moments, Ays' ears ached at the loss. Then, something scratched at the window.

He gasped, suddenly alert and fully awake. He sat up in the bed to see a dark shape hanging down over the glass and thin glowing fingers pressed against the panes. His first thought was of predators and ghouls. The little fingers tapped at the glass. He could see a dark face twisting and grimacing: the face of a malevolent goblin. 'Ays! Ays!' Worse. It knew his name.

He glanced towards the door which he knew to be locked, and back again to the window. The tapping had become more urgent, the creature's palms slapping flat against the glass. 'Ays! Ays!' Soon, the window must surely break.

Ays expelled a sound of anguish. Was he capable of fighting? He eased from the bed, wondering in some futility whether a fresh display of banging and shouting at the door might summon help. The floor felt damp and icy beneath his feet. Wet tendrils of hair or fur were sticking to the window where the creature hung. A face pressed close against the glass, its mouth working, its eyes staring. Ays shuddered, caught in a stasis of terrified fascination. There was something familiar about the face.

For a few moments further, his mind still churned deliriously in withdrawal clutch, before some deeper, saner instinct propelled him to the window. With shaking fingers that were barely able to work the catch, he flung the panes wide. After a short struggle, during which Ays was kicked unintentionally in the face, a cold, wet body fell into the room with a soft thump. Ays found he was giggling uncontrollably. His visitor was Leeth.

'Are you mad? Are you mad?' the girl hissed, on hands and knees before him. She was wearing a tatty black fur coat and her hair hung over her face in lank tassels. The fur on her back, and the back of her head, glistened with snowflakes. She was like an ice imp bringing winter into the room.

The hela-Ays could not recover from what it saw as the hilarity of the situation. Human-Ays hung sadly inside the shaking frame. He was relieved to see Leeth.

'Are you real?' he managed to say quietly through the echoes of laughter.

Leeth pulled herself to her feet. 'Of course.' She squinted. 'Well, it took me long enough to find you! What have they done to you?'

He staggered to the bed and sat down. The cold air from the window seemed to be pouring in to surround his body in a chilling caul. He could almost see it; a tender malevolence.

'I'd better shut the window, the heat will get out,' said Leeth. She mimed a shiver as she pulled the latch towards her. 'Come to think of it, it's colder in here than out there.' She crossed to the door and put her ear against it.

'Locked,' said Ays.

Leeth came to stand before him, her hands on her hips. She shook her head in smug censure. 'Well!'

Ays looked up at her from a posture of submission, his hands clamped between his thighs, his body still shaking from the occasional sob of laughter. 'What are you doing here? How . . .?'

'You are lucky I don't take offence,' said Leeth, interrupting. 'I wondered what that Tollink character was up to when he whisked you off into the city. I was so angry with you! But when I'd calmed down, I started asking questions. Max was vague, and Yemina wouldn't tell me anything. I thought about it for a while, and had to investigate why you'd come to Salaganda alone. Might have known it was something to do with your bad habits.'

'How did you find out where I was?'

Leeth took off her coat and sat down beside him on the bed, so that she could drape him in it. It was snug with the warmth of her body. 'I stayed with the Tollinks for a few days while I made my investigations. They came to nothing. Derrell Tollink was extremely rude to me, and deliberately withheld information. But I learned to keep my ears open.' She explained about the argument she'd overhead between Yemina and Derrell, and how she'd left Radianti the following day. When she reached the part of her story where Panoplidia and Periculus appeared to her, Ays interrupted her sharply.

'What did they look like? Were they the Tampers?'

'Of course not!' Leeth scoffed. 'I would have recognised them. The man was very handsome, but almost completely silent. The woman was beautiful, athletic-looking, and slightly more approachable. They were young . . .' She wrinkled her nose. 'Strangely, I can't really remember their features. I was simply so grateful they'd found me. I asked them if they knew where you were, if they'd help me get to you, but all they did was give me a purse of Salagandan money. It seems so odd: they got me on the city, but refused to do anything more. I do not believe they told me their real names.'

'Perhaps they are opponents of Massifer's?' Ays said. 'Perhaps they disapprove of what he's doing? Massifer has great influence, so his enemies could hardly act overtly.'

Leeth shrugged. 'I don't know what their interest is. I haven't seen them since, and that was months ago.'

'How have you been living?' Ays asked her. 'The Salagandans are not exactly friendly to outsiders.'

'As I said, I had a little money so I was able to get a room. There is one area of the city where few questions are asked, but as you can imagine it is a very small area. Everyone knows about the Oskovelliers, so I was able to learn where their manses were. I made a couple of friends, whom I told about you. They said there were rumours that Massifer Oskovellier kept hela addicts locked up in his house to experiment on. People, especially land-lopers taking a ride on the city, disappear regularly from the poor area. It's said that many of the Magisteri use them for human experiments. Well, that made sense of what I'd heard Yemina say. After that, I thought I'd find you very quickly.

'I walked to the gates of this house a few times, but the guards wouldn't acknowledge my presence. I appealed to them, told them about you, about me. I said I was your lover, and begged them to help me get to see you. Eventually, they drove me off with pikes.' Leeth reached out and lightly touched Ays' arm. 'I was afraid I'd be too late, that you'd be dead.' She stood up. 'For weeks, I watched the guards at the gates, trying to divine if any of them might help me. I had to pick on one, and it's so hard to tell who might have the warmest heart. Still, I couldn't wait forever. A couple of days ago, I gave what was left of my money to the man I thought was the best bet. He took it and opened the gate. He told me to knock at the front door. I did that, and a servant came. He said I must forget you, but he didn't deny you were here.'

'That was Savalin,' Ays said. 'I heard you come, Leeth. I looked out of the window and saw you walking down the drive, but I thought I must have hallucinated it.'

'It's been hard since then,' she said. 'I had to give up my room, and beg food. Even the paupers here resent beggars. Being poor in Salaganda has a different meaning to being poor anywhere else. They don't know the meaning of real poverty here.' She walked to the window and put her fingers against the glass, drew a few strokes in the mist that had gathered there. 'They have slack security here at this manse,' she said. 'Why? Because there is so little for them to fear. Guards on the gates, but a ragged patrol along the boundary. I asked my friends at the inn to help me climb over the garden wall, but they wouldn't.' She laughed bleakly. 'They do not hate the rich here, no. So I walked to the wall, walked along it, and what did I find?' She turned and smiled, with a hint of fever in the smile. 'A rope attached to a grapple hook. Just lying there beside an ornamental shrub. It was bizarre . . .'

'Was it?' Ays had started to shiver again, despite the warm coat.

'I have never been particularly athletic,' said Leeth in a dreamy voice, staring out at the falling snow. 'But tonight, it was as if my heels had wings. It was like being drunk or drugged. I wanted height, I craved it. Scaling the pipes and parapets of this house was as easy as mounting a flight of stairs. I ran across the rooftops. I looked out over the city. I felt so tall. I hung down from the eaves by my feet, gazed into all the attic windows until I found you.'

Ays was hypnotised by the fervid gleam in Leeth's eyes. They were full of swirling motes; the reflection of shining snowflakes.

She turned away from the window. 'We must go,' she said. 'Now, before everything changes.'

'I can't,' Ays said in a cracked voice. 'I have no hela. I need . . .'

Leeth sighed impatiently. 'You must do without. Come.' She held out her arm.

He glanced at the door. 'I'll never make it. I'm too shaky.'

Leeth rolled her eyes. 'Can you make it out of the window and on to the roof?'

'No, not without hela.' He stared at her in appeal. 'Massifer has a workroom. He grows hela there. Oh Leeth, you must get some for me!'

She appraised him in silence for a few moments and then nodded, as she came to a decision. 'It makes sense for you to have your wits about you as we escape. But if

I break into one of the other rooms, I must be quick. I could be heard, so you must give me precise directions.'

Ays' heart gave an involuntary flutter of hunger and hope. 'I will, but there is no one up here to hear you. I know there isn't.'

Leeth sighed. 'This is a stupid risk, but perhaps essential. I certainly can't carry you down to the ground.' She swung up on to the window ledge and opened the panes, crouching there. Ays went over to her.

'The room you need is four down this corridor.'

'How many windows is that?'

Ays shrugged. 'I'm not sure, but it is a big room. A workroom, full of benches and equipment. There is a hela-farm in there – under glass. Grab as much as you can.' Leeth scrambled out of the window and back up on to the roof. Ays leaned out to watch her.

'You are a fool!' she said. 'A sensible person would have overcome their addiction to the stuff before they left Min!'

She disappeared over the slates. Presently, Ays saw a shadowy shape clambering down to a window ledge further up the building. There was a muffled sound of breaking glass and soon Leeth gained access to the room. The wait for her to re-emerge seemed interminable. Horrible images assailed Ays' mind: Savalin asleep on guard in the workroom, woken by Leeth's arrival; Leeth cutting herself on the glass as she clambered through the window, lying bleeding to death on the floor. Eventually, however, she nimbly jumped out of the window and back on to the roof.

'I never thought there'd be a day when I'd be pleased to see you,' Ays said, as she came back into his room.

Leeth made a harsh sound. 'It serves you right. I knew you'd have to, one day.' Ays decided to ignore the suggestive note in her voice.

'Well, do you have it?'

'Here!' Leeth removed a spongy mass of ripped up fresh hela from inside the bosom of her dress. Its yeasty reek filled the room.

Much as Ays longed to fall on the stuff and devour it all, he disciplined himself to chew only a few strands, just enough to restore his strength and confidence.

'Be quick,' said Leeth. 'I feel our time is running out.'

'What time?' Ays swallowed a wad of hela. 'Nobody heard you.'

Leeth wriggled. 'That's not what I mean. Hurry up.'

After only a few minutes, the hela had already extended a benign hand and brushed away any vestige of debility from Ays' body. He felt full of energy, and the night no longer seemed cruel and chill, but sparkling and alive. Leeth had already clambered up on to the windowsill.

'Will you be all right without a coat?'

'I can't feel the cold,' Ays said. For a moment he experienced the urge to thank Leeth, extend some words of kindness which he knew would please her. It was a miracle she'd found him and liberated him from Massifer's employment. Without Leeth's blind devotion, he might have died in Massifer's house or emerged irretrievably deranged. Leeth: his saviour. It seemed outrageous, and yet, wasn't he owed this from her? He followed her out into the night.

Casmeer

Casmeer knew that his stories were heading towards a conclusion. He wondered what point he was trying to make. Perhaps there was none? Sometimes, the stories deliberately excluded him and he could not find the gate to enter their realm. It was almost as if someone else was writing about him writing the stories. He had wanted to be the one to rescue Ays from the Oskovellier manse, but that had been Leeth's privilege. Marvrani had taken control and prevented it. He had not written this, but he knew that it was true. She was becoming stronger, perhaps stronger than Varian himself. He could feel her presence around him, although there was no sense of her in the crumbling roche out in the roof garden. What had he created? He could not write about Marvrani's private life with Varian, because it was unknown to him, a shadowed area. This was preposterous, for hadn't he plucked her being from his own mind?

Despite this rationale, Casmeer felt that Varian and Marvrani interacted on their own level, apart from him. He suspected that they filled in the spaces of their story themselves when his mind was not engaged with them. Varian was Casmeer's fictional alter ego and yet, as Varian's creator, Casmeer was restricted. Sometimes he felt he was excluded from his own fantasy, that it carried on growing and expanding without his creative input. In the cold hours before dawn, Casmeer wondered whether he was the fiction and world of the flat-lands was reality. It was a terrifying thought.

By day, Casmeer worried that he was becoming too involved in his work. He realised that the boundary between fantasy and reality was growing blurred. Occasionally, but with increasing regularity, he thought about giving up on his creation. And yet, it had given his empty life some meaning. How could he live without it now?

Chapter Sixteen
The Heartless One

There was a word engraved on a brass plate attached to the horse's headband. The word was Matanyan. Whether this was name of the animal's previous owner, the name of the horse himself, or the person who'd crafted the bridle, Finnigin didn't know, but he called the horse Matanyan from then on. The animal was a proud and fractious beast, totally unaffectionate and often quite vicious. As they entered the gloom of Overhang, Matanyan flinched at the slightest sound, and shied at the faintest flicker of a shadow.

For three weeks Finnigin rode Matanyan through the labyrinth of Overhang's dry, dark valleys, wondering if, after all, he would simply die of hunger when the supplies ran out. Matanyan had to feed himself as best he could on the pallid weeds and lichens that grew on the rocks, but for some reason, perhaps an unnaturally robust constitution, he did not appear to lose condition. The same could not be said for Finnigin, who felt he could see the weight falling from his bones.

Occasionally, they'd pass an outcrop of rocks that might have been ruined buildings, but fear of what might inhabit them, alive or dead, dissuaded Finnigin from seeking shelter inside. He often found himself thinking of Varian, and as time progressed, was able to ponder the events of his last night in Oubrahani, without his mind flinching away in shame and fear. He had either dreamed of his amorous encounter with Varian, or else Varian truly did possess some unnameable power, a power that could temporarily turn a man into a woman. Finnigin could not imagine why Varian would want to do that. It seemed utterly perverse to him.

When weariness seemed at the point of swamping the last of Finnigin's energy, the path Matanyan was following widened and began to slope downwards. The rocks also changed colour, fading from the depressing black to grey to a pale, streaked sand. Hardy, gnarled trees grew from the rock face. Twice in the space of an hour Finnigin saw a goat leap from his path, and also thought he heard a snatch of bird song. Irrepressibly, his spirits lifted, and he felt sure that Matanyan's step became more jaunty. Was it possible they were at last leaving the underworld of Overhang behind?

Finnigin rode Matanyan down the narrow rocky concourse into an area that he perceived as a new land, even though it was perhaps just as mountainous as the stark crags he'd left behind. Here, however, the bare bones of the rock were fleshed with forests and sloping fields of lush verdure. Pausing among the cover of trees, Finnigin could see evidence of agriculture in the fields below: scattered farm buildings, neat enclosures of pasture, animals browsing in the mild autumn sunlight, fields of corn, orchards, and on a distant slope, vineyards. It seemed an idyllic, peaceful place. This impression was swiftly dispelled. When Finnigin approached the first of the farmsteads, a group of labourers released a pack of yelping hounds to worry Matanyan's heels and then pelted Finnigin with stones. Matanyan galloped away without waiting for a command from his rider.

Finnigin crossed the valley without provoking further

attack, although a group of fruit-pickers shouted abuse at him and waved their fists in a threatening manner. Clearly, this was not an area friendly to strangers.

By nightfall, Matanyan was picking his way up into a dense pine forest and Finnigin had resigned himself to the fact that his dreams of filling his belly with ripe fruit at the hearth of some amiable family were unrealistic at best. In the shelter of the forest, he examined his supplies, the remainder of which were wizened and leathery. Supper was a meagre meal of pine nuts, gathered from the forest floor, and brackish water, peppered with a condiment of dead insects, sipped from the cups of pitcher plants growing around the tree-trunks. Matanyan, more easily satisfied, nipped delicately at the sparse strands of stiff, dark grass growing among the spongy fallen needles.

The following day, Finnigin discovered an overgrown orchard beside a ruined farm and was able to fill one of his panniers with fruit. Rooting around in the jungly remnants of a kitchen garden, he found vegetables and a few straggly lettuces. All of this food, however, was perishable, and would have to be eaten quickly.

For several days Finnigin rode Matanyan along an overgrown roadway, where the forest had at one time been pushed back to accommodate the husbandry of the land, but for some reason all the farms in this area were abandoned and many bore the signs of having been burned. It appeared that no one had lived there for many years. Finnigin met nobody else upon the road, but occasionally heard furtive movements in the long grass alongside that seemed too loud to have been made by animals. On the fifth day, mountains loomed tall against the horizon and the road rose to greet them. The air had become chill and golden leaves littered the path. Finnigin sensed an atmosphere of expectancy, as if he was approaching something. In the night, as he camped among the rocks, shrouded by ferns and young trees, he heard heavy, muffled noises in the distance. The sounds rose and fell on the brisk evening wind. Sometimes they sounded like cries, at other times like explosions. In the dead time before the dawn, a company of riders galloped past, their leader shouting hoarse commands. Black Matanyan was hidden by the shadows, Finnigin crouched unseen; they were not noticed by the riders.

Finnigin decided it would be best to part company with the road, and urged Matanyan up one of the high banks that flanked it. Traffic became thick below them; carts, steam vehicles, horses, and some strange, hybrid creatures that were enormous and wore armour with inbuilt weapons. Finnigin looked down upon these people and animals, but no one paid him any attention. He thought this was strange because the road-users were military, and evidently military that had seen recent action. If there were hostilities going on, why didn't they question strangers? He could have been a spy.

Eventually, the banks declined and Finnigin was forced to ride along the road once more. Horses and vehicles jostled past him, men with dark, cruel faces looked right through him. They all wore black uniforms of leather, resplendent upon the breast with an emblem of red and gold. Finnigin rode unmolested until he reached the lip of a valley where the road tipped over and plunged down towards a scene of carnage. Here, a couple of soldiers caught hold of Matanyan's bridle.

'Are you a commentarist?' one of them asked. His tone indicated he expected the affirmative, so for the sake of convenience, Finnigin answered: 'Yes.' He was unsure what a commentarist might be, but as it clearly wasn't an enemy, it seemed safe to adopt the title for the time being.

'Down there.' The soldier pointed to the left along the slope of the valley.

Finnigin must have looked confused, because the second soldier also pointed and said, 'Where that outcrop of rock is, next to the stand of rubber pines.'

Finnigin peered along the track. 'Ah, yes,' he said uncertainly.

'Well, get going then!' said the first soldier. 'You're cluttering up the path.' He slapped Matanyan's rump, an indiscretion Finnigin himself would never have dared to attempt. The horse gave an indignant grunt and cavorted sideways in the direction of the rocks. Finnigin wondered whether he should have asked questions, but perhaps that would have been unwise?

Finnigin's initial impression of the commentarists was that they resembled a flock of ragged carrion birds, waiting to gorge themselves upon the flesh of the dead. They crouched in the shelter of the rocks, twittering together. Some sketched rapidly upon pads of creamy paper – spidery drawings of anguished faces, twisted limbs, smoke and mud. Others whispered out a frantic commentary which was taken down in shorthand by amanuenses. Finnigin dismounted from Matanyan and tied his reins loosely around a drooping tree branch. A few of the commentarists gave him a quick inspection before turning their attention back to the battle. Finnigin walked towards them and stood looking down into the valley.

It was a scene of utter chaos, the ground churned and gouged by explosives; dead animals and men lying in tatters as if they had been thrown there. It seemed the battle was more or less over as the majority of the fighters were dead, but there were sporadic knots of fighting, where huge guns retched out gobbets of metal, and men fought in hand to hand combat with a variety of cutting weapons. On the opposite slope of the valley, Finnigin could see another group of people sitting down, making notes or simply watching the battle. A thought came to him, as pure and unsullied as a diamond: *this* is madness. He turned to the nearest of the commentarists, a scrawny woman who was frenziedly scrawling a depiction of a dismembered corpse. She used a magnifying optoscope to examine the subject of her drawing – a soldier lying in several pieces near the centre of the field.

'What is all this about?' Finnigin asked her.

She looked up and blinked at him. 'Eh?'

He patiently repeated the question.

'Don't you know? This is the nineteenth battle.'

Finnigin hunkered down beside her. 'A battle between whom, and for what?'

'Where have you come from?' demanded the woman, in a tone that suggested she thought he'd crawled out of the ground. 'More to the point, where have you been?'

'I'm a stranger,' Finnigin replied. 'I am looking for the city of Gleaming Fisk.'

'Way off course!' answered the woman. 'Still, you are lucky enough to be near Phaxteriniad.' She gestured towards the valley. 'Our troops have just annihilated the scum from Plurakelica. All to the good. It was our turn to lose last time.'

'Your turn to lose? I don't understand.'

'It's simple,' answered the woman. 'You've come to the most civilised place on earth. The cities of Phaxteriniad and Plurakelica have always been enemies, and much bloodshed occurred because of it.'

Finnigin eyed the scene below and made a scornful sound. 'Still does, by the look of things.'

'Ah, well that's where you're wrong,' said the woman. 'The Kings of the cities came together some years ago and worked out an arrangement. Battles are still fought regularly, but the outcome is predetermined. Therefore, so as not to risk losing good men, the losing side sends out an army of slaves, miscreants and numbskulls. It deals with the problem of overcrowding in prisons too.'

Finnigin laughed. 'That's the most insane thing I've ever heard!'

'We appreciate it must be difficult for outsiders to understand,' said the woman, somewhat fastidiously.

Finnigin looked over her shoulder. 'Why are you doing all these sketches.'

'The battles have to be recorded,' she replied. 'It's my job.' She made a flourish. 'There now. The Emerald Mines will belong to Phaxteriniad, until the next battle.'

'Why bother even fighting the battles then? Surely, if the arguments are over territory, a political agreement could be made.'

The woman scoffed. 'Ha! What do you know? Fighting is in the blood of our noble sons! If they didn't fight the battles, who knows what they'd get up to?'

Finnigin shrugged. 'That's a valid point, I suppose.'

'It is indeed! Now look, you're getting in my light. Move!'

'Where is the nearest city?' he asked.

'Follow this path to the end of the valley and turn towards the sun. You will see a great mountain that is the resort of the Goddess Scarzanera, our benefactress. The mountain is an extinct volcano, and our beautiful city is to be found in the crater. It is about a day's ride from here.'

'Oh.' Finnigin was disappointed. He'd hoped it would be nearer than that.

'You don't expect the fighting to take place right beneath the King's window, do you?' The woman laughed. 'This is a civilised land.'

Finnigin mounted Matanyan and urged him up the path. He hoped he'd be able to sell the horse once he reached Phaxteriniad. Surely, there would be no shortage of buyers for such a beast in a city that was so keen on warfare.

News of the battle's outcome raced ahead of Finnigin, and his journey was broken by meetings with many individuals celebrating by the side of the road, who were eager to offer their liquor flagons to any passers-by. Finnigin was scornful of their antics – what was the point of celebrating victory when the result of the battle had been known beforehand? Still, he appreciated the sight of friendly faces.

Tall trees lined the roads, obscuring his view of the land ahead. It took Finnigin nearly two days to reach the mountain of Scarzanera, but even before its obsidian scarps came into view through the trees, the evening sky above them was ablaze with fireworks; glittering explosions that dimmed the stars. The citizens within the mountain must be in a festive mood in the wake of war.

The road widened, flanked by tall columns of snowy stone, upon which resided the haughty representations of Phaxteriniad's elite and famous. The trees withdrew respectfully from the road and the magnificent bulk of Scarzanera was revealed, a sheer titan dwarfing every hill and crag around it. The road hugged the mountain-side, winding up to a yawning cavern, flanked by monstrous sentinel gargoyles of polished black stone. Traffic moved freely in and out of the gateway, and there seemed to be little evidence of security.

Finnigin felt excitement mounting within him. He directed Matanyan to increase his pace to a swift trot and soon they were passing into the echoing gloom of the gateway; a wide tunnel through the rock that led to the crater. Finnigin had imagined that Phaxteriniad would be very much like Oubrahani; a place of bare rock. The sight that greeted him, however, was very different. The city was enormous, but dwarfed by the size of the crater, which was no barren landscape, but a fertile enclave. Much of it was forested, but not with the severe, soaring pines of the woods beyond the mountains. The trees around the city were huge, spreading, deciduous, all wearing a riot of autumn colours. The city itself was walled, and festooned with creepers bedecked with scarlet foliage. Enormous sulphurous lamps illuminated the soaring stone and highlighted the disdainful features of gigantic statues that lurked among the leaves.

Finnigin pulled Matanyan to a halt a few paces down the sweeping road that led to the city. He felt nervous, anxious about approaching the gates, even though they stood open, offering welcome. All he could hear were hectic sounds of gaiety and merriment, yet still he faltered. He wondered whether he was simply unsettled by the sheer magnitude of the scene before him; the titanic statues peering from the walls, the massive trees whose crowns brushed the tops of the looming city walls, and beyond them the unforgiving verticals of Scarzanera's inner cliffs. The gates to the city looked like an enormous, hungry mouth; Finnigin could imagine going inside, but hurrying out again was perplexingly harder to visualise. He considered. Perhaps it might be less daunting to enter Phaxteriniad by a less public route, get his bearings a little?

Many narrower roads branched off from the main thoroughfare, leading into the trees. Glimpses of white, suggesting the presence of buildings, could be seen between the wide, moss-seamed trunks. Finnigin urged Matanyan down the nearest of these side roads, where the reaching trees formed a canopy overhead. Beside the road, naked torches on tall metal stems hissed into the night, their smoke scented by aromatic resins. Finnigin's heart slowed its pace. He sucked deep and regular breaths to try and calm his nerves. Presently, he came to a place where the road widened into a circular plaza, lined by trees behind which were tall railings of filigreed metal. Through these, smooth lawns could be seen, and the graceful, colonnaded porticoes of buildings that appeared to be temples or shrines.

Finnigin urged Matanyan into the centre of the plaza. The only movement around him was that of enormous moths shivering around the haloes of the torches. Matanyan snorted and bent his head to scratch his nose on one of his knees. Finnigin dismounted. The gate to the nearest Temple garden stood open. Its bars were intertwined with a creeping vine, bursting with late flowers and heavy, perfumed berries. Beyond, beneath a canopy of leaves, a straight path, plush with moss, led to the steps of the Temple. Oil burned in shallow bowls beside the path, throwing out a flickering yellow radiance. The sight was sensuously inviting, irresistible. Finnigin didn't know what he expected to find within the garden, but he was compelled to enter it.

A feeling of unreality crept over him. The sounds of the city were faint in the distance; the muffled boom, fizz and whine of exploding fireworks, strident music, thin human voices. Here in the garden it was absolutely tranquil. Finnigin advanced up the path towards the Temple. Behind him, he heard Matanyan shake his mane and shuffle his hooves on the plaza stones. These sounds too seemed to come from an immense distance away. As he drew nearer to the portico, a gentle sound of softly chanting female voices could be heard, gradually growing louder as the owners of the voices drew nearer. Presently, a scampering bevy of young girls flickered out from between the columns like a flight of white moths. They carried baskets of winter rose petals, which they began to strew across the path at Finnigin's feet. Their faces were scrolled with intricate patterns that appeared to be tattoos, and their expressions were dreamy, introspective. When they looked at Finnigin, it was as if they were looking into their own dreams. Perhaps they were drugged.

Finnigin was enchanted by the spectacle, and did not speak for fear of shattering the exquisite atmosphere of otherworldly languor. As the girls surrounded him, in a dipping, swaying throng, a group of tall, robed individuals stepped forward from the shadows of the columns. They raised their arms into the air, sleeves falling back to reveal a treasury of golden bangles, studded with precious stones that caught the faint, liquid light of the lamps. An air of opulence and richness stole out into the garden, riding a cloud of perfume, the essence of roses and jasmine. Finnigin was transfixed. It did not occur to him that he might be interrupting some rite of majesty and importance. He felt absurdly a part of the proceedings.

The leading figure, a mature woman of stately appearance, approached him. She was clearly a priestess of the highest order, her head crowned with ivory spikes, a long veil tumbling from the crown to the floor, thrown back from her face. Two acolytes with veiled faces swiftly glided past her and flicked Finnigin with a scented liquor from silver bowls. Finnigin backed away, brushing at his dusty clothes, and opened his mouth to speak, but the woman spoke first. She gestured at the mountain's walls, her eyes raised to the sky.

'My Lady Scarzanera, it is I, Brinorah, Architrice of your Holy Temple! The invocation is complete! By the prophecy of Twillian the Mage, the scryings of Reptilia and Gorgon, all hail to the Great One, the Lord of the Chasms, the Tongue of Truth!'

'All hail!' echoed the company.

'Scarzanera, Great Lady, we humbly thank you for your bounty.' The priestess closed her eyes, lowered her arms and bowed, her veil falling forward over her shoulders.

Finnigin decided it would be prudent to leave the scene. He turned round and a voice cried, 'Wait, he moves! Mark the steps!'

He couldn't resist looking back. His behaviour elicited an astounded but appreciative hiss from the temple personnel.

'Hark! He watches us!' cried the Architrice.

Several lesser officials behind her dropped to their knees. 'O Revered One, speak!' commanded the Architrice in a ringing voice.

Finnigin looked around himself. 'Me?'

Another urgent whisper rippled through the group. The Architrice took a few stately steps towards him. She bowed, performing an elaborate, sweeping gesture with her arms.

'Speak!' she said. 'Enlighten us.'

'Er . . . I don't think I'm who you think I am,' he began.

The Architrice straightened up and raised her right hand. 'Heed it well!' she instructed the people behind her.

'Please excuse me,' Finnigin said, and made a run for the garden gate.

He heard someone shout, 'Follow!' and then a pounding of footsteps. In the plaza, Matanyan, who had been disdainfully nibbling leaves from the lower branches of the trees, struck a pose of alertness as he became aware of the sounds of rapid approach. Finnigin ran towards him, reached out to grab the reins. Matanyan skipped sideways.

'Come here!' Finnigin yelled. The horse refused to

comply, dodging this way and that, thereby evading all Finnigin's efforts to capture him. Panicking, he glanced over his shoulder.

The priests and priestesses had poured into the plaza, and now stood watching him from just beyond the garden gate. 'Behold!' cried the Architrice, pointing. 'He comes to us on a black horse, as it was foretold!' The volume and tone of her voice were finally too much for Matanyan who lowered his head and galloped off up the road towards the city, reins and stirrup leathers flapping. Finnigin uttered a whine of disbelief and frustration. His pursuers had edged around the plaza to encircle him. He was trapped.

'I've done nothing!' he shouted. 'Get away from me!' He ran towards a place guarded only by a couple of girls, but when he tried to push past them, they grabbed hold of his garments.

'Be at peace!' one of them said. 'We will not harm you! We are here to welcome you!'

Finnigin relaxed a little. 'You don't know me,' he said. 'I am a stranger. I don't know who you're waiting for, but it isn't me.'

The Architrice Brinorah approached him. 'O Revered One, we heed your words. They shall be consigned to the Book of Sayings. Let us take you to the city, to your proper and appointed place.'

'No!' Finnigin said, but his protest was ignored. He was lifted into the air by a multitude of hands and, accompanied by the joyful songs of the girls, carried along the torch-lit avenue to the gates of Phaxteriniad.

The streets of the city were thronged with people dressed in festive costumes. Coloured lights sputtered gaily into the night air, garlands drooped from every building. When they caught sight of the approaching parade of priests and priestesses, the crowd began to cheer and wave and clap their hands. Finnigin, dizzy and squirming, saw the world dip and dive around him. Grotesque faces in theatrical makeup swooped towards him; hands pinched his flesh, ripped his clothes, his hair. The further he was carried, the more the clamouring voices sounded like the baying of predatory beasts. He feared he would be torn to pieces at the journey's end. Sobs of terror constricted his throat. Where was Varian to save him? Would Babooshpet appear from a doorway to calm the hysterical crowd? Surely, something would happen. He'd been aided too many times in the past simply to die now.

A blaring peal of trumpets sounded overhead, and a cascade of wet petals poured down to cover Finnigin's body, fill his open mouth, obscure his sight. He could tell those who carried him were climbing steps, and as they climbed, the howls of the crowd diminished. Just as he'd managed to shake the last of the petals from his eyes, he was engulfed by darkness. The only sound was the swishing of his carriers' robes, and the hushed pad of their feet. He was aware of great height and space around him, but could see nothing. He cried out, 'Let me go! Let me go!' and his voice echoed up and up into an endless void. He tried to wriggle, but the hands held him too tightly: there were too many hands. Presently, he heard the sobbing susurration of religious chanting nearby, and the company passed swiftly through a thick, musty veil of brocaded curtains into a vast room that was lit by bowls of burning oil upon the floor. Here, Finnigin was lowered to the ground. He crouched low, rubbing his bruised limbs, his whole body caught in a spasm of shuddering. Oblivious to his mews of distress, his garbled, unfinished questions, two priests came and lifted him to his feet and led him up a short flight of steps to a raised dais, there depositing him in a gigantic throne. Finnigin leaned back against the fusty cushions, the back of the throne soaring high behind him. He felt he would faint at any moment. What were these maniacs going to do to him?

The temple had filled with a shadowy host of robed priests, all of whom stood facing the throne, their expressions those of joy, relief and adoration. Small, involuntary cries occasionally rose softly from their midst. The Architrice stalked to the foot of the dais and turned, in a swirl of robes, to face the crowd.

'My brothers and sisters of the Order of Scarzanera, today the prophecy has been fulfilled, the predictions of Reptilia and Gorgon brought to fruition. As instructed, the Prima Sphere conducted the rites of invocation, and at the appointed hour we went out into the garden. The Tongue of Truth rode to us on a black horse. He came into the garden, and as has been boded, denied himself to our faces. He abased himself, told us he was not worthy, that he was not The One For Whom We Wait. Gladly, we raised him on high and carried him into the city, preceded by his magnificent steed. Now, he is here before you, The Lovely, in all his splendid youth. I have done as should be done. He is brought to you.' Brinorah bowed and turned to Finnigin.

'Speak, O Great One!'

Finnigin groaned. 'This is a nightmare!' he said weakly. 'I am here against my will!'

The priesthood gasped. 'Thus,' said Brinorah gravely, with some satisfaction, 'does he utter the truths that have been ordained. Thus does he, in beautifully simple words, encapsulate the human experience of life on this earth. "This is a nightmare. I am here against my will." The words shall be written in the Book of Sayings!'

Finnigin managed to sit upright and lean forward. 'Stop this!' he said. 'I don't know what's happening!' He struggled to his feet to stand swaying upon the dais. All eyes were fixed upon him in total attentiveness. 'If you were waiting for some kind of holy person, I am not he. I am Finnigin, a terranaut from beyond the mountains of Overhang. I am on a journey of learning, that's all. I have no wisdom to give you.' He noticed that a scribe was sitting at the bottom of the dais, scribbling in a large book. It didn't take much imagination to realise that everything he was saying was being written down. Presumably, that was the Book of Sayings. Finnigin sighed. Perhaps a little cunning was in order?

'I have to continue my journey into the mountains, to enrich my experience. Then, I can come back to you and tell you of all that I see and hear. You must not keep me here.'

'Ah,' said the Architrice, nodding to her colleagues. 'It is as it should be. He is coming into bloom, remembering himself, no longer denying who and what he is.' Everyone nodded in agreement.

'Then I can go?' Finnigin asked, tentatively beginning to walk down the steps of the dais.

The Architrice bowed to him. 'But of course. We ourselves are only too aware we cannot enjoy your presence for more than a hundred days. Then, your journey into the Realms of Scarzanera's Family will continue. But until then, you must let us indulge ourselves by supplying your every need. No demand uttered by the Tongue of Truth is too great. Command us, O Revered One. What do you desire?'

Finnigin considered. 'I am hungry,' he said diffidently.

The High Priestess inclined her head. 'A feast shall be laid out for you.'

'And . . . my clothes are in rags.'

'Sumptuous garments await the blessing of your body.'

Finnigin grinned nervously. 'I would like the best wine Phaxteriniad can provide.'

'The vintners have prepared exquisite liquors in readiness for this very moment,' said the Architrice. 'Already flagons stand in ice awaiting your perfect lips.'

'After I have eaten and refreshed myself, I would like to sleep in the most magnificent chamber, upon the most comfortable bed in the world.'

'Such a chamber lies behind veils of black silk awaiting your arrival,' said the Architrice.

Finnigin wondered whether he dared believe he was so lucky. A hundred days of luxury? Surely, the delay would be worth it. He might think up a few amusing Words of Truth while he was there. 'Then take me to the feast!' he said.

The Architrice bowed yet again, before clapping her hands smartly. 'Attendants, take the Great One to his chambers.'

The ceremonial chambers of the Tongue of Truth outshone even the most sumptuous rooms of Varian's palaces that Finnigin had visited. He was delighted to discover that he had the run of eighteen rooms, which were interconnected and situated next to a wide marble terrace on the third floor of the Architrice's Palace. The rooms were not stuffed with gaudy riches as he'd imagined, and were in fact quite bare, but the elegance and comfort of their appointments provided a greater opulence than swags of hangings or ornaments of gold. Finnigin was taken to the bedroom, while a bath was prepared for him in an adjoining room. Left alone for a few moments, he walked to the long windows and gazed out at the city. Pale muslin curtains, the height of three tall men from floor to ceiling, fretted at the open windows, allowing a cool breeze to ventilate the chamber.

Finnigin sighed. Was this Varian at work again? Surely there was no person alive as lucky as he. At some point – and he was sure the day would come – he would have to speak to Varian, glean the truth of what was happening to him. There must be a greater plan behind all this. He could not believe Varian was acting randomly.

A movement in the chamber behind him prompted Finnigin to turn around. Someone had come into the room; a youth dressed in leggings and tunic of dark purple, his hair a halo of light around his head and shoulders. Finnigin's mouth dropped open. This must be a prince of the city. The youth inclined his head.

'Good evening, Your Prominence. I am Luminar, your personal mantologist.'

Never had Finnigin met a person who seemed so self-possessed. 'Mantologist? What's that?'

Luminar stepped lightly to the windows, performed a genuflexion. 'Your diviner. My speciality is astromancy, but I have knowledge of sciomancy and also a smattering of oneiromancy.' He pointed with a graceful arm towards the sky. 'However, my vocation lies with the stars.'

Finnigin laughed nervously. 'And why would I need a diviner? I'm only going to be here a hundred days. Perhaps you could look into my future and see where I should go next?'

Luminar frowned, an expression so subtle and slight, it would have been easy to miss. 'My function is to work with you, to establish the Truths of your reign. When you speak, I apply your words to the positions of the stars, and thus gain greater insight into your sayings. I am to be your companion.'

Finnigin smiled. 'I could not wish for more gracious company.'

Luminar twitched a nostril and turned away. 'With your permission, I shall now see to the adjusting of my equipment.'

The following morning, after a night of sublimely tranquil slumber, Finnigin was presented to the King of Phaxteriniad, a man named Gorestel. The King came to Finnigin's apartment, surrounded by a clustering entourage, but throughout the introduction he remained invisible behind an opaque screen. The Architrice was in attendance, along with two dozen or so of her immediate cabal. King Gorestel said nothing. Brinorah spoke a few formal words about Finnigin's function, and the inspection was concluded within minutes. After everyone had filed solemnly from the apartment, Finnigin said to Luminar. 'A man of few words, your King.'

Luminar's response was smoothly delivered. 'What has he to say to you who speak the words of ultimate truth?'

Finnigin shrugged. 'A greeting would have been nice.'

Luminar laughed softly. 'Your Prominence, I would be doing you no favour by withholding the information that although your position in this city is one of status and prestige, it is ephemeral. The King has seen many Tongues of Truth. Your words will be written down and pored over by the inner cabals of the Temple, but they will not be read by Gorestel, and no one else will remember them. You are, in truth, a ceremonial decoration.'

Finnigin bridled. 'Surely you should not speak to me this way!'

Luminar shrugged. 'As a mantologist, I shall work my art in the palace until I am dead. I intend to live to a ripe age, and carve a splendid niche for myself in Phaxteriniad's elite. You, on the other hand, will be no more than a memory in this city, once the hundred days have passed. In the meantime, you may enjoy being clothed in silks, applying yourself to gluttonous gourmandising, and lapping up the attention of the Architrice and her cronies, but do not expect respect from any members of the honoured orders of mantologists. I shall fulfil my duty without complaint, for I am honourable, but that is that.'

Finnigin objected to Luminar's insolent remarks. 'I could complain to the Architrice about your behaviour.'

Luminar's eyes flashed, but there was no other indication of displeasure. 'And have me replaced?' He laughed, his eyes surveying Finnigin's body from head to foot in a belittling manner. 'I think not.'

Finnigin felt himself flush. He was unsure how to take that.

'Even the King's third daughter commands my art,' said Luminar.

'Ah, so she appreciates your modesty and vanity-free good looks,' Finnigin said caustically, folding his arms. 'No doubt she wilts in your arms. Am I supposed to be impressed?'

'Our arrangement is not so frivolous as that,' Luminar replied. 'We have a deeper understanding.'

Finnigin made a scoffing sound. 'I think the favours of royalty must be fickle. Don't be so sure of yourself.'

Luminar smiled. 'You have not met the Princess Alomeah. All Phaxteriniad trembles before her.'

Finnigin sighed. 'Naturally. Well, don't let me keep you from your work. Get on with what you have to do.'

'I have to be your companion,' Luminar said, and sat down upon a shawled sofa to regard Finnigin through slitted eyes.

So began Finnigin's reign as the Tongue of Truth. He was dressed in splendid clothes that were stitched from the most costly fabrics. He was fed upon delicacies and refreshed with mellow wines. Daily, he was attended by a team of pages and handmaidens, who cleaned and massaged his body, groomed his hair and buffed his nails. He wandered from room to room in his apartments, drinking copious amounts of wine and uttering whatever thoughts came into his head. For the first few days he enjoyed the proceedings. A clutch of attentive scriveners scurried along behind him, noting his utterances. There were always at least two priests or priestesses lurking around his rooms, forever muttering together every time he opened his mouth. In moments of extreme drunkenness, Finnigin was moved to express obscenities which caused the priest to draw in their breath sharply. 'A time of hostility is presaged!' one of them said. Finnigin couldn't care less. He did not consider that his incautious words might be shaping the city's future.

In the smallest chamber, two rooms away from the bedroom, Luminar set up an astrolabe and other arcane contrivances to do with his art. The priests approached him at regular intervals, to deliberate about how Finnigin's words might apply to the position of the stars. Luminar dealt with them in a cool, indifferent matter. Watching from a doorway, Finnigin wondered whether Luminar truly had any faith in his art. He was certainly cunning, and knew how to use his considerable beauty to secure his position within the palace. Princesses and lesser royalty fawned before him. Finnigin imagined he would recite witty anecdotes about the peccadilloes of the Tongue of Truth to his admirers, eliciting laughter and perhaps a little derision. Finnigin had quickly learned that only the priests regarded him as something special. To others, his function was something of an amusement.

Finnigin was annoyed with himself that he looked forward to his brief meetings with Luminar. He sensed the mantologist despised him, but Luminar was such a feast for the eyes it was hard to dislike him. Beside Luminar, Finnigin felt clumsy and crude. Luminar, with long, cool eyes of darkest green, was usually polite but always distant. He seemed to manifest and disappear at will, or perhaps he used a secret entrance to the apartments? His hands flickered over the complexities of his machinery, administering a caress here, an adjustment there. Finnigin heard his maids speaking of the mantologist in hushed tones, and noticed that they giggled when Luminar came into the room. He would glance at them in surprise, but then pass on. Apart from Luminar, Finnigin's staff treated him with awe and reverence. He stroked his maids and they responded favourably. He knew they would sleep with him if he asked it, but somehow the idea lacked appeal. It was too easy to accomplish.

Each evening, Brinorah and her cabal would convene in Finnigin's sitting-room and ask him questions. One night a priest said to him, 'Tell us of the heart of the third daughter of the King.'

Brinorah cast the man a warning glance, but he pretended not to notice.

Finnigin answered with abandon, careless of what he might say, but also conscious of Luminar's attention from the corner of the room. 'Having never met the woman, I am reluctant to reply, but a princess is a princess. Her heart would be rigid, lacking the tenderness that regular beatings and bruisings inflict upon the hearts of commoners.' He was proud of those words, but wine had oiled his eloquence.

The priest made a sour sound. 'That tells us nothing new!'

Brinorah reprimanded the man severely, but the episode served to instruct Finnigin that Alomeah was not greatly liked by the priests of the city.

The incident must have reached the ears of Princess Alomeah herself, because she made a dramatic appearance in Finnigin's chambers the following day. Finnigin supposed Luminar had said something to her about it, because he knew that the Princess generally ignored the antics of the Temple.

She appeared at sundown in the late-afternoon, accompanied by her two lackeys, Niles and Marmion. That she was a creature to contest convention was obvious from the moment of her arrival. For a start, no female of noble birth should have men as body servants rather than women. She was a slender and striking woman in her early-twenties, possessed of a glorious mane of red hair which she wore loose to her waist. Finnigin could see she was dangerous because of the intelligence that gleamed in her eyes. Here was no inbred lackwit, but he supposed his assumptions about her heart were right; it was clearly an organ of flint.

'So,' she said, prowling around Finnigin where he stood in the centre of the floor, 'here is the Great One, the Tongue of Truth.'

Finnigin said nothing. He wished Luminar was there, but the mantologist had been conspicuously absent all day.

'I hear you have been making pronouncements about me.'

'I say the things people want to hear,' Finnigin answered smoothly. 'That is my function, I believe.'

The Princess raised her brows. 'You can say what you like, but don't mention me. If I hear of any more indiscretions on your part, I will have you poisoned, hundred days or no hundred days. The traditions of the Temple mean nothing to me.' She folded her arms and faced him. 'Still, Luminar was right: you are a pretty morsel. Too pretty. What a shame.'

'I am surprised to hear Luminar say anything complimentary about me,' Finnigin said.

Alomeah laughed. 'Ah, don't be deceived. He is as prickly as a bowl of shards, but he appreciates attractive things.'

Alomeah made herself comfortable upon one of Finnigin's sofas and patted the seat beside her. 'Come here. Sit with me. Let me tell you about myself. I would enjoy doing that.'

Diffidently, he eased down beside her.

The Princess snapped her fingers together. 'Niles, bring us wine. Plenty of it. They say truth resides in the bottom of a wine cup. Let's test the theory!'

Finnigin regarded the Princess' companions nervously. Niles was tall and dressed completely in black leather. He had a satanic face, with a neatly trimmed beard and very dark eyes. His hair fell in oily tresses over his shoulders, and his hands were gloved. Finnigin could imagine the man obeying Alomeah's orders to the letter. Orders such as: 'Kill that worthless wretch for me!' Marmion did not seem so threatening as he smiled continually and had a restless, lively manner. His less sinister appearance, however, was offset by a certain manic gleam in his eyes.

Niles brought Finnigin and Alomeah a cup of wine each. His glance as it met Finnigin's was contemptuous. Finnigin felt very young and naive before them. It was as if Alomeah had his fate dancing upon the palm of her hand. She stretched luxuriously beside him, drawing up her knees beneath her.

'I have already had five prospective husbands disposed of,' she said.

'Congratulations,' Finnigin responded automatically.

Alomeah smiled. 'Yes. I did congratulate myself

actually.' She reached out a slim, white hand and touched Finnigin lightly with her fingernails. 'Don't worry. You're not marked for that fate. My father tolerates my caprices because in truth he is in love with me and can't bear the thought of any man touching me. He is also, I must point out, a rigid and conventional creature and would never dream of making improper suggestions to me. He will suffer in silence, which suits me fine.'

'How do you get on with your mother?' Finnigin couldn't resist asking.

'She is dead,' Alomeah said.

'Oh, I'm sorry . . .' he said lamely.

Alomeah shrugged and sipped her wine. 'Whatever for?' She closed her eyes and then slid Finnigin a sidelong glance. 'So, what have you heard about me?'

'Very little. Only what Luminar told me: he holds you in high regard.'

'How dull! I would have liked you to have heard about my exploits. The ones I'm famous for.' She smiled. 'You don't know how privileged you are having me here. I never bother with Temple tripe as a rule.' She leaned forward. 'Marmion, come here and entertain us.'

Marmion had been slinking around the chamber, examining Finnigin's belongings. He sauntered over to his mistress and performed an elaborate gesture. 'Your Highness?'

'Tell this truthful tongue here about my family, about me.'

'With pleasure.' Marmion raised his hand and struck a dramatic pose. 'King Gorestel of this fair city has three daughters, who are famous from the Tar Cliffs to the shores of Gleaming Fisk.'

'Gleaming Fisk?' Finnigin interrupted.

Marmion gave him an admonishing glance. 'Yes.

Now pay attention. The eldest daughter is the tall and regal Astenia.' He raised his chin into the air and pulled a sneer. 'She struts through life searching for suitors.' Marmion began to parade around the chamber, lifting cushions and drapes, his face set in a disagreeable expression. 'Any men there? Come out!'

Alomeah had begun to laugh. 'La! Poor Asti! Though he speaks the truth of it!'

Marmion straightened up and once again pointed at the ceiling. 'The second daughter is the Princess Povanya, a lady of vanity and, of course, great beauty.' Now, he preened before an imaginary mirror, grimacing horribly and smacking his lips. Then, one hand on his hip, he minced across the room in a splayed-kneed waddle. 'Make way, make way, I'm coming! Look at me, everyone! Ah, that mirror is faulty! It has cracked!'

Alomeah was gripping a cushion in mirth. 'Ah, how cleverly you mimic their little ways! Povanya is no work of art!'

'The youngest and most lovely of the King's daughters is the fair Alomeah,' said Marmion, gesturing at the sofa.

'And are you going to mimic me, dear sweetling?' Alomeah enquired in a silvery voice.

Marmion smiled. 'I think not.'

'Oh, I am sure you can do a good job!'

'I am not worthy. Besides, how could I mirror such wondrousness?'

Alomeah giggled at Finnigin. 'He is a pet!'

'The Princess Alomeah is famous in the city,' Marmion said. 'She is a scholar.'

'That is correct,' said the Princess. 'I am a scholar of pain and death. It fascinates me!'

'Not your own, I trust,' Finnigin remarked dryly.

'Of course not!' said Alomeah. 'I am very interested in anthromancy, the divination from entrails. Luminar is helping me in my studies, but unfortunately I don't have his skill. Yet. I once tried to glean some bodings from the offal of an opened slave, but I could see nothing in the mess! Still, the study is most interesting.'

'Your dedication is admirable,' said Finnigin.

Alomeah nodded. 'I am a person inclined to delving.' She tapped Finnigin's arm. 'I know everything about everyone in this city, from the lowliest scullion to the highest lord. It is very important for a woman in my position to know these things.'

'Absolutely,' said Finnigin. He paused, wondering whether he dared risk the question that sprang to his mind. 'I don't suppose you know of someone called Varian, do you?'

Alomeah frowned prettily. 'Varian? The name means nothing to me. Why? Who is he?'

'He is a very rich man, I think. I met him on my travels, and for whatever reason he became interested in my . . . future. He claimed to have palaces everywhere, and the ones I've seen were certainly no mean hovels. I last saw him in Oubrahani.'

Alomeah grimaced. 'Terrible place! Whatever were you doing there?'

Finnigin shrugged. 'It was just a port of call. This Varian appears to have a great deal of influence in every city I've visited. His powers are almost magical.'

'Hmm,' murmured Alomeah. She summoned her companions. 'Have either of you heard of this man?'

Niles and Marmion had not. 'What does he look like?' Marmion asked. 'It's possible he lives here under a different name.'

Finnigin described Varian as best he could.

'He sounds very striking,' Alomeah said, 'but that description could apply to many young dukes and barons of Phaxteriniad. Mystery and aloofness are popular fashion accessories at present.' She smiled.

'Perhaps I could make enquiries?'

'I would be grateful,' said Finnigin. 'He has meddled in my life a great deal, and I'm curious as to why.'

'You had better tell me about it,' Alomeah suggested. 'Perhaps, with my intelligence, I could help you?'

Rather reluctantly, Finnigin outlined his travels and Varian's appearances in them, neglecting to mention the most personal aspects of these episodes.

'This Varian seems a fascinating character!' Alomeah declared. 'I shall apply myself to his discovery at once.' She stood up. 'Ah, it's a shame you're confined to these rooms, Tongue of Truth, otherwise I could take you to one of my mantic events. I'm sure it would interest you.'

Her words brought a chill to Finnigin's flesh. 'Confined? I don't believe I am. The Architrice told me my every wish would be granted while I am here.'

Alomeah laughed. 'That was perhaps an exaggeration on her part! Still, it will be entertaining to see what you do – in the end.'

Finnigin disliked the sinister note to Alomeah's voice. 'Surely you can ignore any of the Temple's decrees?'

Alomeah shrugged. 'I expect so, but I'm more intrigued by observing you at present.' She turned to her companions. 'Niles, Marmion, precede me! We are leaving.'

'Wait!' Finnigin cried, but Alomeah merely waved a languid hand at him and left the apartment.

Finnigin stood indecisively in the middle of the room for a while and then, mustering resolve, marched to the main doors. He opened them and faced a clanging of crossed spears. Two guards regarded him impassively.

'Let me through!' he commanded.

The guards ignored his words, continuing only to

stare at him. Finnigin pushed against the spears, but was shunted back into the room. Fuming, he slammed the doors.

Behind him, he noticed a furtive movement: the scriveners. He marched towards them, where they cowered unobtrusively among the curtains. 'What is the meaning of this?' he demanded. 'Why can't I leave these rooms?'

The two scriveners both raised their arms in gestures of helplessness, and displayed their mouths. Finnigin saw that they had been rendered mute; their tongues were missing. Also, they seemed almost witless. His attempts to chide them into writing messages came to nothing. Still furious, Finnigin marched to the room where Luminar kept his mechanisms, hoping the mantologist might have come back to the apartments by some unseen means. But the room was still unoccupied.

Sighing, Finnigin peered through various view pieces attached to the astrolabe. He had been foolish to believe there wouldn't be a price for receiving all this comfort and attention from the Architrice and her people. He remembered how he had greeted the rhukahas when they'd accosted him, his naivety then. Had he learned nothing? But surely, Varian would appear soon and take control. He only had to wait.

In the early evening, Brinorah and her staff appeared to speak with Finnigin. Before they'd even sat down, he demanded to know why he was being kept locked in.

Brinorah raised her brows. 'It is tradition,' she said in surprise. 'You don't want distractions. Your thoughts must be an unswerving stream.'

'Alomeah was here today,' Finnigin said.

Brinorah hid her reaction, if any, to this news. 'She is a restless, inquisitive young woman. And very imaginative.'

'I want to go into the city tomorrow.'

Brinorah turned away to select a comfortable seat. 'No.'

Finnigin refused to speak until the company went away. Far from being put out by his behaviour, the priests contented themselves with interpreting his restless body postures and sighs. This did nothing to improve Finnigin's mood.

After the priests had left, whispering among themselves, Finnigin stalked out on to the terrace to seethe alone. His scriveners hovered by the doorway, apparently discomfited by his temper. Finnigin leaned over the balustrade and considered whether he'd be able to escape by climbing over it.

The city was a blaze of coloured lights below. Two storeys beneath the terrace, a paved plaza with a central fountain provided an area where palace residents could stroll in privacy. Beyond the plaza, a wall separated the palace from the city streets. Finnigin wondered whether he could get away by making a rope of sheets and curtains and climbing down to the plaza. From there he could run to the wall, and perhaps avoid detection. However, a sudden rustle behind him reminded him he was never alone. Tongueless or not, one undesirable move on his part and the scriveners would rush to the guards on duty outside and attract their attention. Finnigin sighed and rested his chin in his hands. 'Varian,' he murmured, 'where *are* you?'

Presently, Luminar came out on to the terrace. 'Ah, there you are! What are you doing out here? There's an untouched meal laid out in there, and we both know you are hardly a person to deny your stomach.'

Finnigin gibbered an irritated complaint.

'Oh dear, a sour mood,' said Luminar, leaning beside him on the balustrade.

'Yes!' Finnigin snapped. 'I am a prisoner here!'

'Oh, you've only just realised that?' Luminar laughed. 'You are such a child!'

Finnigin wheeled round, his fist raised. He was pleased to note that Luminar jumped back, his expression one of alarm. 'I was kidnapped!' Finnigin cried. 'Kidnapped and dragged here against my will!'

Luminar raised his hands placatingly. 'That is not my fault.'

'I never said it was,' Finnigin said, lowering his fist and flexing the fingers. 'Just don't be so condescending.' He sighed. 'I have to get out of here! If only Varian would come now.'

'And who is Varian?'

'A friend of mine.' Finnigin couldn't resist intimating he had also found favour with the Princess. 'Alomeah said she'd find him for me.'

'Ah, yes,' said Luminar. 'She did mention something about it to me earlier. The mysterious man. He sounds like the sort of person you'd invent, if you didn't know him.'

Finnigin flicked Luminar a narrow glance, but was too weary with the mantologist's manner to shout. 'I have not invented him.'

'You're too touchy. I never said that.'

'You implied it . . . Anyway, where have you been today? I suppose you knew Alomeah was coming to see me?'

'It was I who suggested it,' said Luminar. 'As to what I've been doing, it's none of your business.'

'I thought you were supposed to be my companion?'

Luminar shrugged. 'We all need time alone.'

'I don't need your company at all!' Finnigin said. 'There is nothing pleasant about having you around.'

Luminar smiled. 'Come inside,' he said.

Finnigin refused to eat any of the food and skulked restlessly around the room, while Luminar sat down at the low table and fastidiously helped himself to small portions of the repast. Whenever he paused to dab his mouth with a napkin, he glanced up at Finnigin, shook his head, and smiled in a bemused manner. Eventually, he pushed his plate away.

'Sit down, Finnigin Truth-Tongue. Your antics are giving me indigestion.'

Finnigin gave a frustrated growl. 'Sit down? How can I? I can't relax at all. All I can think about is what I can do to get out of this place!'

'Well, you can't at the moment,' Luminar said. 'So you might as well resign yourself to the fact. Come and sit here on the floor by me. I'll massage your neck for you.'

Finnigin pulled his lips back into a snarl. 'What's this concern of yours, all of a sudden?'

Luminar shrugged. 'I'm not concerned. I simply want to touch you.'

Finnigin was silenced.

'Well?' said Luminar. 'Sit down.'

Finnigin gestured at the scriveners. 'What about them?'

'Watching me massage your neck won't hurt them. Come here at once.'

Grudgingly, Finnigin sat down on the floor at Luminar's feet. 'Brinorah and her cronies are planning something terrible for me, aren't they?' he blurted out.

Luminar stroked Finnigin's hair from his neck. 'So that is your fear.'

'Deny it, then.'

'Whatever they're planning, you have your friend Varian who will no doubt appear in the nick of time. Relax. You are full of knots!'

Finnigin leaned back against Luminar's knees, allowed himself at length to take pleasure from the touch of Luminar's fingers.

'I am your friend,' said Luminar softly. He bent forward and kissed the top of Finnigin's head.

'Has Alomeah told you to do this?' he asked in a slurred voice.

Luminar laughed. 'She never tells me what to do. I follow my own heart. You must trust me.'

He slid down to sit beside Finnigin on the floor. They embraced. In the silence of it, Finnigin could hear the scratch of pens on paper, further up the room.

Casmeer

The next episode of Ays' life came to Casmeer in a dream. He awoke from it terrified, and yet was unable to resist rushing to his workroom in order to write down what he'd dreamed before the details vanished from his mind, or – worse – before some other character in his story intervened and changed it. The story was incomplete, and at first he thought it signalled the end of Ays entirely. Was Finnigin to be the one to continue the story? Had Casmeer unconsciously made a choice between the two?

He knew that he preferred Finnigin's character, which was altogether warmer than Ays', but Ays was a more complicated person. Ays had great potential, Casmeer felt, and his cold aloofness was a façade that could be shattered.

Over the last few days, Casmeer had not left the house. He found he was eating less and less, and that his fear of the outside was gradually widening to include the streets of the city itself. Would he starve to death because of that? He resolved that the next day he would force himself to go out and collect food. He had more than enough in his larder for today.

His anxiety at the way his stories were obsessing him

had abated as his agoraphobia increased. What else had he to fill his life with? he reasoned. Even if he ended up totally deluded, living entirely in his fantasy world, what did it matter? There was, after all, no one around to object.

The plumosites now came confidently inside the house. They had appropriated some of the wall hangings, which Casmeer did not protest about. Babooshpet had shown an interest in Elini's jewellery, but when Casmeer had offered it to her, she'd shied away. She had squatted on the stool before Elini's cloudy mirror, in order to sniff the dregs of the perfume bottles. Standing behind her, Casmeer was impelled to pick up a tortoiseshell comb and apply it to the long fur on Babooshpet's neck. She had looked up into the mirror in surprise, her owlish glance meeting that of Casmeer. But she did not move away, and allowed him to groom her. After a while, she became bored with the attention and climbed down from the stool. Casmeer felt very tired. He had to lie down for a while. His limbs felt stiff and ached intolerably in the joints. Was he getting old at last?

The plumosites scampered around his room as he dozed. He could see the shadow of their shapes through his closed lids. Presently, he wept, and they sang to him. For the first time in many years, Casmeer thought about death.

Chapter Seventeen
Beyond the Brine

The frozen water stretched as far as the eye could see, although there was a smudge on the distant horizon that might have been the shadow of mountains. Leeth climbed a small hill near the sea-shore and stared out over the ice. She had left Ays huddled in a hollow overhung with rattling, dead grasses, in order to escape his moans, his haggard face. Leeth felt powerless in the face of her companion's torment. She'd always disapproved of his addiction and had been sure he'd be able to overcome it with her help. That had been before Ays' meagre supply of hela had expired. Now, despite Leeth's fervent inner prayers and persistent faith that she could best the evil bitch of his cravings, she had to accept that Ays was no longer the man she had fallen in love with. Mara hela was stronger than she was. The skeletal creature Ays had become, of peevish moods, flaking skin and hollow bruised eyes, was a stranger. How they'd managed to travel this far up the Skine was a miracle Leeth could not fathom, but she suspected it had been her will alone that had kept Ays alive and moving.

She breathed deeply of the chill air with its ghost of salt. Despite her grief and frustration, her body felt dynamic and tall; her limbs strong and lithe. The cold energised her. Her hair whipped forward across her face and shoulders, tangling with the ragged black shawl she'd wrapped around her body. Her feet were alternately numb and throbbing, but she did not register the discomfort. Inside, there was a budding feeling that some kind of end was fast approaching. She felt excited, eager.

They had left Salaganda with comparative ease, clambering down an oily rope-ladder that was presumably used by engineers. A couple of mechanics hanging in the city's machinery noticed their departure, but made no move to prevent it. An air of magic surrounded their escape. Leeth and Ays had dropped down to a hard, cold ground and the true depth of winter. Deprived of the city's shelter, Leeth had set about acquiring the things they would need for their journey. Mara hela had not been on her list, but even if it had been she did not uncover a source. Ays had been euphoric at first, ignited with hela energy, and it had been Leeth who'd suggested prudence with the scant supply of hela she'd managed to uproot for him from Massifer's workroom. Leeth took it from Ays' pocket and put it in her shoulder bag. When he asked for it, she would assess his appearance and decide whether or not the dose was vital. She'd anticipated trouble from him about that, but there was a weariness about Ays that had not been present before he'd entered Salaganda. He eventually told her all about Massifer's experiments, causing Leeth to wonder whether some of them might have permanently damaged his mind and body.

Water nomads wintering on the Skine were helpful, and took pity on her when they caught sight of Ays. She told them he had a wasting disease. Some of them must have guessed the truth, but they did not comment on it. Leeth worked hard, helping to repair the long, narrow boats that, during the summer, plied the Brine of Reconditities and congregated around the water markets. In return, the nomads equipped her with winter clothes and a small, leather tent. Although they were not generous with donating supplies, they explained where Leeth could find food and how to prepare it so that it wouldn't poison her. They gave her salt and a generous portion of dried milk, but that was all. Leeth had become quite friendly with a couple of the girls, who attempted to dissuade her from leaving them until the spring. She confessed to them about Ays' condition. Because Ays had not yet reached the nadir of his deprivation, and was still attractive, the girls were eager to advise Leeth in how she could find spores. Now, she knew what to look for, and how to harvest it, although she resented having to do so bitterly. Her instinct was to burn any hela spores she found, and she'd have been quite happy to spend the rest of the winter hunting them down.

As they travelled down the Skine, Leeth became quite adept at locating bitter root vegetables growing wild along the frozen river banks. On sunny days, she would walk out on to the ice, right to the place where it became uncertain and thin, and the deep river current held sway in the centre of the flow. Here, sluggish, oily black fish rose to the surface, seduced by the deceptive sunlight, and Leeth could catch them by dangling the ends of her hair through a hole in the ice, and spearing the fish with a sharp stick when they came up to nibble at what they mistakenly perceived as insects. Ays would huddle miserably on the frosty bank, hugging his knees, his cheek resting on his hands, his eyes unfocused and wretched. At least he did not seem to hate her any more. She was encouraged by this at first, until it became apparent that he was too listless to feel anything at all.

The water nomads had told Leeth about the Brine,

but she was not sure whether she believed their tales. They said that, as the sea froze, all the sounds in the area – those of birds, animals, fish and retreating water nomads – were trapped in the ice. They warned her about lingering there in the spring. 'We never go there until the trees are in bud,' they said. 'Because the sounds coming out of the melting ice drive people mazy.'

Now, Leeth stood on the seaside hill, and wondered if she could smell the approach of spring in the air. She looked around at the leaning, whip-branched shrubs that clung to the grass-covered dunes. Their branches were red, crowned with tight, pink buds. Everything sealed and gummed. Leeth was reminded of blood and birthing. Was the approach of spring bloody rather than green? The nomad girls had told her that hela spores lived in the ice. She did not want to scratch them free, and yet the grotesque that Ays had become was unbearable. If she wanted the beautiful Ays back, she must give in to the wicked demands of the drug. Feed me. Feed me. Ays had rambled about how the hela had taken control of him, lived inside him as a separate being. Leeth had privately scoffed at that, but now she was not so sure it wasn't true.

'Leeth! Leeth!' The cry was thin, pitiful, querulous, demanding: the cry of an old man.

Sighing, she trudged back down the dunes to where Ays was crouching. He looked like a wizened little animal; repulsive, yet heart-wrenchingly pathetic. He wore a thick woollen hood to protect his scalp from the cold; most of his hair had gone. Leeth went to him and held him close. He never objected to that now.

'I thought you'd left me,' he rasped.

Leeth squeezed him tight in reply, said nothing.

After a few moments, Ays pulled away. 'It's too late. Even if we find the spores, it's too late.' He held out his hands. 'Look at me.' He wore gloves usually, but had obviously been driven to take them off and examine his skin. Leeth was frightened by the black patches on his fingers. What if the fingers should fall off in her hands? She shuddered. No, don't think that.

'It's not too late,' she said. 'I'll erect the tent, build a fire, we'll have a drink, then I'll start searching.'

Ays made a pitiful sound. 'It's too great a task.' He made a feeble gesture towards the sea. 'The spores could be anywhere out there.'

'I'll find them,' Leeth said firmly. She stood up in a purposeful manner.

'Leeth . . .'

'What?'

'Why are you doing this?' Surprisingly, it was the first time Ays had asked that question. Leeth had imagined he'd simply accepted her assistance because he knew how she felt about him.

'Don't be silly,' she said briskly.

Ays struggled to his feet. 'I'll help you.'

'There's no need. Stay here and rest.'

He limped forward. 'I'll help you.'

Together, they erected the tent and Leeth stowed their few belongings inside, lacing the flaps against intruders, although it was clear there were no animals or people around. Ays stood gaunt and shivering, warming his ruined fingers in his armpits, while Leeth unrolled the small pouch of tools that she'd been given by the nomads. She laid them out on the ground; a couple of metal spikes that could be used as picks, a chisel, a hammer.

'Remember we have to look for rust patches just below the surface of the ice,' she said. 'Let me know if you spot any. Don't try and excavate them yourself.' She already knew that once they'd located spores, a whole area of ice would have to be removed and melted slowly, to prevent damaging the hela. She had visions of Ays frantically gnawing the ice if he found any spores himself, and wished he would be content to sit here and wait for her. Still, she appreciated his eagerness to take part in the search.

By nightfall, no spores had been found, and Ays was delirious with exhaustion. Leeth helped him back to the camp and prepared a small meal. She had little appetite herself, and Ays had to be forced to eat anything at present. All night, she held him close against her body, kept awake by his mutterings and twitchings, and also a fear he might die while she slept. Before dawn, she napped briefly and woke refreshed. After giving Ays a warm drink of dried milk and melted ice, she gathered a large bundle of twigs and driftwood, which she tied securely together, and then took down the tent.

'What are you doing?' Ays asked her blearily.

Leeth was strapping the tent-leather to her body, so that it billowed behind her like a vast cape. 'Climb on,' she said brightly. 'I'm going to drag you across the ice.'

'You can't . . .' Ays began to protest.

'It will be quicker,' Leeth argued, 'and you hardly weigh anything. Hurry up. We need to get moving.'

All day, Leeth marched doggedly towards the distant mountains, staring down at her feet for tell-tale patches of red, until her eyes ached. She carried their belongings on her back, wrapped in a coat, and dragged both the fuel and the tent behind her. She refused to pay attention to the pains in her muscles. It was time to get this over with. They had to find the spores quickly and move on. This was wasting precious time.

After two days of travelling and pitching camp at night on the ice, there was still no sign of any hela spores. Leeth didn't want to light a fire on the ice, but she knew it was important that Ays had warm drinks.

As a precaution, she lit her kindling on a metal plate which she hung from a tripod she'd constructed hastily from wood and cord. Her little fire seemed to have no effect on the thick ice. The food supply was running out, and there was nothing but a vast frozen desert ahead. Sometimes, as she warmed the milk, she thought she detected the ghosts of sighs and laughter. She would look around herself nervously, her skin prickling, but never saw anything. Perhaps the nomads' tales were true, and the small heat of her fire had released a few trapped sounds. It made her feel uneasy. The thought of being surrounded by a cacophony of such sounds was terrifying.

Occasionally, as they travelled, very brief spasms of fear and powerlessness about their situation attempted to assault Leeth's persistence, but she fought them off. By the third day, Ays was too weak to move, and Leeth could only wrap him up in coats and secure any openings with thongs. Camping that night, Leeth was seriously considering turning back come morning. She wondered whether she should take one of the spikes now and put Ays out of his misery. There was so little of him left anyway. She fell asleep sitting up, with her head on her knees, and awoke before dawn.

For the first time, she felt real anguish and went out of the tent so that she didn't have to look at the husk of Ays' face. Outside, the light was bluey-grey, and the sky showed a narrow yellow-pink flush on the horizon. The air seemed full of echoes which had just died away. Leeth shuddered and sighed. She'd come so far, and failed. Why? She'd been so sure she'd succeed. A red ray of light cut across the ice in front of her, and for a moment she thought she saw the bulk of a vast, sleeping animal ahead. Then, she realised it was an island. They must have approached it unaware in the dusk the day before. She'd stared down at her feet for too long. With a renewed lightness of spirit, Leeth scampered towards the rock, towards the dawn. It wasn't until she put her hands against the first stones of the island that she realised the ice beneath her wasn't flushed simply with the colours of a new day. It was red ice. Blood-red. Mara hela.

The island was small, but there were a few stunted trees and shrubs growing on it. Leeth was pleased to discover a shallow cave. Without waking Ays, she went back to the tent to collect her tripod and the remains of the fuel, and returned to the cave to build a fire. Turquoise amphibians were hibernating in hidden niches. Leeth killed them before they woke up. After laying the bodies in a neat row on a rock shelf, she went down to the ice with her tools. At the shore, she carefully removed several shallow circular segments of ice, which she carried back to the fire. She wrapped her shawl around her ears in case anything loud and sudden came out of the ice. In the event, all she could hear were a few faint mutterings, which might simply have been the hissing of defrosting hela. Her fingers shaking in excitement, she adjusted her tripod so as not to burn the hela and then steeled herself to return to the tent. A part of her was afraid that Ays would have died in her absence, and she hesitated before dodging beneath the leather flaps. She knelt down beside him, and uncovered his face. It was hardly more than a parchment-covered skull. Gently, she shook him.

'Ays, wake up.' At first, he didn't respond, but then his cracked lips dropped open and a whining sigh escaped them. 'Ays, I've found them.' Leeth's voice was no more than a whisper. He groaned and turned his head slowly from side to side. Then, he opened his eyes. 'I've found spores,' Leeth repeated.

Ays could not speak. His lips tried to move, to smile.

'Wait here,' said Leeth. 'Oh hold on, my love. Wait for me.'

When she returned to her fire, the spores were lying in a pool of water on the metal plate. They were a tangled, spongy mass, like chopped hair mixed with weeds. Leeth poked them with a stick. She needed Ays now, to tell her what to do with the spores. It seemed unlikely this putrid mass could somehow sprout into a living fungus. She removed a small amount of the spores and carried these back to the tent, keeping them warm in her clenched fist. She wasn't sure whether it would do any good, but opened Ays' lax jaws and placed the spores on his tongue. She hoped it would revive him enough to help her. Ays frowned and chewed weakly, making odd little grunts through his nose. Leeth sat down to wait beside him. After a few minutes, he opened his eyes and turned his head to look at her. He was breathing rapidly through his nose, although his mouth hung open.

'I need your help,' Leeth said. 'I've found the spores, but I don't know what to do with them.'

'Was that spores you just gave me?'

Leeth nodded.

'Help me up.' Ays struggled to rise and Leeth leaned over to assist him. 'The effect of the spores will be transient. I need young hela growth. We need to encourage germination on my clothes, somewhere they can incubate.'

Leeth nodded. 'I thought as much.' She opened the flap of the tent and pointed at the island. 'Can you make it to there?'

Ays was filled with new strength, either from the effect of the spores he'd chewed, or simply because an end to his torment was in sight. He leaned against Leeth; so little weight. 'I can make it.'

Leaving Ays to sow his spores, Leeth gutted and

prepared for cooking the amphibians she'd killed earlier. She built a larger fire on the floor of the cave, near the entrance, so that smoke could escape. Still, a woody fume blew back into the low cavern, which made her eyes sting. Ays seemed oblivious of such things.

'How long until the spores grow?' Leeth asked.

Ays looked up from his work with red-rimmed eyes. 'A day or two. We should harvest more than this. It's likely I'll kill the first crop, because I'll have to take fronds from it so quickly.'

'Well, there's plenty of spores around,' Leeth said. She felt subdued and depressed. Ays would soon be restored, but she resented the fact that hela would be responsible.

He reached out and feebly squeezed her arm. 'Thank you, Leeth. You've saved my life.'

She shrugged. 'Well, according to you, I've risked it often enough, so now there is no debt on either side.'

Ays withdrew, and she wished she hadn't sounded so sharp.

Ays' recovery was swift in one respect, but very slow in another. The spores gathered from the frozen sea were vigorous and fecund, and grew with almost indecent haste next to the feverish heat of his body. As he'd predicted, he ravaged the first, delicate growth by ripping it savagely from his coat and stuffing it into his mouth. Leeth looked on in distaste. Luckily, several new crops were already sprouting in different patches, and eventually Ays was able to control his personal farm, and thus maintain a balance between growth and need. He felt overwhelmingly grateful to Leeth, so much so that it occluded all his original despising of her. It surprised him that he did not feel resentful. She had exhibited patience and endurance to supply his needs, ignoring her own, other than the need to love him. Neither could he feel guilty about that. He and Leeth had attained a level of understanding. He felt very close to her now. But it was a platonic closeness. For her part, she seemed content with that, or had at least resigned herself to enjoying what Ays was able to give her.

His clarity of mind returned rapidly, and a superficial, sizzling strength in his limbs, which unfortunately burned itself out quickly, and left him exhausted. He knew his body had suffered greatly from the ravages of withdrawal clutch, and even admitted to himself that he might never again enjoy the same good health he'd had before. His stomach had trouble coping with solid food, even though he clearly needed intensive nourishment. There was some food to be harvested on the island, but the tough roots and wild vegetables Leeth dug up did not agree with Ays' delicate digestion. He lived on thin soups, which tasted acrid and made his mouth dry.

As they melted the ice to release the spores, both Ays and Leeth listened for the soft, ghostly sounds that floated up on the steam. 'Are we imagining them?' Leeth wondered. 'If the nomads hadn't told me about them, I might not have noticed them.'

'I can hear them,' said Ays.

'It scares me,' Leeth admitted. They only melted ice during the day.

After five days on the island, Leeth and Ays had a discussion about what they should do next. It seemed obvious that they should walk towards the nearest shore and trust that they'd come across human habitation shortly. The supplies they could gather from the island were limited, and lack of fuel would soon be a problem. Leeth was concerned that Ays might deplete his fragile stamina, but agreed they had no choice but to keep moving.

It took much less time to reach the shore than it had to find the island. Leeth and Ays were almost in celebratory mood when their feet climbed the frosty dunes, and they surprised a fox, who had just made a kill. When the animal fled, the travellers appropriated its prey – a large hare – which they promptly cooked.

'This is a good omen,' said Ays, as he bit into the fragrant meat.

Leeth smiled at him. Was she imagining it, or had his face filled out a little?

They continued to travel towards the east, around the edge of the sea, in the direction of the mountains. There were no cities around, which indicated the terranauts had migrated them all to a less harsh climate. Neither Leeth nor Ays knew much about the weather conditions of the flat-lands.

'I thought my father had taken me to far spots,' said Leeth, 'but I realise now how limited my experience is.'

'The same goes for myself,' said Ays. They were approaching the summit of a dune. 'Look at us! Look at what we've been through! I could never have imagined such adventures back on Min.'

Leeth nodded. 'My world seemed so small before.' She frowned. 'In fact, I have difficulty remembering much of my life before I met you. Even my time on the *Rush* seems dim and vague.' They both stopped walking and stared at one another. A strange feeling shivered between them, as if a half-grasped truth had just revealed itself. Leeth held out a hand and Ays grabbed hold of it. Neither could speak, but their eyes were wide with unfathomable knowledge.

'Over the dune,' Leeth said breathlessly, at last.

Ays nodded.

Hand in hand, they walked towards the next story.

Moblinske was a foundered city. At some time, it had

faltered at the edge of the Brine and sunk to its knees, abandoned by terranauts and movement. Ays had come to believe that such events presaged the death of a city, or else the fragmentation Bockstave had told him about. Moblinske, however, was perhaps more tenacious than most cities. Its tiered platforms listed at an alarming incline, and all of its original buildings had collapsed. Now, new constructions reared up from the precipitous streets. From a distance, it was an astounding sight.

Leeth and Ays approached it in the afternoon, both overawed by what they saw. 'It is dead,' said Leeth. 'I have never seen anything like it before.' She shuddered. 'I have a feeling no one is supposed to see a thing like that either.'

Ays put an encouraging hand on her shoulder. 'It's not dead,' he said, pointing. 'Look. There are people there, and those buildings didn't just tilt themselves like that when the city keeled over. No, those are new buildings.'

'Surely, that's not possible,' Leeth said, frowning.

Ays laughed. 'We should realise by now that anything is possible in this world.'

Sweeping flights of steps had been constructed, which led up to the city streets. The original perambulatory mechanisms had mostly been removed, and what were left were covered in evergreen vines, with rusty metal revealed where growth was sparse. Ays and Leeth climbed the steps warily, for there were a lot of citizens about, but most people nodded cheerfully in greeting, and one woman, who was carrying a pannier of winter vegetables, stopped and spoke to them.

'Well, you're a sight coming in from the frozen places! We don't see many travellers at this time of year. My, you look as if you've suffered hardships!'

Ays nodded. 'That's true. When we left the last city

we visited on the Skine, we had no idea we'd have to travel so far before we found another. We have been virtually starved.'

The woman pulled a sympathetic face. 'You poor things! Listen, I am not a person to be close-pursed. Come back to my house with me, and I'll give you a hot meal. I am Furia Mendle, by the way.'

Ays and Leeth introduced themselves and in weary relief followed Madam Mendle back to her home.

The sight of a roaring stove, and the smell of cooking food was almost enough to make Ays keel over. Leeth helped him on to a sofa in Furia's living-room, which doubled as a kitchen. Most of the buildings in Moblinske were narrow, but tall, and all were constructed of wood rather than stone or brick. A typical dwelling comprised a single room per storey, with three or four storeys being the norm for domestic dwellings. Foundation platforms were built beneath the buildings, but the floors of Furia's house still sloped alarmingly. She busied herself with preparing a meal, and answered her guests' questions with frankness and pleasure.

'Moblinske has been here for nearly a hundred years,' she said. 'When the city foundered, history has it that a great many people panicked and fled. But some remained, and saw no reason why adjustments couldn't be made and the city still lived in. The farms and power systems continued to operate, after repairs. The people simply needed to accommodate themselves to a new way of life. As you can see, they were successful. We have extended the city to form a port out over the Brine, and now enjoy a rich relationship with the water nomads. The surrounding hills have been mined – an occupation that would have been impossible before the fall. Nobody would want to return to the old days. We have far more mobility now, because we can extend wherever we want to. Hills were off-limits in the days of Moblinske's slavery to the terranauts.'

'I must admit your society seems a lot more relaxed than those found on the moving cities,' Ays said. 'We've had some very peculiar experiences on them.'

'I've no doubt of that,' Furia replied. 'Inbred and isolated; that's what they are. Maziness breeds maziness. It takes the tranquillity of immobility to encourage real mental growth and profound philosophies.'

'I'm sure you're right,' said Ays. 'Although I've heard that cities are supposed to fragment when they founder, so that new cities can form.'

Furia frowned. 'Is that what you've heard?' She shrugged. 'Perhaps Moblinske was too lazy or too strong to have such a fate? Perhaps cities fragment only because their people run away from them in terror when the change occurs? And our ancestors strongly believed the ceasing of movement should be looked upon as a change, rather than an ending. I think we Mobles are more hardy than other city-dwellers, and certainly more sensible.'

'I'm inclined to agree with you,' Ays said.

'So, are you heading anywhere in particular?' Furia asked.

'Not really,' Leeth answered. She glanced at Ays. 'Perhaps we need to think more about settling somewhere?'

Ays frowned slightly, but made no comment. He was thinking about how he'd felt when he'd first come down from Min, his commitment then to his quest for answers. It all seemed so futile now. If he'd learned anything from his journey, it was that life was chaotic, and the reasons for existence were perhaps more subtle than could be appreciated by a human mind. Did he want to settle down somewhere with Leeth? The idea seemed preposterous, and yet he could see the sense of it. Leeth was young; she might get over her adoration of him. They could live as siblings. No. The notion did not feel right. There was something else waiting for him, something beyond Moblinske, and he was unconvinced that Leeth was a part of it.

After they had eaten, Furia offered them a bed for the night, and made many suggestions about how they could find work in the city, and accommodation of their own. Leeth was enthusiastic about the idea and, in the bedroom they were allocated on the second floor, spoke excitedly about the future. 'I like this place,' she said to Ays. 'I want to stay here.'

'Then you should,' he answered shortly, sitting down on the bed to remove his boots.

Leeth hesitated, her eyes suddenly becoming fearful. She went to sit beside him. 'Surely, you don't intend to continue travelling? Haven't you been through enough?'

Ays shook his head and looked away, throwing his boots into a corner. 'I'm not sure,' he said.

'If you leave, I'll have to come with you.' Leeth's voice was a sorrowful murmur. Her shoulders were hunched; she was gripping her hands with her thighs.

Ays sighed, and lay back to rest his head on the pillows. 'Leeth, I don't want you to think I don't care about you, or that I'm not grateful for what you've done, but the truth is, I still feel there is some purpose behind my travels, and I haven't faced it yet. I don't want to keep travelling simply to annoy you, or hurt you, or get rid of you. I need to keep going because I am driven to. I'm telling you the truth. Also, I really don't feel there's any future for you with me. If you like Moblinske, you should stay here. You'll make friends, find work, build a new life.'

'Ays, I love you,' Leeth said hoarsely, and desperately.

He blinked slowly. 'I know. I know. I can't help that. I'm fond of you too, but in a different way. You'll get over me. Remaining as my companion will do you no good, I'm sure.'

Leeth put her fingers against her eyes, and by the way her shoulders trembled, Ays deduced she was weeping silently. He sat up and hugged her, but her body remained stiff in his arms. 'Leeth, Leeth,' he crooned. 'It is for the best.'

She pulled away from him. 'I won't let you leave me! I can't!'

'Leeth, don't be stupid.'

She bunched her hands into fists. 'I'll follow wherever you want to go! You can't stop me.'

Ays regarded her dark, determined face. Sometimes she still resembled the crabbed girl he had first met. Relenting, and realising the futility of argument, he nodded. 'Very well. If that is your wish. But please remember you are free to go at any time.'

She wiped her eyes with the back of her hand. 'I know. Thank you.'

He rolled his eyes and made a languid gesture with one arm. 'You are an obsessed fool, my dear.'

Her voice was watery with tears and relief. She lay down beside him. 'I don't care.'

Later, Leeth would punish herself for allowing Ays to take such a large dose of hela that night. She sat and watched him as he broke off a copious hank of strands, and then ate them one by one. 'Isn't that rather a lot?' she'd ventured, nervous of invoking his anger, for she had learned he was very touchy about his hela habit.

'I need it,' he said. 'Leave me in peace and go down to talk with Furia. I need to relax and think.'

Reluctantly, Leeth got off the bed. 'Then think of giving up your insane desire to travel. Think about life here in Moblinske, summer walks among the hills, your own house.'

'All right.'

She'd left him then, and went downstairs, her breast filled with condensed anger and frustration. She was angry that Ays wanted to keep moving, and angry that she couldn't simply let him go. She knew he was right. She should stay here in Moblinske. The people were friendly, and Furia had made it plain she would be happy to help Leeth get set up. Her love for Ays was pointless, she knew that, but she couldn't bear the thought of a life where she'd be unable to see him every day. And he would be beautiful again soon, she was convinced of that. Would she grow old following him? She wanted him to touch her in love, and although that seemed unlikely at the moment, perhaps if she stayed with him for long enough, he'd eventually turn to her for affection? If she let him go on alone, that slim possibility would never happen.

Furia appeared pleased that Leeth wanted her company, and got out a bottle of wine for them to drink. Leeth muttered something about how Ays had gone to sleep. 'He's been very ill,' she said.

'I can see that,' Furia replied. 'He needs to rest. You should hobble his feet!'

Leeth grinned weakly.

Furia told Leeth she'd lived alone since her daughter had left home. There was no mention of a husband or lover. Leeth drank the wine and was aware that her jaw was clenched, almost as if she was cold. She couldn't dispel a feeling of dire foreboding. Perhaps her inner self was more upset about Ays' refusal to settle than her conscious mind had admitted?

Furia chatted on happily about her neighbours and friends, telling Leeth how she'd introduce her to everyone the next day. 'You'll love it here,' she said.

'Moblinske is a genial place.'

Leeth nodded, wondering how Furia could be so oblivious to her anxiety and uncertainty, which she felt shone from her eyes. In the early hours of the morning, Furia's conversation petered out and she began yawning. Leeth took the cue. 'I'll be off to bed now. Thanks for the company, and the wine.'

Furia stretched and yawned again. 'You're welcome. I'll let you lie in tomorrow. Get up when you feel like it.'

Leeth mounted the stairs to the second floor with a heavy heart. She didn't want to see Ays snoring and twitching in hela-rapture on the bed. She hoped the strike had subsided a little, and that his sleep would be normal. Moonlight fell into the room so brightly, there was no need to turn on a lamp. Leeth crept in and wondered whether she should undress. She'd slept in her clothes for too long, and cherished the thought of being able to press her skin against Ays' body. She noticed he was lying on top of the bed, fully clothed, his limbs spread out to claim all the available space. There were no snoring sounds. Bathed in the moonlight, Leeth slowly disrobed herself, making a ritual of it. She imagined Ays opening his eyes and seeing her, his expression changing to that of desire. She could see the dark hole of his mouth, which hung open, and the caverns of his eyes, which were closed. It would take something cataclysmic to wake him now, she thought bitterly.

It was only once she'd climbed into the bed that she realised something was wrong. Ays' body rolled in a disturbing way when she tried to push him over to the other side of the bed. Panicked, she leapt up and fled to the light switch. Yellow radiance flooded the room. Leeth's hands shot to her mouth. She wasn't sure whether she wanted to be sick or scream. Ays' eyes were not closed; they were open, but sunk so deep in their sockets, it had been impossible to see that with the light off. They had a glassy sheen, a dead sheen. His skin was grey, completely grey, and it looked as if his face had somehow collapsed inwards. He could have been dead for years.

Leeth ran naked from the room, down one flight of stairs to Furia's room, where she banged frantically on the door. Furia opened it, belting a dressing-gown around her.

'Grief, child, what is it?'

Leeth babbled hysterically, pointing to the room above. Frowning, Furia marched up the stairs with the command, 'Wait here!'

Leeth stood sobbing and shaking on the landing outside Furia's room while her hostess inspected the contents of her guest room. A few moments later she came back down the stairs, her face grim. 'In there!' she ordered, pointing to her room. Leeth obeyed.

'Is he . . . Is he . . .?' she stammered.

Furia draped another robe around Leeth's shoulders, and then took hold of her hands. Her voice was soft but adamant. 'Now listen to me.' She tugged on Leeth's hands for emphasis. 'You're going to have to be strong, my love. Your friend has gone.'

Leeth retched out an agonised wail and attempted to struggle from Furia's hold.

'Now calm down, calm down,' Furia said, pulling Leeth against her with strong arms. 'Weep all you want for a moment, but you have to remember there are things to be attended to.'

Moblinske was a happy, friendly city, but it was not totally devoid of strange customs and beliefs, such as those which permeated the societies of the moving cities. One of its traditions involved death, and the treatment of the dead and dying.

In the centre of the city was a pyramidal building which soared towards the sky. It was a charnel house, but they called it the Temple of Immortality. Whenever a resident of the city became fatally ill, they were conveyed to the pyramid and there incarcerated, amid mementoes of their lives, scarlet hangings and a wealth of silk poppies. The theory behind this was that because no one could ever really be sure whether the invalid had succumbed to their illness or not, they must neither be dead nor alive, but simply experiencing another aspect of existence. If this theory was incorrect, however, it would mean that whoever was incarcerated in the Temple would starve to death before whatever illness affected them took its toll. Everybody in the city believed in the theory of immortality, and as no one actually entered the Temple, it was never contested. Naturally, occasions of sudden death were tragic affairs, and bodies were carried to the Temple of Immortality in the hope that the benign spirits who protected the place would perform miracles to transform the corpse into a transcendent form. Had Ays been in the position to appreciate it, he would have noticed the parallels between Moblinske's customs and those of Min. Both involved a hastening of death, a refusal to let nature take its natural course.

In the early-morning, monks from the Temple arrived in response to Furia's urgent summons. They were silent, intense individuals, whose magnificent robes of voluminous scarlet voile, emblazoned with poppies of a darker crimson, seemed quite at odds with their lean, stern faces. Leeth disliked their swarthy skins, their narrow eyes and stubbly chins. She did not want them to touch Ays' body, and made a nuisance of herself at the door to the stairs. Furia took control of her in a competent manner, and kept her from leaving the room. 'There are some things a young woman should not dwell on,' she said, as the monks filed past her up the stairs. 'The appearance of the body of a loved one being the first of them. Remember him as he was, before he was ill.' She guided Leeth to the sofa, firmly pushed her down, and then went to fetch some articles from the kitchen; plain, homely things that were only sinister in the context of what had just happened: an old enamelled basin, torn rags, a jug of steaming water, sachets of herbs, a needle and thread. She followed the monks to the bedroom.

Leeth sat in numbed stupor in Furia's living-room, sipping the wine which her hostess had shrewdly left on a tray for her. She drank until intoxication blunted the sharpest blades of her grief. Occasionally, she wept, unable to comprehend that Ays had gone for ever. Surely, there was a mistake, and the monks would soon come down to tell her that Ays had revived, his terrible pallor merely the result of hela-strike.

Presently, Furia came back downstairs and summoned Leeth to her first-floor bedroom. 'Soon, we must accompany Ays on his last journey,' she said. 'Go and wash your face and hands in my bathroom, and then let me brush out your hair. Be strong, dear. You must look lovely for him.'

Leeth obeyed meekly. In the bathroom, her face appeared unrecognisable in the mirror, but there was a maturity to her expression, and also a bizarre serenity. She couldn't help feeling she looked beautiful. Was that a terrible thought?

Back in the bedroom, Furia dragged a brush through Leeth's hair, attacking tangles that had resisted all grooming attempts for years. At the end of it, Leeth's scalp was burning, and she was filled with a sense of having been cleansed. As she followed Furia back to the living-room, her hair seemed to float down the stairs behind her like steam.

Furia opened another bottle of wine. 'I'll need more from the back,' she muttered. 'Folk will flock after the walk.' She turned to Leeth. 'They'll all rally to you, my dear, all my friends. A sudden death is a terrible thing. We'll all walk with you.'

Leeth stared at her, blinking numbly. What was she talking about?

She and Furia sat together in silence, drinking the second bottle of wine. Presently, one of the monks came into the room, a signal which prompted Furia to stand, dragging Leeth up beside her by the elbow. The monk stood to the side of the door, and his colleagues came heavily down the stairs and into the room, carrying something long and bulky, which was wrapped in a red sheet bearing arcane symbols in black embroidery.

Leeth stared at the red-wrapped bundle in mute horror. She wondered what Ays' face looked like inside it. Had they closed his eyes? Furia came to hold Leeth's shoulders as the body was taken into the street. Friends and neighbours of Furia's had already gathered at the threshold, to provide a respectful entourage for Ays' journey to his last resting place.

Furia led Leeth outside, her arm protectively around the girl's shoulders. They led the way, walking just behind the monks. As the party passed houses along the way, people came outside and made sad, sympathetic gestures. Some picked tiny, red winter flowers from their window boxes – flowers that grew tightly, without foliage – and threw them on to the body. Leeth felt she must be dreaming. All of this had happened so quickly. Her life had changed irrevocably. She looked back over her shoulder and saw the expanding group of followers behind her. When they caught her eyes, they touched their brows and blinked faint smiles at her. I am one of them now, Leeth thought. One of them already. It is very strange.

Only immediate family were allowed into the Temple itself, but Furia was allowed to accompany Leeth, so that she did not have to be alone with the monks. Once they were inside, the great sloping doors swung back, and all were encased in a brownish gloom. There was a strong smell, but it was not of death. It reminded Leeth of something very old, something she should recognise, but the memory escaped her. Ays' body was placed upon a flat surface which could be slid through heavy, crimson curtains into an unknown space beyond. The leading monk took down a circlet of cloth poppies from a hook on the wall and placed it over where Ays' face would be. A coronation of the dead. He uttered a few words and then gestured for Leeth to come forward. Furia pushed her gently. 'Go to him,' she murmured. 'Say a few last words. Kiss the shroud.'

'I don't want to,' Leeth whispered fretfully.

'You must.'

Leeth reluctantly approached the corpse. She suddenly felt angry that strangers had taken control of her life like this. She wished Ays had died out on the ice, so that she could have performed her own private obsequies for him. Not this. Not this.

Her eyes glittering with an arcanum of unshed tears, Leeth let her hand hover over the shroud. 'Good bye,' she said hoarsely. 'I'll not forget . . . You will always be a friend to me.'

The curtains drew silently back and the table slid through them into darkness. One of the monks played a sad tune upon a small pipe. Another rang a tiny, tinkling bell; slowly.

Then it was over. The doors behind them creaked

open once more to let in a wan winter sunlight, and Leeth was led by the arm into a new life.

Casmeer

He could no longer write, for his hands hurt too much. Now, the stories were created and expanded within his own head, although he spoke them aloud to the plumosites when they came to visit him. I am ill, he thought. Am I dying?

Babooshpet seemed to appreciate his declining state. She brought him food now, fallen fruit from the city orchards. When she realised he had difficulty chewing it, she masticated it first in her own mouth and then regurgitated it into her hand. He could swallow the pulp more easily.

'I have to finish it,' Casmeer told Babooshpet. 'I mustn't die before the story's finished.'

She hooted softly and stroked his hair with her claws. The images were so real to him now, and entering into the world of his story was like waking up in the morning, refreshed. In contrast, Thermidore seemed like a grey hallucination around him. He could not see the corners of his room. All was dark and indistinct.

When he wept, Babooshpet extended her long, black birdlike tongue from her beak and gently licked up his tears. She obviously liked the taste of salt.

Chapter Eighteen
The Drowning

Sixty-eight days of Finnigin's reign as Tongue of Truth ticked by in the city of Phaxteriniad. Every morning, he awoke with a feeling of chilling presentiment in his chest; a feeling that became more intense with each day that passed. His mouthings to the Architrice and her cronies became more garbled, more furious. He asked them the same question again and again. 'What are you going to do to me?' They would not answer.

Luminar too proved reticent about providing information on the subject. Whenever Finnigin voiced fears about how he suspected the Architrice would sacrifice him at the end of his reign, Luminar would answer, 'But your friend Varian will come. Hasn't he always done so in the past?'

'Yes, I suppose so,' Finnigin would reply. It was his only hope, and because he had faith in it, he did not make any serious attempts to escape.

The long, white fingers of winter grazed the soaring crags of Scarzanera, and let its cruel softness fall down in flakes over the city. Phaxteriniad became a place of enchantment, its spires and domes and sloping roofs furred with snow and studded with the black commas of marching rooks.

Finnigin stood on his balcony and thought: Day sixty-nine. A rook called hoarsely and Finnigin saw a brindled cat run low across a roof below.

Frozen life. Who will rescue me?

He had not seen the Princess Alomeah again, but he had heard stories about her. A merchant had come from a far city named Pavarentier. He dealt only in poisons that twisted the human face into various grostesqueries. Gossip had come back to Finnigin via Luminar who often spoke of the Princess and her caprices. She had commanded the merchant to experiment with his merchandise upon a gaggle of ladies-in-waiting whom the Princess felt did not like her.

'The results were outrageous,' Luminar said.

'Did they die?' Finnigin asked listlessly.

Luminar laughed. 'No, but I'm sure they wish they had.'

An army came back from a battle with a gang of bandits in the mountains. They were starved, tired, and comprised mostly slaves and miscreants. Alomeah went to view the troops. She wore a fur coat, with nothing beneath, and walked barefoot through the snow before them. One of them she made lick a powder from her breast. He died ejaculating at her feet.

'She has an unusual wit,' said Finnigin, wearily.

'Indeed,' replied Luminar.

Day seventy dawned. A maid came into Finnigin's room as he was being dressed and announced that he had a visitor.

'Who?' Finnigin demanded.

'Sir Niles,' replied the maid.

Finnigin's heart fell.

Niles was standing beside the window in the main chamber, staring out over the city. Even faced with the man's back, which was covered with the serpentine coils of his long, oily hair, Finnigin felt young and awkward. Sir Niles had killed people. Sir Niles joined in with Alomeah's atrocities. He was a dangerous man.

'Yes?' Finnigin said, in a voice he hoped sounded arrogant and aloof.

Niles turned round and raked Finnigin with a withering inspection. 'There is a spectacle she wants you to witness,' he said in a monotone.

'The Princess Alomeah?'

Niles did not deign to answer, obviously considering it a waste of breath to do so.

'What spectacle?' Finnigin demanded.

'She thinks it will interest you.'

'Oh?' Finnigin advanced to the window. He could see little of the plaza below the terrace from here, but even so thought he detected an increased activity there.

Niles folded his arms, and spoke in a drawling voice. 'Incidentally, Her Highness has asked me to tell you that she has news concerning a certain Varian.'

A swift, brief flush of heat snaked up Finnigin's spine. 'She has found him?'

'She believes so.'

'Where is he?' Finnigin could not repress the soaring feeling that took flight within his breast. He could almost feel the flutter of wings against his ribs.

'In the city,' said Niles. 'A guest of my lady.'

'Is he someone she already knows? Where did she find him?'

Niles grinned sardonically. 'I suggest you put these questions to her yourself. She will be here shortly.'

'I cannot go to her spectacle,' Finnigin said. 'She knows I cannot leave the apartment – or is she prepared to flout the Temple law for me?'

'There is no need to flout any law,' Niles replied. 'The spectacle is being brought here to you.'

Alomeah, escorted by Marmion, arrived soon afterwards. Luminar was again conspicuous only by his absence. Finnigin wondered why he avoided the apartment when Alomeah came there, since he claimed to be an intimate of hers.

Alomeah was wearing an outdoor coat; a sumptuous garment made from the pelts of rare animals. She wore a necklace of ruby beads that looked like drops of frozen blood, almost uncanny in their perfection, lending a flush to the pale flesh of her throat. Her eyes were outlined heavily in black, and her blazing hair was confined at her neck with a black silk scarf. She looked splendid, oozing an air of seductive cruelty and deadly calm.

'Hello, Tongue of Truth,' she said, peeling off a pair of pale leather gloves and laying them on a table. Finnigin had heard about the gloves; they were reputedly made from the skin of a badly behaved servant boy. Alomeah was said to have consumed the rest of him at a banquet she had thrown for her closest friends, none of whom had suspected the origin of the contents of the casserole pot. Of course, it was possible these tales had been invented by Alomeah herself, although Finnigin felt it would be perilous to let himself think that. He also thought that it would be a frightening thing to be a person Alomeah considered a close friend.

He bowed respectfully. 'Your Highness.'

Alomeah strode past him to the windows and threw them wide, letting in a punching gust of freezing air. 'Ah!' she said, breathing deeply. 'Frost and blood: what a happy combination!' She walked out on to the terrace.

Niles gestured for Finnigin to follow her.

'I need a coat,' he said peevishly.

Niles frowned at one of the servants hovering by the door to the bedroom, who ducked back to fetch the required garment.

'Come here!' Alomeah commanded. 'Come here

quickly, Tongue of Truth. There is to be a thrilling exhibition!'

Finnigin pulled the collar of his coat – a fur of lesser quality – close around his neck and went out on to the terrace, realising too late that he was only wearing flimsy slippers on his feet. The snow had soaked their thin brocade within seconds. He joined Alomeah at the balustrade.

Below, the plaza was a muddle of trodden slush, but slaves were wheeling carts of new snow through the wall.

'At my signal, the snow shall be scattered,' said Alomeah grandly, extending stiffly fanned fingers towards the plaza. 'Then, we shall have a semblance of unviolated purity beneath us.' She laughed. 'But not yet. The preparations are not complete, the major players are yet offstage.'

Finnigin wondered what ghastly demonstration she was about to present. He could not stomach observing any sickening events, such as the ones Luminar had told him about. He wasn't squeamish, but neither was he barbaric.

'So what is your programme today, Your Highness?' he enquired.

Alomeah cast him a lascivious glance from beneath downcast lashes. 'My, you are impatient! I would like it to be a surprise.'

'Sir Niles told me you'd found Varian.'

Alomeah looked distinctly irritated. 'Don't spoil everything, Tongue. Be quiet and watch. We can talk later.'

Finnigin sighed and leaned on the balustrade. A frosted coating of snow crunched beneath his sleeves. Below, people were gathering around the edge of the plaza, apparently directed there by palace guards. They had a distinctly herded look to them. Like him, they were obviously present only at Alomeah's command. Their clothes suggested they were individuals highly placed in Phaxteriniad's society. Were they Alomeah's so-called close friends?

In the centre of the plaza, a tall cross of wood had been erected that suggested a crucifixion would be involved in Alomeah's entertainment. Before the cross, four short stakes had been stapled to the ground. Finnigin couldn't imagine what their function might be, and thought he'd rather not find out.

Varian, Finnigin called plaintively in his mind. Reveal yourself. Walk on to the terrace now. Stop this abomination, whatever it is.

He jumped as Alomeah suddenly emitted a hoarse and manly burst of laughter. She slammed her slim hands down upon the balustrade, dislodging a smoke of fine snow. 'Bring me wine. Bring me fine red wine!'

Marmion, who had been hanging back conferring in low tones with Niles, sauntered into the apartment without any show of urgency, presumably to gratify his mistress' request.

Alomeah made a gurgling sound in her throat, and wheeled around in a spume of fur to face Finnigin. 'Are you excited?' she asked. Her eyes were alight, her lips wet.

Finnigin was afraid of her. If he said the wrong thing, he imagined she'd order Niles to throw him into the plaza, or worse. 'Yes,' he said lamely. 'Yes!'

'Ah!' Alomeah threw up her arms and turned around to face the gathering crowd once more. 'My friends!' she yelled. 'My friends!'

Everyone in the plaza seemed turned to stone by her words. They looked hunched and miserable, their expressionless white faces turned towards the balustrade.

Someone should kill her, Finnigin thought. Why

hasn't someone killed her? Is her father so weak to let her act this way? Gorestel, he had realised, was hardly more than a name. If anyone wielded power in Phaxteriniad, it was Alomeah, and all the courtiers she had under her dominion. Luminar had intimated that her famous information network had guaranteed her considerable influence over the rich and prestigious. And who but Alomeah could perpetuate the ridiculous charade of the regular battles with neighbouring cities? She went to observe the slaughter with the same desire for entertainment as ordinary folk went to the theatre.

A tumbril was being driven haphazardly into the plaza, drawn incongruously by a team of enormous snow-white panthers. They were an unruly company, snarling hatefully at one another, lashing their tails, ignoring the driver's whip. The driver was a female dwarf, bedecked in festoons of coloured ribbons and wearing a high, complicated wig of coils and ringlets. The cart made little progress owing to the fact that no two panthers wanted to proceed in the same direction. The tumbril was covered by a cage of woven withies. Shadows moved half-seen behind the bars. Finnigin saw fingers gripping the withies. Victims. He felt his belly constrict.

Marmion returned with a tray of wine, and dispensed goblets among the company. Finnigin's fingers were shaking with cold and nervousness, and he had to hold his goblet in both hands. Staring down into the jewel-depths of the red liquor, he was sure it would taste like blood when it touched his tongue.

Alomeah, perhaps thinking the same, quaffed her goblet with gusto and then gestured imperiously at Marmion to refill it.

Beneath them, the rear gate of the tumbril was being lowered.

The prisoners were presently goaded out by guards

who stabbed through the withies with their pikes. The first to emerge, staggering and tattered, was a woman. She fell to her knees, her head lowered. When her companion – a man – stumbled down from the cart, it became clear that it must have been the woman's hands that had grasped the bars of the cage, because the other prisoner's arms were tied to a thick wooden bar which lay across his shoulders. His head too was bowed; long, filthy hair hung over his face. But despite the wretched condition of these people – innocent victims of Alomeah's greedy, heartless curiosity – their appearance still struck a chord of dreadful recognition in Finnigin's mind. He stared at them in confused misapprehension for a few moments. Then he said a single word in a voice bled of power or emotion: 'No.'

Alomeah giggled. 'Isn't this fun? Enjoy, my little Tongue! Enjoy! You may have a heart upon a plate if you wish.'

'It can't be,' said Finnigin quietly to himself. 'I don't believe it. It's a joke; can't happen.'

'I said I'd find your friend for you,' said Alomeah.

In the plaza, Varian, bound to a wooden bar, was goaded towards the cross by the guards. He slipped in the wet snow, staggered. But he obeyed them. He did not, or could not, fight them.

Finnigin tried to rationalise. That man looked like Varian, but it couldn't possibly be him. No. Varian was powerful, surely more powerful than the abominable Alomeah. He would never be subjugated by such a creature. And the woman down there. Could it really be Marvrani? She had a similar build, but it was hard to tell. Her hair hung in matted rags over her face.

Be sensible, Finnigin told himself firmly. Alomeah is tormenting you. She wants you to think she has Varian at her mercy, but it has to be someone else.

He managed to stretch his rigid lips into a smile and

slowly took a sip of wine. It ran like acid down his throat. 'Very amusing,' he said in a cold voice. 'You surpass yourself.'

Alomeah looked momentarily nonplussed. Had she expected Finnigin to throw himself at her feet and plead on the prisoners' behalf? Very likely. Well, he wouldn't play her game.

'The best is yet to come,' she said. 'Drink your wine, Tongue of Truth.' She turned back to face the plaza with a set expression on her face.

Finnigin felt he had scored a point. He downed the wine in several gulps and copied her arrogant gesture to exact a refill. Humming beneath his breath, Marmion insouciantly complied, although he allowed a splash of red to fall across Finnigin's hand. 'Oops, pardon me.'

Finnigin ignored him and pressed himself close to Alomeah's side. He wanted to make her feel uncomfortable.

In the plaza, the male prisoner had been released from the wooden bar. He stood drooping, witless from either exhaustion or pain, and made no attempt to resist as the guards stripped him naked before the crowd.

On the terrace, Finnigin called for another goblet of wine. His head had begun to feel blessedly numb.

The guards tied the prisoner to the cross. Finnigin had expected a nailing, blood, screams. He steeled himself, drank more wine.

The female prisoner, in the meantime, had also been unclothed in a rough and brutal manner, and was now being tied, supine, to the four stakes before the cross. Finnigin could see her struggling, and could hear that she was uttering enraged curses.

'Oh, look, the bitch has spirit,' said Alomeah. She unfastened her coat. Beneath it she wore a long red sheath-dress of supple silk.

Soldiers were unloading metal cauldrons from the tumbrel. Torment by fire? Finnigin wondered. Brandings? Burnings?

'Hurry up!' squeaked Alomeah, quivering with excitement. Finnigin moved away from her. Clearly, his close proximity did not upset her. She seemed unaware of it. 'Snow!' she cried. 'Fresh snow!' Slaves hurried forward at her command and began strewing the contents of the barrels around the cross. Their movements were erratic, their hands fumbled in their terror of the woman on the terrace. Desperate to obey her command, they threw the snow about haphazardly, so that even the female prisoner's body was covered with a fine coverlet of white.

She must be so cold, Finnigin thought, so cold. His lips felt numb.

Once the scenery had been completed, both slaves and soldiers moved back, and turned their faces expectantly towards the terrace; the slaves crouching, the soldiers erect and tense with the hunger for action. Alomeah put down her goblet, and gracefully raised her left arm. It hung poised in the air for a moment; a red streak against the grey-white sky. Then it fell in a blur of colour.

At her signal, one of the soldiers briskly stepped up to the cross and removed something from his belt. His body obscured whatever action he took from Finnigin's sight, but suddenly there was another arc of red streaking out into the white winter day.

Finnigin's stomach roiled. He fought nausea, averted his eyes. Beside him, Alomeah was wriggling and tittering in pleasure. 'Cut an artery!' she yelled. 'Make it spurt!'

Finnigin thought he would faint, and yet his eyes were drawn back irresistibly to the scene below. The male prisoner was being bled to death, his jetting ichor caught in the cauldrons held up by the soldiers in an attitude of grotesque solemnity. The soldiers crouched motionless, seemingly oblivious of the fact that they were being showered in blood. Around them, the newly-cast snow was splashed with patterns of red. Finnigin thought he could see it steaming. It was all too much.

The next moment, Finnigin found himself crouched behind the balustrade, his vision eclipsed by boiling motes of light. He could hear the laughter of Alomeah and her companions. Someone kicked him.

'Get up, Tongue of Truth! You grovelling coward!'

Blearily, Finnigin glanced through the squat columns of the balustrade. He felt numb, immune. He watched, but his mind had turned off; he was merely a machine of sight, without feeling, without judgement.

How long does it take someone to bleed to death in that way? Finnigin would later be unable to recall how long he crouched there, watching the prisoner die. Vomit pressed against his gullet, but his muscles had become nerveless. He could not expel it. He noticed movement in the crowd below; others had been affected by the proceedings. People knelt in the snow, friends leaning over them, arms offering comfort.

'Look at them,' Alomeah scoffed. 'Sheep, all of them. Only half alive.' She sighed. 'Well, it is all but over. Let us see the rest.' She made an abrupt gesture. 'This is the boring part, I feel.'

On the plaza, soldiers carried the slopping cauldrons over to the prone female. Finnigin heard her utter a thin scream; just a single cry. Thankfully, the soldiers' bodies hid most of what happened next, but Finnigin saw them tip the cauldrons, guessed what they did to her. When, after a few minutes, they stepped back, the woman's head was red, her hair a gory trail on the ground behind her. They had drowned her in blood.

The body of the man hung motionless on the cross. He did not look noble, or pitiable. He looked like a slaughtered animal.

Alomeah clapped politely, and presently the crowd below raggedly joined in with her. Niles and Marmion hauled Finnigin to his feet. He realised then how drunk he was, and was grateful for it. He would not look at the plaza again.

Alomeah made a rapid, waving gesture at someone on the plaza. Then she turned to Finnigin.

'Well, what did you think of that?' she asked brightly, and then pulled a rueful face. 'Oh, you didn't enjoy it.' She sighed. 'Still, it is an acquired taste, I suppose, and not for the faint-hearted.' She laughed and put her slim fingers against her mouth. 'Oh, but what a clever trick! In thirty days' time, my sweet boy, Brinorah will weight your feet with gold and have you cast into the bottomless pit at the centre of the city, in order to appease her petty gods! And guess what, there is no Varian any more to come and save you!' She threw back her head, and emitted another grotesquely masculine laugh.

The information she'd given him did not come as a surprise. Hadn't he always known, in his heart, that the end of his reign spelled death for him? The prospect of his own death did not alarm him any more. The possibility that Varian was dead was far more terrible. He had to make her tell him she had tricked him. Had to. 'That was not Varian,' he gasped. 'You cannot fool me.'

Alomeah frowned. 'I'm afraid it was, Tongue. It was quite remarkable how I found him. He actually came to my father's palace, two days ago. Strangely enough, I had never met him before. I suppose he must have come to secure your release.' She smiled in rapture at her own thoughts, and gazed up at the sky. 'My beloved father – he never denies me anything. I asked for Varian and his whore to be incarcerated, and of course he was happy to oblige. He was a beautiful man, your friend. I am quite overcome at the spectacle of his gorgeous death. Such beauty, such glorious red, such a body. I reserve such fates for only the most handsome creatures.' She glanced at the apartment windows. 'Ah, good, our refreshment has arrived.'

One of the soldiers, fresh from the plaza below, walked towards them across the terrace. He was bareheaded, and his long, silky blond hair was splattered with blood, as were his chest and face. He smiled steadily; a creature of considerable beauty himself.

'My favourite,' purred Alomeah, and held out her arms.

Into her waiting hands, the soldier placed a large, golden goblet. He bowed. 'For you, Your Highness.'

Alomeah raised the goblet to her nose, and sniffed the contents deeply. She gasped and threw back her head, her eyelids fluttering. 'Such a vintage!' She turned to Finnigin. 'Tongue, you shall have the first taste.'

Drunk as he was, Finnigin yearned for more alcohol to obliterate the last trace of reason in his mind. He reached eagerly for the goblet, but the soldier would not let him hold it. He simply held the cup up to Finnigin's mouth. A sacred wine.

When the first mouthful hit the back of Finnigin's throat, his body finally found the strength to retch. Bright red vomit splashed onto the terrace tiles. He heard a strange high noise, like a pig being slaughtered, or a child in terrible fear. He knew it was coming from deep within his chest, although his body could not feel the physical sensation of screaming. He fell to his knees.

The mad woman stood over him, laughing in delight. 'What other ichors of Varian's did you taste, I wonder? Does it choke you, his blood?' She turned away. 'Give me the cup! Let me drain it.' There was a moment's silence as she emptied the goblet. Then she sighed. 'Take the Tongue inside. He is quite worn out.'

Marmion and Niles once again lifted Finnigin between them, and dragged him back into the apartment. For the first time there were no scribes in the room, no priests. Niles and Marmion dropped Finnigin on to the carpet, and left him lying there. He did not notice them leave.

Finnigin lay alone in silence. He did not move very much for several hours; his mind was empty. Sometimes, he hummed tunelessly, and traced patterns in the carpet. He hiccuped, tasted blood. A rusty crust dried around his lips.

Darkness fell, and in the moonlight, with the cold coming in great draughts from the open windows, Finnigin sat up on the floor. He felt very cold and stiff, but his mind had become astonishingly clear. In some ways, he felt he had experienced a release. If Varian really was dead, then his life was his own again. And he must save it for himself. He realised he felt very similar to how he'd felt on the morning when Oubrahani's army had attacked Rodarigo's enclave; calm, detached, and somehow protected. He stood up, and went through the darkened bedroom into the bathroom. Here, he washed his face and drank as much water as he could. Then, he returned to the bedroom.

Something dark lay on the bed. No doubt that was Luminar. Finnigin despised the mantologist now. No intelligent person could put up with Alomeah's manias. No sane person. His friendship with Finnigin had been a game, nothing more. He suspected Alomeah had designed the moves too. Luminar had probably reported back to her in minute detail. Finnigin made a growling sound and turned up the lamps. He intended to tell Luminar what he thought of him, order the mantologist out.

The aura of protection condensed around him, holding him tight. What he saw could not affect him. Not any more.

Luminar did indeed lie upon the bed. As a mark of respect for his craft and past service, perhaps, Alomeah had not killed him in a messy fashion. Strangling, maybe, or suffocation. He lay entwined in the arms of another man, another dead man, whose body was cut and covered with blood.

Utterly detached, Finnigin walked over to the bed. He knew he had to be sure.

The face was Varian's; there was no doubt. All of his fingers had been hacked off; the wonderful jewelled rings were gone.

Nervelessly, Finnigin pulled the sheets from beneath the bodies. He found a knife lying in a bowl of rotting fruit. He began to rip and tear. Then he began to knot.

He was halfway across the plaza before they caught him. He fought valiantly, possessed by a lunatic strength, but there were too many of them. It seemed they had been waiting, watching. Alomeah was not there.

Brinorah walked across the plaza, muffled in a thick cloak. 'It is too dangerous for you up there,' she said. 'We are taking you somewhere else.'

They let him drink as much as he liked in the bare cloister that was his prison cell. He drank and did not count the days. The scribes were there. They wrote everything down, everything that he said. And Finnigin had much to say during those final days. He felt he had somehow become prophetic. He cursed Alomeah, and hoped the curse would hold. Brinorah visited him regularly as before, listened to his rantings, and seemed, in her silence, to approve.

A beautiful young servant girl brought him his meals. He slept with her because he felt he should. She desired him; he accommodated her. Soon, he would die.

Spring had not yet arrived when the priests and priestesses came in a great twittering crowd to escort him on his last journey. Finnigin had lost count of the days, but could feel no surprise, nor even any fear. He let them bathe him, dress him in robes of darkest indigo, crown his head with twisted evergreens.

Brinorah came through the crowd that had cramned into the cell. They parted for her reluctantly.

'Do not let my death be for nothing,' Finnigin said. His voice was low and serene. 'Let it be the catalyst for the fall of the insane monster who holds this city in thrall. Something . . . something must happen.'

Brinorah eyed him placidly. 'You have a last request? We shall grant you that.'

Finnigin held her glance. He nodded. 'I want her there. Make her tie the weights to my body.'

'I am sure she will be more than happy to comply,' said Brinorah with the faintest hint of a smile.

They led him out into a day of pale sunlight and old snow. Crowds lined the streets, as when he'd entered the city, but this time they were silent, watching. He felt very powerful; death did not frighten him. They took him to the pit, a depthless pool of milky, green water, at the crater's heart. A terrace, approached by steps, jutted out over the water. The ice on its surface had been recently broken. Even the sad, emasculated King was there to watch the ceremony. The company of priests and priestesses mounted the final stairway, Finnigin in their midst.

Why don't I feel afraid? he wondered. Life seemed so precious once, but now . . .

Alomeah stood proud upon the terrace, her head held high. She wore a long coat of black fur, and her hair was loose around her like a veil.

'We meet again,' she said sweetly

Finnigin said nothing. He was aware of the sardonic smiles of Niles and Marmion who stood, as usual, behind the Princess.

Brinorah stepped to the brink of the ledge and threw up her arms to address the crowd gathered below around the edge of the pit. She uttered a long, formal speech, the words of which made no sense to Finnigin. It was unimportant to him. His mind focused only on what he hoped to achieve in the very near future.

Once the speech was concluded and ritual flowers and grains had been thrown down into the pit, Brinorah turned to face Finnigin.

'Can I push him in?' Alomeah asked the Architrice in a bright, resounding voice.

Brinorah winced only slightly. 'If you wish, Your Highness. But first he must be weighted with the gold.' She gestured towards the floor, where the priceless bricks were attached to ropes of silk.

Alomeah giggled in a girlish manner, and cracked her knuckles. 'I shall tie the knots with loving care.' She squatted down and picked up the first rope.

Finnigin let her do it, watched her tie the ropes of silk around his body. He did not move a muscle, aware of every fibre of his being, the importance of what he must do, the precise timing of it.

Once the weights were in place, Alomeah stood up, her perfect mouth stretched into a grin, her eyes alight once more with a killing lust. 'I regret I will not see your face as you die,' she said. 'Unfortunately, the gold will take you quite from our sight.' She reached to touch Finnigin's still, pale cheek. 'I will not forget you, Tongue. Ah, you would have made a good candidate for the bleeding. I would have . . .'

Her words were cut short. Finnigin grabbed her in a tight embrace. He kissed her savagely upon the lips, noted her expression of surprise and, yes, even now, delight. 'Together,' he said, and mirrored her insane smile. Then he threw himself over the edge of the terrace. Too late, priests rushed forward, but somehow they managed to obstruct the guards who'd been alerted from the moment Finnigin had grabbed the Princess.

Entwined together, the two bodies plummeted downwards, until the holy waters accepted them, as a sacrifice to surpass all others.

Casmeer

When evening came, Casmeer tried to rise, because he wanted to be near his books; he wanted to touch them. If death was waiting at his threshold, his body must be abandoned next to the things he loved.

Babooshpet made soft flutings of distress, and several of her attendant males came into the room. Together, the plumosites helped Casmeer from the bed, and half dragged, half carried him to his workroom. He did not have to speak now; they understood his thoughts.

Gently, they manoeuvred him into his seat, and arranged his stiffening limbs into a comfortable position. Babooshpet offered fruit pulp, but Casmeer closed his eyes and mouth to indicate he did not want food any more.

I shall wait, he thought. Here. I shall wait. Tears

escaped his heavy eyelids, slid down his face like molten glass.

The plumosites threw back their heads and began to keen. It was a mourning song.

Chapter Nineteen
Blind Orifice

In the land of the dead there were distant sounds: scurryings; faint, maddened laughter, quickly stemmed; a sad, soft moan.

In the land of the dead there were quaint perfumes; reeks, not of decay but of desiccation.

The light was brown – yet glowing – and seemed to be full of floating motes that hung like a veil before perception.

Ays became aware. He noticed the hollow echoes of the space around him, perceived its colour and texture. He heard a sound like water dripping, but dry as the imperceptible shiftings of attic dust. *Where?*

He tried to sit up, but something restrained him. Was he bound? Memories of how he had come to this place were vague; shimmering doubts at the fork of his perceptions. He seemed to recall a landscape of ice, a dark girl, like a crow, flapping over him with protective wings. Again, he tried to rise and noticed a tearing sensation; whatever held him was friable, could be breached. Two more attempts and he pulled free, with a stomach-churning wrench, a grip at the back of the throat, a sucking of eyeballs.

He was standing upright on the floor of a vast hall whose walls sloped inward to an invisible point, high above his head. The walls were terraced with a multitude of recesses, on each of which reposed indistinct shapes that did not move. Scores of mechanical limbs swarmed up and down the walls, like immense insects, inserting glowing optical fibres into the niches, and moving on. They were a dull flash of gunmetal in the autumn gloom of the hall.

A sound behind Ays incited him to turn, but as he did so, he was strangely unaware of movement. Nearby was a wide stone table, on which lay a long bundle wrapped in red cloth. Its shape, clearly revealed by the sheer, clinging fabric, was that of a gaunt, human frame. Its face was covered, but bore a circlet of gaudy imitation flowers. As Ays observed, jointed, mechanical limbs sinuously emerged from apertures in the walls and, with an air of stately disdain, began to inspect the wrapped corpse with shivering, fibrillated palps. *I must remember how I got here . . .*

Ays' instinct was to approach the corpse and reveal its face, feeling it must be pertinent to his situation. Perhaps, when he saw it, he would recall what had happened.

The mere act of thinking this caused an instantaneous proximity to the slab where the body lay. It was like being in hela-rapture, hallucinatory; this movement without effort.

The moment when he realised he was consciousness without form occurred when Ays tried to reach out towards the shrouded face. He had nothing to reach out with, other than a pure desire.

It was then he knew, without visible proof, that the body on the slab was his own. He was discarnate; a ganglion of impulses, memories, information.

A deluge of panic, without fibres or fluid to impede or contain it, swept through his awareness in a swiftly cresting wave, and departed as swiftly; a thought, an emotion, ebbing away to commingle with every other vagrant human feeling that saturated the air. With vacant tranquillity, he directed his observance to the space around him. It was empty of intelligence, but for the limited, insistent beat of the machines, servicing the nooks and crannies of the oppressive walls. The multitude of slowly shrivelling corpses that peopled the vault slid softly to powder in a soulless void. The sounds he had perceived were no more than rogue emotions and memories, echoing from wall to wall.

This was a station, a limbo; no storehouse, but a refuse heap.

Ays moved his consciousness towards the opposite wall, obeying an urge to depart, but unaware of how to find the exit. He passed several bodies that had fallen out of their niches on to the floor, their broken limbs positioned in attitudes of despair and terror, their crushed faces expressing the most appalling horror. These were the remains of those who had been incarcerated before death, who had been deposited in niches by the attentive machines, only to claw their way from their shrouds, struggle and plummet to extinction. The machines clearly were not designed to deal with that eventuality, and as the people who built them never entered the vault, no one ever discovered these accidents or was able to devise a method of preventing them.

The stone floor was littered with the dried petals of ancient flowers, scraps of withered cloth, fragments of bone. Ays' passage caused a spectral breeze that worried the carrion dust up from the smooth slabs in eddies and swirls.

In the centre of the floor, several stone slabs were missing, so that a gaping, dark hole was revealed. Ays intended to pause at its lip and extend his perceptions over the edge, but the pit was the spiritual drain of the place. He was drawn to it and sucked in, as water from an unplugged basin is dragged irresistibly down into the effluent pipe.

He experienced a feeling of descent, which became more rapid as time passed, but the fall might also have occurred for an eternity. Everything around him was completely black. Was this death, this unending plunge? Was there nothing more to it than this? Again, the transient tide of panic made its presence known and subsided. Passionless calm came once more to replace it.

Down. Down. Memories of Min sped by invisible. *What of my mother*? What . . . He could hear the fluting horn of the *Whiteknuckle Rush* and an unseen recollection of Leeth's face went by. Leeth! A tug.

In Moblinske, in Furia's house, Leeth experienced a fleeting shudder as Ays' spirit memory touched her heart. She wept anew for his passing. Ays felt this as if it was happening right next to him.

Down. Down. Cities sped past his awareness: great colossi, darting hamlets, foundering leviathans. He was conscious of spires, minarets, castles, palaces, bridges, nets, streets, trees, hanging gardens, temples, theatres, factories, statues, gargoyles, crematoriums. All this faded, as if a page of history had turned.

Down. Down. The face of the Blue Feather Man appeared, and this seemed to hang like a torch before him; as real and visible as if appraised by living eyes. Surely he was an angel of death who had recognised a feyness in Ays, and had followed him, biding his time until the final reckoning. But the face simply smiled in a faint, cynical fashion and slowly dimmed to blackness, absorbed by the hungry dark.

The impact of collision with an unexpected destination eclipsed all Ays' awareness. When it returned, he was in pain. He tried to extend his thoughts in the silky transition through space that had already become familiar, but his efforts were thwarted. He felt constrained, claustrophobic, heavy. He felt flesh.

He found he had eyes to open and opened them. All was dark. The only sound was his own panicked gasping, which echoed as if he was in a large enclosed space. Had all that happened been a hideous hallucination invoked by overindulgence in hela? Ays groaned and tried to move. Every fibre of his being ached; nerve-ends shrieked in displeasure. Hesitantly, he patted his body with palsied hands. His skin felt smooth, almost excoriated. A memory assaulted him; that of sickened flesh, falling hair, collapsing features. Oblivious of the pain, he sent his hands flying to his face and found it whole. He plunged his fingers into his hair, and it was thick and slippery against them. Healed or reborn?

Eventually, Ays managed to position himself on hands and knees. There was coarse rock beneath him, which was damp to the touch. He patted the ground before him, and slowly began to inch forward. *Am I alive?*

His knees and palms were rubbed raw by the rough stone, but he was afraid to keep still, afraid to rest. After what seemed an eternity of agonised crawling, he became aware of light. Its source was invisible, and although very dim, partially revealed his surroundings. He appeared to be in a vast cave which extended in all directions. Any walls were hidden in shadow. Reassured, Ays paused and sat down to rest his knees. The darkness was spooking him now; he suspected he was no longer alone, even though he could hear no tell-tale sounds that might suggest other creatures were nearby. The darkness was electric, almost vigilant.

He stood up and began to walk, quickening his pace as he went. It seemed he himself was the source of light, for it surrounded him, extending to a distance of several feet on all sides, providing just enough illumination for him to proceed. Presently, he saw a rock-face ahead, with a dark patch on it that indicated a tunnel mouth. The floor of the tunnel was smooth, as if carved. Ays walked along it quickly, the ceiling of it nearly touching his head. He came to a place where water dripped down the wall, leaving a trail of slimy lichen. The sight of it ignited a parched longing that was almost maddened. He put his face against it and licked and sucked until his arid mouth was full of liquid. It tasted bitter, but in his thirst he did not think about the possibility of poison. He swallowed, and moaned as the fluid forced his withered gullet apart. He wet his hands and wiped his face and neck, before taking several more mouthfuls. Already, he felt stronger, more alert. He remembered a room, high in a stranger's house, and the taste of hela on his tongue. It was then he realised the pull, the ache, the yearning for hela was no longer with him. He was neither aware of its presence, nor terrified of its demands. He stopped dead in his tracks. *What has happened to me?*

A great sense of freedom pealed through his mind like the victory of bells.

He laughed aloud – a nervous, cackling laugh – and the sound of it seemed to break through the surreality of his situation. He heard dripping water, and a distant, thundering clatter that suggested great rocks clashing together. There was a metallic screech, like an iron door being dragged across stone, and a patter of footsteps up ahead.

Ays walked towards the sounds. He felt wary, but not afraid. Surely, whatever lived in this place had preceded him from the hall of the dead. He was kindred to it. There was no need for fear.

The tunnel opened out into another cavern, and here

Ays paused to appraise the astounding sight before him. It looked as if, at some distant time, a city had crashed through the earth and fragmented. Now, in a chaos of tilting streets and buildings, it occupied this hidden realm. The cave was enormous, its rocks coterminous with the ruins of the city. The earth and the city had become one; a mutant creation. Ays saw figures moving on the hanging streets. He saw white faces at windows. Were these *his* people?

He approached the city, but as he moved forward, it seemed the inhabitants retreated, repelled as if by a magnetic force. He could not reach them. When he called out to attract their attention, his voice was blown back into his throat. Also, his feet could not find purchase on the leaning streets and he was continuously forced back to the cavern floor. Eventually, Ays abandoned any attempt to climb up, and instead skirted the islands of cityscape, finding a path between them that led across the cavern. When he turned round to look, he once again saw white faces peering in stillness from high, insanely angled windows, and diminutive bodies climbing up and down the almost vertical streets.

Not his people, then.

After what seemed to be several hours, he reached the farthest edge of the city and here found a fecund patch of mushrooms growing in sewage mulch on the cavern floor. For a moment, he hesitated in picking them, absurdly afraid they might be related to mara hela, but hunger overcame his objections and he greedily tore up handfuls of the fungus and stuffed it into his mouth. It tasted musty and dry, but at least stilled the demanding pangs of his belly. Soon afterwards, he heard the sound of crashing water and came to the bank of a wide, cataracting river of obsidian black water. Here, he knelt to drink, and as he leaned over the water, noticed something sparkling just beneath the bank. The water was shallow there, so he put in his hand and withdrew a large chunk of crystal. He held it up to examine it, and was surprised to see that it appeared to have been carved into the shape of a human heart. No detail had been spared: every vein, every contour, had been carefully reproduced. It was a beautiful thing of transparent rosy quartz and Ays wanted to keep it, but he reasoned with himself that as he had no clothes, he'd have to carry it in his hand. He needed no unnecessary burdens. Reluctantly, he raised his arm to throw the crystal out into the river, but it was as if someone was standing behind him and stayed his hand. He lowered his arm, flexed his fingers about the crystal, and began to follow the river upstream.

Ays came to a place where a great, arched viaduct crossed the river, and he could see, on the opposite bank, the vast and crumbling structure of an ancient Temple. Its stones, like the water, were utterly black. He mounted the worn black steps to the viaduct, where two statues of begging lions frowned down with wasted faces. High walls enclosed him, and the sound of rushing water was muted. As he stepped on to the ancient thoroughfare, Ays was sure there would be someone standing before him, someone to block his way. But there was only a feeling, and that was easily passed. He crossed the river.

The temple looked long abandoned, its columns crumbling, its roof half-fallen.

When Ays crossed the threshold, the vibration caused by his feet provoked another pillar to fall. He jumped back in alarm, wondering whether it would be too dangerous to continue exploring. And yet, he felt strongly that the Temple was a significant stage of his journey, and could not be passed unheeded.

Beyond an entrance hall filled with rubble, Ays followed a short passageway which led to a chamber that was mostly intact. Light was provided by baskets of burning bones. Skulls grinned from niches in the wall, presiding over offerings of braided, hairy plant-roots, which suggested the Temple was still in use, for all its appearance of neglect. On the far side of the chamber, bowls of lighted oil on the floor illumined a ragged curtain which was drawn across an alcove. Ays experienced a deep feeling of recognition. He knew that he was in the home of a god, and that he had been there before.

As he drew nearer to the curtain, he could see that it was comprised of layers of ripped black netting, into which had been woven the bodies and wings – separately – of large, glittering insects, which hung in the net like jewelled brooches. They were accompanied by tiny bones – perhaps of rodents – and twisted fragments of tree-root. Ays reached out and, with the hand that clutched the crystal heart, impulsively tore the curtain aside. Bones rattled and fell; fragments of sparkling insect husks flew up into the air.

He expected to see an ancient idol, shawled in dried blood or wreathed in human hair. He expected to witness the final shattering image of his journey. He thought he'd reached his destination.

In the alcove, upon a seat of crumbling marble, sat an aged woman. Her head was sunk upon her breast, as if in sleep, her hands laced loosely in her lap. She was naked, but veiled by a mat of tangled grey hair. Her face was like the pleating in an ancient tree, almost too wrinkled and gnarled for features to be recognised. She wore a necklace of iron, studded with crudely cut chunks of turquoise.

Ays gasped and stepped backwards, and his movement roused the crone. She lifted her head and opened her eyes. They were the eyes of a young girl; clear and sparkling, a vivid green. The sense of familiarity intensified. Ays dropped to his knees.

'Mother Darkness,' he murmured, lowering his eyes from the holy countenance.

The crone shifted upon the stone and champed her toothless gums together. Her voice, when she spoke, was the voice of a maiden; mellifluous, full of the sensual confidence of a woman who knows she is beautiful.

'A wayward son,' she murmured, in a musing voice. 'A visitor.'

Ays dared to look up at her. He saw cruelty in her face and a tenderness too great to be born. He saw the balance of life and death swinging within her expression; the fate of love upon her brow. 'Mother, am I dead?' he asked.

The crone smiled and slowly shook her head. 'Who am I to answer your question? I am not sure myself what comprises the states of life and death. And yet, this is indeed the Dominion of death in all his forms, in all her forms, for there are multiple types of death as there are of life.'

'What type of death have I?'

'That is for you to decide.'

'I am on a journey. The purpose of it was to discover my origins. Have I achieved that?' He looked around himself uncertainly.

'I am not the author of your life, so it is impossible for me to know the end of your story,' said the crone.

'Are you Mother Darkness?'

'I am known by many names, some of them quite forgotten now.'

Ays stood up. 'Where do I go next? How do I reach the surface?'

The crone frowned. 'Surface?' She laughed. 'Oh no,

you cannot go there. You can never go there. This is the underworld, and no one escapes it. Where you go from here is entirely your decision, but one thing I can tell you – the way marked "up" is forever barred to you.'

'I must go there,' said Ays. He sensed a barrier, but also that it could be surmounted.

The crone eyed him speculatively for a few moments. 'In my youth, there was a game I played with my sisters. It was called "Pass Me By".'

She paused, and Ays sensed he should not interrupt. He gripped the crystal heart tightly, felt its broken edges, the torn stone arteries and veins, bite into his palm.

The crone shifted upon her seat, and the movement caused a waft of stale meat to escape her body. It was mixed with the memory of incense. Ays did not flinch.

'In my youth,' said the crone, 'the floors of this temple were so highly polished you could see your face in them. Many white bodies came here, bewildered visitors drifting by . . .' She nodded in recollection. 'Yes, they always wanted to know the way; the way up, the way back. It is an addictive substance, life.' She sighed. 'Pass me by . . .' Shook her head. 'The essence of the game was this: whoever could answer a simple question in the correct manner would be given the secret, the knowledge of the way back.'

'I want to go there,' said Ays in a low voice. It was the persistent demand of a child who has not yet learned the cruel realities of life.

The crone smiled. 'Let me touch you.' She leaned forward and Ays went towards her, allowed her twigged hand to stroke his hair and face. 'You are a perfect creation, a template. I do not feel you are lost here . . .' She sat upright, her mouth moving rapidly in a chewing motion. 'Yes, I shall ask you a question.'

'I am ready,' said Ays.

'There is a solitary figure, sitting alone in a bleak and abandoned place, where the light is harsh. He is very lonely, and yearns for company. Beyond his harsh environment is a busy world teeming with people. All he has is a net of dreams and a bagful of memories, yet he does not move from his dreary locale. Why?'

Ays considered the crone's words. A riddle. Was the answer predetermined, or would inventiveness and imagination be taken into consideration? His mind felt very active, and the crone's words invoked a host of rapidly moving images in his head. His strongest thought, however, was of the solitary figure who had pursued him, or had appeared to: the Blue Feather Man. He attempted to discard this image in favour of something more pertinent, but was unable to do so. He opened his mouth, and words came out. 'The man uses his imagination to follow an object of fascination. He is tantalised by the chase, but also tantalises the prey. He does not want to move from his lonely home, because the reality of life might not match up to his imagination.' Inspiration came to him. 'Therefore, he does not move because he waits. He is waiting to be found!'

The crone nodded, smiling. 'Succinct and acceptable,' she said. 'Perhaps the riddle was too easy for so keen a mind as yours.'

'I am sure there could be many different answers to it,' Ays said.

'True, but I like yours because it is genuine.'

Ays frowned. 'Genuine? How? Is there really a lonely man sitting in a bleak place waiting to be found?' He thought of his mysterious pursuer. Could the bleak place be a symbol for the Blue Feather Man's own mind? Physically, he moved freely about the world. Unless the riddle had nothing to do with that. Still, the image had been strong.

The crone leaned back in her chair. 'So now you want the map of the territory.'

'I answered the question as you directed,' Ays said.

She nodded. 'Yes, you did. And I believe the answer you gave could not be delivered by a person whose life above is over. However, it has to be said that Death can be a cruel trickster, so it might well be your fate to die before your time.'

'You promised me the information!' Ays scrambled to his feet. 'I have to find out the truth about myself! I have come this far!' He could not believe that the lightless and empty reality of the underworld was to be his for eternity. He felt too vibrant, too immediate, for that. 'This is not my world! I know it isn't! I must leave!'

The crone listened to Ays' ardent outburst without interrupting. Then she nodded to herself. 'My dear boy, your search for your origins is pointless.' Her bright eyes flicked upwards. 'You live only in the imagination of the one who created you, and have no past other than that. Your life is a bright, fluttering dream, a butterfly against the sky, a spiralling petal falling down from a high branch, a falling snowflake approaching a hot coal. No more than this. You have never been truly alive.'

The crone's words hung on the air as if she'd scrawled them in light. Ays sat back on his heels. The information, surprisingly, did not sound shocking to him, and yet he believed her utterly. 'As a child, I simply woke up on Min one morning . . . manifested there . . . Is that what you're telling me? And the people of the temple, of Mother Darkness, found me there?'

The crone laughed softly. 'Perhaps, though I feel the fiction began much later than that. A fiction with memory.'

Ays regarded the crone with a clear gaze. 'But, if I have never truly lived, how can I die? Your words only reinforce my belief I do not belong here.'

The crone put her head on one side. 'Are you not distressed by what I have told you?'

Ays frowned, considering. In his heart, he could not believe the crone's information was anything other than metaphorical. 'Not yet. I have to go back . . .'

'You are a hungry soul.' She sighed. 'Still, if you find your creator, who knows, you could ask them to perfect the details of your untrue history. You could invent whatever you like and make it real . . . Give me your hands.'

Ays knelt down again and extended his arms, still gripping the crystal heart in his left hand. The crone took hold of his hands, apparently ignoring the fact that one fist was closed. 'If you can survive a journey to the surface, then I suppose you have rightly earned your passage back. Your trial will be by water.'

'I am ready.'

The crone released his hands. 'Go through that passage there on the left, between the fallen idols. You will come to a well that was once a sacred place. You must lower yourself down the well and swim along the passage you'll find there. If you come to any forks, always take the right turn. You must swim across the wide lakes. Often, there will be few opportunities for you to breathe air, so that you must regulate your breathing carefully and replenish your lungs wisely.' She reached behind her among a tangle of ancient netting and tattered cloth. 'I shall give you this.' Into Ays' open right hand, she placed a ceremonial knife.

'It is beautiful,' he said, holding it up to admire, 'but why shall I need this?'

'Why should you not?' replied the crone. 'Don't

question my generosity. Such gifts should be accepted without argument.'

Ays felt he should return the gesture. 'Can I give you this?' He held out the crystal heart.

The crone looked at it steadily for several long seconds, and then shook her head. 'No, thank you. It is not mine.'

'But I would like to give you something for your help.'

'I am beyond receiving gifts,' said the crone, 'but perhaps you could one day do something for me?'

'Anything.'

She nodded. 'When you find him, tell him the joke is over. He must release me.'

'When I find who?'

The crone leaned back. 'You will know. Just remember what I said to you.'

Ays got to his feet. 'Am I to go naked into the world?'

'At some time, everyone has to,' answered the crone.

'But it is wintertime, up there.'

'Are you sure of that?' The crone sighed. 'I have done my part. Be off with you. Practical problems are not within the scope of my interest.'

A ragged curtain suddenly tumbled down from overhead to obscure the crone from Ays' sight. He had a feeling she had scuttled away somewhere. With the knife in one hand, the crystal heart in the other, he left the chamber by the door she had indicated.

He found the well without delay. It was situated in the centre of a small chamber that was empty but for two skeletons that appeared once to have belonged to sentinels who'd guarded the door. Their armour of leather and metal scales was still mostly intact, and Ays appropriated a belt from one of them, ignoring what the crone had said about nakedness. The belt was hung with several leather purses that could be shut tightly with thongs. He put this about his hips and secreted the knife and crystal in the purses.

The well was a black tunnel, going downwards. Had the crone tricked him? What if this led only to another, deeper level of the lightless lands? Rusting metal rungs were set into the wall of the well, and faintly luminous fungus grew among the rough stones. Ays climbed over the lip, gripped by a brief, nauseous vertigo, and swung himself on to the rungs. He hung there for over a minute, his heart beating wildly. Coarse flakes of old decaying metal pressed painfully into his forearms, his chest, his belly, his thighs. Then, feeling tentatively with his feet for footholds, he began to descend.

There were no visions to experience during this descent, and soon he became tired. His arms ached from supporting his body, his thigh muscles contracted. Gobbets of light flashed before his eyes, but this was only a physical reaction to the complete darkness. Eventually, as he stopped to catch his breath, his right arm hooked through a rung, he thought he could hear the faint, distant sound of running water.

It came upon him without warning, an engulfing cold wave. Ays spluttered and floundered in the water, panicking. His hand groped for the last rung of the metal ladder; if he lost that, he would be unable to judge direction in such darkness. His hand found the wall, so that he was able to feel his way around it. He was afraid to let go of the rung, but if there was any exit, it was beyond his reach, hooked as he was to the wall. Summoning shreds of courage, he released his hold and the water took him instantly, before he could press himself against the wall. He flailed his arms in wild terror, kicked his legs, found no resistance. The water sucked him under and propelled him forward – to the right? He could not think of air, and yet the desire for it consumed him utterly. Just as he was about to give in to the demands of his lungs and helplessly drown himself, his head struck stone and he swallowed a great lungful of air. There was not much room above the water, maybe only six inches before the ceiling began. Encouraged, Ays began to swim, his movements aided by the river's flow. Presently, the underwater channel sank once more and there was no more air, but he kept on swimming, trusting there would be other places further on, where he could gasp a few breaths. He tried to relax and exert himself at the same time, maintaining contact with the channel's ceiling, alert for a drop in the water level.

It came sooner than he expected – perhaps only seconds after the first time. The river spilled out into a vast lake, with a sandy shore that was dotted with constructions that appeared to be small, hastily constructed shrines. Torches burned on the shore, but there were no people around. Ays swam towards land, and emerged to lie on his back on the damp sand to catch his breath. He was alert for sounds – though there were none – and the only smell was a fresh brininess, underlined by an earthy tang.

Just before he slid back into the water, he heard a far booming sound, far overhead. The towering rocks of the cavern wall seemed to shudder, and there was a sound of small stones falling. An echo of the boom came, and another. Then, silence. Ays held his breath, waiting for something else to happen. But, other than another brief fall of stones and gravel somewhere nearby, all was still. He wondered whether what he had heard indicated that a city was moving far above him on the surface, and whether the resounding thunder meant that it had foundered, or collided with another city. He felt that the sounds of life would not reach this far down, but the sounds of death would.

The water was not uncomfortably cold. Ays swam lazily, yet moved with speed. Slimy, undulating forms wove between his legs, caressed his flanks, but neither bit nor constricted his limbs. On the other side of the lake was a cave mouth, water lapping right into it. Before he entered its shadow, Ays glanced back at the cavern he was leaving. He mourned the loss of light, but braced himself for another more difficult stage of the journey. The ceiling sloped downwards gradually, as if teasing him. He kept taking long, measured lungsful of air, sure that every one would be his last, only to find there was time to take another. Then the stone kissed the water, and he had no choice but to descend, feeling blindly with his hands, kicking with his feet. The tunnel was wide and the water moved lazily. Occasionally, the ceiling rose upwards to provide niches into which a swimmer could ascend. Ays felt the smooth stone above his head with his fingers. It was seamed with thread-like crevices, through which he presumed breathable air must pass. It seemed likely that at one time, human hands must have carved the rock. But if that was the case, why hadn't they simply raised the entire roof? Perhaps it had religious significance, a relic of some long-dead rite of passage? He sucked air and descended, careless now, confident of another stopping place nearby. This time, it did not manifest.

At one point Ays was able to purse his lips and extend them beyond the water's surface, into the narrowest possible margin between water and stone, in order to sip a few precious breaths of air. It was stale, unfed by crevice or seam; there was little to be had. He plunged onwards, trying to calm himself with the remembrance of the crone's words. Use the breathing places wisely. Had he been too nonchalant? Had there been some precaution he'd overlooked? Then, the channel opened out abruptly, and there was no stone above his head.

Gratefully, Ays felt around himself for air, but found only water. He must rise then. He was able to see, which was certainly a good sign, but the water was murky, filled with debris, so his sight was limited. Ays expanded his mind with the single thought: Up. He relaxed, and felt his body ascend, as if drawn in by a rope from above. His vision became cloudy, sparkling. His lungs screamed for breath. His head was filled with a bloody beat. Soon. Soon. Do not give in, do not give up. He reached upwards with his hands, reaching for light, for air.

Just when it seemed he must break through the surface and avail himself of the welcome wine of air, something heavy and dark came plummeting through the water, and collided with him. Ays nearly sucked in water in shock. Whatever missile had hit him, now bore him downwards beneath its weight, back into the darkness, the airless murk. Ays struggled to free himself from beneath whatever obstructed him, and in the muddy dimness, he could make out that the heavy shape had a human face whose mouth was open, as if screaming, its eyes starting from its head. The body turned in the water, limbs bumping against Ays' body. He thought – surely this was impossible – that the creature possessed two heads. A mass of long hair streamed behind it. The eyes of the second head were closed, and a thin jet of bubbles poured from its mouth. Wet cloth entangled Ays' legs. He was being engulfed and pushed down by the two-headed beast. Instinctively, he reached for his knife, fumbled for fractions of a second with the thong of the purse, tore it loose. He stabbed frantically at the thing that surrounded him, tore the blade through cloth and hair and flesh. One part fell away, in a languid, dead flailing of limbs and hair. The other still gripped him, and even though he had stabbed a limb, would not release him.

Time stood still, ignored the event.

Even as his brain screamed for air, and his head felt it was about to explode, Ays was capable of realising that what he had thought to be a two-headed monster was actually two separate people, one of whom had now sunk to the bottom of the pit. The other was still dragging him downwards, hanging on to him in obdurate persistence. Ays saw a glint of gold. He saw ropes hanging from the legs of his assailant, attached to the gold. He did not think or reason, but merely, with detached calm, slashed at the ropes with his knife. Quickly, the gold fell away, and then, as if they were somehow suddenly made of a lighter substance, Ays and the other shot upwards. They ascended in a shroud of hair, in ribbons of blood, up through the milky water. And it was not so far.

When they hit the surface, Ays had to remind himself consciously to breathe. He opened his eyes and they became filled with light and colours. For a while, he was unable to recognise shapes within them.

All that he was sure of was that he had achieved his objective. He had life. He had gained the surface.

Chapter Twenty
Merging

It had never happened before. Never, in the history of Phaxteriniad, had an offering to the Goddess re-emerged from the sacrificial pool.

There had been mayhem on the platform after Finnigin had taken the Princess Alomeah in his arms and jumped into the water. The King had seemed to wake from an abiding lethargy. He had leapt to his feet from his cold ceremonial throne, and had pushed people aside as he ran to the edge of the platform. Brinorah, watching nearby with perhaps suspicious stillness, thought she had never seen him move with such animation since the Queen had died. Now, she thought, with a little weariness, it was over; all of it. Brinorah felt she could rub her hands together and a scale of evil would fall from her in flakes; a taint she had not accepted intentionally, but which she was aware had besmirched her as much as any other who had stood by and allowed Alomeah her bloody free rein. Gorestel, she knew, must have his own reasons for the apparent apathy concerning his daughter's behaviour. Once the commotion following Finnigin's unexpected manoeuvre had died down, Brinorah had little doubt that Gorestel would start talking of debilitating grief over his wife's death – or at least his aides would.

She glanced around her. Hysterical people bustled past, their faces displaying shock. Later, relief might replace those pained expressions. In the disorder, a couple of courtiers had actually fallen over the edge of the platform, and were now splashing about, yelling, in the water below. Mercifully, for dignity's sake, the King was not one of them. Brinorah saw him straighten up slowly from his contemplation of the pit's surface. He stood with his back to the Architrice for a few moments, but she was well aware that he sensed her presence, her eyes. Presently, he turned and looked at her. She admitted it took some effort to return the stare, but she felt that she had nothing to feel guilty about. Could he really be sorry?

Still staring at Brinorah, he gestured at the guards. 'Send divers!'

Brinorah spoke. 'I feel, Your Highness, it is too late for that!'

'We must try,' he said.

There was no desperation in his voice and, as yet, no grief, but Brinorah knew that would change. At the moment, he only looked as if a favourite brooch of his had fallen from his tunic into the water. And yet, his eyes were full of hate as he looked at the Architrice. A man of conflicting feelings, Brinorah felt.

'Of course you must try,' she said firmly, and then paused, wondering whether she dared to speak the words that came to her tongue. 'Everything happens for a reason, Your Highness. Our Lady Scarzanera would have it no other way.'

'I don't want to hear it,' snapped the King and strode off the platform, heading for the stairway. Behind him strolled his two other daughters, decked out in their ceremonial costumes, their veils prudently across their faces, although Brinorah could feel their euphoric smiles nevertheless. A blight had just been purged from their lives; a bitter torment expunged.

Beauty is a dangerous thing, thought Brinorah as she moved towards the steps, her priests falling into line behind her. It dazzles us. We tolerate so much more than is healthy from those who are beautiful. They are life's blessed, there is no doubt of that.

She noticed that Niles and Marmion, Alomeah's lackeys, were hurrying off in the direction of the stables. With smug satisfaction, she realised she was looking at them for the last time.

And then a roar came from the brink of the pit. Brinorah's heart seemed to turn to stone within her. A pain shot up her left side. Had the bitch surfaced? Oh, Goddess, no! It must not be so! The Architrice ran down the last few steps of the Sacrificial Way and, holding up her robes, hurried to the water's edge, pushing pressing bodies from her path. If Alomeah had reappeared, she would risk all and jump in and strangle the monster with her own hands! She would . . .

It had never happened before.

An angel of the Goddess had caught Finnigin in its arms as he descended. Clearly this was what had happened. The angel had cut the ropes and carried him to the surface. It bobbed there now, its hair a streamer of gold on the pea-green water, Finnigin in its arms. Why? The Goddess had rejected the Tongue of Truth, or spared him? Had Alomeah been accepted in his place?

Palace officials were busy giving orders, and guards were forcing the curious back, so that the King and his immediate court could approach. Brinorah took advantage of this to attach herself to the entourage. Naturally, no one questioned this, although her acolytes were prevented from accompanying her. She moved without obstruction to the King's side. He was conferring with his aides.

'Without doubt, a messenger of the Lady,' said Brinorah, to the King.

He turned and looked at her, scepticism uncontained. 'An accomplice,' he said, voice like rock.

Brinorah patiently shook her head. 'Impossible. There is no other way into the pool; none, that is, which a frail human body could negotiate. The lady has spared the Tongue of Truth. She has delivered him from the pit!'

The King bared his teeth. 'He murdered the Princess. That is treason. Now . . .'

The sentence was never spoken because Brinorah interrupted quickly. She knew that once the King had uttered such a decree, it would be virtually impossible to reverse. 'The water accepted our beloved Princess. Finnigin was weighted. Alomeah was not. I think the facts speak for themselves.'

The King held her eyes. She could see she had not swung his opinion, and realised impetuous action was necessary. Raising her arms high over her head, Brinorah cried out in a clear, ringing voice that echoed around the pit. 'All hail to the Tongue of Truth, the Deliverer! All Hail to the Great Goddess who in her wisdom has immortalised the offering! Let flowers be strewn! Let the bells be tolled! All hail!'

Around her, others took up the chant: 'All hail! Scarzanera! All hail!' The crowd, already excited by the sacrifice and subsequent events, were in a mood ripe for further hysteria. The excitement coursed like a hot wave around the pit, and the populace of Phaxteriniad all bellowed praises to Finnigin and the Lady's avatar, who was still bobbing in the water, as if unsure what to do, whether to emerge or not.

The King eyed Brinorah without warmth. 'You are a scheming bitch,' he said, in a low voice.

Brinorah did not react. 'What must be must be.'

The divers who had been ordered to search for Alomeah were now assisting the heavenly saviour of the Tongue of Truth towards the edge of the pit, still with Finnigin in his arms.

'They must be taken to the Temple immediately,' said Brinorah in a loud voice. She noticed several of the King's aides nodding in agreement, their faces set in earnest expressions. They were sheep, all of them. Perhaps Gorestel and herself alone were wolves, now that Alomeah was dead.

'He should die! Him and his demon!' muttered the King, for the ears of a select few.

'That is out of the question,' said Brinorah smoothly. 'Of course, I understand your distress, but this is a religious matter, and thus beyond the jurisdiction of the state. It might cause civil uproar, should any rash action be taken before the mantologists can examine the matter and divine its significance.' Without waiting for a response, Brinorah turned away and with great dignity, summoned her acolytes to precede her to the Temple palace. She felt the eyes of the King boring into her back, making the skin between her shoulder-blades prickle. Let him think what he liked. She knew she was right. Later, the mantologists might discern sacred meanings in the episode, but even if there were none, Finnigin had done the city a service. He had been given a second chance and deserved to live, in her opinion.

Chapter Twenty-One
The Alliance

'You could be twins,' said Brinorah. 'Are you?' The naked youth had been dried and clothed. Unlike Finnigin, who was still unconscious, he seemed none the worse for his experiences in the pit.

Ays shook his head. 'No. I've never met him before.'

He had laughed when the priests and priestesses, clustering round him with fluttering hands and twittering voices, had suggested he was a heavenly messenger. His laughter was the result of euphoria at finding himself alive and above ground. 'I am Ays,' he had told them. 'I was drowning.'

They had seemed oblivious to his explanations, and had insisted on showering all manner of pampering upon him which Ays had accepted, simply because it was easier to do so than resist. He had been installed in a room in the Architrice's palace, and now Brinorah had come to interview him. He realised at once she was no fool, and also that he must keep the bulk of his history secret. He told her he'd become lost in some caverns and had escaped only by swimming through underground channels.

'I had no idea where I'd emerge.'

'Where do you come from – Plurakelica?'

Ays shook his head. 'I am a traveller. I have no home city.'

Brinorah decided to play a card of high value, and test her luck. With careful words, she related all the events leading up to Finnigin's throwing himself into the pit. She wanted to observe Ays' reactions. 'I cannot help wondering how you managed to be in the water at exactly the same time,' she said. 'Seeing as no one has ever discovered an underwater entrance to the pit.'

'Coincidence,' he said.

'But why did you bring Finnigin to the surface with you? Surely, it would have been easier to ascend alone?'

Ays shrugged. 'I had no choice. Your holy man grabbed hold of me, perhaps because, in the confusion, he thought he was still holding on to the Princess. I stabbed him, in order to rid myself of him, but he still would not let go. Therefore, I could do nothing but cut the ropes of his weights. After all, I had no idea what was going on. I only wanted to get to the surface, and quickly.'

Brinorah nodded. 'Hmm. It would be best if you did not discuss this with anyone but myself,' she said. 'For Finnigin's safety, and perhaps your own, I feel everyone should carry on thinking some supernatural agency was at work.' She eyed Ays sharply. 'In spite of what you've told me, I'm still not convinced there wasn't.'

He ignored the last remark. 'Don't worry. I won't say a word to anyone. I'm just grateful to be alive.'

'It is indeed a miraculous coincidence,' said Brinorah. 'And whether you deliberately involved yourself or not, significant.'

Ays shrugged. He was confused about what had happened, and it was difficult to think straight, to plan.

'You saved Finnigin's life,' said the Architrice. She was surprised to discover how fond she'd become of the erstwhile Tongue of Truth: She had hardened her heart, because of the necessities of the ceremony of sacrifice, but she couldn't deny the exhilarating relief and joy she felt at his escape from death.

'How is he?' Ays asked, because out of politeness, he thought he should.

'He was nearly dead, but luckily our physicks have managed to revive him. However, he has yet to regain consciousness.'

'He was lucky,' Ays remarked. His voice sounded incongruously cold.

'Very.' Brinorah hesitated. 'I would like you to meet him when he comes round.'

'Whatever for?' Ays himself had no interest in meeting this person. The thought of it made him feel strangely unnerved and anxious.

'I would like to observe it,' Brinorah replied. 'I think it might help Finnigin if he met you. As our guest, it is the least you can do.'

Her tone was not lost on Ays. He inclined his head abruptly. 'As you wish.'

Ays felt he could do nothing but comply with the wishes of these people. He needed more information about where he was before he could make decisions about his future, and the hospitality of Phaxteriniad was most useful at present. He had survived the ordeal by water, but had no idea where he had emerged. Perhaps this was a different world entirely to the one he had inhabited before? Perhaps he had become mythical, and was therefore creating myths? As soon as such ideas came to his mind, he chastised himself severely. Fanciful thoughts should have remained in the underworld. He wanted only straight reality now. And yet, everything about his past life seemed so vague now; the flat-lands but a dream. He felt as if he'd been reborn mentally, but refused to entertain the thought that the body he'd inhabited in Moblinske was dead. No, hela had addled his brain back then. There had to be a rational explanation for what had happened.

When Finnigin awoke, it was as if the last thirty days of his imprisonment had not existed. He awoke raw with grief for a man he had barely known. He awoke weeping and raving, Varian's name on his lips.

They fed him sedative potions, and rubbed his body with healing oils. They stitched the wounds in his arm, inflicted by Ays' knife. His body felt stretched, used up. Breathing was painful. A young woman who wore a royal diadem leaned over his bed and whispered in his ear: 'She's dead.' He felt her lips against his brow before she withdrew, leaving only a faint sandalwood scent behind. Nothing could relieve his grief. When Brinorah appeared at his bedside, it almost drove him mad. He could not bear the sight of her face, because he knew she had been aware of what Alomeah had planned, and had done nothing to stop it. No one ever had, until him. And his actions had been taken too late to save Varian and Marvrani.

Brinorah seemed unaffected by his incoherent abuse. 'A higher dose,' she said gently, and inclined her head towards the glass tray where ranks of potions waited to be administered.

'Are you recording this, writing it all down?' Finnigin cried.

Brinorah sat on the edge of his bed. 'No. That is all over. I only want to see you well.'

'Before you only wanted me dead.'

She closed her eyes briefly, as if in pain, and shook her head. 'You must understand. You were part of something, and miraculously you survived that part. I respect that, we all do. You must not fear us now.'

'I wanted to die,' Finnigin said. 'Along with my reason for living.' The words sounded strange to him, but he felt they were true.

'You should not reject the gift of the Goddess,' said Brinorah gently. 'She has given you life, and no doubt for a reason.'

Finnigin blinked at the ceiling. 'I saw myself down there. Naked. Myself, but somehow lighter, more golden.'

Brinorah reached out and lightly patted his hand where it lay above the blankets. 'Not yourself,' she said, 'but a young man who inadvertently became entangled in your fate. You are right, though. He does look like you. It is uncanny.' She stood up. 'Now, you must rest, and later, I will bring this person to you. His name is Ays.'

'I don't want to see him,' said Finnigin, suddenly afraid. With acceptance of fear, he realised he must still want to live. A person yearning suicide is afraid of nothing, surely. And this incredible twin, rising up through the water wearing his own face, seemed a terrible thing. He was afraid of losing himself to the vision, the bright Finnigin that had risen to rebirth.

'I am sure you will soon feel differently,' said Brinorah briskly. 'Now have something to eat, something light.'

'I don't want anything.' Finnigin turned his head on the pillow, a mulish child.

'Don't be silly,' said Brinorah in a harder voice. 'You have survived and that is that. Don't be a fool.'

Finnigin said nothing.

'I will come back later,' said Brinorah. She made to leave and then paused. 'Finnigin, you experienced some dreadful things in this city which were not meant to be. People became interested in you, who shouldn't have. I deplore the incident in the plaza which resulted in your friends' deaths and wish to assure you my hands were tied concerning it. I had no wish for your reign to be anything other than pleasant, as it is traditionally meant to be. The people of this city are grateful to you, and appreciate your sacrifice is perhaps greater than if you'd simply given your life. It is regrettable that innocents become embroiled in the great rituals, but the will of the gods transcends our petty lifetimes, our meaningless thoughts and desires. You have been touched by sacredness, and have passed through a holy sphere intact, and incarnate. Do not be bitter, but at rest. I do not ask you to be grateful, or even relieved, for I understand you had no wish to be part of our world. All I ask is that you live, and live fully . . .' She sighed. Words seemed inadequate. The exhausted young man on the bed had his eyes closed tight as if he could shut out the sound of her voice in that way. Perhaps the speech had not been for him, but for herself?

Ays was nervous of meeting Finnigin. At the time, he'd been too wrapped up in a panic of survival to notice, but Brinorah had told him how, when he'd emerged from the water, he seemed to be carrying a darker replica of himself in his arms.

'I do not remember his face,' said Ays.

'You will see,' said Brinorah.

Devoid of acolytes and attendants, she shepherded him along the lofty, interminable corridors of the palace. 'You have been part of something wondrous.'

'This is not my world,' said Ays.

Brinorah led him to a door where a guard stood on duty, looking bored. She stood to attention at Brinorah's approach, and opened the door with a measured bow. Brinorah nodded at the guard and swept into the room beyond, Ays following.

'I have never seen a place like this,' he said. 'It is magnificent.'

'It is very old,' Brinorah replied, 'and has been

embellished and expanded over the years.'

They had entered a comfortable sitting-room where a priest sat reading by the window. He stood up quickly when he saw the Architrice.

'How is he?' she asked.

The priest wiped his lips nervously before speaking. 'He will not eat or drink, but he has stopped raving.'

'That is good news. I bring a visitor.' Brinorah walked to a door, which stood ajar. 'Come along, Ays.'

He was still nervous of this meeting. He wasn't exactly sure why this should be, but wondered whether it was because he feared witnessing madness, a reminder of days gone by. He thought of a wasted face lying upon a pillow, hair coming off against the sheets. The image made him shudder.

'I can't see what this will achieve,' he said, but he approached the door. Brinorah stood aside to let him pass, and followed discreetly.

Finnigin was awake. He could not prevent his head from turning instinctively when he heard voices at the door, even though he had told himself he wouldn't look, wouldn't react. His first thought was: He looks nothing like me, but there was something about Ays that reminded him instantly, painfully of Varian. It was nothing to do with appearances.

Ays walked towards the bed, and stood over the person lying in it. He was relieved to see there were no marks of decay upon the youth, only seams of sadness in his face. 'It seems you owe me your life,' Ays said. 'But my act of deliverance was unintentional.'

'I will not thank you,' Finnigin replied, 'because I wanted to die anyway.'

That, Ays thought, was all that could be said. He made to turn away, when Finnigin said: 'Are you from the flat-lands?'

Ays turned back to him. 'Yes. Why?'

Finnigin stared at him. 'I don't know. I thought . . . We do look alike. I wondered whether you were a terranaut, like myself.'

'You are a terranaut?' Ays took a few steps back towards the bed. His old fascination with terranauts was rekindled instantly, and he wanted to examine this prone example more closely.

'Yes.' Finnigin attempted a weak smile. 'At least, I was. I'm not sure what I am now.'

'I am not a terranaut,' Ays told him. 'I am a traveller. I abandoned my city.'

'Which city?'

'Min.'

Finnigin shook his head slowly. 'I have not heard of it.'

'It is a flying city.'

Finnigin frowned. 'What are you doing here?'

Ays shrugged. 'I don't know. I am lost.'

'Do you intend to return to the flat-lands?'

Ays paused. 'I have no idea. I have no plans.'

As he heard these words, something became clear in Finnigin's head. He realised that he himself did have plans. He wanted to retrace his steps to Oubrahani, find the house that Varian owned there. The journey might simply be a pilgrimage to exorcise his grief, or he might learn something useful and significant. As to what he'd do after that, he was yet unsure. The idea of returning to the flat-lands in order to attach himself to a terranaut group and spend the rest of his life planting pilot-stones, seemed anticlimactic at best. He looked at the beautiful youth standing over him, and observed the ghost of himself in that face.

'We are so much alike,' he said, and then his eyes widened, seemed to clear as if a film had been blinked away. 'Come closer.'

Ays leaned over the bed, so that Finnigin could

whisper to him. 'Were you sent here for me?'

Ays glanced over his shoulder at Brinorah who was straining to listen although politely keeping her distance. 'I . . . don't think so,' he replied.

'Did Varian send you?'

'Who's Varian?'

'A man. A very powerful man. Ever since I began my journey from my people, he has followed me, observed me. He has helped me often.'

Ays experienced an intense shock which tingled through his body from head to foot. For a few brief moments, he remembered an image of a face hanging before him in utter darkness. 'That is something we share,' he murmured. 'I too felt I was being followed. I called him the Blue Feather Man, because of his hat.'

Finnigin's face had gone sallow. 'Varian,' he said in a soft murmur, to himself. 'What did he look like, this Blue Feather Man?'

Ays' face twitched. 'He was tall, dark-haired. More than that, I can't really say. I never saw him properly.'

'Where did you see him, and when? What happened?'

Ays found Finnigin's urgency a little distasteful. He drew back a step. 'It is a long story . . .'

'You must tell me.'

Ays frowned. 'I'm not sure whether I want to. I'm no longer sure what is real or illusory, and it seems unfair to delude you.'

'I won't be. Tell me your story.' Finnigin tried to struggle upright in the bed. Brinorah summoned the priest who hurried to help Finnigin sit up against the pillows.

'You must drink,' she said, and snapped at the priest, 'Bring warm milk!'

'The man who was following me,' Ays began, sitting down on the bed, 'I never learned his name.'

'And you are sure you can't remember any details of his appearance?'

Ays shrugged. 'He was generally cloaked, his face obscured by hood or hat. I think I only spoke to him once.' Suddenly, Ays sat upright, his eyes staring wildly. His hands were clenched against the bed-spread.

'What is it?' demanded Brinorah, and to the priest, 'Is he having a fit of some kind?'

Both hurried forward.

Ays felt as if the blood had dried up throughout his body. The shock of realisation was made worse because he had not thought of it before. He said in a vague voice, 'I think I saw the Blue Feather Man die once.'

'What?' Finnigin reached out and clutched Ays' hand in a painful grip. He was as stiff as granite.

'In Min,' Ays said, his throat convulsing. 'It was in Min!'

'Varian died about thirty days ago,' Finnigin said quickly.

Ays needed to stand, to move. He was thinking of the man who'd instigated his travels, his last client in Min. It seemed so obvious now. Why hadn't he realised that before? He shook his head fiercely. 'Thirty days ago? No, this was months ago, perhaps more than that.' He put the heels of his hands against his eyes, wresting himself from Finnigin's grasp. 'Oh Blessed Mother, something strange is happening,' he said raggedly. 'Why can't it be over?' The echo of his desperate cry hung in a breathless silence.

Ays suddenly leapt to his feet and walked to the window. Outside, lamps burned in the cold darkness. His whole body felt uncomfortable, almost as if it was dematerialising. He had to grip the window frame to keep a grip on reality. He put his forehead against the cool pane. He knew, without a shade of doubt, that the

Blue Feather Man and the person Finnigin called Varian were the same. The coincidences were staggering. Ays and Finnigin looked alike, they were both travellers, they had both been followed by a mysterious stranger. Their diverse paths had conjoined in the dark waters of Scarzanera's sacred pit; one plunging to death, another rising to rebirth. Ays felt sick.

'What is it?' Brinorah asked sharply. 'What's wrong?' Her voice seemed to come from very far away.

Finnigin's voice came anxiously from the bed. 'Ays, we have to talk. Ays, come back.'

'I can't!' He ground his forehead against the glass, but it did not break. Brinorah came up behind him and took hold of his shoulders, pulled him away from the window.

'Sit down,' she said, in an officious tone. 'Have a little wine.'

Ays sighed and relaxed, weakly allowing her to lead him back to the bed. He accepted the goblet which the priest put into his hands but he could not drink. It would be too sour. It would burn. Strong emotions pounded through his blood; he hated the sensation of that. He could not control it. Helplessly, he looked up at Brinorah, who stood over him frowning. He felt drawn to her femininity, as if seeking an echo of his goddess. It took him a while to expel the words, but when they came to their lips, his voice was steady. 'I was dead,' he said. 'I died.'

Brinorah took a single step backwards, her hand fluttering to her mouth. Then, she collected herself. 'No, no, you didn't die, Ays. You just thought you were drowning there in the water, that's all.'

He shook his head. 'No, you don't understand. I'm talking about something that happened before I went into the water.' He shook his head. 'No matter how strongly I try to deny it, to explain it, I feel I have to say the words. I died in a city called Moblinske – far away. My spirit went into the underworld, and there the Mother sent me into the water, so that I could be reborn in flesh.'

'The Mother?'

'The Goddess of the Underworld. She made me answer a riddle, concerning . . . I think it was concerning the Blue Feather Man. Afterwards, she let me go free, told me the way back to the surface.' He put his head in his hands. 'Oh, Goddess, let it be a dream, let it all be a dream. I don't want it to be real, because if it is, then it isn't over.' He sighed deeply and murmured, 'Oh Leeth, Leeth!' The memory of his lost friend rose up from his mind and encircled his heart. He yearned for her comfort. Why now did he have to appreciate what he'd had in her? She was grieving for him somewhere, he knew it. And he could not reach her.

Finnigin reached out hesitantly, and the tips of his fingers rested against Ays' arm. He did not speak.

Brinorah gazed down upon Ays in shock. The words he had spoken were outlandish, insane, yet in the tense atmosphere of the room, entirely believable. She wondered whether she should summon scribes to notate what had been said. Instead, she went to the connecting door and closed it.

Chapter Twenty-Two
Turning to Stone

Ays and Finnigin stood side by side against the balustrade of a terrace, which was almost identical to the one from which Finnigin had witnessed Varian's murder. It overlooked a pleasant walled garden where, from its atmosphere of tranquillity, it was obvious that no one had ever died in a horrible manner. Finnigin and Ays had spent the last few days in deep conversation. The stories had been told, compared, the similarities mulled over. Ays was very interested in the fact that Finnigin was a terranaut, and hoped that he could learn some of the terranauts' secrets. But Finnigin didn't seem to know any; neither was he interested in discussing the matter. His sole concern of the moment was Varian. 'If there are answers to the mysteries of the world,' he said, 'then Varian can give them to us.'

Us? thought Ays. He quickly realised that Finnigin believed them to be allies.

'Could we be brothers?' Finnigin wondered aloud.

'I suppose it's possible,' Ays replied grudgingly. He looked at the young man standing beside him. Physically, they were very alike, but for the colour of their hair and skin. Finnigin was much darker than Ays. What do people think when they look at me? he wondered. Do they feel as I do now? Half of him wanted to pull Finnigin close, absorb his flesh, because of their similarity. The other half of him was repulsed, unnerved. Finnigin's expressions, being more mobile than Ays', seemed a parody.

'In that case, could Varian be our father?' Finnigin murmured, his eyes burning.

Ays sighed. 'I was looking for a mother. It was her forgotten image that haunted me.'

Finnigin didn't appear to have heard the words. 'He isn't dead, Ays. I know it.'

Ays gave him a narrow glance, uncomfortable with the fanatical edge to Finnigin's voice. 'I understand why you want to think that, but you must face the reality that you did see him die with your own eyes.'

'So did you.'

Ays made an irritated gesture. 'I was overcome with emotion when I said that. It has to be very unlikely . . .'

Finnigin uttered an exasperated snort. 'How many times are you going to change your mind about what happened to you? One day you accept that something miraculous occurred, the next day you rant about hallucinations and delusions! Ays, wake up, it happened. We don't know how or why, but we must find out. Only Varian can tell us.'

'Dead Varian,' Ays said mulishly.

Finnigin rolled his eyes and shook his head. 'No! I know in my heart Varian is stronger than life or death.' He wrinkled his nose in vexation, struggling for words to frame concepts he barely grasped. 'He exists beyond both. I saw such strange things in his house . . .' His eyes widened. 'We must find him, Ays! We have to know the answers, and why he's been following us.'

'Finn,' Ays began, 'how could it have been the same man? We were at different ends of the flat-lands.'

Finnigin shook his head, his mouth drawn into a determined line. He hadn't told Ays or Brinorah about what had happened that night in Varian's house, so he realised his apparent obsession with Varian must appear deranged. He had never spoken of love. 'It was the same man. I know it was.'

Ays sighed heavily. 'I thought my search was over. I'm tired of travelling, of looking for invisible things.'

'But you haven't learned anything!' Finnigin said hotly. 'How can you believe it's all over? If anything, it's just beginning. For both of us.'

Ays visibly winced, and then looked up at the sky, as if searching for the shadow of Min. 'There is nowhere for me to go back to.' His voice was wistful. He stared at Finnigin intently. 'Perhaps I was wrong to seek a way out of the underworld?' He slammed his closed fists against the balustrade. 'If only I could have had oblivion. Nothingness! At this moment, it's hard to find a reason for carrying on.'

Finnigin looked aghast. 'You mustn't think like that!'

Ays laughed bitterly. 'It's how I feel. I feel tired.' Impulsively, he reached out and lightly touched Finnigin's arm. 'Don't look so afraid. Whatever my jaded heart feels, my instinctive desire to survive is much stronger.' He smiled, anxious to change the subject. 'Just think, Brinorah's people will write about us, make us into legends. How we rose from the bottomless pit.' He rested his chin in his hands, and stared out over the garden. 'Still, I can't help wishing that another Priest or Priestess of Hands had attended to the man whose words propelled me from Min. I was given a sign at the door to the hostel, but I ignored it.'

'I believe you couldn't have heeded it, even if you'd wanted to,' Finnigin said earnestly.

Ays glanced at him, almost embarrassed by Finnigin's fervour. 'I would like to be at home now, sitting with my friends . . . or making love. It is an eternity since I touched someone in that way.'

Finnigin turned away. 'I understand that, but I've learned that the meanderings of destiny are often inconvenient. I think certain truths in our lives yearn to be uncovered, regardless of circumstances.'

Ays made a scoffing sound. 'You are speaking, of course, of Varian. Again.'

'Together, we shall find him,' Finnigin said obstinately, as if he expected argument. 'I am quite sure of that. Why else would we have been thrust into one another's lives?'

'Coincidence,' Ays said bluntly. 'Anyway, how can we look for this person? We have no leads. Nowhere to look.' He laughed cruelly. 'Other than the prisoners' death pit here in Phaxteriniad!'

Finnigin flinched, briefly touched his mouth as if to repel nausea. 'You already know Brinorah thought of that . . .'

'And she found nothing,' Ays added. 'Very well, that might be seen as a clue, but Alomeah could have done anything with the bodies. Eaten them, even!'

Finnigin shook his head. 'You don't mean that. We do have a lead to go on: the house in Oubrahani. We must go there. It is not a moving city, so we will be able to find it fairly easily.'

Ays pulled a disagreeable face. 'Brinorah will not want us to leave.'

'I know. But she won't stop us either.' Finnigin offered Ays a look of naked appeal. 'Will you come with me? Please?'

'Why is my company so important to you?'

Finnigin looked away. 'Even if you don't have the slightest interest in finding out about Varian, which I think is unlikely, what else is there for you to do? Do you want to stay here in Phaxteriniad?'

Ays grimaced. 'Well, not really. But I could.'

'I don't believe you are a coward, so you might as

well travel with me to Oubrahani.'

Ays nodded thoughtfully, and then sighed deeply. 'I know Brinorah would expect me to go with you.' He smiled tightly. 'But of course, she'll make us promise to come back one day, to tell her what we discovered.'

Finnigin grinned, sensing submission on Ays' part. 'And we will promise to do so.'

Ays frowned. 'Do you think we'll keep that promise?'

'I think we might try.'

Ays sighed and threw up his arms. 'This is bizarre! All of it!'

Finnigin put his hand over Ays', said nothing for a while, and then: 'We have each other now. We have discovered each other.'

Ays withdrew his hand hastily. 'I'm not easy to travel with.' He paused, remembering Leeth. Of course, there was no hela problem now. Perhaps it would be easier this time? 'You will hate me by the time we reach Oubrahani.'

Finnigin made a firm decision. 'We shall leave here as soon as we can.'

As he did not have access to a Temple of Mother Darkness where answers, however oblique, could be sought, Ays opted for the next best thing, and requested an interview with Brinorah. She, after all, had heard the bulk of his history, and he knew she was fascinated by it. She received him in an informal parlour where dark red drapes were drawn against the evening.

'Finnigin wishes to leave within the next few days,' Ays said, as he sat down.

The Architrice nodded. 'Naturally. He is fired up with the belief that his beloved Varian may not be dead.'

Ays pulled a sour face. 'I can't help feeling it's nothing to do with me. I haven't the slightest desire to go hunting this Varian down.'

'You are afraid,' announced Brinorah.

Ays glanced up at her furtively. 'I admit to an element of fear, but that is not the whole story.' He shook his head. 'I have been forced into a kind of fraternal closeness with Finnigin, yet we are strangers. We look alike, true, but what else do we have in common beyond that?'

'A shared fate?' suggested Brinorah. 'Oh, come now, Ays. How can you ignore the way in which you and Finnigin have been thrown together? Nothing in common? Pah! It sounds to me as if you are simply making excuses.'

He shrugged. 'I don't know what to do. Even if this Varian character is still alive, we might not ever find him. There has certainly been a dramatic conclusion enacted here in Phaxteriniad. Perhaps he is bored of us now? I can't believe he'd ever explain everything to us if we found him. The mystery was part of the story . . .' He assumed a wistful expression. 'I have left people behind me. Perhaps I should return to them? There was a girl . . .' He paused and then shook his head. 'No, that wouldn't be appropriate. She's done with her mourning, no doubt. She will have another man by now. Besides . . .' he visibly stiffened 'I do not love her.'

Brinorah gave him a knowing glance, but he did not notice it. 'Are you asking *me* to decide your future for you?' She wondered whether she should talk to Ays about the problems he had with his emotions, but then igniting any suppressed feeling for this unknown girl might prove inconvenient to Finnigin's plans. She remained silent on the subject. 'I hardly know you, Ays. How can I presume to direct your destiny?'

'You directed Finnigin's well enough,' he remarked dryly.

Brinorah shrugged without awkwardness. 'That was different.'

Ays sighed. 'I want a normal life. I want to forget all this.'

'That's virtually impossible for you now!' Brinorah felt he was deceiving himself. Did he really need her to refute his words? She shook a finger at him. 'You have responsibilities, Ays; if not to Finnigin, who through your agency was snatched from death, then to yourself. From what the crone told you in the underworld, I must agree with Finn. If I were in your position, I'd want to find this Varian. It seems clear he has some peculiar influence on your life.'

'You believe that?' Ays slumped. 'I can't be sure. I never knew his name . . . the other one.'

'I doubt if there are two such men.' She leaned back in her seat, and gestured at the window. 'I saw them die, you know, Varian and his companion. A beautiful, proud man, and a striking, fierce woman. Such a waste. They seemed very human . . . and yet . . .' She shook her head. 'Who knows? A sacrifice rises from death in the arms of an angel. And an inspection of the corpse pits reveals no corpses.' She grinned. 'Ays, you will go with Finn, you know you will. You have not come here for my advice, but merely a sympathetic ear.'

Ays grimaced ruefully. 'I miss my goddess, and my friends.'

'If you truly believe in your goddess, then she is always with you,' Brinorah said gently. 'And you have new friends, Ays. Myself and Finn, at least.

'You do not know me,' he said abruptly.

Brinorah ignored this remark, and leaned forward to clasp his arm. 'Be kind to Finnigin,' she said.

Ays blinked at her. 'I'll try.'

* * *

Matanyan had been kept stabled in the royal livery, and had in fact been appropriated by the King's Chamberlain who was reluctant to give the animal up. Tersely worded orders from the Temple, however, brooked no argument.

Despite Matanyan's difficult temperament, Finnigin was determined to ride him out of Phaxteriniad, as he'd ridden him in. Ays was equipped with a palfrey, a gentle chestnut mare named Floriella who had once belonged to Alomeah. He was unsure whether this was a deliberate gesture, or simply convenient. He'd never ridden a horse before, but fortunately Floriella was compliant and predictable in temperament.

The Architrice convened a priestly parade to celebrate the departure of Finnigin. This was attended by Alomeah's sisters, who undoubtedly harboured a deep gratitude towards him. They stood upon a high balcony outside their royal apartments, muffled in furs, and waved scarves in a slow and wistful manner, their faces invisible behind concealing veils. The King made no appearance.

Two pack horses had been provided, laden with generous supplies, a capacious tent, fleece-lined sleeping bags and every conceivable garment they might require. Ays and Finnigin trotted their horses through the streets of Phaxteriniad, showered with benisons by the populace. Ays was silent, apprehensive, but Finnigin waved cheerfully at the crowd, and blew kisses to people who took his fancy.

We are so different, Ays thought, or are we?

They rode out through the main gates, where Finnigin increased their pace to a canter, up to the sheer walls of Scarzanera. Ays clung gallantly to Floriella's saddle, praying he would not fall off. Winter was losing its hold on the land, but very gradually. It would not be an easy journey.

'We should have waited until the spring,' he observed as they emerged from the volcano.

'Why?' Finnigin asked.

Ays did not bother to reply to that. 'How long will it take us to reach Oubrahani?'

'A few weeks.'

'Are you sure of the way?'

Finnigin reined Matanyan in to a trot, and the other horses automatically slowed down, without any commands from Ays who was supposedly controlling all three. Finnigin made a careless gesture. 'We shall find the right path. We have a map.'

'I have seen it,' Ays said caustically. 'It leaves much to the imagination.'

'I will recognise landmarks.' Finnigin leaned forward and patted Matanyan's thick neck. 'You'll know the way, won't you? You'll know the way home.' Matanyan flattened his ears and took two skipping steps sideways to signify his displeasure. Finnigin laughed aloud. 'This animal is a real character!'

The journey across the fertile lands was accomplished swiftly and without remarkable incidents, other than Ays realising he was irritated both by his companion and his companion's horse. He kept quiet about the soreness his new method of transport had inflicted on his body.

Finnigin, wholly recovered from his ordeal and vibrant with hope, wanted to talk the entire time. Ays, naturally reticent, hated the way Finnigin continually repeated himself. He ignored this at first, but eventually could not help himself saying things like, 'Yes, you've told me that. Yes, I know.' Finnigin seemed oblivious of Ays' exasperation. Matanyan, Ays thought, was an evil, cantankerous beast. Initially, he and Finnigin had agreed to take turns in caring for the animals each evening, but after repeated attacks from one end or the other of Matanyan, Ays refused to have anything to do with the animal.

'You don't know how to handle him,' Finnigin said primly.

'I don't dispute that.' Ays glanced pointedly at Finnigin's arm, where he knew a large bruise to be concealed, in the shape of Matanyan's teeth. Floriella had also suffered from Matanyan's brutality. She bore the marks of kicks and bites, and the sight of Matanyan meanly baring his teeth at her, while she shied away in miserable terror, made Ays go cold with rage.

'That beast should be hobbled well away from the rest,' he said, one evening. 'We should tie it up somewhere.'

'He likes company,' Finnigin said.

'Don't be absurd! It's an animal, not a child, and I deplore your habit of treating it as human. Besides, it upsets Floriella. She is a kind and willing creature, and I won't have her abused.'

Finnigin laughed. 'It is you who are absurd, my friend. Anyway, Floriella provokes him; she's a flirt. The other horses don't cause any trouble.'

Ays glowered in silence, infuriated further by the fact that Finnigin would not enlist in the spirit of argument. He continued to address Ays with a stream of inane remarks, apparently determined to ignore any atmosphere of ill humour.

In the mountains, Finnigin lost their way. He was blithe about this, and insisted on letting Matanyan have his head, convinced the horse would find his way back to Oubrahani. After a week of aimless wandering, during which Finnigin admitted the landscape was completely unknown to him, Ays remarked, 'It seems your noble beast is reluctant to go home.'

'He might be going a different way.'

Ays only growled in response.

The landscape became increasingly bleak. Sheer, jagged cliffs rose all around them, eclipsing the sky, muffling sound. Both Finnigin and Ays began to feel jumpy. The rocks were too vigilant, too silent. The horses shied continually at nothing, and even Matanyan became subdued and appeared grateful for Finnigin's proximity, pushing his heavy nose affectionately into Finnigin's body whenever he dismounted. Floriella trotted along nervously in a perpetual sweat, her ears flicking back and forth, while the pack animals pulled against their leading reins and bickered between themselves. Both Finnigin and Ays had to curb an urge to kick the animals into a mad gallop to escape the oppressive surroundings. They could not risk harming the horses, and the narrow path underfoot was treacherous with loose stones.

One morning, Ays awoke at dawn and crawled out of the tent without waking Finnigin, who was still snoring rapturously in a deep sleep. Ays stretched into the chill air and breathed deeply, savouring the solitude, the absence of dull chatter. They had camped on a rock ledge, the horses hobbled below on the path. In the night, one of the horses had managed to stretch up and dislodge some of their fodder from the ledge. Ays knew this had to be Matanyan – who was both the largest and the bravest – and grumbled in annoyance when he realised how much of the compressed hay had been gobbled up. If he and Finnigin didn't find a settlement soon, the horses would starve, never mind the fact their own supplies were also becoming perilously scant.

Ays cursed himself for having agreed to this insane

journey. Varian had become an obsession with Finnigin, his image expanded into some kind of demiurge. Ays could not share this conviction. Neither could he wholly agree that Varian and the man who'd haunted the flat-lands were one and the same. Ays knew from experience that many eccentric individuals lurked in the spaces between the cities. Anyway, if Varian had ever existed, he was certainly dead now. Hadn't Brinorah seen the murder with her own eyes? The best Finnigin could hope for was to ransack Varian's abandoned house in Oubrahani, but most likely it had already been appropriated by Oubrahan citizens, the spoils divided.

Ays went to pet Floriella, who whickered sweetly as he rubbed her ears. He hadn't the heart to take the remnants of hay away from her. She seemed, that morning, more at ease than since they'd left Phaxteriniad. He clucked soothing words at her, kissed her soft-maned brow. Matanyan eyed them coldly, chewing deliberately as if defying Ays to scold him.

Suddenly, Floriella tensed and her head went up, ears forward. She made a querying noise in her chest. 'What is it?' Ays asked. The other animals had also assumed postures of alertness. Then he heard it too: a scream, almost human, shattering the silence.

'What, in the name of the Mother, was that?' Ays murmured. Several answering cries came from the high rocks, and he saw a blur of swiftly moving shapes pass by against the sky. Predators? With reluctance, he went to wake Finnigin. The horses were all whinnying in consternation and pulling against their hobbles as he jumped back up to the ledge. The last thing he and Finnigin needed was for the animals to panic. He roughly shook Finnigin awake.

'There's something outside.'

Finnigin sat up, blinking. 'What?' he asked in a husky voice.

'I don't know. Animals. The horses are spooked.'

Finnigin crawled out of his sleeping bag and went outside barefoot. 'Where?'

Ays pointed vaguely. 'They were over there, screeching.'

Finnigin shaded his eyes. 'I can't see anything . . .' he dropped his arm and glanced at Ays '. . . or hear anything.'

Ays waved his arms emphatically. 'Look at the horses!'

Finnigin peered over the ledge. 'They are eating what appears to be the last of their fodder.'

Ays made an angry sound. 'I saw something!'

Finnigin went back into the tent. 'All right, all right. Let's make a move before breakfast. Perhaps there's a settlement, a city, nearby?'

The city, when they found it, appeared dead. Its walls had mostly crumbled away, and were almost covered by unruly groups of animals, which the travellers deduced must be the same species Ays had glimpsed earlier. They were bizarre creatures, at once birdlike and simian. When they caught sight of the small party of horses and riders, they jumped nimbly down from the ruins, bounced for a few steps, and then ran towards the horses, howling loudly. But when Ays and Finnigin shouted back and waved their arms about, the creatures raised their eyebrows in a comical fashion, and scurried off on feet and knuckles, flapping their leathery wings together over their shoulders, uttering panicked cries.

The city must once have been a splendid sight, and even now, in its decrepitude, inspired awe in the hearts of its discoverers. It was constructed on many levels, seemingly from the bedrock of the mountains themselves. The buildings, what remained of them, were graceful and symmetrical; the streets were wide and paved in marble.

'Oubrahani?' Ays enquired laconically.

Finnigin did not reply. 'Let's hope there's food inside. Perhaps a few people still live there.'

'Remember the rhukahas,' Ays said, glad to be able to use Finnigin's own experiences to chide him. 'We should be cautious.'

They rode up to a fallen gateway where monstrous stone beasts glowered at the ground from broken faces. A group of the bird-monkeys, impatiently and inexpertly dismantling what appeared to be a defence catapult on top of the walls, observed them curiously. A few of the smaller ones shook clawed fists at the travellers, whistling harshly through their beaks, but the horses did not seem overly concerned about them, so presumably they offered no real threat.

'I suggest we catch one of those scraggy beasts and eat it for breakfast,' Finnigin said.

'If you like.'

Ays stopped the pack horses and went to investigate the high domes of baggage. Weapons donated by Phaxteriniad included a crossbow. Neither Ays nor Finnigin had ever used such a contraption before, but with luck rather than judgement, they managed to fell one of the bird-monkeys which they dragged into a nearby building. While Finnigin set about skinning and gutting the beast, Ays explored their surroundings. He thought the building must once have had an official use, for its entrance hall was large and flanked by windowed booths whose glass was broken. The upper floors had fallen through, and now littered the lobby, along with fragments of what had once been furniture. The stairway, however, still swept up grandly from the ground floor. Ays mounted it, and stood at the top looking over the vertiginous drop. He wondered what would happen if he should take a step forward. Would he fall to his death, or find himself walking on air, crossing the ghost of a fallen chamber? Because the urge to do this became distressingly compelling, Ays turned away and ran back down the stairs. Finnigin looked up at him, crouched in bloody debris, his forearms red.

'This is a vile task,' he said.

Ays said nothing. He picked his way over the rubble, looking for items of interest, but found nothing.

The meat from the bird-monkey was tough and stringy, but tasted delicious. 'We cannot stay here for ever,' Ays said, licking his fingers.

Finnigin poked the remains of their fire, built from broken wood they had found among the debris. 'We need to get to Oubrahani,' he said. 'Perhaps we should look at the map?'

'Done it already,' Ays replied. 'This place is not marked. I don't know where we are.'

'Perhaps I should look.'

'Suit yourself.' Ays stood up. 'I'm going to take a look around.'

Finnigin frowned. 'Is that wise? I don't think we should split up. We still don't know if there's anyone else living here.'

'I feel it's all right,' Ays said tetchily. 'I want to . . . I want to be alone for a while.'

Finnigin shrugged. 'I fancy a look around myself.'

'Then we'll go separate ways.'

Ays derived a feeling of satisfaction from knowing he'd annoyed Finnigin. He wasn't sure himself why he got so irritated with people, but Leeth had had the same effect. He went out into the wide street thinking of her. Strange how he should remember her with wistful regard. At one time, he'd feared he'd never be rid of her. Now, he would almost welcome the sight of her thin, dark face. Ays was sure that, should Leeth be travelling with them now, she'd find Finnigin just as irritating as he did. He would have had someone to complain to.

He climbed a soaring flight of steps which led to a wide terrace, bordered by fallen columns. The view was stunning from there; a seemingly limitless vista of past wonders. Occasionally, one of the bird-monkeys would flap and scurry from cover, only to dive into the shadows soon afterwards. The animals called to one another continually.

Ays sat down on the edge of the terrace, with his legs dangling into space. It was time to think. Idly, he picked up a stone beside him, and was going to toss it down to the street far below when a glitter in its depths caught his eye. He examined the stone, and after a few moments rummaged in his jacket pocket for the crystal heart he'd found in the underworld and which he still carried with him. Comparing the two, he was sure they were of the same material. An unusual form of crystal, at once clear and opaque, with a suggestion of light moving electrically through its core. Ays put the second stone into his pocket along with the heart.

I need to decide upon a course for the future, he decided. No more of this aimless wandering about. The desire to seek his roots, discover the place or agent of his birth, seemed ludicrous now. The world was too large, and events within it were too random. It was likely the woman who'd mothered him had forgotten him now, or had died. Sitting there among the ruins, he became aware of his individuality, his oneness upon the face of the earth. Perhaps what he'd been seeking was simply his own self, and he'd been guilty of reading omens into events and places?

In Phaxteriniad, Finnigin's obsession had led Ays to believe that the last man he'd stroked to death in Min had been the person who'd appeared to follow him across the flat-lands, but that was impossible. Such mazy thoughts had obviously contributed to his feelings of being lost, but now he felt confident that he'd found himself. No more doubt. He would banish it. No more worrying that the unbelievable had happened. Whatever it was he'd experienced since Moblinske, he'd been given a second chance. There was no point in trying to analyse it. That would only rekindle anxiety. He could live his life in a straight line now, if he wanted to.

Finnigin was not assailed by such introspective thoughts. He rooted through the ruins, composing conversations in his head that he would have with Varian when the opportunity arose. And he was convinced it would. As he advanced further into the city, he made an astounding discovery which successfully expelled all thoughts of Varian from his mind for a while. The streets were littered with pilot-stones, some of them larger than he'd ever seen in his life. And these were stones vivid with the living fire which glowed so subtly and so faintly in the stones that drew the cities. His first instinct was to gather up as many as possible, but after his pockets became heavy, he realised it was a futile act. When, in the near future, would he be in a position to use them? Still, the urge to acquire the stones reminded him how strongly the compulsion to direct the movements of cities ran in his blood.

He came to a large house, set back from the road, that was mostly intact. Finnigin climbed in through a window which was slightly ajar and spent a few minutes gawping in wonder at what he saw within. The room was large and mantled with the dust of centuries, but the furniture was unbroken, and enormous tapestries still adorned the walls, their images hidden behind a shroud of dust. Finnigin began to tiptoe across the room. He saw a chair by an empty hearth, and his heart began to beat faster. Something was sitting in the chair; a dead thing, its features swathed in a caul of webs. An image of Varian's house in Oubrahani, the dreadful puppet-thing that had worn his face, flashed before his mind's eye. He was convinced the two events were related. He'd brush the dust from the face and see his own features – or Varian's.'

Expecting dead flesh, something like wood beneath his fingers. Finnigin jumped back in alarm when his hand touched the still form in the chair. It was harder than wood or mummified skin. Hurriedly, he wiped its head with his sleeve, and uttered a cry of shock when he realised what he was looking at. An enormous pilot-stone was sitting in the chair. No, not sitting, that was impossible. Someone had put it there. How strange. It was the size of a grown man, the most immense pilot-stone Finnigin could imagine. What was it doing here? Suddenly, the dusty shapes in the room assumed new significance. Finnigin ran about; wiping them clean. Several of them were stones; one by the window, another lying fallen by a doorway, two more upon a brocaded sofa. They were roughly humanoid in shape and held the vestiges of features upon their faces. Statues, he thought. Someone once carved them into statues. What sacrilege! He wondered why he should think that. The piloting of cities had barely entered his life; it had happened in the background, the province of adults. Among his own people, he'd had no reverence for the stones, and had hardly touched them. Now, he was aware of a distinct feeling of revulsion boiling within him. The sight of the stones did not feel right to him. For the first time since he'd left his people, he found himself wishing an elder of the troupe was with him. Someone should know about this.

He climbed out of the window again, and decided to go in search of Ays. He needed to talk about what he'd seen. Ays, he knew, would be indifferent, and yet who else was there to confide in? Once outside, his eyes were drawn continually to the gaunt, leaning shapes that dotted the landscape. So many stones. So many huge stones. Disquietingly human in shape, poised as if listening, as if waiting. Finnigin emptied his pockets of the stones he had gathered earlier, threw them away. Then he began to run, willing the rising tide of panic in his guts to abate. He must not lose control; it would be too terrible. His footsteps echoed through the streets. The flesh of his back prickled.

'Ays!' he called, desperately, uncaring of whether his cry roused someone, or something, else.

The single word rolled from wall to wall. Finnigin felt he should duck to avoid the impact as it was thrown back to him.

'Ays!'

A movement nearby sent him cowering into the shadows of a gaping doorway.

'What is it?'

Finnigin looked up. Ays was standing high above him, on the edge of a hanging terrace, his hands on his hips. Finnigin could not speak, but for the single word. 'Ays.'

Ays turned away and disappeared, presently to emerge from round a corner. 'Whatever's the matter? You look grey. What have you seen?' His voice seemed absurdly languid.

'This place . . .' Finnigin stammered. 'It's . . . it's full of pilot-stones. They're all around us!'

Ays frowned. 'So?' He put his hand in his pocket and offered his open palm to Finnigin. 'Are these what you mean?'

Finnigin flinched away. 'Get rid of them!' He could not bear to look at the coruscating crystals lying on Ays' hand.

Ays put the stones back in his pocket. 'I thought terranauts considered themselves the sole owners of the pilot-stones. What are you so scared of?'

Finnigin shook his head, rubbed his face. 'I don't know . . . It's just . . . not right. There's something not right here.'

'Let's go back to the horses.'

Finnigin looked around himself hurriedly. 'I don't want to stay here.' He looked at Ays in bewildered agony. 'Now I've stopped running, I don't think I can move.'

Ays sighed and rolled his eyes. 'Don't be stupid. Come on.' He grabbed hold of Finnigin's arm and began to drag him down the street, talking in a soothing monotone. 'There's nothing to be afraid of. I'm sure this place is empty. There's no one here. Only the bird-monkeys. It's empty, dead. There's no one here.'

The horses had found some herbs to munch, which were growing on the inner walls of the building where Ays and Finnigin had hobbled them. They seemed unperturbed by the atmosphere, which Ays had to admit reassured him a little. Finnigin's panic had touched him; it was contagious. He left Finnigin sitting against a wall with his head in his hands, and went to explore the adjacent rooms. In one of them, a window-door led out to an enclosed courtyard, with several doors leading off it. Ays went inside the rooms beyond, discovering that they had once been living quarters. One of them was full of store chests and cupboards that were mostly intact. He found heavy curtains of velvet, wrapped in coloured paper and strewn with aromatic herbs that still gave off a ghost of scent. In another room, presumably once a larder, were ancient bottles of something brownish in colour. Ays threw one on the floor. A disgusting stench assailed him. Mouldy pickles. Whatever else had been stored there had long rotted, but there was a shelf that held a filthy array of china goblets, exquisitely shaped, and stacks of old plates.

Down some steps that led to a basement, Ays found racks of bottles. One of them, he broke against the wall, and the heady perfume of good wine filled the room. This was more promising than the pickle store. He took two bottles from the rack, paused, then took two more. Retracing his steps, he appropriated two goblets and wrapped them up with the bottles in one of the curtains. Then he went back to Finnigin.

'Treasures, look,' he said, unrolling the curtain.

Finnigin raised his head and spoke grimly. 'A sight more welcome is difficult to imagine.'

Ays smiled. 'Well, we are in accord on that score.' He broke the top off one of the bottles and filled the goblets, which he'd previously dusted off with the edge of the curtain. He and Finnigin took the first sip simultaneously.

'Good,' said Finnigin.

'Mmm.' Ays sat back, supporting himself on his arms. 'Well, do you feel all right now?'

Finnigin nodded. 'Better. I felt as if a ghost was in my hair out there.'

'It's an eerie place,' Ays agreed.

Finnigin poured himself some more wine. 'Ays, I've been thinking.'

'Me too.'

'I've been thinking about Varian.'

Ays grimaced. 'Oh.'

'No, listen. It's about us too. I have a theory.'

'Tell me.' Ays felt that any uncomfortable revelations Finnigin might come out with would fail to touch his new resolve. He was capable of humouring his companion now.

Finnigin screwed up his face before speaking. 'It's this: we discussed the possibility we could be related. You began your journey because you wanted to find out who your mother was . . .'

'It was more involved than that,' Ays interrupted. 'But it's irrelevant now, anyway.'

'Just listen. We could have the same mother, or the same father.'

Ays' instinct was to silence Finnigin with a sharp remark. Then he remembered he could not be unnerved now. 'It seems too coincidental,' he said haughtily. Then he smiled. 'Mind you, the terranaut I met called Oon did say she thought I might have terranaut blood.'

'That's very possible. I don't know who my parents were either.'

Ays raised his eyebrows. 'Really? I thought you said your mother was a woman called Leeara.'

Finnigin shook his head. 'No. I said my carer was called Leeara. That's different. He brought me up. We don't stay with our parents after we're born. We live with carers.' He poured more wine into Ays' goblet. 'I've been trying to make sense of what has happened to us both. I know you don't agree with me, but I'm convinced that the traveller you did your . . . well, that priestly thing with in Min, was Varian. He influenced you, infected you with the desire to travel, seek your roots. With me, it was slightly different. I was driven to the mountains, lured there as if I was a city following a trail of stones. I feel we were not so much destined to meet as organised to meet.'

Ays took a long drink of wine, mustering patience and tolerance. 'In that case, Varian's directorial abilities include a precise ability to synchronise events.' He pulled a face of disbelief. 'I can't accept it, Finn. I really can't.'

'But there is a pattern. It's so simple if you stand back from it. I think the reason for our journeys, for our being drawn here, has something to do with the pilot-stones, and therefore with the cities of the flatlands themselves.'

'Aha!' Ays grinned. 'We are part of a great plan? I see!'

Finnigin frowned, as if suspicious Ays might be humouring him. 'I wish you wouldn't make fun of this. I'm serious. Why can't you accept that something magical has entered our lives?' He gestured emphatically. 'For you, more than me! Ays, you experienced death and rebirth! That is incredible, yet now you refuse to accept anything other than mundane explanations for what has happened.'

Ays sighed. 'Finn, I was an addict of mara hela. I'd been very ill, had almost died. I woke up in some kind of mausoleum, with my sense of reality in tatters, my mind in a knot of confused perceptions. I wasn't dead, but hallucinating wildly. It's obvious now. I didn't fall for as long as I thought, and no doubt knocked myself unconscious when I landed. When I woke up again, the effects of the hela had diminished . . . That's all there is to it.'

Finnigin shook his head. 'Stop deceiving yourself. As you said, you were an addict. How come your addiction just disappeared?'

Ays snorted impatiently. 'I've no idea. There could be a simple explanation. I'm not a physick.' He stood up and began to pace the floor, flinging out his arms as he spoke. 'Some subterranean society might have healed me while I was unconscious. I could have been out of my mind for months. How can I tell now what really happened? It's all too confusing.'

'What are you afraid of? Why can't you admit that . . .'

'Shut up!' Ays cried. 'Just shut up! I've had enough of this crack-brain talk!' He was furious that he had allowed Finnigin's mazy gibberish to get to him.

Finnigin's eyes widened, yet his face became still.

'I'm sorry.' Ays rubbed his face wearily and sat down again. 'Give me some more of that wine. Open another bottle.'

Finnigin began knocking the glass neck against the wall. 'Tonight, we get drunk,' he said, and then added warily, as if fearing a furious response, 'and tomorrow, we will explore the city. Properly. There are clues here for us, I know it.'

'It's your search, not mine,' Ays said, 'but I'll go with you if you want me to. From the state you were in today, I don't think you'd be capable of wandering around on your own.'

'Thanks for your concern!' Finnigin grinned.

Ays fought an irritable retort, and grinned back fiercely. 'You're welcome.'

The wine was potent, and after most of it had been consumed, Finnigin became maudlin.

'There is something I haven't told you,' he said. He was lolling against the wall, occasionally hiccuping.

Ays was lying on his back on the floor, a blanket over his body. 'What?' he asked in a sleepy voice. The tone of his voice held a warning, but Finnigin did not notice it.

'Varian and I . . . I slept with him once.'

'Oh, Goddess,' Ays sighed. 'The picture becomes more vivid now!'

Finnigin knew that if he should explain in detail what he thought had happened that night, Ays would be scornfully sceptical, and might even laugh. He resented

Ays' cynicism. 'You are a cold, broken stone,' he said at last.

'I know,' Ays replied. 'You are not the first to say it.'

Finnigin crawled over to sit beside him. 'Have you never been in love?'

Ays pulled the blanket over his face. 'I don't know. There are other things to life.'

'It seems a shame that such an attractive person as you should have a frozen heart.'

Ays laughed. 'Please don't. It really isn't worth it.'

Impulsively, Finnigin reached out and pulled back the blanket, touched Ays' face. He realised as soon as he'd done it that it had been a hopelessly stupid thing to do. Ays reared up and gripped Finnigin's hand in a painfully tight hold. 'Don't ever presume!' he said in a low voice. 'Don't ever!'

Finnigin pulled himself free and leapt to his feet, consumed by bitter embarrassment and self-recrimination. He ran towards the door, out into the cold night street. Behind him, he heard Ays call, 'Finn, come back! Don't be a clenchpoop!'

He ignored it and ran down the street, letting the long shadows of the ruins dapple his body. The moon was full, hanging heavy in a star-crusted sky of deepest black. Everything seemed stark. Moonlight glittered in the depths of the pilot-stones. They glowed like the eyes of beasts everywhere around him.

'Finn!'

He realised Ays was following him. What am I doing? he wondered as he ran. Do I want him to catch me? What then? What then?

He veered off up a narrow side-street, his feet slipping on the cobbles which were damp with dew. Crystalline gleams stared at him from empty windows. His breath sobbed in his chest. He knew he had drunk more than Ays. Ays was always cool, refined, whereas he himself was a hot, grubby maelstrom of unwise words and actions. He despised himself.

Ays, strong and sober, quickly caught up with Finnigin. He grabbed hold of his jacket and then pushed him against the wall of a house. 'What do you think you're doing? Have you gone really mazy, instead of only slightly mazy?'

Finnigin felt like weeping. He was sick of other people making him feel insignificant and useless. 'I'm running away from you, and I'm not mazy at all,' he said.

'Why are you running away?'

Finnigin could not easily escape the cage of Ays' arms, even though they did not touch him. Ays had his hands planted firmly on the walls of the building behind them; those hands that killed without thinking. If he tried to duck beneath Ays' arms, Finnigin knew Ays would restrain him more forcefully. 'You are a killer!' he said.

Ays raised his eyebrows. 'Really!' He laughed. 'Poor little Finnigin. Alone with a murderer. Do you think I shall stroke the life from your body now? Don't be absurd!'

'Leave me alone!'

'No, I won't. You made me come with you to this accursed place. I don't want to be alone in it now. Perhaps I'm as frightened as you are?' He made a loud, abrupt growling sound and laughed when Finnigin flinched. 'You see, there are creeping, slithering things in every corner, eyes in every shadow. So scary!'

'Stop playing with me!' Finnigin put his fingers against his temples. He felt incapable of handling a person like Ays.

'I was trying to cheer you up, actually.' Ays lowered his arms and folded them across his chest. 'Look, I'm sorry I snapped at you. I wasn't expecting you to do what you did.'

'It was nothing.'

'I know. I over-reacted.' Ays looked up at the building behind them.

'I didn't mean to offend you.'

'Forget it. Look at this. What a strange, narrow house.'

Finnigin turned round and raised his eyes, accepting that the subject of their argument was closed as far as Ays was concerned. 'This place is almost intact,' he said.

Ays grinned. 'Well, here we are having an adventure. Why should we waste any opportunity? Shall we explore?'

'This house?' Finnigin sounded uncertain.

'Why not?' He walked to the door, which was slightly ajar, and examined the wall next to it. 'There is a plaque here.'

'What does it say?'

Ays peered at it. 'I can't tell. It looks as if the words have been rubbed away. Perhaps, in daylight, we could read it?'

Finnigin pushed the door open. 'It's very dark in there. Are you sure you want to go in?'

'Yes.' Ays' face had become very still, although there was an expression, deep within his eyes, that was both fearful and relieved. 'This is the place,' he said.

Finnigin frowned. 'What do you mean?'

Ays pushed him gently. 'We're here,' he said. 'You were right. Walk over the threshold.'

Inside, the house appeared to have been vandalised. Furniture and wall-hangings were strewn about the floor. There was a strong smell of stale food and animal droppings.

'Someone has been here recently,' Ays said.

'Perhaps the bird-monkeys?' Finnigin suggested.

Ays nodded mutely and picked his way over the broken furniture. He looked up and then disappeared around a corner. Finnigin hurried after him, nervous of being left alone. The atmosphere in the house was tense, as if someone was watching them. Ays was mounting a narrow staircase.

'Be careful,' Finnigin whispered loudly, following.

Ays glanced back once and then continued to climb. They emerged on to a landing with rooms to either side. Another staircase twisted round ahead of them. Finnigin looked into the rooms. One was a bedroom where an overpowering stink of human waste made him back out in disgust. The bed was filthy, soiled, as if someone had been sick for years and then died in it.

'Not just bird-monkeys have been here,' he said. Ays pushed past him into the room, and began to examine the items of clothing strewn around the floor and bed. Suddenly, he uttered a short, shocked cry.

'What?' Finnigin took a deep breath and went back into the room.

'Look at this!' Ays held something up.

Finnigin went over to him and looked at what he held in his hands. It was an ancient, battered wide-rimmed hat, with the remains of a once splendid blue feather in its band. Finnigin said nothing, but stared at Ays with bewildered, round eyes. 'It's the same,' Ays said, gesturing with the hat. 'Older, but the same. I'd swear to it.'

Finnigin had begun to tremble. Ays put down the hat and put his arms around his companion. He whispered two words, barely audible: 'Forgive me.' Finnigin found that Ays too was shaking.

'What's happening?' Finnigin asked. 'Has he been here ahead of us?'

'Sshh.' Ays squeezed Finnigin briefly and then released him, as if the fleeting contact had renewed his courage. He went back out on to the landing, and approached the next flight of stairs.

'Ays, I'm afraid,' Finnigin said.

'And I,' Ays replied. He paused. 'Finn, I think I've been in error . . .' He shook his head, and then began to climb.

Long window-doors in the workroom gave access to a small roof garden. When Ays stepped into the room, there was a scurry of panicked movement and a dozen or so bird-monkeys fled out into the night, to hurl themselves off the roof. Ays jumped in alarm, and almost fell backwards into Finnigin.

'What is it?' Finnigin cried.

Ays collected himself. 'Bird-monkeys,' he said. 'That's all.' He laughed nervously. 'Gave me a fright, but it's nothing.' He ventured into the room.

Moonlight fell in through the open window-doors and danced an ecstatic saltation within the depths of a crystal statue that sat in a high-backed chair facing the window. On a table in front of the chair were several enormous books. One lay open, and beside it was an inkgoblet and a pen. One arm of the statue lay across the open pages.

Ays was filled with a profound emotion that he could not name. Slowly, he approached the statue and stood before it. 'Finn,' he said softly, and sensed Finnigin's presence creep up behind him. 'Look. Look at this.'

Finnigin uttered a soft cry of wonderment. 'Varian! It is a statue of Varian!' He pushed past Ays and went to examine the statue more closely. Ays did not move. His heart seemed to have frozen in his breast, yet it was the warmest it had ever been.

'Finn . . . There is something wrong.'

'He has left this here for us . . .'

Ays shook his head. 'Look at that thing! Really look at it!' The darkness of the room, despite the moonlight, made it difficult to discern detail, but by peering closely at the stone, Finnigin could see what caused Ays' concern. The surface of the crystal was opaque and appeared to be expertly carved in a perfect representation of Varian, down to the last hair on his head. But when he looked closely, he found himself wondering how any artist, however accomplished, could work crystal into the semblance of human eyelashes. The hair on the head was not just a clever representation of such, but a mass of individual crystal hairs.

'By daylight,' Ays said, 'I think we would be able to see organs within the flesh, crystal blood. That is not a statue, but a corpse!'

Finnigin drew back, perplexed. 'I don't understand.'

Ays gestured wildly. 'Neither do I, but I know I'm right. Finn, just look at that thing! It's like some sort of mummy; preserved remains. Oh, I don't know!' He looked around the room, at the thick volumes that lined the book-shelves. 'But I suspect the explanation is here.'

The gas-lights did not work, but there was oil in a table-light and tinder in a desk drawer. Finnigin attended to the lamp, while Ays perused the volumes. 'They are all hand-written,' he said. 'And seem to be in the same hand.'

'A life time's work,' said Finnigin.

'More than that.'

When the light bloomed in the opaque glass hood of the lamp, Finnigin dared to look at the statue once more. He could not believe what Ays had implied, that this had once been a living person. It was not Varian, it could not be. If it ever had been alive, it was clear it must have been a long time ago. Neither was the strong, obsessive conviction in his heart that Varian still lived affected by what he saw before him.

'We'll never be able to read all these,' Finnigin said, gesturing at the books. 'Are you sure what we're looking for is here?'

Ays was scanning the first volume, which he'd pulled down from the top shelf. 'Well, this is a start.' He scanned the lines quickly, turning pages. After a few minutes, he looked up. 'Finn, I can tell you now exactly what the statues in this city are.'

'Read it to me,' Finnigin said, sitting down on the edge of the table, with his back to the statue.

Ays began to speak.

He read the first few pages, which in a bald narrative style described the events which led to the roching of the citizens. He looked up. 'I wonder how long ago this happened.'

'Is there a date in the book?' Finnigin asked.

Ays went back to the first page. 'Yes, but it means nothing to me. Ownhaven 12, 78.'

Finnigin picked up one of the books from the table, a more recent tome. He examined the first page. 'This says Mesthaven 3, 490.'

'If we assume the date follows the pattern of the calendar of Min, which was very similar to the one they used in Salaganda, then that means over four hundred years have passed between the first volume being written and that one you're holding there.'

'Can't have been written by the same person then,' said Finnigin.

Ays looked back at the book for a few moments, spoke bleakly. 'I'm afraid it can. His name is Casmeer. Look.' He went to show Finnigin the page. They both glanced at the statue in the chair.

'Is that him?' asked Finnigin in a low voice.

They read together how Casmeer had become the sole occupant of Thermidore, and how he had resolved to write its history in order to pass his lonely time. Ays made an irritated sound. 'This is rambling,' he said. 'It tells us nothing more.' He gave the book to Finnigin. 'This is the one I want to read.' He began to tug the most recent volume from beneath the arm of the statue.

'Don't!' Finnigin cried. 'You might break him!'

'I'll be careful.' He gently pulled the volume free.

Finnigin uttered a panicked sound. 'It moved! The fingers moved!' He pointed at the table.

'Don't be stupid!' Ays admonished, although his voice was uneasy. He turned his back on the statue to examine the book.

'What does it say?' Finnigin asked. He had unconsciously moved towards the door.

Ays' face was perplexed. He scanned the pages, turned them quickly, his movements becoming faster and faster. Then he paused and uttered two slow words. 'My Goddess!'

'What does it say?' Finnigin repeated.

Ays turned to look at him. His face was white. 'This is insane!'

'What? What?' Finnigin ran to where Ays stood, took the book from him.

'It's about us, Finn! About us!' Ays cried, and then his eyes strayed to the statue. 'And . . . *him*.'

There was silence as Finnigin perused several pages at random. In between the stories about himself and Ays were diary entries, the thoughts of the man who'd penned the book.

'He was roching,' Ays said. 'All the time.'

'What does this mean?' Finnigin asked. 'What does it *mean*, Ays?' His voice was high with fear.

Ays shook his head. 'I don't know. He must have observed us, somehow. I don't know!'

'But if he was Varian, and he followed us, and we

saw him, touched him, how could he be this . . . *thing* here?'

They stared at one another. 'The clues were there all the time,' Ays murmured. 'The mention of stories, of authoring.'

'Are you trying to say he *created* us?'

Ays threw up his arms. 'How do I know what I'm trying to say? I'm attempting to make sense of what I heard in the underworld, the riddle I answered. The crone virtually told me everything there, but I thought it was just another riddle.'

'But we're *alive*, Ays!' Finnigin cried. 'We exist. We're not stories! And Varian was alive, a person of flesh and blood.'

Ays rubbed his face. He looked exhausted. 'Panicking and wild hypothesising will not help us,' he said. 'We must sit down and read that book now. From beginning to end. Then, we can think about it.'

In the morning, Ays was the first to go down the stairs and into the back yard behind the house. There was a water butt there, which, although rather stagnant, he put his head into, to try and clear his mind. It was an impossible task. He rested his brow against the cold bricks of the house, and resisted the urge to bang his forehead repeatedly against the stone. A movement behind him made him turn round in alarm. A plumosite had come into the yard and was standing in a crouched position with raised wings, regarding him steadily.

'Babooshpet, is that you?' Ays asked.

The plumosite waddled over and paused a few feet in front of him. Ays sat down against the wall. 'You are looking at a fiction,' he said, and laughed aloud. Presently, he put his head in his hands and wept, filled with a grief so profound it threatened to burst his body from within. The plumosite squatted down and watched him.

Finnigin, staring blindly at the last entry in the book upstairs, heard Ays' cracked sobbing and put the book aside. Numbly, he went down the stairs and into the yard. The plumosite uttered a screech when she saw him, but Finnigin had eyes only for Ays.

'We're alive,' he said, and then again, more firmly, '*We're alive!*'

Ah, the cruel visions of sickness, Casmeer thought. Phantoms had surrounded him all night, images of his creations flickering across his sight. He'd felt fevered, yet somehow desiccated. The visions had spoken to one another, even raved at some points, yet he'd been unable to decipher their conversation. It was as if Finnigin and Ays had crawled from the page before him in order to torment him. He'd wanted to shout, 'Wake me! Wake me! Touch me with your hands!' But of course, it had been a dream, and he hadn't been able to move a muscle.

Now, he felt so stiff, he still couldn't move. A cold, night draught must have frozen his bones. Perhaps the wan sunlight would thaw them out. And where was Babooshpet? He felt hungry now, needed fruit pulp to wet his tongue. And yet, when he tried to call for her, he could not make the sounds. Even the act of thinking felt strange, somehow brittle. But, despite this constricting inflexibility of thought and action, he was sure he felt better than he had the previous day.

Someone stepped into the room, bringing a morning freshness with them, a breath of cold air. Although he couldn't turn his head, he knew that it was a female. It must be Babooshpet, although the unseen figure had seemed to stride purposefully in behind him. Babooshpet always jumped and scuttled. To his utter astonishment, a clear feminine voice fractured the stillness of the room.

'Oh, please!' she announced. 'What are you doing there?'

Elini? thought Casmeer, unable to pronounce the name. Madness, then, and ghosts. He must be doomed. Why should he be tortured by this incongruous lightness of spirit, when it was so clear his body and brain were deteriorating?

A woman stalked into his line of sight. She shook her head, causing a mass of glorious shining hair to shift across her shoulders.

'You are a pathetic sight,' she said. 'Get up!'

Casmeer experienced a shock deep within him, like a muffled explosion. 'Marvrani?'

The woman waved a graceful arm to indicate the entire room. 'Varian, this place is a dump. Will you please rouse yourself, and get moving? I've had enough of Thermidore. It is a tomb, and very dull.'

Casmeer wanted to blink, but couldn't. Marvrani seemed too solid, too vibrant to be a ghost. Could it be he'd imagined sitting in this room, writing his stories; imagined all those long, lonely years? Had he simply read about it? Was he Varian, rather than Casmeer? A wave of disorientation coursed through him. Marvrani was staring at him in an impatient manner, her hands on her hips, her chin thrust out. His voice, when he heard it, hardly seemed to come from his body. 'I can't move.'

Marvrani threw up her arms and tossed her head. 'Of course you can!' she snapped. 'Varian, you are wasting time. There are things you must attend to. Those delightful little playthings of yours are here. Downstairs. They're in a terrible state. I really think you ought to have a word with them.'

'Ays and Finnigin?'

'The priest and the puppy, that's right!'

'Have you spoken to them?'

'No. That's your job.' Marvrani folded her arms and went to look out of the window. 'Your scruffy plumosite pets have made a foul mess of the garden.'

'What am I going to say to them?' Varian thought, and heard the words whispering around the room.

Marvrani looked at him severely. 'That's your problem. You were the one who led them a merry dance. Now, I expect, they want an explanation. I myself am waiting to hear it. No doubt there will be complications . . .' She began tapping her foot. 'Well? What are you waiting for?'

Varian became impatient with the sluggishness of his body. He forced – willed – himself to rise.

'That's better,' said Marvrani. 'Are you ready?'

Varian extended his hands, examined them. The rings gleamed voluptuously upon his fingers. His clothes were clean, new. Marvrani laughed and tossed him his hat, which he caught in one hand.

'My, you're a handsome creature!' she said.

Before he left, Varian couldn't resist glancing back, even though some part of him was afraid of looking at what sat in the chair behind him. He felt buoyant, light-footed, very much alive, and wanted nothing to spoil that.

He had nothing to fear. The roche was motionless in the chair; dull, dead stone. It was not part of him, and he could leave it behind easily. He directed one last glance around the room. So many memories. At the moment, he could not decide which set of memories he owned were authentic. Perhaps, ultimately, that did not matter?

Marvrani had already left the room. He could hear her running down the stairs. One last look, that's all, he told himself. The roche creaked and a splinter of crystal fell off it on to the filthy carpet. Quickly, Varian turned away, and followed Marvrani downstairs. His heart was beating quickly. He was exhilarated by the prospect of the meeting that would soon take place, but he was nervous of it too.

In the old workroom, the last volume of Casmeer's work lay open on the floor. A sharp gust of wind from the roof garden gusted into the room, and fretted the pages of the book. A crystal finger fell from the roche and marked the place of the final written word. Presently, a page turned over; blank.

This blank page was destined never to be seen by human eyes. Soon, the city would collapse slowly into the mountains, as if the very force which had kept it standing had been suddenly and inexorably withdrawn. In the place where it once stood, there would be no sign left of the human dramas that had been enacted within its walls.

Still there it was: potential. An empty page. A new story waiting for a thought, a heart, desire.